Serpent in the Wishing Well

BY

SAMUEL L. MCGINLEY

Grosvenor House
Publishing Limited

This book is published by
Grosvenor House Publishing Ltd
Link House
140 The Broadway, Tolworth, Surrey, KT6 7HT.
www.grosvenorhousepublishing.co.uk

A CIP record for this book
is available from the British Library

ISBN 978-1-83975-743-3

To the McG3.
All I do is for thee.

Cast of characters

ഔ൧

Bailly, Charles, *Catholic Envoy*

Beale, Robbie, *Mathematician, Servant and Chief Espial Agent*

Beauvery, Hannah, *Whore and Agent*

Blythe, Edmund, *Trawlerman and Agent*

Bridle, *Catholic prisoner*

Cecil, William, *Queen's First Minister, Chief Privy Councillor*

Dee, John (Doctor), *Astrologist, Mathematician and Scryer*

Dudley, Robert, Earl of Leicester, *Privy Councillor*

Essex (Lord), *Privy Councillor*

Essigia, *Whoremaster and Agent*

Fallburn, Olias, *Parish Constable*

Frinscombe, *Gaoler of Portsmouth*

Fyson, Soborn, *Barber Surgeon*

Hendon, Emmanuel, *Pastor*

Herle, William, *Captain of the Griffin and Agent*

Howard, Thomas, Duke of Norfolk, *Privy Councillor*

Jennings, Isiah, *Customs Adjutant*

Kitchener, Jack, *Whitehall Agent*

Levet, Agnes, *Wise-Woman*

Ludlow, Martin, *Privy Councillor*

MacKinnon, *Catholic prisoner*

Masterman, Lynas, *Court Rider and Agent*

Nevon, Titus, *Bear wrestler and Agent*

Porter, Reeburn, *Barber Surgeon*

Rhy, *Rhyming Whore, Agent*

Ridolfi (D'Ridolfi), Roberto, *Merchant banker*

Smythe, Thomas, *Clerk of the Privy Council Chamber*

Snurle, Harry, *Privy Council Agent*

St. Barbe, Edith, *Maidservant to the Walsinghams and sister to Ursula*

Stimpson, Edward, *Manservant to Francis Walsingham*

Stow, John, *Historian and Surveyor of London, Agent*

Traske, Theophilus, *Gaol Carpenter*

Tudor, Elizabeth, *Queen*

Walsingham, Frances, *Daughter*

Walsingham, Francis, *MP Lyme Regis and Proposed Secretary of Intelligence*

Walsingham, Mary, *Daughter*

Walsingham (nee St. Barbe), Ursula, *Wife of Francis*

Williams, Walter, *Actor, Espial*

If all the swords in England were pointed
against my head,
your threats would not move me.

Thomas Becket.
Immediately before his brutal murder.

෨൦ඥ

PART ONE

Blood Circle

June 1553 – March 1570

෨൦ඥ

I

Castle Baynard Ward –
St Paul's, London

8th June 1553

෨ ൬

Death knocks loudly on London's doors this day, he laments, watching the convoy of chaos rage by him in furious revelry. It meant there was going to be more fire. What else could he do but follow, never once suspecting it would forge the unlikeliest of bonds.

'Heretics.' Someone screams as rushed feet slip on the mucky lane. Ranks of guardsmen with murderous intent clasp their flaming torches and hurry along Paternoster Row, near the dominating cathedral of St Paul's. He looks up to its mighty square steeple and wonders whether God could ever forgive them when his 'holy work' was about to be done with such ferocity. Twenty or so guards and their ruthless captain rush on, determined the burnings will proceed. He cowers momentarily behind his high collared cape – remembering it is now lethal to be Protestant. Following the fury of noise, he sees the crowd build like a blocked river and it squalls with intense blood lust as two prisoners are dragged through the muck, the blood and the cheer, barely able to keep pace for the sufferings of beatings and malnourishment they have endured.

Swarmed by the gathered, baying at them like the countless kites of London's sky and streets might flap at the markets of Cheapside – jabbing, tearing and cawing at the sacrificial flesh to be devoured. Just as the refuse-eating birds help keep the lanes and courts of all London's wards clean, the angry crowd believe they are ridding the streets from another kind of filth. Their scared Protestant faces lost all hope but of a mercifully quick killing.

Francis Walsingham behind his fine velvet red cape is twitchy, nervously caressing his wispy beard, suddenly feeling foolish as his concealment is tugged and torn by the heaving crowd. At 21 he is tall and awkward, not yet comfortable in a full man's body, unable to hold steadfast against the surging crowd, their scent heavy with ale and the dung of horse. Seeing the petrified captives, and fearing he recognises one of them, he shouts through clenched teeth, 'John? John Warne?'

Behind bruised and watered eyes, John looks up and around, identifying the voice, a sooth Psalm in the chaos, 'Francis? Is that you?'

Young Walsingham cannot believe his eyes – days earlier Warne was delivering newly upholstered chairs to his Grays Inn office, now he was a ragged ruin. Francis lunges towards him, 'What be your crime?' He asks, shoved back by the Guardsmen for his trouble.

'They mean to find us all.' John manages, just as one of the Guardsman starts to panic, fearing the impassioned swelling crowd will overcome the deathly intentions.

'Captain we need to begin: the crowds endanger the effort.' He shouts, imploring to the distance – Francis follows the direction and can just make out Captain of the Guard, who hurriedly barks the prisoners' charges over the screams of anticipation.

'Like Nicodemus, these pretenders of faith shall perish.' Captain spurns, cueing his men to bind John Warne and the other prisoner at their stakes.

Francis has tears of powerless fear in his eye. Warne, perhaps catching this, cries out, 'Leave our realm, Francis.' The other prisoner, with impending realisation, faints, so a Guardsman awakens them with an almighty back-handed slap.

'In violation of the Heresy Acts,' the Captain of the Guard continues, trying to maintain a sense of judicial majesty, 'the Catholic faith and Good Queen Mary, these heretics shall burn in the fires of hell. Eternity will not assuage them.' He gives the signal to begin.

With the use of silver birch from Smithfield, tar, pitch and tallow, the flames enliven immediately, and the prisoners are engulfed in a gusting thump. The crowd are stunned with the alacrity in which the flames get to work, as if the prisoners had been well oiled beforehand, which Francis knew they might have been. He can no longer bear to look at his burning friend, who tries to brace himself from screaming out in the scorching fire. For the time being, at least, his bravery works.

Francis distracts himself, looking anywhere but at Warne's face, so peers down…only to behold the victim's feet blistering like joints of meat on a skillet, beginning to fizz, pop and blacken – an unholy roast for the fire to devour. All their torment was far from over. In the throes of an inescapable and cruel death, Warne's screaming finally begins. It is expected, almost palatable, to hear women scream, wail and yap their pleas in the calamity of Tudor London, but to hear a man do so was to scratch the throat of Satan himself. Even the craving of the crowd subsides in numb shock as Warne wails to the heavens. It takes a full four minutes for him to die, the screeching was unbearable for all who could hear. Francis knew it would never leave his ears, but he also knew he had to bring himself to look just once more at his friend, the face now like shrivelled leather. This would remain with him forever. What stunned him next, though, was Warne's last moment on this earth, shrieking from the inferno, 'I am no Nicodemus...leave England... return only to complete God's true work.' Then the unnatural fire hears enough of this pathetic mortal and snarls around Warne like nets tightening fish. This horrifying succumbing only serves to re-excite the hordes' savagery and they relentlessly holler for more.

As if driven by a will to please the crowd, the Captain of the Guard shouts, 'Hunt down the heretics, they are among us.' His Guardsmen then indiscriminately rip into rows of people. Francis realises his grieving would have to wait, for Warne was right: it was his time to leave.

In his panic and anger, the gangly youth forgets how to be conspicuous, turning and barging people out of his way. Immediately he is suspicious and five Guardsmen begin pursuit. Backing up to Trinity Lane where the alleys narrow between Old Fish Street and Thames Street, Francis scrambles through courtyards, slipping on rancid haddock guts, slapping into stacked crates of skate, but he knows where he is headed. Caring less about indignities, he careens around the mess, down another alley and bundles himself into a familiar basement dwelling. The Guardsmen see.

Inside it is smooth and dark, smelling like old wet stone. Despite the sparse mess, it is clear someone has ransacked the place. Amongst the pathetic array of furniture and belongings strewn, there is a whimper. Francis gently approaches the bleak corner, 'Robbie? Dear boy.' He sees the child of no more than nine years, clearly beaten, scrunching and scared.

'They sought for you, but I did not betray.' Robbie stutters in between tears.

'I'm so sorry, my little, brave man.' Francis' heart yanks, knowing he has not the time to be all tender mercy because outside there are screams as stalls and tables are hurriedly broken. The Guardsmen are close. 'We must leave England.' He insists, grabbing Robbie's limp hand, but has to let go when, with such force, Guardsmen smack the door from its hinges, bouncing him apart from Robbie who falls away, and his pursuers lurch through, faces hungry for their prize. There is no time to think as one of them makes a leap for Francis, grabbing him, but he is a little lucky as they cannot gain purchase on his thin wrists and he spins just at the right time, slamming them both through a thin plaster wall and out onto the floor of the backyard. Even in this speedy happening Francis gives thanks for his uncle making him learn to wrestle on the farm as he skilfully vaults the Guardsman off, crashing him into the pig's trough. To Francis' horror though, three of them have Robbie. Now suddenly hectic with fury, Francis makes a charge for them. Click. One of the three Guardsmen primes a musket, pointing it right at him. He does not aim and the youthful Walsingham darts out of the way, up a wall and the shot misses, blasting a hole in the bricks. No one would have believed he was merely an apprentice to lawyers – no sinewy clerk is as tough as this.

Francis looks back to Robbie, petrified and pathetic, another Guardsman primes his musket. If he attempts rescue they both may die, if he leaps to safety, they might let the boy live. All is lost and Francis has no choice other than to vault away, crashing through filth and fences, so Guardsmen bound after this new enemy to Mary's Catholic state.

Deflecting and bobbing people aside, the young clerk steers through teaming cargo wagons and Stevedores lining Queenhithe's wharf on the north of the river as he speedily meanders along Thames' path. He is not losing his trackers. Ahead is a small merchant vessel readying sail and, just as he nears, its gangplank is being removed. Guardsmen are too close for him to start negotiating with the crew so Francis turns and sees a wagon being loaded and dives amongst its covers. They scoff at his poor show of escape, surround it and, drawing their swords, plunge them deep into the flax sheets.

The cunning apprentice lawyer wriggles beneath a cart, like an errant child on feast days crawling under rows of benches. He has bought himself valuable seconds as he sees the merchant vessel creep away from the wharf's edge, this is his last chance. He snatches off his red velvet cape and with his long legs runs for his life.

Racing to the edge of the wooden pier, he hurls himself with all the thrust God gives him, managing to just catch the stern rigging as he hurtles downwards. Slapping into the arse of the boat, he clutches whatever he can and holds tight to it. The rope is coarse like splintered wood and his sweaty hands fail his exhausted arms and he falters to support his bodyweight upwards. His feet are wet and he feels himself slipping, hands in tearing pain, the Thames' cold water ready to gladly subsume his weighty clothes and certainly leave him no chance to struggle against survival. It is then, behind his eyes, he sees John Warne's face screaming and then little Robbie's tearful eyes. His determination reignites. In one deep breath his arms tussle the rope and he does well to just hold, not daring to look back wharfside.

Guardsmen are shouting after him, replacing their swords, poising muskets.

Francis dangles there like a clipped partridge on a gorse bush, looking up at the protruding belly of the boat he must climb to live, this could be the last sight he beholds. Oak beams and grey sky gyrate in his view, a messy farewell, when suddenly a fat Stevedore leans into view with a big greasy smile gawping down and reaching for his hand – 'Tell me why I shouldn't throw you back?' He asks gruffly.

Walsingham cannot help but let out a single breath of boyish glee – never has something so ugly been so beautiful. Then, with the calm that will, in years to come, instil fear into many a man's soul, Francis smiles thinly and says, 'One day you will need a powerful friend.' The Stevedore laughs heartily and yanks him so forcefully he flies up and nearly kisses his brown teeth. Liberation is only a short, sweet release though as Francis can do no more than hug the brute, fully embracing his herring enriched apron, before looking tragically back to Queenhithe's wharf and the embittered Guardsmen...they smirk, in realisation they hold the cards...as Captain of the Guard arrives by horse, with a limp cargo draped over it as if it was stolen linen: Robbie. Francis cannot believe his eyes and scrambles to the aft.

The boy is thrown to the floor, the Captain dismounts and places his sword in a nearby fire grill. Francis stares helplessly on at the rear of the boat. They force Robbie to kneel. Captain of the Guard retrieves his sword, searing red like the sun at Summer dusk. Francis, only hours ago an apprentice lawyer of the respected Grays Inn now a religious fugitive, watching despairingly as the sword scalds Robbie's naked arm with a singing fizz. The boy screams, collapses and howls so sharply the Captain's horse whinnies and yanks up on its hind legs. This is not how farewells are supposed to be. Right there in the wind billowing up from the Thames' estuary, Francis swore, through anguish and shame, he would return and avenge the contorted face of little Robbie Beale's pain; and that of John Warne's too.

The tears come fat and plentiful now as Francis cannot bring himself to look anymore, other than to catch one more glimpse of the Captain of the Guard, sneering as the Pagans might have once done when honouring their dark Gods with a sacrifice. Seeing that face and those demonic eyes feels to him as if Beelzebub had plunged a horn-rimmed hoof into his soul.

This day, he decides, shall never leave him.

II

*Seething Lane, Tower Street
and Aldgate Ward, London*

11th March 1570

ℰↃ ℭℛ

Watching the posy delicately fall into what she thought must be the centre of the earth, it occurred to Frances in her nine years of wise living this might not have been the right thing to do after all. Ripples of dark water spread ominously in the puddle at the bottom of the deep hole – its grassy lips guarding the top of the throat into the depths. A creature of the deep earth, some leviathan, she gasps, suddenly feeling as if there was an awakening beneath the water. Was an unstoppable entity from the very depths of the underworld ready to arise? It was only supposed to be a jape, a harmless charm, but as she looked across London's three hills from the wasteland beyond their yard near Tower Hill on this grey morn, hearing no song from the birds, and seeing her little sister's sad eyes, these ill omens filled her with foolish gloom. What had she done? What had she unleashed?

Linden leaves, Thyme sprigs and the small written parchment that had tightly bound the posy together now flaked apart in the disused well, floating with hopeless irretrievability.

Frances asked herself whether at nine years old should she have known better. Feeling her body becoming a woman, this was not the responsible actions of a young elder, she thought. Looking over at Mary, her sweet younger sister by four years, she guiltily asked herself if it be fair she shares the blame for this misdalliance? Frances listened as the little girl obediently recites the rhyme she had taught her.

'On parchment my wish is told, but I shall not say what my heart withhold, I beg haste a quick mission, so my life will match my vision.' Mary cooed into the deep hole, proud of her perfect recitation of what the old Crone from Cheapside had told the sisters to say.

Frances was struck cold and deep with the uncertainty of what may come of this. It was her that had promoted her naïve sister to caster of charms, only too eager for the task. Poor Mary – how could she share blame, never knowing what words matter or their intent. Frances pitied her and, glumly watching the ripples spread further, accepted it was her alone that would face any repercussions to come.

Completely unaware of her sister's dreadful forebodings, Mary looks up to her and asks, 'Why throw the Tussie-mussie into the hole?'

Frances smiles bravely, 'This is how you cast good luck charms.'

'Why?'

Normally she would have answered that their endeavors would be paid off with getting exactly what they wanted.

Frances and Mary peered down into the 30ft chasm.

'If I were to fall I should not come out alive.' Mary says with mock alarm. They smile.

'They say it's as old as London itself.' Frances marvels out loud, enjoying her elder status to frighten and amaze her younger sister a little too much.

'Do fairies live there? How did it get here?' Mary asks, all a muddle with intrigue.

'Dropped to earth by the old Gods.' Frances was purposefully evasive, knowing perfectly well that it was a Roman borehole dug thirteen-hundred years before. She was doing this on purpose, building little Mary's wonder, about to offload her own fears onto the forgiving shoulders of her motley-minded foot-biter sister. 'You cannot betray the secrets of the old Gods, can you Mary?' She asks knowingly.

'No, not ever...and not I.'

'Then we must not discuss evermore what happened here today.' Frances stares right at her with the roundest and brownest of eyes, incarnate of her father, like Kestrels they are, people would say – both intimidating and captivating.

'I shan't.'

'Then we shall hear from the old Gods no more, lest you break that promise.' Frances says, as Mary violently shakes her head in agreement. As the posy wilted into the water, Frances gently tugged her sister's arm to move away, time to get home. She did not want to think what spirits, what magic – white or black – had been conjured and awoken from beneath them. They stand and look once more into the shaft's blackness, and the parchment, sprig of Linden and Thyme have disappeared. Frances could not resist dramatically concluding, 'The Gods have swallowed our charm.'

'Were they listening?' Mary asks, a little worried. 'How do we know?' Her questioning did not stop as they walked the short distance home.

Frances ushers her sister back through the fence panels, the tiny apple orchard and into their yard. Mary's questions were relentless and unceasing, but Frances let her whitter on, unanswered.

'Well, I could always ask Papa.' The five-year old says, annoyed at no response.

Father. Frances suddenly tingles with horror. Maids, mother or the pastor she could handle, but the disappointment from her father she could not.

'Mary, you must not tell Pa-pa. Not any soul.' Frances chugs throatily to her sister.

'Why?'

'Because...the charm will break.'

'Will we get into trouble?'

Frances swallows, 'Yes. Verily.'

He is waiting for them. At the far end of the orchard, ready for their Wednesday walk, he slowly raises both arms by his side, as his daughters approach, tentatively, never sure how to read his over bearing eyes. Unfurling his black cape, he swallows them both whole in a swooping hug, like a raven swaddling its chicks.

He knows not, Frances gleefully thinks as she nestles into his strong stomach in the blackness of his embrace. Their Wednesday walk would go unspoiled. As they left their house, Frances and Mary held little chilled hands aloft to tuck into their father's, as he leads them around the lane towards Tower Hill. Thoughts of charms and old Gods had left both girls as they skip out of Seething Lane, revelling the prospect of his stories from old, their favourite being how the son of Venus, daughter of

Jupiter, had built London. They always giggled at the silly names and were rapt with his deep, calm voice, impersonating the peaceful giant race who had first constructed their city.

Hopeful sunlight glimmers from the lead guttering on the two small parish churches that buttressed either end of their street. The sisters were convinced this was a sure sign today was anointed in joy. Frances' anxieties from the old Roman wellspring were dissolving away, just as the Tussie-mussie had done so into the water. The ever-brighter sun and building breeze distract her.

With animation, their father begins a story, 'The giant stamped and the earth shifted and shuffled. In this way the beast as large as forty men had created the third hill of the new city, calling it Trenovant. It would later become Londres, which means fierce.' His daughters grinned excitedly as he went on, 'The red clay of our soil, being the blood of his very toil. The river is said to be the water unwanted by his body.' This causes squeals of simultaneous disgust and delight from his daughters, giggling it all off, knowing this was a wonderful private moment that he would never have shared in front of mother. Ecstatic and adoring, Frances and Mary marched merrily on, not wanting this day or his nonsense stories to end.

As they turned, eastwards onto Tower Street, a wind suddenly blew up Francis Walsingham's cape, and it flapped at the girls, who laughed startlingly up into his egg white face with paintbrush thin goatee and leather brown eyes, their hero.

Then the moment suddenly soured. For the girls' optimisms, like the glowering sun, quickly cowered into shadows and became a colder reckoning. Beneath the imposing steeple of All Hallows Barking, John Stow was stood waiting to greet their father. Like a blunt thud, these doting little girls knew right there and then that his awkward smile and the way he stood meant ill tidings. Some men just have that look, Frances thought. Worse, he was there to rob them of their father's attentions.

'Francis...your charming daughters.' He says, like a man without his own children might forget the names of others' – as if they were a superfluous accessory. This really vexes Frances and even Mary begins to understand, as both furrow their brows when he crouches to meet their eyes, 'Miss Walsinghams. May I join you this morning?' They were not quite old and bold enough to decline the offer, so he takes their tacit consent and leads on with their father. The sisters find each other's eyes in downright consternation – what had they done to deserve this invader – before then being tugged along by their father's long arms. As their sore minds temper, both pairs of eyes widen and intensify with the same terrible thoughts: could their casted charm have started to enact its ungodly price on them? Was this man their punishment? Frances takes a breath and sees panic in her little sister's face, but she stares her down and gives the signal to speak no more of it. They now listen confusedly to their father, having missed the early part of his conversation.

'Did you hear me girls...' Their father says, as they traipse grumpily along, 'Gentleman Stow graces us this morn as a master of antiquity. He writes and publishes, near to St. Paul's cathedral.' He nods their attention down to the east-west thoroughfare running from that great Norman keep, the white Tower of London, on towards St. Paul's in a hope they might appreciate not only the odd and incredible view the calamity and chaos of London holds but also how important this new visitor was.

They nod quickly, uninterested.

The girls, he thinks, are somewhat distracted today. Perhaps he should remind them in this moment of how formidable a place the city was with its constant dangers and keep his daughters in check, as a father should. Walsingham would remind them they should not be too complacent and proudly point out their residence was in a well-appointed street, with houses large and fair, being close enough to the main arteries of Leadenhall, Cheapside to St. Paul's and yet sufficient distance from the lawless low-biters that prowled Bridge Within Ward by the river. Having lived in London for most of his life, he would always say, he knew the insidious rogues and vagabonds thereabouts would sooner cut your throat than cut your purse, and always reminded his daughters of this if he felt them lackadaisical.

As the sisters passed the churchyard and turned their gazes back towards home with its visible yard, they yearned to be there, in the small apple orchard chasing clouds from the sky because this day was not at all what they had expected.

We walk this way, they heard their Papa explain to this new man, adding that he liked to remind my daughters of consequences.

Then their eyes fell upon it. The sisters' tummies fluttered as they beheld the great white tower peeking up from the horizon and their heads bobbed in anticipation of glimpsing what frightened and excited them: the gibbets; execution scaffolds; and blocks that pockmarked the steep hill – crooked teeth in the jaws of hell.

'The flat crosses.' Mary pointed out to Frances. 'How many bodies today?'

'A score or more?' They look at each other in revelry.

The four of them stopped for a moment. Tower Hill was both marvel and intimidation. Pageants to portent, Walsingham would always say under his breath whenever he saw them and did so now in his reverently calm voice.

Flies whirred manically around one soul's remnants, as the girls left their father's side and counted twenty-two traitors in various stages of transience. Wind then licks up the hill and one cadaver twists around, its face lolls down at them with gloopy green eyes and black tongue. Frances and Mary do well not to squeal, reasoning it was not watching them, but, just in case, they dash to clutch their father's hands, having to settle on a finger or two. Any clasp of safety will do since they had long past All Hallows church on their street corner.

'You should not have thrown that charm into the water...I told you not to.' Mary scolds her older sister as quietly as she can behind her father's black cape, flitting in the breeze.

Frances sneers at her amongst the ruffling of his cloak, silly little girl for thinking such things work. They don't...do they? She spars with the ideas in her head, looks back to the green-eyed man, just as a raven perches on his shoulder and jabs at the eye's sloppy socket. Frances thought about the church of All Hallows again, then her house, its yard and that hole in the fence they climbed through to get to that old Roman watering hole. She winces and asks herself angrily why she had done it, then mouths to the heavens, 'Sorry,' and closes her eyes, praying the trouble away.

Stow was impressed with how the girls were inquisitive around the bodies. Look, one was even praying for their salvation he motions to Walsingham, seeing Frances in passionate prayer.

'Death, salvation and spectacle lies at every London street corner.' Walsingham says airily, before adding, 'These are trophies of treason. I like to remind my daughters of the perils of pride.'

As Mary gawps again at the scrags dangling on timber frames, Walsingham never once allows them to wince from whatever unsightly mess Queen Elizabeth's policy had made of some poor wretch. It was not that he ever took them to an execution, the great Elizabethan pastime, but only to rue the remnants of mistake. His lesson of comfort to them that this was unquestionably God's work. Warnings must be heeded because ignorance of them was no defence. To appreciate life – a Godly life – their Papa preached, they must revere death.

As their Wednesday stroll carried on in the sun-grey morning, John Stow listens with an intrigued smile while his new friend explained to the girls there were five ways an Elizabethan could be put to death: hanging, beheading, pressed, burning or, the most feared of all, hung, drawing and quartering.

Frances winced as she wondered which would be the quickest and which she could endure. Mary was stuck imagining being pressed to death was like the apples being squashed under the cider press on the family estate in Kent.

Walsingham smiles with pride as both daughters listened intently, as if he was pointing out the providence in the stars at night time or explaining how rivers began. These, they knew, were the real facts of life. If only she knew the real facts of her own life – for already hers was a lie. In the Parish registers she had been mis recorded as being born in 1567 when it was in fact 1561, the Parish Warden's withering hand making a flick of the quill mistake. It was one her father chose not to correct, for reasons he kept to himself. He would school them in the ways he knew how. Punishment was savage, he would say, and the humiliation insurmountable, searing the memory of all souls who witnessed them, his hushed tones transfixing them. Their father took delight in their seeming lack of worry – while John Stow shuddered – for Walsingham had so clearly convinced them that his, and theirs, was the righteous way. What, of course, he kept from them was his own puzzlement: for no matter how savage and abominable these punishments were, crimes failed to dwindle in number. It was this very thought that had brought him to Stow and their meeting on the breezy morn.

He admired the young historian and surveyor, knowing John was well educated, fastidious and could care less for fashions. This made him deeply unpopular with the Clerks and quill scratchers of Parliament but endeared him to Walsingham who enlisted his help in custom warrants and information gathering in and around the city. When he had heard the progeny was compiling tallies of London's misconducts, ill deeds, misdemeanours and crimes, this greatly intrigued Walsingham and he pressed him on the analysis. Initially, he had quaked when it became apparent crimes against persons and, most alarmingly, the state, were actually increasing. Stow was no narrator of his times – a mere recorder, he had humbly joked – so when Walsingham pointed out to him that whether life was so tragically hard or the people so mindlessly fearless and reckless, the consequences were somehow worthwhile for their meagre causes, their mutual understandings had then bonded them. Walsingham had concluded that punishments did not serve to prevent these dangerous, determined people. Remedy for the state could, he reasoned, be found only in protection and forewarning of such crimes. Stow had agreed, flushing with admiration for the wisdom Walsingham, only a few years his senior, exuded. But how can you forewarn or how can you prevent? Stow pondered aloud.

As the men chattered on, it was still not at all clear to the sisters why this fellow had come to see their father, nay ruin their day. Surely Papa had not requested to see him...on this...*their* morning walk? Frances swallowed deep – was it really the charm going wrong?

Walsingham stops to regard the square white tower, some hundred yards at the bottom of the hill. Impressive, impregnable. It was a monument to power. Guardsmen were moving barrels within the keep. Another delivery of gunpowder, Stow points out. Walsingham wonders, 'How, whenever the government twitches, it buys gunpowder but shoots no man.' John looks between him and his daughters.

'There are two reasons men will create insurrection.' The historian says, before turning directly to Walsingham. 'In desperate want of water. Or when he feels threatened.' He then crouches to address the sisters, 'Has your Papa told you of London's great mayors?' They now smile for the first time since meeting him and in unison shout "Dick Whittington." John laughs, of course. The most famous, he tries to explain, should be Henry Wales because he was the first to ensure a cistern of lead built into the stone walls served as a great conduit for bringing fresh water into the city. It had an incredible 1,096 rods, he went on, mistaking their agog looks for astound. When one of the girl's yawn, he is not insulted, because their father understands. He stands back up and points out that was in 1282, so why, almost two hundred and ninety years later, do Londoners and Englanders twitch with rebellion?

They both look across Tower Hill and down to the great Norman keep once more, standing brazenly across England's capital, daring to be challenged.

'We are not in want of water, Francis, mayors greater than Richard Whittington saw to that.' Stow says quietly.

'Security.' Murmurs Walsingham.

Perhaps Stow heard him, 'You and I understand three things: history, mathematics and the law. Alas, they do not govern all men. For my part, I am a humble surveyor. These three can show us when we are being threatened, the realities of how it will work and how we must protect. It is you that has the ear of government and positioned to use them for change.'

'I am but in the further benches of Parliament, nay more.' Walsingham despondently declares.

Frances and Mary tug at his arms, they now really dislike this man who speaks ill of Dick Whittington and has distracted their Papa for long enough and have decided they just want to go home.

'You are the one, the only one, who speaks of grave concerns that impede England's realm. It is you who understands.' Stow presses.

'It is my folly for doing so. Look where I am – asunder from power and without potential.'

'You and I are the only ones to see sense on the Catholic rebellion from last year.' Stow says imploringly.

'Since the rebellion of the Northern Earls a year past, Her Majesty's government has decreed there is to be no more talk of England's dangers, threats, perils or plots. The treacheries committed in 1569 and the resulting trials were as if they had never unfolded. Silenced.' Walsingham says pinchingly, looking around at the grisly corpses, 'The dead speaketh not of their lost chances.'

Stow knows he has to try another tack, 'Why did you first request my parley?'

'To examine those very trial's typescripts, to understand what exactly transpired.'

'And why so? Did you not support your government's ruling?' Stow asks with plain revelation.

The girls were getting impatient but knew a comment may render them with a smack to the scalp.

Walsingham was already testy and shouts, 'I did not believe it could happen in England.' Then, with a calmer sting, 'An error of investigation so damnable a court fool could do better.'

John nods solemnly and, with a sense of achievement, says, 'Why is none of the Privy Council asking this? Forget not that anger. And all your others too.'

Walsingham feels he should know what he means. He looks down to his impatient daughters and nods they will hurry along shortly. 'Rumours forewarn of a great announcement from Rome.' He says, as if he was talking about rain on the horizon.

'Queen Mary of Scots is housed in England. In England! I beseech you. The papal pincers are closing. The government is blind to threats and wades in the mud of obscure denial. There is perhaps only one thing that we can learn from the Northern rebellion trials…?' Stow scoffs.

'There are few in the governing orders to be trusted.' Walsingham angrily concedes.

'Indeed. Who, though?'

'The implications from the Northern Earl trials were of numerous well-connected men but who have since convinced Her Majesty of innocence. All now once again at large.'

'In our government.' Stow says with a disbelief and tone that indicates Walsingham should resolve it. 'They need to be found.'

Walsingham turns to him, shaking his head, saying, 'I am but poor and in lack of allies, against inexhaustible resource and networks so tightly woven even the Pope's prick is restrained.'

The two men's eyes smile at the insinuation, which the girls did not hear.

'Inexhaustible? This was what the Viennese thought about the Ottomans. They found a way.' Stow says and looks to Walsingham's daughters, 'I have taken too much time,' before turning to him, 'and you must now use yours wisely. Find a way to find them – or we both know it will happen all over again…and Catholicism and all its terrors will once again choke this land.' He abruptly leaves and heads south to the river, never once looking back.

Walsingham turns and dawdles his daughters away. Amongst the rotting flesh flopping over timber scaffolds like bare autumnal trees, wilting and cold – the poisoned fruit on England's prickly branches – he contemplates last year's trials. Yes, the 1569 Catholic rebellion had been quashed with minimal civil violence, which was a victory, but the lessons that needed to be learned had been swept away by the contentment that its leaders were quickly executed or had fled from England to the Highlands. A danger no more. This had been foolhardy to think so. The trial had failed to ask from where these schemes had been devised. In the loud huzzahs of victory, reason and understanding had been deafened out. Whether or not the defence forces were mustered and utilised correctly in response to the rebel Earls of Westmoreland and Northumberland, Walsingham ashamedly had no idea. He was quick to rationalise, therefore, that the market for militaristic strategy was not in need of his lacklustre skills. Prevention, however, had not been. It was this murky world of betrayal, plots and treachery he was now debating whether he should plunge himself into.

His girls' hands limped lazily in his, rather like the government's policy on security, and it was dawning on him that, even with his meagre experience, nobody in Whitehall was talking about this to solve long term. As a member of parliament, he had no clue what their design was, only that William Cecil could get the government to react to any serious threat. This was only as much strategy as seeing a bandit approach with a club so you arm yourself with the same in the hope you hit back just as hard. He looked back at the dark and still bodies hanging in the sunny breeze, their scent like sour bacon. Did it ever need to take so many deaths? The less, it seemed, that Her Majesty's government knew, the more they killed in response and reprisals.

Walsingham realised now with agonising clarity that intelligence and information was the only future for England's stability.

III

ℰᴑᏆ

Walsingham barely noticed the evening give way to darkness as he solemnly sat in his study. Stow's comment to him several hours earlier that he should, "Forget not that anger. And all your others too" makes him think through his entire life. The still room twitches in the night as his unease rubs shoulders with memories in the flicker of candleflame. He fidgets in his chair and it creaks in complaint, heightened in the dark by the wood crepitating so sharply that it shudders right through him, as if one of his own bones had suddenly snapped.

Bones do snap, he states quietly to himself. They neither crack nor splinter like twisted branches nor pop like a dropped glass vial. He knows this. For he has heard them in the screams of men. Snap they go in angry protest of something suddenly being in two. A memory from twenty years previous at the butcher's bench suddenly comes to him. Sinew wrangled from pork loin. He could see the cleaver swiping swiftly down and splitting the bone apart. Snap. That was the noise. In all that changes, sounds you never forget. Their voice never failing to bring some alarm from the past. His past. An alarm for the future too. Memories now barge into his mind, dense and loud –

* * * *

Stand back, he as a little boy was told, while the old man with thick forearms steered him away, beyond full reach of the hand that clasped the sharp blade. It swung round in a wide arc and, with a sound like treading on icy mud, tore into flesh and prized it effortlessly apart. The pig's bowels spilled onto the floor as the blade slid up the belly to its neck. His father had insisted the boy Francis be shown every manner of the farm's workings: crop rotation; fallowing fields; hauling of dung; the stables and livery. The overseer for this job fell to his uncle, a stout bearded man with limbs like logs. Butchery fascinated the boy most of all, with its deftness – and indifference – to danger, the richness of blood and the glistening black wet leather of the tannery. Their darkness mesmerized him. Until he was shouted at.

'By what tide you opportune to finish, boy?' His uncle would remonstrate, bidding his daydreaming nephew's work rate increase.

'Look at it.' The young lad would say, holding up stained skin or glistening innards, their glimmer captivating him.

'Aye, tis dark, nothing more.'

Yes, young Francis Walsingham thought, but you do not see what I see.

Puzzled, the uncle watched his nephew revering its gloomy sheen, and tried to break him out of it, 'Darkness there and nothing more.'

Walsingham back in the solemnity of the study could now see his younger self revere its mysticism, and this clarity of thought within dark would never leave him. He let his memory continue –

'This here be the tough part. Remember, stand right there.' His uncle says, as the young boy watched with macabre fascination the forearm thicker than his own leg get to work. A vigorous sawing motion hankered into the pig's throat and head. Long dead, it shook as if writhing from post-death pain. Sinew is thickest here, he could hear his uncle, the artisan of flesh, tell him, his arm pumping yet harder when, as graceful as picking an apple from a tree, the knife suddenly swipes out of the animal and with sheer momentum swings speedily towards the boy, the man's bloodied arm at full stretch, clasping the crimson blade, stopping just an inch from his face.

'That,' the old butcher warned him, 'is why you stand such distance.' The blade's tip pointing right between his eyes. Francis nodded earnestly as it was reiterated to him that mess, danger and life are never far apart but need never cross paths. 'Any knife wielder can chop or slice, but it takes great skill to cut with care. Butcher's need to trust each other. Nay, any man does in such life endangerings. Always remember: the blood circle.'

Young Francis adored watching his uncle at work. He knew from then that butchery was not merely hacking meat, but discipline and talent. The pig was majestically laid out on the table, a great drape of meat, flopping over at the corners. The bigger the beast the easier it is, he was told. Hares and hens were where the real art lay. His butcher uncle wiped his sweat with his other almighty forearm and, seeing the boy was keen, beckoned his nephew into the yard where chickens were cooped. Nay slip on the guts, Francis was told, so he trod carefully over the disembowelment beneath him, shining on the grimy floor. A mill pond of death. There is a clean way to do dirty work his uncle remarked. Advice he felt was given to dwell with him throughout the rest of his life. Francis was keen to learn.

He had helped his cousins feed the chickens and detested their noise but, seeing his sturdy uncle approach, the birds fell silent and herded to the furthest corner. They knew. Even when they look slaughter in the face, he was telling his nephew, you have to make them feel comfortable. Francis had laughed at this ridiculous notion. Entering the coop, the birds flapped and hopped over each other. Food, Francis was sure, would settle their terrors and said so to his uncle. Do that once with their feed and they won't eat again – and all you have is weak birds, bad eggs and scrawny meat, he had responded. His uncle did not mind explaining and encouraged Francis' curiosity, but in this moment made him watch and listen to what he did next. The old wise executer of animals collected some old feathers lying on the ground into a bundle, knelt to the floor and offered the handful to the birds. Slowly, a couple of the old hens came to inspect. I shall pick the oldest one, her egging is done. Look, he was saying, she is sniffing the feathers in my hand, probably thinks it be one of her chicks, and, as gently as he was speaking, with his other hand he scooped the bird up underneath its hind and soothed it, rubbing down the breast. Tis the only part of their body they can't muzzle themselves, he explained. They then walked calmly out with the unsuspecting chicken, it never making a fuss, remaining intrigued with the feathers.

Breaking its neck had to be quick, no second attempts – for the old meat was tough enough but doing this wrong would tighten its sinews with panic and no length of cooking would make it chewable. He continued to soothe the bird and was looking at Francis while telling him to be quick and sure, lest supper be ruined. With his soft little hands, the boy then stroked its breast, plump and soft, up to her neck and in an instant grabbed, twisted and yanked it down hard. She was no more. A floppy cushion. His uncle smiled, surprised.

Francis could only stare at his pale and bony hands, claiming their first life. He was surprised to see how clean they were, having done this dirty, necessary, work. They took the warm bird back to the butcher bench, where he was handed the cleaver and was prompted to show his uncle what he had learned. Francis, now apprentice butcher quickly becoming a man, swiped it into the backbone, smartly snapping it in two. Clean, dirty and necessary work, he thought, turning to his uncle, holding the heavy blade at full stretch, his uncle out of reach.

'The blood circle.' Was all he said.

* * * *

These many years later he could still hear that snap of the chicken's neck sat in his dark study. Walsingham smiles with the odd fondness of how people reminisce about what used to shock or worry them. His past now more at the forefront of his thoughts. Why today? He took some comfort in a phrase he heard – the more uneasy the future, the more men sought answers from the past.

His cogitating glare is broken by Ursula, his stout and large-bosomed wife he has come to adore. She brings a replacement candle and places it on his desk.

'There is no need, I shan't rest here long in want of more light.' He says idly. Ursula smiles, knowing that to be a lie.

'Light or no, I offer chance to think.' She whispers, securing the candle into place by its stem.

'We can't afford the wax.' He says looking glumly up to her with his generous eyes.

'Then we should consider retiring to the estates in Kent,' she jibes, half sighing, 'sell them over for sheep farming.' At awkward angles they turn and look to each other, Ursula cannot resist a chuckle, which rustles her breasts the way only big women manage. Everything about her comforts him.

'Sheep farming.' He tuts, half knowing it was indeed the easier fortune to make, just not the labour of dutiful servant to the realm, God or Queen. That is the order of things, he affirms silently.

'I hear there's profit in such ventures.' Ursula adds, by this time at the door, about to go back downstairs but sees the joke has worn thin and so offers genuine consolation. 'You're a first term member for Parliament. Patience, Francis.' Leaving, she smiles deeply.

He calls after her, 'Perhaps a wife should say that.'

From the creaking walk downstairs she retorts, 'Well perhaps a husband should make his opportunities, not just wait for them.'

Walsingham exhales deeply, she is right. As a middle term Member of Parliament for Lyme Regis, his career should be beginning to peak, but as he looks over the shelves, empty of folios, and oak trunks sparse of scrolls, all staring back at him like emblems of lack, mocking his underachievement, he wrestles and succumbs to doubt's firm clasp of just why he has worked as hard as the Devil to get nowhere? In one final indignation his own bronze seal stamp, glistening with almost virginal pride, not yet being soiled with the stamping approval of rampant communication, shines scornfully back at him. Surely his sole function is not merely to concern himself with the excise duty on fisheries or the yield of farmsteads, but that of a truly greater purpose. He fights the melancholy. Ursula is right. Opportunity is only ever made.

His talk with Stow earlier on Tower Hill now forces him to think anew: can he really make an opportunity from England's threats? Someone has to because no one seems to know. He turns to his ornately detailed map of *merrie England* sprawled across his desk. Certainly there is work to be done. Whether it is assuring Her Majesty's subjects are free from religious persecution and coercion, to assessing threats from hostile foreign states or even in the preventing of subversive attacks against England's sovereignty and Her Majesty's person. There would be an abundance of intelligence to harvest. In so doing, he and Stow had agreed, England's prosperity would be secured.

He was excitedly convincing himself, but where, how to begin…and who with? Answers he knew did not lay in the peaceful cobb and quay of his Dorset harbour town nor in the lowly bench of Parliament. Shadows danced on the wall from the candle's flicker as his legs fidgeted impatiently. Looking for concentration away from the map, the orange yellow glow on the wall pulsated disquietingly.

Memories began to re-intensify in his mind. He could now see himself as a wispy bearded 21-year-old, the summer sun coming back so vividly that it brought about perspiration under his doublet in the cold study. Closing his eyes, as if to invite more, his head jarred as he recalled how England in June 1553 was a very different realm: today he was free to worship how he pleased. In those turbulent Summer months the sun was not the only heat searing through London's streets. Fire, with its hellish grandeur would take hold, metaphorically and literally, clasping men's souls.

Following the not too far gone days of Edward VI's reign when Protestants could be forgiven for believing their new Jerusalem would flourish evermore and the vile and corrupt Catholicism would forever be banished and burned on the realm's long pyre of superstitious legacies. England rapidly became a confused, nervous and growling nation when Edward died prematurely and Mary Tudor, his devout Catholic sister, acceded the throne. She promised to scratch back all previous gains of the religious reformation and sought completely to remove all memory of Protestantism permanently – and by burning if necessary. Queen Mary would, she advised her Privy Councillors, enact her own *holocaustum* should "the need be so prudent." Holos meant the whole and caustum: to be burnt. The pyre would certainly be stacked ever higher, for this was no temper tantrum, but dangerous sincerity, prospering into royal policy.

Fidgeting thoughts still jerked him, for this night was not yet done with Francis Walsingham. Amidst the flickering candle's flame there began to brew more nightmares from his past. In this deepest dark of night, mystical and menacing, those days of peril in the middle months of Summer 1553 came roaring back to him, frenzied and toxic.

Walsingham wakes, crying out in haunting lamentation, which quickly trails when he realises his distress is over and those terrible visions of fire are through. The darkness, however, was not, nor would ever be. Was this what Stow had meant when he said, "Forget not that anger. And all your others too."

With these troubling visions of fire from his past came a realisation of purpose: commencement. Should it be that England simmers towards a scalding of the pure once again, then, he decided, tempering these growling forces was going to take commitment. The kind demanded by initiating his own blood circle.

IV

፠ᘒ

Ursula was late readying a breakfast of oat bread and cheese when she bustled up to her husband's study on hearing his restless wake-up cries and fussing away his daughters, telling them not to worry for their father. Helped by Edith, her younger sister, Ursula saw to it that Edith was treated as all other servant girls should be, according to the etiquette demanded by London's near-wealthy households. Until, that is, she became a man's charge, and the family would be relieved of her.

Climbing the stairs, Ursula unfolded some black velvet as she went while Edith knocked apprehensively, and then they enter.

Walsingham was stood in his under-vestments staring out towards Tower Hill. 'I slipped and startled myself. Nothing more.' He says, knowing they were about to ask. Ursula did not mind the lie, wanting her to retain thoughts of gallantry, as the man of the household should.

'Come, have some hearty fayre to set the day forward.' She dotes, looking to her sister the servant to set out his meagre meal. A thin legged and scrawny-armed girl with broad breasts, Ursula always marvelled how Edith never toppled. Right now she was hiding her fury at why her sister had made the breakfast late – how hard would she have to hit her today, she considered. Not that Walsingham himself minded this particular morning, clearly preoccupied.

'No fish.' He observes sorrowfully.

'The trawlers not yet returned.' She too could lie.

'The household budget run aground more like.' He yaps, evidently she is not very good at it.

'Hither, let me tailor your gown.' Swaddling him in the black velvet of his new robes and stepping onto a standing stool to ease the height difference, it gives her the opportunity to kiss him on the lips.

Edith, thankful her mistress sister was not going to take a swipe at her for tardiness, curtsies her escape quickly and leaves.

'Good morning, wife.' He smiles, before chewing at the tough bread. 'In want of fish, this dry wood.'

'Hush and let me finish your gown to send you complete for your...your – what is thine intentioned purpose for the day?'

'Petition to Privy Council.' He smiles at her ever-dutiful service. Walsingham would never cease to view the world through the eyes of servitude. We all have masters; he always took the time to remind his daughters.

A manservant's voice throbbed up through the floor below, announcing his steward had arrived. Ursula brushed him down and beheld the masterpiece, how stately and resplendent he looked, pleased she knew exactly how to stitch the seams so that it would fold and sway to match her husband's gait; melodic, smooth and purposeful, like a bird of prey.

Walsingham held and kissed her, then walked down the stairs, his long cloak making him look as if he was floating. He remembered it had been near seventeen years since he had last seen him. Although in reality it was almost every night: that little tortured face; that scalded arm; that memory at Queenhithe wharf.

Stimpson, Walsingham's deaf manservant, shook Robbie's hand. They mouthed pleasantries to each other, and both understood. Stimpson leaves them with their reuniting.

The two men beheld each other, Robbie Beale no longer the boy from his dream, but coltish young man with eyes that told the world he should be taken seriously. Love and loyalty effortlessly seeped from his smile that was exaggerated by the fashionably thin moustache and smooth rounded chin. Edith was in the background, hiding, but keeping an intrigued eye on the new addition to Walsingham's retinue.

The steward's master was overcome with relief and managed to say and do what he had wanted to after all these years, clasping both the young man's arms, simply saying, 'Robbie, dear boy.' They hugged as if to warm each other from a long cold night apart, now in their morning of togetherness. 'It is delightful to have you in my midst once more. Now that London will be my seat I shall never abandon you again.'

'And I you…?' He faltered slightly – the convention of how to address him, his master, steward, surrogate father.

'Francis. Always Francis.'

'Yes, sir – Francis! You shall always remain my master and I your servant.' Loyalty, Walsingham beamed from the inside, never dies.

'Let us walk awhile and I shall share my speech of petition to the Privy Council.'

They left the house and headed south towards London Bridge, they were going via Southwark, no short cut, Robbie noted – evidently this was going to be some speech. He was surprised, then, that as they ambled through the growing busyness in the lanes, Walsingham did not speak for some time, merely holding a reflective gaze as someone might when they are pondering news that will deeply and long-lastingly affect all they care for.

Robbie was keen to catch up on lost time and though they had corresponded over the years nothing could replace face to face conversation. He wanted to update his mentor – for there really was no other word to describe someone who had taken pity on him when, at the age of six, Francis had seen him gutting eels for a fishwife at Billingsgate. One slap with a wooden spoon too many saw him snatch the boy from the earthen wench and instantly employ Robbie into his servitude: menial jobs at first but then it was obvious the boy had charm, wit and a deductive mind. He set him to task with numbers, collating orchard yields, recording their prosperity, before evolving him to victualling excise duties and timber stocks from the Baltic states, forecasting profits. Robbie thrived in the work and, though he could not yet scribe, his reading of English, Latin and French was proficient, and he could record number ledgers as well as any clerk of the exchequer at almost two decades their junior. Words would merely confuse the boy's mathematical mind, Walsingham would explain to Ursula, perplexed to see how holding his learning back could "better" him. By the time the boy was nine years old, and before those tumultuous days of 1553 when their destinies were sliced – more seared – apart, he was already a mathematical virtuoso.

In the absence of his master's exchange on this extensive stroll, Robbie decided to just go ahead and talk, picking up from that long ago day at the wharf when Francis had looked back to him from the trawlerman's boat. Walsingham listened and heard him say how he was kicked from Captain of the Guard's possession as a useless wharf rat but, despite his scarred arm disabling him for a long time, he was able to prosper with the skills endowed to him by Francis. He eked out a survival by helping minor merchants with their counting and approximating of stock, even journeying as far as the Baltic and the Azores. Robbie would even see from time to time that rotten shit sack woman who beat and rebuked him mercilessly at Billingsgate. Jovially approaching her one miserable day, with every right to thrust his fist into her ill-fitting nose, he instead paid her handsomely for the most expensive eel and oysters, only to give them to the next starving sufferers in her charge. He never did lay eyes upon the Captain of the Guard again.

Walsingham nodded intently but remained pensive as he glided over the filthy muddied tracks in his newly tailored cloak and gown, heading down onto London Bridge. He had been so keen in his correspondence to learn more of what the boy was doing to advance his mathematical skills, Walsingham more recently even setting him problems, predictions and patterns to figure out, but Beale knows not to be bruised by his inattentions.

'Left ho.' A loud voice belches to the hundreds that were now teeming onto the only thoroughfare joining either bank of the Thames. London Bridge was so busy that its traversers were told which side to walk or drag their cart. Walsingham watched them mindlessly starting their day.

Robbie, gabbling through his own history monologue stopped only to amaze Walsingham that the bridge itself had not sank for it seemed with each month there were more lofts and rooms built ever higher. One of his friends, Beale excitedly recounted, had taken comfort with a whore that dwelt right at the top of one of those lofts and, he had heard said, it took all this man's ingenuity to get where he wanted. Walsingham chuckled, it was a good pun he admitted. It had the added value of being true, Beale went on, explaining the poor chap really had to aid his ascent with the climbing of ladders and rope bridges. He saw Walsingham smiling, still listening, looking up to the extensions of gabled wooden garrets now stacked and staggered upon high.

Other than height, not much had changed in near two decades on the bridge – there were still taverns, guest lodges, communal toilets where you shat straight into the river, Robbie mused, right next to merchant stores, galleys, although there was a tobacco leaf seller now. It took them about an hour to cross as London was now fully awake. All this time Walsingham remained quiet. As they headed to the bustling south side, Robbie wondered how much he had truly listened. He must have looked to him with anticipation or concern because Walsingham, taking his cue, then immediately took out his scroll with an apologetic smile and started to read. Robbie Beale looked ahead to the boisterous crowd and wondered how practicable this was going to be and warned him so, but Walsingham was not concerned.

'England is a Protestant country, but far from being at peace.' Walsingham announced, as he walked, shifting between bumps and barges from the people around who cared less for what or who he was. As they passed *Dead Man's Place* along The Bank walk, mounting crowds and passers-by began to jeer Walsingham in his finery and grandiose voice – as Beale knew they would any gentleman. Rehearsing his speech was going to be problematic after all, but he was determined to continue, much to their joyous amusement. Trying to ignore them and appear unphased, even as women began to slap his arse and flash their gussets, Walsingham spoke with surprising calm. Beale tried, where he could, to combat the growing attention, and to push them away in hope of saving blushes. One man tries to snatch the parchment from Walsingham's hands, dancing around him, regurgitating arse-spitting noises in outlandish mockery. Beale fizzes with anger but Walsingham paws him back, and they continue.

He reads on unabashed, he will finish his rehearsal, 'Paranoia of plots to murder Queen Elizabeth are rife, denying us fact or meaningful intelligence. This, I will change.' Instinctively they turn right, towards Southwark's wharves, and he then stops them right in the middle of the hustling.

Beale is initially puzzled and awkward as they stand between moving crowds that bump and shuffle them, then looks at Walsingham's position and realises why he has stopped. They turn and have a long view of the bridge's south side entrance with its three-hundred-year-old barbican, above which traitors' heads are trophied on spikes, eyes absent and flesh eaten away, rancid reminders of ill-chosen destinies. Beale cannot help but think how odd their reunion is today, when his father figure solemnly nods as if to point out how the lesson within his speech was so far being ignored and sidles away. Worried how this walk could get more challenging, Robbie looks on down the lane towards

Southwark, where it was certainly less busy, though somehow more disorderly. He mentally rolls up his sleeves for a fist fight, what with all these spittle lickers out in force, he thought. It was still only morning tide and already there was huckstering, whoring and drinkers frothing insults at no-one in particular. Beale notices many centring around a fenced-off pit and believes they may well get through unmolested.

Walsingham decides it is time to read on, his voice stern and sure, 'Twelve years hence, since Her Majesty succeeded the throne, alack, the tyranny of Catholicism has yet to be expelled.' He is interrupted by a beastly snorting sound. Thinking it another rude interjector, he ignores it and proceeds with his rehearsal, 'Gentlemen, England is in peril.'

Robbie hears the grunting continue and tries to be attentive to Francis, but sees it is coming from a cage where the morning shards of light blind his sight to what is inside. Another growl, this time hollow and deep. What monster lurks there, he trembles, as the crowd's shouting around the pit grows louder. Uneasy at the sense of possible danger, Beale looks hesitantly to Walsingham.

'It is a peril that terrifies us, like some demonic beast, from the shadows.' He continues to intrepidly read, just as –

With a frightening roar, the cage crashes open and an almighty bear lurches high above the crowd, who scream excitedly with bloodlust, their faces mean and horrifying.

Startled, Robbie yelps and instinctively yanks Walsingham's arm like the little boy from years gone by, forcing them to stop and take in the phenomena.

Leashed bull mastiffs bark wildly as if their very existence was being challenged, which it was. There was six of them, plunging and jabbering in such ferocious unison it looked like a gang of labourers hacking hoes at wet soil as the possessed dogs slid, darted and stammered in the mud. The huge bear, now arched up on its hind legs, dominates its territory. This did not concern the slathering baiting dogs who were unleashed and flew into the black beast with their jaws poised. In one almighty swing, its paw digs one of them into the ground, dead.

'You've seen a bear baiting before?' Walsingham asks, amidst the riotous shouts, noting Robbie's shock. He lies and nods. 'Wait until the wrestler takes the beast on, that is a fine sight, I am led to believe. Come, let's away from this rabble.' They push on with iron shoulders, and Walsingham can finally finish his speech in between the continued jarring shoves to his sides and back. Beale cannot help but look around with interested horror but is unable to see anymore slain animals – or the wrestler of bears. Walsingham skips back over his last sentence: peril...terrifies...demonic beast...the shadows, before finishing, 'What I propose will lift the veil on this menace: a secretariat dedicated to gathering real intelligence for the Crown.' Mentor looks to Mentee for approval. 'The beast will be bested and tamed.'

Beale, flitting his eyes between the baiting and Walsingham, stutters in response, 'It is well written, my Lord. Bold.'

Walsingham was more talking to himself when he replied, 'My first petition to the Privy Council – nevermore has the need of boldness been so prudent.'

Savage purveyors of cruel sports that they leave behind, celebrating or consoling their bets won or lost on beast's mastery over one another, are now behind them as Beale says, 'I doubt any here realise the danger we all find ourselves in.'

'Mine is to worry whether or not they care. Oblivious in oblivion.' Walsingham says with cool alarm.

In a sudden smack, one drunk reveller barges at both gentlemen, so bewilderingly inebriated his eyes goggle as he tries refocussing before attempting to stagger away. This is one too many impertinences for Beale to accept and, furious at the ill-mannered wretch, snatches him back, inadvertently rolling up his own leather tunic revealing his boyhood scar. He is about to demand an account for the goggler's poor conduct when, without remorse, is burped at.

'What game's this?' The Drunkard asks Beale feebly in a slur, his eyes reeling, seeing several of them both in his midst.

Beale knows any attempt to gain an apology is useless, so settles to venture putting their theory of ignorance to the test. 'What do you know of Catholic plots and rebellions?' Predictably, the reveller looks blankly back.

'The Earls in the north? Percy?' Walsingham adds. Still nothing.

Beale suggests, 'Westmoreland? Essex?'

'What about Sussex?' Walsingham hopefully suggests.

Drunk reveller scornfully looks them up and down, 'You want I sucks it? – dirty bastard, you need Gropecunte Lane for that.' Beale slams him away with both hands, very nearly starting a riot had not the Drunkard's more reasonable merry-making accomplice warded him off belting the well-bred gentlemen.

Walsingham sighs. 'Yet one more ignorant in the cesspit of unthinking imprecision that is London. This, our intended holy bastion of England, rapidly losing its way as the new Jerusalem.'

'And we concern ourselves with protecting such toothless, slug-breathed wretches.' Beale states sorrowfully, wondering whether or not any will ever care or understand.

Walsingham, sensing his apathy, reiterates their duty, 'Our Queen loves her people. And we love our Queen.' He sees Beale roll down his sleeve covering the scar – that reminder of torment from Catholic times past. 'I didn't return from exile just to see Catholics subjugate England once more.' He takes Beale's hand, looking between his eyes and the horrific scar, before earnestly promising, 'And these perpetrators will pay.' Beale is struck by the tenderness and danger in Walsingham's voice. He solemnly accepts his master's vow.

'Your petition could change everything.'

'I am prepared to get my hands dirty for England, Robbie. Are you?' He knows full well the answer but waits for Beale, who nods passionately, and they then walk to their wherry to take them back across the Thames, westwards to the Parliament palaces of Westminster.

Beale breaths in the sharp Spring river air and with complete clarity can see both why they took this longer route and how everything Walsingham does – or says – has purpose. For the twenty-minute wherry bobble across the water, Beale regards the man sat before him looking away upriver in its breezy lapping. With his black skull cap pinning thin brown hair that tries to escape underneath the white trim lace, Walsingham's black cape billows around his black doublet and a small white ruff like a shelf for his tiny beard on a triangle chin, like a resplendent bird atop a branch on a windy day deciding when to fly, he thought. Beale feels the awe pump through his heart, gushing to himself how truly magnificent he looks – and is. Whatever the dirt may be, he promises silently to Francis with his eyes and soul, his hands are ready for it.

V

Westminster

૪૭૮૨

Arriving at the thoroughfare outside, both men breathe in Edward the Confessor's abbey. A pantheon of piety still standing immensely strong after four centuries. Walsingham observes its immensity and cannot help but speculate if the old king would turn in his tomb to see the anthill anarchy his holy ground had become. Might the Anglo-Saxon saint see the irony as Hawkers harry with Whores while Butchers bump into Bishops on his consecrated highway, rubbing awkwardly together like stones in the smooth silken slippers the old pious prince used to wear?

Beale listens as Walsingham, staring upwards, says, 'His Roman God fumbling and faltering in the new age, destined to reveal their foibles.' Glancing thoughtfully and reverently up at the medieval buildings, it is all so clear in Walsingham's mind. When bringing God to the people, they should choose. Let them. Let them not be leant on by mighty buildings or the gold of its decorations. He has followed this growling maxim all along – not to be imposed upon by unflinching Catholics, for Englishman had not fought on battlefields or over legal precedents for their liberties to be policed in the most important part of their lives. It is now the enormity of the day gushes over him in realisation of what he is about to do. His heart pumps hard.

'Now we begin. Do you remember your undertaking?'

'To listen.' Beale says, proving his dedication, and then loses himself amongst Westminster's swarm. Walsingham watches him trot gayly off to a nearby tavern, sure he will ingratiate himself into the coteries of the other Parliamentarian stewards for any morsal of information they could use to better understand the perils facing Her Majesty. He would need to listen very carefully indeed.

Ambassadors, Servants, Clerks and Parliamentarians form a jumbled cortege heading into the beehive of government business. Walsingham joins them, comfortable blending in for now. His scroll could make him not only stand out, but possibly ostracised. Someone needs to take a stand; so, he strides in with conviction.

Entering under the shadow of God's great edifice and the palace of Westminster's portico, he listens to the murmurs of how and why the Queen has called her Parliament – is it because her Papist cousin, having sought refuge in England these last months, has come with a plan to take back her Scottish throne? Will Mary Queen of the Scots ally with Queen Elizabeth, finally ridding England of the danger of France and possibly Spain? Will the Queen herself be speaking in person? All hushed questions with profoundly loud urgent anticipation. Walsingham keeps his sentiments to himself. As a staunchly loyal monarchist and Parliamentarian, Walsingham felt conflicted in the manner with which the Queen calls Parliament – so far in her reign it had been a mere four times. He would never question, out loud, Her Majesty's ability to govern but she famously avoided – nay, ignored – her duty on calling the Commons to hear from the people.

Disappointingly for him it was usually when she needed taxes levied or laws to be introduced and therefore any other topic concerning the realm was not up for discussion, including the most important: religion. Parliament was never going to be the place where ideas were discussed and negotiated, being merely the belly of England to be filled when the Queen grew hungry. Herein lies the near unsolvable puzzle, he thought. There was no question of accepting her assertion of divine right, meaning she could rule unquestionably. The Captain need inspect the ship to see how she sails, and if Her Majesty pacified Parliament their winds would gust favourably. Sighing as he trod slowly behind all the other serviles, Her Majesty merely seemed content riding her luck in the storm.

Filing down into the depths of the building with its many dark caverns, the cortege pass countless Clerks undertaking the actual role of governing England by busily scratching their quills on parchment, recording and instructing each and every village, town or shire. Walsingham is careful not to slip on the smooth damp cobbles that slide down to the nadir of this stony palace, nearing England's permeation of power: the Privy Council Chamber.

Reaching the small vestry-like room where the Queen's handpicked ministers discuss pertinent matters of state with – sometimes without – Her Majesty, Walsingham veers away, gliding away from the main trail. As they head onwards, approaching the Commons Hall, Walsingham, with scroll in hand, makes his move. As expected, the door he approaches is manned.

Clerk of the Chamber is a stout auburn man, whom Walsingham could imagine commanding Highlanders

– all hair and tough unyielding brawn of muscle. With ill matching eyes and angry eyebrows that confuse his disposition, he looks both vexed and dim-witted.

Walsingham addresses the inferred Scotsman with subtle confidence, 'Honourable Clerk of the –' but before he could complete his introduction –

'What do you want?' Interrupts the gruff Northumberland accent, without even looking up.

Walsingham tries not to let this flummox him, 'May I make my introduction, I am...' he calmly begins.

'No, but you can answer the question.' He realises the Clerk must have heard this routine a thousand-fold.

Ever determined, Walsingham proceeds, 'I would like to leave my petition to the Privy Council, where I outline numerous –'

'They go over there.' He motions to a huge basket, brimming with scrolls. If he cannot even get to finish his plea then this was going to take far longer than he had first thought, but, ever the servant of protocol, he dutifully places his scroll on top and moves away. He does not care to glimpse back and see if the bombastic brows had finally bothered to look up. They did not.

Walsingham has no time for gloomy reflection on his decreasing prospects for a sudden commotion breaks his negative consternation when several prominent people begin arriving. The long line he had been part of now swells around him as they surge forward to see. He is inadvertently pushed near to the front. A small path clears for the eminences to progress through.

As they approach, hush and bows tell Walsingham exactly who it is, and he reverently whispers to himself, 'The Privy Council.'

A fat Parliamentarian joins his side as he bows, having heard this and, wheezing heavily, says, 'Nay more than peacocks.'

Half amused, he says smoothly, 'That as may be. Beauty and statecraft are hand to hand.' Still bent in half, he dares to peak a look at them passing, seeing Robert Dudley, the Earl of Leicester, parade by as gorgeous as a Greek God.

The wheezer beside him decides he will not be out-witted by this new, slopey-nosed fellow with the big dark eyes and black skull cap, so retorts, trying to impress, 'Rumours abound he's the Queen's fancy.'

Petty knowledge for gossip was not Walsingham's style and he contemptuously side-glances him, looking back to the entering Privy Councillors, mystified by their magnificence. The Earl of Essex hobbles past them but managing to do so with a glorious air. 'I've only ever seen their portraits.' He says, rather too obsequiously, remonstrating himself – for surely his portly companion must have heard and will inevitably respond.

'Swollen-headed prigs.' He leers predictably. Walsingham could perhaps accept that for Dudley, as charismatic as he was, but the Earl of Essex was, in his mind, a battle strategist of incredible capability.

'Essex is a true defender of the faith, and Her Majesty.' Begins his validation. 'Vanquished the papist northern rebellion not a year gone, sending them running to their Hibernian hideouts.' Still in their bow, they exchange glances which tell Walsingham they should never exchange names.

As if posing a challenge, the stooped fat man asks Walsingham as the next councillor approaches, 'And what say you of Thomas Howard?' Walsingham watches the Duke of Norfolk lumber along, unwilling, it seems, to acknowledge anyone else is there, with eyes bright and devious that say the sooner this jape was over the better. You could hear his contemptuous grunt with each step.

His eyes.

Walsingham flinches, almost forgetting himself and about to stand to catch a better glimpse, stopping just short of irrecoverable embarrassment at poor etiquette, and remains arched over, twisting his neck to follow him. No parlour portrait he had seen contained that face, although he could now only see the ermine shawl draped over his back as he walked on. Whispers grow, distracting him, as William Cecil approaches. First the clapping was slow and uneven, then it was excited and joyous.

Smaller in stature than Walsingham had anticipated, Cecil walks humbly behind the dozen Privy Councillors. Wisdom gleamed from his eyes and the authoritative gait made Walsingham's knees tremble. If Parliament was the belly of the country, Privy Council the pounding heart, then Cecil was the brain. Though the man himself would invariably have argued he was merely its constitutional common sense.

Walsingham knew Cecil's lawyering and legal thinking required betterment, having read the dispatches of the trials following the Northern Rebellion of 1569. The Queen's First Minister, as was his formal title, was in such a rush to convict Westmoreland and Percy that several powerful men were never held accountable. Dudley, Essex, Norfolk and Ludlow among those never punished. These names, as magnificent and historic as they were, are not to be trusted. All now walking past him.

Remaining stooped in genuflect, he suddenly thought of his father feeding him honey for the first time – he would always want to taste it again, never forgetting its potency. He could feel himself growing lustful to have it in abundance. Power, he knew, lay with these thirteen gentlemen. A dull clanging soon interrupted his relish and everyone stood back up straight.

The Clerk of the Chamber thudded his brass-tipped staff onto the stone floor signifying the Privy Council were in session and reverently closed the door. Their peephole into power, gone.

'Is that it?' Walsingham says surprised, the honey no more dripping down his throat but the taste very much alive in his senses.

'Oh not to concern yourself, we shall know when we're needed: to collect taxes. Needed just to be informed we are not needed.' Parliamentarian says, now being joined by other sympathetic thinkers, for their sighs betray apathy and hopelessness.

'What about our petitions?' Walsingham wonders. The responding sniggers making him realise he was sounding like an apprentice.

'Their chamber fires will always need stoking. Come, even a lowly MP, like you, knows that.' One of the men snides. Before Walsingham can register who, a bell sounds, the hall goes quiet.

'Here come our orders.' Parliamentarian chimes in sarcastically.

Clerk of the Chamber strides forward to address them all, his northern accent like wind pinching through sails, 'Gentlemen, due to the rising problem of vagrancy in our parishes, shires and towns, the Queen requires you to fix new poor rates on your townsfolk.'

Walsingham looks at his acquaintances' told-you-so eyes. Clerk turns away, signaling their dismissal, visibly twitching when he hears disappointed rumblings from his pronouncement.

Walsingham starts to move away from his naysayers, but holds back when one man near him that stunk of spoiled wine moans to no-one in particular, 'What care do we merchants have for Vagrants? – To prosper trade we need tax levied to create armies for protection.'

'My constituents need grain.' Fat Parliamentarian scoffs, now beginning to sound remotely human.

'Nothing changes.' One Ambassador says dejectedly. Not by staying out here, thinks Walsingham, looking towards the small, closed Privy Council chamber door.

'Five years my parliament robes have swept these floors, waiting.' Complains another Parliamentarian.

'We should choose our moments wisely.' Walsingham says.

'You've not been here five minutes.' Jibes one, trying to take him down a notch or three.

'And I intend not to waste any more time.' Walsingham counters without even looking at them and gliding to a dim corner, ridding himself of these distractions once and for all. He perches on a small bench behind one of the many dark stone pillars bedecking the corridors, taking it all in as if he was watching chess for the first time. How commanding and invincible the pieces impose themselves at the commencement of the game: one ill-conceived move and the campaign was hopelessly lost. Hubris could be the toppling of his pieces. Strategy, then, would be mastered before any opening moves are made. How could he endear Cecil's confidence – and once he had, who could he trust amongst the Privy Councilors? In the bleak arches and shallow ceilings his senses would once again glisten alive, vivid and sharp, as they had in the days working with his uncle – mysticism and clarity within the dark. He smiles as his father's words echo forth in his mind, with the lesson he would consider the most important: forming the blood circle.

Hours pass and Walsingham remains on the bench. The smoke from the day's candles, fire torches and hearths create a disquieting murk of blackness. Having had a great deal of time to think, he still feels the pangs of his recent nightmares churl in and out of his mind like a bad play from a second-rate acting troupe. It was his proposal and thoughts of what England needed for the good of the realm and the security of his most beloved Majesty that weighed heavier on his mind. What would keep England safe from all its foes, its papal enemy, the long years of ignorance or just plain cowardice in facing up to the reality of what could lurk and strike at any terrible moment? Now was the time to embrace the dark of uncertainty when no one else wanted to. Too long had been spent waiting, hoping diplomacy would buy time with proposed marriages to France or Spain so Elizabeth could ward off the devilish threat to England of once again returning to Catholicism. Walsingham clasped his knee: never. Pure Protestantism should flourish and Elizabeth's England will be free from the corruption of the anti-Christ in Rome. There would be no more sufferings the like of which Warne, Robbie and hundreds of others had endured in the name of this treachery to God, the Bible and Christendom. He saw too how the country was perilously vulnerable with its guard lowered by underestimating the potential

Mary Queen of the Scots was as a rallying cry for Catholics who thought Elizabeth had gone soft with her middle way on religion.

His nails dug into his clothes, piercing his skin, and his heart beat fast. He knew his battle lay in combatting ignorance and that his scroll was a declaration of war to exactly that. He was going to ensure England had an informed Queen, a warned government, and a purist Protestant country, kept safe by his own army: intelligence. They had been hiding under bed clothes, convincing themselves no terrible beast lurked in the shadows – no one could fight an enemy they could not see any more than they could find a foe that they did not know how to look for. Walsingham was supremely convinced he could change this, convinced you can learn to see in the dark.

VI

৩০ ৫৩

Following the smell of salt and wet wood down through the tangled alleys unravelling at the wharf, he could hear the shouting at the water's edge. It made him smile to think of the confusion amongst gathered Londoners hearing the ancient and mystical sounding language.

'Taht hsif si dlo.' Someone bellows, as Walsingham proudly recalls what that meant, once again thankful for his days on the family's farming estates where he picked up this skill at the market fairs. That fish is old. Is what they had shouted. Versed as he was in the archaic *Rehctub* – the backwards language of Butchers and Fishmongers.

Through the early morning fog, he could now see the men between boat and dock prattling on at each other in this disguised seller's dialect, as stocks of fish are launched wharfside. A gruff voice shouts from the boat, 'Lles eht dlo tab taht eno.' As another crate is chucked. It took Walsingham a moment to undo the puzzle missed by the ageing woman buying her early morning fish.

With no wind, the cold early morning fog crippled the servants of London's noble and merchant elite who queue along the wharf, the women's woollen shawls damp and heavy in the mist. A brawn Trawlerman glances upon them, but could not see who he was looking for so carries on unloading his slippery salty cargo. Disgruntled and damp, a Kitchenwench, disappointed at the choice, shouts up to the boat requesting Dutch cod.

Trawlerman grabs a different crate and lands it at her feet, saying, 'Ehs nac evah kcoddah. Ti skool eht emas.' The fisherman stood near lets her grab two fistfuls for her basket and she hands over some coin and walks happily away, none the shrewder for it.

'French prawns?' Another woman shouts. He grabs two smaller crates and heaves them on the quay, landing imperfectly as grey langoustines spill onto the cobblestones.

'Yeht yap elbuod.' Fisherman takes the woman's money, but signals it costs more. She refuses and crosses her arms.

Trawlerman sees this and shouts down, 'Taorg rof eht tol.'

Fisherman holds up four fingers to her and she hands over two more pennies.

Stood looking down from the boat, Trawlerman cannot help but chortle, with many of London's elite abiding by the laws and not eating meat on Wednesdays, Fridays and Saturdays they enjoy a lot of fish and are not prepared to pay too steeply for it. It is then he sees him – it has to be – a figure bedecked in black glides past the queuing women who scoff and leer at him, not because they think he is muscling in on their patient wait, but because they know this is no place for a gentleman.

Fisherman on the wharf shouts up to Trawlerman, 'Eht dlo hsif si enog, teg eht hserf.' Another two crates are launched down to him, almost hitting the swathed black figure. Walsingham removes his hood and smiles familiarly up to Trawlerman who jumps down and lunges a greeting hand towards him. As they embrace amidst the smell of fish, it reminds Walsingham of their first encounter near seventeen years ago as he was hauled up and rescued. Edmund Blythe had changed little and even the wrinkles of age had been kind. They walk away from listening ears.

'Your own trawler.' Walsingham discerns.

'We are both men of changing fortunes, no?'

Walsingham can tell he had not forgotten his promise, but serves to remind him, 'We are at the turning of the tide. It is all our duty to play a part now.'

'Fishing is but scathing labour.' Blythe mops his brow, then with relief, says, 'I received well your message.'

'Robbie Beale is a most trusted servant, in times when this necessity is scarce. I knew it to be greeted well.' Walsingham's last words sounding more hopeful question than convincing statement. 'Your station has destiny and I am yet in greater need of your help.'

Blythe takes him in closer, saying, 'Then it will please you and your trusted steward to hear news I bring. Amidst the sea of England and France not two nights past, we offered succour to a lowly trading vessel who had on board captured cargo. They sought freshwater and purchased fish, being want of avoiding entering London's ports should they be searched. They did not show me but their piss purse of a captain boasted a French prisoner. Blythe checks over his shoulder, 'A Catholic sayeth he. They are to berth at Henry VII's naval dockyard. For what purpose I did not ascertain.'

'An interrogation?'

Blythe nods, possibly, then whispers weightily, 'Blast a shit from Satan's anus if I did not ponder they be plotters, Francis. I only fear this news may be too late for whatever your purposes be, but I venture it is important enough to know?' Walsingham combs down his beard and thinks of the past four weeks inaction since placing his scroll with the Privy Council. Already too much time to lapse for the Devil's schemes.

'Two nights past?'

'Aye, supplies enough only for three maybe four days.'

'You have done well Edmund Blythe.' Walsingham shakes his hand. 'And I shall never forget. If you write, do so only to me by way of Beale.' He gives the old stevedore, now licensed trawlerman, who rescued him all those many years ago a writ waiving customs duty. 'This will save a small fortune.' Blythe merrily returns to his slippery silver prizes from the sea.

Walsingham calculates the captain would have docked by now and a messenger deployed to the court to arrive by noon tide. He must get to Whitehall.

Arriving within the hour, relieved the day had yet to break, his body thinned with the sting of the early morning chill. Condensation was making it difficult for the servants to keep the embers alight in the grills. The mix of vapour and dampened smoke reminded him of the peat-burning bogs in the New Forest that he would pass on his infrequent visits to Lyme Regis. Crouching beneath the wafting smoulder, he took up position in the cloudy shadows near the Privy Council Chamber door and could see a little clearer when he sat. He waited, watching servants coming and going, removing platters and goblets from within the brightly lit room that plunged the rest of the hall in darkness as its door closed. For all his own ambition and determination, it was these toilers who had more access to the other side of that door than seemed ever possible for him. He suddenly felt pathetic, like standing at a well with a broken bucket, so close yet not to be. He shifted and fidgeted upon the wooden bench until it got warm and he was able to regain calm, consoling himself that he was making an opportunity by just being there. Everyone else in England was asleep. Except the Privy Council.

He would need convincing. They were not going to just let him in and preach his protectionist policy then send him on his way to conduct his enterprise with free reign and endless funds. Not that he was after financial sponsorship, he and Beale had plans for that too. What he needed was the Privy Seal. That elusive formal endorsement of her Majesty's government, the eminent signifier of power stamped in wax, which was carte blanche authority across the realm. It was worth more than a bagful of silver bribing groats. Its value was such that forging the seal came with a monstrously high penalty. Walsingham winced as he remembered one man having his testicles pounded off with knotted rope for attempting it. If a woman were caught her breasts would be sliced out.

Just then two Spit-Jacks take their rest and sit themselves across the hall to sup ale and tug their teeth on leftover oat bread, never once thinking they were being watched. Their murmurs drifted to Walsingham of Parliamentarians who'd sooner throw cess at them than a tip. Though coarse as common cursitors, he smiles fatefully, these are the kind of men who lend better ears to the street than any of their Whitehall superiors: honest, unflinching and aware. There would be time when he would heed their hearsays, but the entrance of a Court Rider changes his priorities. The man had clearly ridden all night to get here, his satchel had Hampshire livery. Edmund's intelligence was right.

Walsingham observes him absorbedly. The Rider's cape was drenched, not with rain but sweat and the early morn's settling dew, giving it a mottled look as if it mapped the stars. Exhausted, Rider gathers and smartens himself before approaching the Privy Council Chamber door. His pretty young face is weary and worried. Spit-Jacks ignore him, being the same station, he is of no concern to them, but Walsingham rises slowly, quietly, and moves unseen nearer to where he is headed.

From the dimness, Walsingham watches Clerk of the Chamber take the message packet into the Privy Councillors. Rider rubs his journey-weary eyes and anticipates the worse. Walsingham thinks to himself what error he must have committed to be worried when, incredibly, William Cecil, the eyes and ears of the Queen, emerges, but his view is restricted by a pillar, so Walsingham focuses his hearing more intently – this will be crucial.

Rider instantly drops to one knee, stammering nervously, 'My Lord Minister...'

'This is the news you bring?' Cecil rattles the packet at him as if it was rancid meat for a meal. 'Nothing? Even after an interrogation? You have come with nothing?' In a rare moment of fury, he throws the packet at Rider, who ducks, mightily embarrassed and floppy in his knees.

'They be the only transcripts on my person pertaining to her majesty's causes, my lord.'

'Useless, I might throw them on the fire and you afterwards.' Cecil turns back to the small chamber, signalling Clerk to send him away. Rider is left stood there, suddenly ludicrous and obsolete. Walsingham smiles – a unique look that some know as his hallmark smirk: an opportunity. He makes his move, beckoning one of the Spit-Jacks, who jumps up as the other scrambles away thinking they are in the deepest of trouble –

'My Lord Member? – I reasoned none were here to serve.'

'An ale for our Court Rider.' Walsingham flicks his hand.

The Spit-Jack is deeply affronted, fetching after an equal low-born subservient, but he has no choice, as Rider looks delighted. 'Yes sir.' He concedes, as if he has just bargained away his mother for a button.

'Heartily appreciated, my lord...?' Rider begins.

'Walsingham, Parliamentarian for Lyme Regis.'

'Never been.' Rider says, perhaps a little too honestly.

'But you have been working hard. Protecting the Queen.' He coos, leading him towards the galley.

'Yes sir.'

Spit-Jack returns with the ale, offering it to Walsingham who nods it towards Rider. It is handed over with disdain.

'And some venison?' Walsingham asks, 'Still roasting on the spit?'

Spit-Jack cannot believe it and Rider licks his lips. He skulks away, stunned he has to wait on this messenger again, but has little option than to usher them, 'This way.' Wishing he had run with his friend into the caverns of Westminster Palace, he looks back to Rider, who grins like a pig in shit.

The basement kitchens are a furnace, the heat stifling Walsingham as if a bucket of sand had been thrown over him. He ushers Rider onto a small stool and Spit-Jack brings some steaming mutton ends.

'No venison.' Spit-Jack half smiles, a small victory. Rider does not care, he scoffs into it, unashamedly ravenous, Walsingham relieves him of the letter packet and wanders slowly away.

Opening the mangled scroll, he notices Cecil's torn seal. Cecil did not need to use the Privy seal – he had his own. The document was an elegant verbatim script of an interrogation aboard a ship, the Griffin. No specific purpose of the prisoner interview was mentioned, which aroused his suspicions immediately as it should be stated in formal correspondence: it was to be secret then. The scribing was easy to read, an apprentice wanting to impress no doubt: *Interrogation aboard a frigate, The Griffin, off Portsmouth Point, taken this day of our Queen, 1570.* But no specific date.

As he read on, Walsingham imagined a majestical 20-gun carrack listing and yawning as below deck lanterns gently sway in the calm night, crews' faces swelling in the shadows. He continued hungrily reading:

The Frenchman was brought before the Captain and Boson to be questioned further, alack – so buckled were the prisoner's knees with exhaustion, two sailors were employed to traverse him forth. Speaketh only in his native tongue for which, it please your Lord Minister, is translated here:

HERLE: You have been brought forth to discern your interests in travelling to London?

PRISONER: Merchant interests.

HERLE: In lack of ledgers, contracts, letters of introduction and absent of specific contact names and locations to visit?

PRISONER: I have a broker.

HERLE: Alack, missing specifics. You will forgive our consternation to disbelieve you. Now your truths shall begin and will enlighten us on your designs of your profane Catholic faith.

Walsingham realised he was not reading the questions of a skilled interrogator here – there was no building of a story to later break down and scrutinise.

PRISONER: Never – English heretics. Never.

HERLE: 'English heretics' sayeth he.

PRISONER: Catholic faith is the one true religion.

The French prisoner had a face well bloodied and in want of rest but the Boson was ordered to administer further punishment, the crew in need of entertainments.

Herle, Walsingham had heard tell, was a brute of a man, oak blocks for hands and a thunderstorm temper. There was little doubt in his mind, Herle had already given the Frenchman a masterful beating and his growling crew were hungry and impatient for more.

HERLE: I know you understand English. You will speak, Frenchman.

Where are the Catholics plotting?

The Prisoner remained silent and an order to tighten was given from the Captain.

Tighten? It could only mean thing: woolding – the cruellest and most brutal of interrogation devices. Walsingham betrayed a respect for Herle using this most risky torture device whereby rope is bound around the head and a tourniquet gradually tightened until the information needed is extracted. One quarter turn too much and the skull crumples.

> *So intense did he suffer, the prisoner screamed for goodly several moments. Then, holding firm, he bemoans from his guts --*

FRENCHMAN: *Beak. All I can report is beak.*

HERLE: *Who leads the plot, ye traitor of faith?*

FRENCHMAN: *I am no Nicodemus.*

HERLE: *Tighten.*

> *Henceforth the application was made, the Captain encouraged the pursuance until the Prisoner ceased to talk but spew supper onto the decks and wasted his vestments with his own blood.*

There his torment and the questioning ends. Walsingham could hear the crack of the skull in his ears, or, should he say, the snap. An eye would most certainly have popped out. He knew this from Flemish soldiers who used to toy with Catholic runaways in the Delft market squares, which he himself had seen as an outlaw during the panics of Queen Mary's reign. Doubtless wretch the Frenchman was, Walsingham realised from the abrupt end of the interrogation, his thoughts or words would now no longer be his own to control. At the bottom of the transcript there was a short, but incisive, note –

Addendum: Herle questioned the word 'beat' but to his consternation the gathered here witnessed it as 'beak.' Alack, the prisoner was no more of word or deed to either confirm or deny.

This was not incorrectly recorded phrasing. Walsingham was convinced the Frenchman had said 'beak' for it was not uncommon that messages would be sent encoded and that animals, particularly birds – for their numerous varieties – were often used. Of course, he knew it could mean anything – *Beak* was a derisory street term for Jewish financiers or for the curved knife used to skin deer. It could therefore be a contact, a place or even a resource. If only that dumb pig Herle had more gently tortured the Frenchman they could know proof positive. Little shock, then, that Cecil had thrown this seemingly useless interrogation back at the Court Rider.

Walsingham rolled the scroll away and stalked out into the dark day, mist and moisture ensconcing him in his black cape like a wet dog's fur.

By the time he reached Seething Lane later that evening, Ursula was fast asleep in their cot and had been for some hours. She had left a candle in his study and it was half burned through. His eyes grew tired as he once again tried to find solace from the day in the candle's flame.

This time his night visions start not with Warne, but the Captain of the Guard and Warne's feet sizzling and popping in the flames, as if he was on hades' stove. He is back there. All night.

The following morning, heart pounding, ear humming as his neck and chest pulsates, Walsingham wakes. From behind the door, comes a rattled voice, 'Francis, Francis?'

'Enter.' He mumbles, disillusioned by the dawn enlightening the dark room. Beale pushes open the door.

'Cecil has called an assembly.'

'My petition?'

Arriving by mid morn he sees the entire Commons gather, ceremonially stood in the long Westminster Hall. The House of Commons chamber was too small a meeting point for the entirety of the governing classes. As Walsingham enters and looks up at the ribs of ceiling beams, his mind spins in three directions: what were the fragments of his night visions to mean; what would be his response to Cecil if pressed on ideas within his scroll; and why was that interrogation so important? Murmurs amongst the gathered swell, like the distant sound of an approaching army, rhythmic and portending, united by the same question: would the Queen be speaking?

The latch on the Privy Council Chamber door flunks and clicks open, a breathless moment. Walsingham, the only one to move, slides back to his dark corner. William Cecil walks out and, as he stands and waits, an expectant hum rumbles around England's frustrated and obedient servants of government.

'Gentlemen, there is alarming news from Mediterranean ports.' Cecil knew how to stun into silence. 'From Rome, a Papal Bull that slanders our beloved majesty and will soon be read in every market square, parish church, alehouse and bordello across Christendom.'

The chests of men now fill with outrage, as one bravely and loudly scourges, 'Papists.'

Walsingham smirks, the rumours he heard and mentioned to Stow were proving themselves true.

'Turn your tempers to rebelling factions in England.' Cecil says, annealing them down. 'These traitors will unite under this treasonous declaration. With Mary Queen of Scots now domiciling in England we have to be ever more watchful and act with swiftness. Go to your Parish Constables, Nights watchmen: we need intelligence.' To his surprise there are groans of disappointment – this tired message again. But in one shadowy corner, dark brown eyes look to Cecil and around the room and give a convincing smirk – England, thinks Francis Walsingham, will obtain just the man.

As Cecil turns back towards the Privy Council, the Clerk of the Chamber announces the dissolution of Parliament.

Cecil walks through the door and quicker than the flap of a bird's wing there is a whirl of bright amber just as the door shuts, the Commoners surge forward with the same tantalising question – was that the Queen? Gasps of pleasure and amazement fill the Commons meeting hall as almost all the gathered tug at each other's gowns with their feet and fall over themselves to see Her.

In a blink, she is gone and the door once again slammed shut and all are left hopelessly wanton.

Walsingham's eyes catch Beale entering. Despite being in the far reaches, he is bobbing his head up in the excitement to gain a glimpse that is long gone. Beale bounds over to him, darting through the directionless crowd, licking his lips. 'Did you see? Was that...? Did you see her?'

'Robbie,' He calmly thwarts him, 'it is beginning.'

Beale shakes his head, has he not been listening, 'But Cecil, you must go back to...Parish Constables, Night's watchmen?'

Walsingham takes him deeper into the sides of the hall, 'What do they know of intelligence. Half-pissed toss pots. How quickly can you ready a coach and horse?'

'Tonight. Why?' Beale, not seeing any sense in his master, distracted by the possible presence of the Queen.

'I have my suspicions on where plots awaken the Catholic menace – and precipitously where information can be gained. 'We can thwart them,' he says, 'but we need to take someone with us. Robbie, you won't like this...' Beale's face turns from consternation to open rebellion –

'No.'

'Find him.' Walsingham sternly says.

Shaking his head in abhorrence, 'What do you want with a drunk – and an actor at that?'

'Go to the taverns and listen.' Walsingham urges, softer, like a father encouraging his child to try again at some failure.

'He's nothing useful to say.' Beale knows his protests are irrelevant, but it feels personal.

'Not to <u>him</u>, to the scroll readers.' Walsingham looks back at the closed Privy Council door, fetishizing the power within.

Beale a little concerned, asks, 'Francis, I know funds are sparse, but if I am to be replaced...?'

'I need you Robbie. Now more than ever.'

VII

୫つ୦ଽ

Twining alleyways knot the magnificent medieval cathedral of St. Paul's as if tangling a tree's ancient roots, choking it with printers, pamphleteers and preaching. Beale loosens his cape as he walks through the jostling and huckstering of anti-Catholic furore and Puritan idealism, as if he was warding off the strangulation of threatening notions. He fears that ever since Queen Elizabeth's official *via media* religious policy had loosened the reins of censorship and created in this part of London a daily battle of posturing opinions unleashing brand-new ideas. He stops and takes off his cap to mop his brow, the curly blonde hair matted to his brow above bright blue eyes that squint to take in the tight-packed taverns, parchment makers and pressers of Paternoster Row. The noise was incredible and he puffs with concern at how it had become a bull ring of discussion and debate, The sheer mess of paper, the excess of pamphleteering strewn about showed him clearly ideas are not won by the loudest shouts alone. He had heard it rumoured so many were produced each day and left unread that kitchenhands snuck back there after dark to help stoke their fires and some even used them to insulate their bed sacks. Artless anus suckermates, he froths, sheafing through littered parchment with his buskins.

As he moved to the Ink and Quill tavern, Beale winces at the squeals of preachers and purists he passes, like a noisy hissing fire, and just as dangerous. Then there are the ridiculous, hearing one warn all to 'beware the demonic voice of the Pope.' Another hollering, 'Mary Queen of the Scots must be cast out, thine harbinger and rallying cry to Catholic plots.' As he gets to the door a Versifier, squat drunk on the lane outside, sings darkly:

> *Die, but yet before thou die,*
> *Make her know what she hath gotten,*
> *She in whom my hopes did lie*
> *Now is changed, I quite forgotten.*
> *She is changed, but changed her taste,*
> *Let her burn in that hellish place.*

Beale fumbles and fidgets with his cap, hiding the fact he does not know if he should be impressed or pity the beggar singer: their life all lost of purpose. Passing him going into the tavern he sees there is no "V" branded on his forehead so he may still be on his first chance warning from the authorities. He has at least one more chance before a hanging. Beale has no time to report him to the Parish Constable and continues into the tavern, cursing aloud that England is a mess.

Inside, Chancers, Prostitutes and Gamblers, argue and scheme their next desperate enterprise. Amongst the rogues, he could not yet see him, not helped by the gloom – the tavern not yet lit its evening fires. He could barely make out the Reader on the small stage, though his voice carries well.

'Elizabeth, the pretended queen of England and the servant of crime has ejected bishops and other Catholic priests from their churches.' He echoes around the murky arches and snugs. Beale understood this was no opinion but word for word the Papal edict Cecil had warned Parliamentarians about. His ears were now attentively pricked, though no-one else was taking it seriously, barely listening even. A little shocked, Walsingham's mentee glances about the tavern, its patrons slurping conversation into each other's ears as ale and mead drawled from their heathen gobs, ignorant of the hatred and hostility spewing forth from Rome – or even right outside the door from where they drank. Reader blithely continues, 'You must take up against her the weapons of justice. We charge and command all and singular the nobles, subjects, peoples and others afore said that they do not dare obey her orders, mandates and laws. Those who shall act to the contrary we include in the like sentence of excommunication.'

Beale now sees him. Walter Williams. Tall with broad shoulders and fine blond hair behind his ears that, along with his thin facial hair, makes him resemble more a Plantagenet king than out of work drunkard actor. Beale sees he is camouflaged in conversation with a caped man, ugly in nose and teeth. Walter notices Beale and they know not to give each other away because, despite being free to speak in Elizabethan London, it did not mean with whom you were free to do so. With every master having a servant informer it was best to be cautious. Beale sits at a corner stool, Walter slips away from the caped man, sidles in next to him and both pretend to listen to the Reader's address before they feel comfortable to talk.

'What poxy errand has he got you on?' Walter asks from the side of his mouth. Taller than Robbie, he has to lean slightly in to him. To anyone watching it would seem a drunken threatening gait and although there is history and familiarity between them, unease is putting them on edge.

'We both serve our Lord Walsingham.' Beale dutifully says.

Walter scoffs, 'I serve the fattest purse of groats.'

Beale knows this is the truth, but ignores it and nods at the Reader, distracting their conflict, 'Anything useful to know?'

'Drivel direct from the Pope.' Walter says, like an apple pip has got caught in his teeth.

'Walsingham will want to see the text.'

'Tis but horseshit. All of it horseshit.' He says, as if he could smell it right there under his nose. 'Politics, plots. Rather spray mine own puke onto new buskins. Sod Catholics, and sod Protestants, sod God.' They look at each other and half smile. 'Time to execute my destiny Robbie. Theatre. One may be opening in Southwark.'

Beale shakes his head, 'Never catch on, London has too much taste for cruel blood sports. Bear baiting pits abound I note.' He shivers at the thought of the bear in Southwark gardens. Walter looks to him and Robbie sees his intent. 'Just come to Seething Lane, see what he has to say Walter, you owe Walsingham that much.'

The Reader is getting to the end of the declaration for the second time, threatening the sentence of excommunication, before signing off 'Written at St. Peter's of Rome, on 25 February 1570.'

Beale, a little frustrated and worried, 'It has taken just two weeks for this to spread with such ferocity to England's shores.' He gets up and approaches Reader before he can stop him.

Williams, embarrassed, watches him ask for the scroll, and is rudely refused. He tries to insist, going to snatch it and is pushed away. Reader adds to this shame by shouting that Walsingham could sup from his chamber pot.

Caped man and Williams share looks, which Beale sees, distracting him from the Reader who skulks past him out of the tavern.

Beale, then Walter, instinctively follow. As they do, Beale flushes with humiliation and looks to Walter twitching his head to the caped man, sneering, 'Is that who pimps your loyalty this week?' Now both their bloods are boiling as they leave.

Outside the tavern, Walter, visibly reeling, scorns, 'Unlike yours, I have only one loyalty: our beloved Queen.' He then snatches Reader back, who looks round, dazed, up to Walter's furious face leering over him, the drunk Versifier still singing:

> She is changed, but changed her taste,
> Let her burn in that hellish place.

Williams has heard the final insult and decides to now lunge for the tuneful drunkard, picking him up and, with one angry slap, crashes him to the floor. Reader cowers, decides the scroll is not worth a cracked jaw and willingly hands it over, losing himself amongst the crowds. Beale scours at Walter, perhaps he went a little too far, as they both look down to the Versifier, shaking himself awake.

'I entreat your forgiveness, but you sing treachery.' Walter says, as the poor fellow spits out teeth into the dirt and they help him to his feet.

'I but sing for my supper.' He stammers with blood slurping between his lips. Williams smiles and gives him a chunk of bread for his troubles. 'How do I eat absent of teeth?' They leave him, staring longingly at the food he cannot chew.

They walk together through the chaotic chorus of St. Paul's alleyways and lanes without speaking, then stop at where they should part. Beale looks to Walter and refuses to give up, 'This is the freedom of speech England so wants!'

'It leads to the day of judgement.' Walter sighs.

'Then let us help Francis prevent it,' Beale lingers with an imploring smile, 'together.'

* *

Inside the dark caverns of Westminster's halls, the fire dances its last in the grate with two blackened faggots. For as long as it took those logs, each as thick as his arm, to burn through, is how long he had been waiting near the Privy Council Chamber door. Their charred brittle remains a transient reminder of time.

Walsingham remembers as a boy seeing heretics from Henry VIII's reign having to carry burned faggots in the streets – a warning of the fire that would claim them for hell should they continue with their apostasy. John Warne and many others had no such caution under the Catholic zealot Mary Tudor. As far as he was concerned, Warne was one more martyr to Mary's blood-soaked crusade. His death will not have been in vain. All Protestants should be free from persecution to practice their faith without harassment, he asserts, clenching his fist. Burnings at the stakes he was no longer prepared to sit through – but waiting, he was. This was no cutting the head from the beast, but he could set a trap. If you want blood, his father had once wisely said to him, you must make a cut.

Finally, Clerk arrives and Walsingham inches up to him with such stealth it startles the man, 'Sufferings of Beelzebub,' the poor fellow yelps, 'don't tell me, you want a response to your petition to the Privy Council?'

'If it has not yet warmed a Councillor's feet by the fire.' Walsingham says drily, sensing a grin from the Clerk.

'With haste, sir, account me with what you want.'

'I can convince our Lord Cecil to re-interrogate the French prisoner at Portsmouth.' Walsingham declares comfortably.

'Convince Cecil?' Clerk laughs. 'First you have to convince me, and I don't even know your name. Second, how in the steps of hell do you even know there was an interrogation? Intercepting Her Majesty's communications breaches the law, punishment for which I needn't...' – Walsingham has to think with surging immediacy as two nearby guards move closer –

'The legal precedent already exists.' He interrupts with smooth calm. 'Magna Carta.'

Chamber Clerk will not be made fool of, and starts back, 'A three hundred and fifty-year-old obsolete contract?'

'But there were addendums, provisions and contractions over time. One such was the Blenheim Principle.' Walsingham says in such a way as to prompt the Clerk of the Chamber's memory from some ancient schooling. He is momentarily stumbled, so Walsingham eases the road, 'It was made prudent for intercepting any communication pertaining to assassination.' The unease that final word leaves with the Clerk makes him look back to the Privy Council chamber door, this is no time to discount assaults on Her Majesty – what if this large-eyed upstart dressed in black with unfashionably cropped hair was right? Walsingham can feel his feet slipping towards the door and feeds off the old man by pressing the point, 'Time pressure is always mounting. Even if evidence is not.'

* *

Williams and Beale are sat twiddling thumbs, waiting, nosing about Walsingham's study. Noting the empty shelves and portfolios that nightly mock him. 'What are we even doing here, Robbie?' Williams says with hollow care.

Ursula enters, 'My husband will be certain of good reason to invite you here this eve tide. I shall be in pursuit of your manners that they prevail and wait his return.' She says. It embarrasses Williams a little, so he nods graciously. 'Shall I fetch Edith up with some supper?'

Williams politely declines but Beale gleefully accepts. Ursula leaves smiling at Beale like older women do, understanding some of the ways of younger men's worlds.

Bending into Beale, Williams is jocular, saying, 'Edith - now we know why you're here. I shall let you eat and sup whence I bid you away.'

Beale says nothing and so both men just sit in perfect candlelight, no flicker from the settled London evening outside, the sound of the streets as gentle as a baby's sleeping wheeze.

Edith soon enters and Beale watches her, thinking to himself what a beautiful young maid who does not yet know how to smile properly at a gentleman, what small round cheeks, pointy nose and soft lips. At eighteen she would have long ago been mothering children were she of poverty, but being of gentry townsfolk, as the Walsinghams were, Edith was now at prime betrothal age. Beale's keen eyes following her as she brings in supper. He sits upright, giving Walter the upper hand at his friend's affectionate unease. She pours the ale from a generous jug, her slender arms with hands that look as if they have been washed with stones and sand. Beale guesses she has been in service since she was five and is alive at the thought of ending all that for her. Too slight for Walter, 'I like tummies and tits to bounce and round thighs to slap as I spear my prey.' He surly smiles, and lets the young buck have his dream. Beale wants to thank her, to start a familiarity, but even that would break protocol and heartless mockery would no doubt ensue from Walter. He can only watch as she breaks the bread and spoons the lard, trying to steal a glance.

'Feast well, sirs.' She says, ending her look with Beale.

'On supper, I assume.' Smirks Walter, never taking his eye off their immature ritual. She smiles thinly. If she had not, Walter would be within his right to beat her, being his employer's guest.

'Thank you, Edith.' Beale says, before kicking Walter under the table.

'You're welcome, sir.' Said in a way that could have five different meanings, never losing her smile to him as she leaves.

Walter laughs, while saying, 'Be done and sard the poor wench.' Beale rolls his eyes and eats slowly – what is keeping Francis?

* *

Closer now. His feet nearly shuffling against Clerk's. He could even hear the rumble of voices through the thick oak door. Lesser men would crumble into their already buckling knees. Walsingham had not felt like this since his return to England in 1558: trepidation at the uncertain. It had taken him twelve years of meandering through petty politics and the lacklustre pursuits of Parliamentary business, until this moment right here outside the door to the Privy Council. Yes, perhaps he was about to enter on flimsy pretence that he could save the realm – from what, precisely, he could not entirely make clear – but he unshakeably believed you do not have to see danger to know it is there.

Chamber Clerk, probably going to regret it, knocks the door, as they tread carefully forward, pauses, so conversation within can halt, and with a deep breath ushers them in.

Instantly Walsingham gulps in the room's detail: quickly counting twelve men sat round a surprisingly simple slim oak table, small archway doors either end, scrolls scattered across the room and a huge leather-bound ledger, which is shut by Cecil, bringing complete silence and focus upon their entrance. Eyes bear Walsingham down, no creaks from this fine furniture. Cecil clasps his hands to bring about an air of repose. Ludlow is sat closest to him, bland and charmless, his inheritance being his only qualification to be here.

Dudley, Essex and Howard are the furthest from him and it feels as if one of those should speak first. Clerk approaches Cecil, whispers in his ear, then motions Walsingham to step forward, but he stops when Cecil begins speaking –

'Gentlemen, our member of Parliament for scrumpy orchards and milk maids wishes to establish a secretariat to gather intelligence for the Crown.'

Despite the mock grandiose and snide chortles, Walsingham does not flinch and he sees three Councillors sit up straight as they shake their heads chuckling sardonically. Their laughter is meant to hurt but it eases him, men are always just men, although he notices Howard, Essex and Ludlow laugh hardest of all.

'You should try sheep farming.' Howard blurts, performing now.

'Woolingham.' Ludlow jibes. Booming Howard into laughter, while all the others only grin tiredly. Walsingham braves on; never surrender the high ground of the right and true he repeats over and over in his mind, offering his pouch of papers to Cecil, which Clerk takes from him.

'These transcripts from the interrogation off Portsmouth have merit.' He manages to say without faltering.

'Merit?' Cecil splutters, 'These are near two days past, you would tell the farmer it rained last week so cover the feed today? We do not guess nor bumble our intentions, sir. Serious business is conducted here.'

Walsingham quickly senses losing the room. 'Your agent did not fulfil his obligations, my Lords.' He suggests, stopping all grins and Howard's chuntering. Cecil stands, gives him a look that could emit thunder, the utter gall of this man. 'If it please you, my Lords.' Walsingham adds quickly, yet still not showing signs of desperation. 'He foundered, sirs, in his modest chore that was his undertaking.' Dudley drinks from his goblet, hiding a grin, he will hear more of this impetuous and amusing fellow.

'Get him out.' Howard snaps, done with this lowly MP from the-Lord-only-knows-where.

Surprisingly it is Essex with his firm eyebrows that betrays a look to Cecil and convinces Walsingham he is not on shaky ground. Cecil acknowledges, giving Dudley the opportunity to invite more.

'No. Speak on, my dear fellow, you ruffle enough feathers here, some are ready to be plucked.' Dudley nonchalantly says, lingering evocatively on his last word.

Cecil does not ease in directing his attention from Walsingham. 'You question an agent of the crown? Of mine? And just what do you propose to do about Herle's error?'

Walsingham clears his throat and looks them all in the eye. Every single one of them.

* *

Their feast has finished and ales sunk. Walter stands and looms over Beale, 'I am wasting my time. You are wasting your time.'

Out of his own frustration with Walsingham's absence – and Williams' impatience – Beale quickly entreats, 'One last chance.' It is not clear if he is asking for Walsingham or himself and Williams can only shake his head. Beale is much stronger in his conviction when he adds, 'You owe him this much, Walter.'

'In a lifetime of luck,' Williams says with a tired frown, 'Walsingham has run his last.' He makes a move for the door.

'Don't make me get the papers.' Beale warns quietly, about to close his eyes in regret when –

Walter sneering with disbelief, says, 'Loyalty is not earned through fear, Robbie.'

Beale stands. They look bitingly into each other's eyes: Beale's ever so slightly watery and Walter's dry and piercing. Seeing into Beale's, Walter relents and decides manners dictate he should wait, though the threat he cannot forgive.

* *

Dudley and Essex sit back, impressed by Walsingham's articulate proposal from his original petitioning scroll. Even Ludlow seems bought. Cecil looks to Howard whose answer is clear, muttering this impostor is a naïve, obstinate fool.

To Walsingham's relief the rest of the table take their lead from Dudley and Essex, one even going so far as raising his goblet in consent, though no-one would be as foolish as to speak up in support of a lowly Parliamentarian.

Howard cannot bring himself to say it is as near to open rebellion as they had suffered in the Germanic states three decades past – and that led to civil war. Instead, he pinpoints his glare at Cecil who has let this farce go on for too long. The wise little man shrugs it off like his pony swiping horseflies with its tail and moves to approach Walsingham, veering him towards the door from where he entered, away from prying ears.

Bracing for rejection, he is almost wrong-footed by Cecil's tactile holding of his forearm as they step gently to the door. Softly, Cecil murmurs to him, 'You shall leave with one piece of advice: return with value.' A chair creaks as one of the Privy Councillors leans in to hear the exchange, as Cecil continues very quietly, but no less earnestly, 'Or a mountain of shit fall upon your house, sir, and I shall be the first to drop my breeches and defecate.' Cecil's eyes let him know this is half jest, tightening the grip on his arm and they lock gaze, as he goes on to say, definitively, 'Why is it some sparrows succumb to the sparrow hawk and others do not? Understand this, Francis Walsingham MP for Lyme Regis, should you founder in your "modest chore" now in your charge, I cannot protect you from the wrath of this Council nor our favoured majesty, should your designs perish to fortuity.' He motions subtly back towards the table, 'They are your hawks. Do not give them opportunity to devour.'

Walsingham glances back to the dispassionate faces then focuses on Cecil's fixed eyes and knows from this moment he would never be able to read them accurately ever again. As squires adored to serve their lordly knights in histories long since gone, he had quickly found himself wanting to please and impress this most humble and powerful man of all England. And he knew how he could.

VIII

⁂

Beale had done his best in the time he had – it was by no means a stagecoach, more wagon with propped canvas roof, like a moving bivouac, but it appeared stable as it was pulled slowly along by a lagging horse. Walsingham smiled appreciatively at their moving shelter, convinced it would shield them from the night rain that he could smell was on its way. As they clumped and jolted along the ancient roads away from London, rutted hard with centuries of timber wheeled carts, Walsingham read by lantern light the Papal Bull Beale had taken from the Reader earlier that day. Beale admired the ornate papacy seal as Williams sat and sulked.

'Thank you for joining us, Walter.' Walsingham says, without looking up. Williams shakes his head, huffing through his nose. 'You listened to every word in the Ink and Quill tavern?' Walsingham asks them both. They shift uneasily.

'We…were…reunited.' Beale offers. 'It had been such time since we had last spoken.'

'There were songs to listen to.' Walter says, catching Beale's eyes and they cannot resist smirking.

He then says each word clearly and scoldingly, perhaps more so at Beale, 'You are my eyes and ears.'

'Nay do folk in taverns listen, just talk.' Walter says defensively back.

Walsingham points them to a passage in the scroll, which states *cross into England, take up against her the weapons of justice.* They suddenly feel as if tricked by a penny Counterfeit Crank at some cheap wharfside bagnio. 'This but caused no reaction in the tavern?' Walsingham asks. 'It is a call to arms.' They know it. He burns a look at them. 'At this moment it is we three who are to record and analyse the threats made to her Majesty. Yes, the court is full of informers and messengers for countries and factions alike. Some spy on each other. None, not a single one, operate for a unified purpose, content squabbling like little children over who picked the biggest apple. Distracted in their short-sightedness while threats to Her Majesty's person loom ever larger and the nation's security unravels, leaving just the chaos of a civil war.' Walsingham takes a deep breath knowing he must relent his scathing tongue, although his remonstration is not lost on them and they listen intently as he continues, 'I advise again, we, this humble three, can stop the monstrosities of ignorance and hate from overwhelming our land. We must listen, see, record and react.' After a moment he asks deliberately, 'Still thinking of becoming an actor, Walter?'

Williams cannot believe Beale, how could he betray trust like that. 'I thought you were resigning from us.' Beale defends limply.

'Resigning from what? There's no stipend to behold nor timely reward.'

'Perhaps not instantly, in certainty, there eventually will.' Walsingham says, giving Williams quill and parchment, which he looks at in hostile bemusement – what in Mary's holy snatch is he supposed to do with these? 'We now commit from memory each utterance and every passing jest from all, friend or foe· that pleasures our acquaint.' Walsingham tells him.

Williams is still puzzled, 'Why?'

'So Francis can cross reference them.' Beale says, half hoping to impress Walsingham and to convince himself.

'I mean, why are we doing this?'

'Intelligence transforms knowledge. And knowledge is power.' Walsingham asserts, opening an empty wooden chest and placing his parchments in, adding, 'And we will become the most powerful of all.'

These are the last words they dwell upon for some time while the coach trundles south through Kingston's woods.

The swaying and lolling of the cart as it picks up speed sends them all to sleep for many hours where they eventually rest the horses at Petersfield.

Early the next day as dawn is yet to break: all three men slouch as the wagon stops, thick fog seeping into their carriage the way steam lips from copper broth pots. A Night-watchman thrusts his bulbous head inside and, with rancid breath, demands, 'What errand here long after curfew?'

Disorientated, Williams can only muster, 'Where in the wretched depths are we?' None of them seem really concerned with the official's demand, so he asks again, as if they were suspicious in some smuggling enterprise.

Beale reminds the man of his station introducing Francis Walsingham as Member of Parliament, on Her Majesty's Privy Council business.

'Dawn within the hour,' the Night-watchman replies, looking them up and down, 'until light can nay vouch for your sirs safety. Privy, Parliament or nay.'

Walsingham ruefully shakes his head, this clearly remains one of the most perilous places within England's realm. Williams peeks out of the wagon, he smells mud and sea. The Night-watchmen waves the wagon through and they move slowly over a wooden bridge entering the town's gate, leaving behind sprawling morass, boggy mud and ugly distant dark brown hills.

Still with his head outside, Williams hears Walsingham from within the wagon, 'The French call this place fossé de l'enfer.' He brings his head back inside to hear him say, 'It means Hell's Ditch.' Williams looks out again and Beale joins him, united in their meek glum faces. 'Welcome to Portsmouth.' Walsingham adds.

From their entrance at Landport Gate they plod slowly onto High Street, the main thoroughfare, a half mile of darkened timber and stone houses. The jutting market stalls eerily quiet and ominous, as if wooden spiked Frisian horses guard positions on the battlefield, defensive and imposing. Amongst the countless alehouses and brandy shops, there are still some lit lounges with faces glaring out. Nothing goes unnoticed in this paranoid town. During daylight hours, songs are sung of joyous times in bordellos and bawdy taverns, of unbounding loyalty to their Queen. Sailors who put their lives on the line see it as their birth right to enjoy such indulgence. As night arrives, it changes and the town twitches like a trapped adder, unpredictable, spiteful and poisonous.

Hooves thud slowly in the dirt of the commercial street, causing a few shutters and window rugs to crease ajar with curiosity as the wagon nears the quay. Beale and Williams take in the wooden sally ports that claw out into the dark cold Solent, calm as a mill pond. Neptune sleeps soundly in the still night's sea. They turn to Walsingham with equal uncertain eyes – what are we doing here?

'Now, Walter, you perform.' He says.

'Perform what?'

'An actor you were, an actor you shall always be, in the greatest play yet: find the Catholics and we foil a plot to assassinate the Queen.' His two counterparts sharpen their senses with the solemnity in Walsingham's round eyes as he begins to tell them of their purpose in this dangerous town.

The wagon stops and Williams leaves them, losing himself quickly in the pre-dawn mist, exuberant in his mission. He takes on board what Walsingham said about knowledge having too many weeds that entangle the hasty harvester, so brevity is key.

As Walsingham and Beale move out of the wagon, they see berthed alongside a wooden quay, the Griffin. Water lapping slow and thick against her as if black tar glooped on to the ship's side. Beale steps down from the wagon, checking his dagger is accessible before aiding Walsingham out, giving grace to the gentleman's exit. He chucks the driver a groat, which is gratefully received, and who loses no time in tying the horse and heading for respite, licking his lips in excitement for a well-fired hearth, jug of ale and some Poll's warm hands to play with his balls.

Cautiously, Walsingham and Beale approach the Griffin's gangplank, not a soul to be seen. Looking at the thicket of boats without sails dockside it is as if they are walking beside a wintertime woodland. Click – they hear a musket being primed. Both stop sharp, although Beale subtly readies his hand on his concealed blade. Behind the blackness of ropes tangled amongst the mast and beams, a serious voice warns, 'From fifteen feet I can spat your brains against the quayside.' Beale's hand clutches his dagger.

With the swift calm of a bird of prey, Walsingham rounds the gangplank and replies, 'I hope you account one degree of accuracy for every foot your spinning shot takes. For then you must act with haste, whence it will take 50 seconds to recalibrate your weapon. In which time my companion shalt dash aboard and disgorge your bowels.' They can almost hear the invisible lookout play this out in his half-drunk mind. 'May I instead propose you take me down to Captain Herle and avoid such calamity.' The voice presents himself from amongst the vines of rigging, nods them on, and underneath.

Below decks it is every bit as dark as Walsingham had imagined reading the interrogation transcript and Herle, though a little worse for drink, does not disappoint his vision either: like a bear at Southwark's blood sport gardens. 'Get these men some ale.' He barks at his lookout. Beale, for the first time letting his dagger go, and smiles appreciatively, licking his lips in anticipation.

'No, thank you.' Walsingham politely says. Beale, rasping, and disappointed.

'Puritans?' Herle grins.

'Where's the prisoner?' Walsingham asks, as if suddenly assuming command of the ship.

'Why?' Herle reminding with bluster who is the Captain here.

'The Queen's orders.' Walsingham says, knowing he cannot draw a card to beat that.

'What be Her Majesty's assignation with he?'

'Re-interrogation.'

'Re-interrogate?' Herle can only snort. He gestures for one of his sailors to fetch the prisoner. This is power, Beale thinks as he regards Walsingham.

Sailor leads Frenchman out like an ageing dog on a leash. It is a miracle he still walks, merely a ghost of a man, head bowed and moaning. Strange vile deeds done by man to man, as the sight shocks Beale to his linen stockings. 'Beelzebub, is he poxed? Witchery?' Beale rattles. His concern has Herle spitting laughter derisively.

'Worse I wager.' Walsingham says knowingly. 'Woolding.'

Sailor stops, twists the rope, and Frenchman halts, with a half writhe of muted pain.

'It could be said he has...an ache of head.' Herle says sinking his ale.

'He'll answer no more questions.' Beale frustratingly points out, tired and aleless. 'What are we to do sir? A wasted journey.'

'Price paid for being of France. What do you expect?' Is all Herle has left on the matter.

'That's Queen's witness you've spoiled.' Walsingham says, spooking Herle enough to stop him drinking. 'Are you sure he said "beak?"' Herle now uncertain of what answer is good or bad decides not to reply.

Beale grinds his teeth, 'Your indignity is an insult, sir.'

Herle stares this uppity sinewy seaweed down his broken fat nose. Walsingham watches the Frenchman moaning, his bowed head lolling and swaying. Sweat matting his hair, blood clagging his ears and neck, but he is drawn to the lolling head, an old scar amongst its mess. Walsingham approaches the prisoner, dormant for the indignities he has suffered. He looks over his head, running his fingers over its contours as if appraising a fine trinket.

Beale has had enough of Herle staring derisively, 'Sir, let me run this fool through.' Herle huffs in retaliation, as if that could happen.

Not taking his eyes off the Frenchman's bloodied head and knowing how to bay Herle's aggression, Walsingham glibly says, 'My Lord Cecil will see fit to punish.'

Herle looks straight to Walsingham, 'In shite he will.'

'I shall take the prisoner.' Walsingham declares, meeting Herle's glare.

The drunk captain knows any more bluster here is foolhardy. 'Any error is mine alone, but our slave stays.' Herle says soberly.

'Then you will leave me no choice but to report your Catholic sympathies.' Walsingham coos.

The humiliation on Herle is too much for him to take in front of his crew and he rushes for Walsingham, but Beale is quicker, barging between them whilst jamming his blade up against Herle's neck, scraping his stubble. Herle's crew pausing nervously, poised, ready to run these bastards through, should their Captain give the nod, but it is a nod that would slit his own throat.

Walsingham has not once lost sight of Herle's bulging eyes, rampant with hatred. He stands firm, 'Beale here does clasp a Grosschedel from the Armourer of Landsehut that, being present in the hands of an astute swordsman, can part a bull's skull in two with one strike.' He says gliding between the two straining men, 'You granting us passage will be much cleaner and my Lord Cecil need never know your defiance.' Walsingham soothes diplomatically.

Frenchman continues to loll and moan, unaware of the intense standoff he is in. Herle looks to the dumb beast, there is only one right decision here.

* *

Wagon rider whips the horse hard, too hard – he had managed the ale and warmed his feet but, he grumbles, his balls were still cold.

Under their canvas cover, now dully illuminated with the morning light, Beale looks perplexed to Frenchman, like a spooky statue, head bowed in paralysis. 'How will this dumb beast serve our purpose?' He asks Walsingham, sat pleased that this has been a profitable scheme.

'On him depends our entire endeavour. Now, pray, tell me what do you see within his written interrogation?' Beale reads over the parchment Walsingham had taken from the Court Rider with Cecil's privy seal.

'Who is Nicodemus? – Obviously Biblical…but what is the pertinence?' Beale asks.

'Nicodemus refused to worship Christ in the open. Resorted to a closed, secretive faith.' Walsingham a little disappointed he had not schooled the boy properly many years ago.

'A code?'

'Not of any great secrecy, no. Meant as heresy, religious treason.'

As the wagon grinds its way back up High Street on the long journey home, they hear a commotion break out in an alehouse. The fracas is no more serious than is usual for this ferocious place, but Walsingham looks out in a way that suggests it was about time.

Night-watchman drags out a drunk and wields his halberd like a penny juggler, then smites the bewildered fellow with one clean clock over the head, and he crumples to the floor. Stunned and bleeding, the drunk lofts his head and they see…Walter Williams, before he is then dragged away by his ankles, scooping a path out in the muddy track. Walsingham sits back, content all takes shape.

* *

Pigs and dogs snuffle and traipse together in the sodden straw-matted cobbled floor, united by hunger in their stone-walled cell of the town gaol. The local rakes and roustabouts call it *Lucifer's lobby,* having long being a holding place for stray animals as well as suspicious rogues. In the almost constant dark, the smooth cobbles glisten with moisture, some say from the sweat of demons trying to break in to collect their own.

Frinscombe, the irascible no-nonsense gaoler, knew that because it was situated so near the sea it was liable to seepage and the occasional flooding. Such briny sediment meant that his prisoners had to buy their water and not collect moisture from the walls as they might in other gaols. This money-making perk had its price though. With the occasional flooding, the worse prisoners in the lower dungeons would be entombed and not discovered until weeks later when the waters receded and left nothing but the putrid rot of beast and men. Frinscombe took a fee so his guest might not be placed in the gaol's depths. Williams has no such fee.

The rancid smells seemed never to leave the subterranean dungeon and sear Williams' nose and throat as he is dragged into the bleak grotto – his beaten swollen eyes blurring his view. How long would he be in this infernal place? Frinscombe throws down his ankles and kicks him down into his gaol. Williams, as tough as leather armour, did so but made it look like it was an ordeal. For this, he was shoved down the stairwell, smacking each step with every part of his body as he went. At the bottom he glared up at the walls, but lost focus and fell unconscious.

He imagined a goose feather pillow to comfort and nestle into, with a plump hessian straw-stuffed mattress to soften the rock-hard floor. Instead, he woke with his face glued to the cobbled floor with dried blood and his own ripped cape for a covering. As he slowly prized his face from the caked blood, he could make out his tiny cell with two other prisoners present. There was a flunk-clunk sound. His captor trudged down the steps, towards him, slowly spinning his halberd and letting it scrape and prang on the floor – flunk, clunk it was going. Williams could just make out his leather boots stopping over him. Then, like a Roman builder laying a foundation stone, his halberd was pile-driven onto his head. Welcome, traveller, to Portsmouth, smirked Frinscombe the Gaoler. Walter would be out cold for twelve hours with no feather pillow to soften his calamity. But, he was in, such had the great actor convinced his audience.

IX

∞)(∞

Walsingham and Beale, tired with their 4-day journey, enter the Palace of Westminster with the leashed Frenchman. The rain Walsingham had smelt in the air on the way had waited for their return and had slowed their track halfway back from Portsmouth at the Devil's punchbowl. They were forced to sleep in the wagon overnight, stuck in the quagmire of sludge. They were cold and hungry – and now frenzied by their absence from London all these days.

Entering the dank cavernous building, the suffering Spit-Jack catches sight of them and, determined to avoid Walsingham, darts into the dark. Beale sees and orders him back. Jolting and rolling his eyes at this dreadful misfortune, he has no choice but to do his unwanted master's bidding. Again. After Beale requests a meal and cleaning water, Walsingham watches the servant go and makes sure there are no other ears, 'Now Robbie, the real work begins, you know of Fyson?'

Beale has to think, 'The...Cheapside barber surgeon?'

'Take him the prisoner.'

Looking at the Frenchman and, with disbelief, he quips, 'For a beard trim?'

'Fyson should undertake with care removing all hair.'

'All of his hair?'

'The message will be revealed.' Walsingham hurries him along for fear of prying ears.

Beale shakes his head in disbelief, relieved the tiredness is clearly not just affecting him. Walsingham hears closing doors and voices from the distant Commons Chamber and motions for the Frenchman to be led quickly away. Beyond this smaller hall and the Privy Council Chamber where Cecil gave him his deadline that he is hearing the carried voices, suspicious in their low tones. There is no one else about so he heads towards the conversations, seeing the entrance doors ajar. He slides himself in.

* *

The servant Spit-Jack returns with ale, pottage, cheese and a wooden bowl of water with a cloth swab, looking about for his neediest and tiresome of masters. Realising his absence, he is half relieved but half furious – all this work for nothing and curses Satan's anus. Where could he have gone to? In his silent anguish he too hears the low hush of voices and turns to their direction. The door is open slightly.

* *

Within the shadows against the wall, Walsingham surveys the dark Commons Hall as best he can, being just a long room with two huge oak tables at each end and benches running up the entire length on either side. At the far end, gathered around the only hearth is where the conspiratorial chatter comes. He grazes his body quietly along the wall, remaining in the blackness, though still able to make out the black and white chequered floor upon which the two equal rows of benches face each other, enough to house the arses of 200 parliamentarians, whenever – and if ever – Queen Elizabeth decided to call them.

It does not take him long to slink closer to the small group of gentlemen, skirting almost the entire length of the room and, as such, can now make out their features. They have not noticed Walsingham penetrate their privacy. He stops and remains at a good vantage point from within the shadows. What he sees is about eleven men, some foreign ambassadors, noblemen and merchants conversing intently around the burning-out hearth. Such was the inertia of Parliament that this great hall, which should give voice to the people of England, now seemed nothing more than an ad hoc conference room for the whining privileged. He recognises several merchants from his days of excise duty management at the docks. Unmistakably there was the Conte d'Rouen, whom Walsingham had once privately heard referred to as the Ruined Cunt, on account of the French diplomat's poor financial affairs.

It was another, far more impressive figure, however, that caught his eye. Whether it was the ostrich feather adorning his hat, the embroidered tunic or the pin sharp moustache and jet-black hair, he had always been impressed by the Mediterranean types. Possibly Genoese, he squinted, from the red velvet shoes he wore. Walsingham knew he had not been far wrong, when he heard his name, though was a little surprised as it was one of the more famous foreign names of London – Roberto d'Ridolfi, the Pope's financier and merchant banker. Despite never seeing him before, Walsingham recalled that this Florentine was stunningly wealthy and was renowned with his generosity to English trade, which endeared him corruptively close to the city of London's guilds. He could not quite make out their conversation because of their differing dialects, so he deferred to another of his talents: lip-reading. His manservant, Stimpson, was deaf and Walsingham had made him teach him this art, being the perfect skill of statesman to read when one failed to hear. Unfortunately, the dialects still made this a struggle. Needing to get into a better position, he found it difficult to move as the conversation lulled and he did not want to make any noise. He decided to stay put for the time being.

Ridolfi's were the only lips he could see clearly and, in between him preening his moustache, Walsingham picked out words and phrases: there was talk of silk, citrus fruits and wine to be transported at oddly low rates from the ports of the Mediterranean. Nothing unusual in this, he thought, as trade negotiations were conducted in this way, not on the shores and in ports, but in quaint rooms and galleries between high born gentlemen. It was not their conversation that intrigued him at this moment, but whom the gathered were and for whom they were waiting, clearly idling away the moments with trader's small talk.

As he adjusted to the dark, some of their faces were definitely familiar and he recalled disagreements over the years on his climb of the splintery ladder of his government career: licences to extend fishponds in Southwark, reduced tariffs on Ottoman tapestries, letters of marque to import Baltic timber. Fripperies of administration, he had always complained to Ursula. However, the more he brought to mind these faces the easier it was to see what very different banner they united under on this cold evening: religion. It must be. These were men who had been early vocal sceptics of Elizabeth's attempted reconciliation between squabbling Catholic and Protestants. None he recognised from the

Puritan prophesying assemblies he attended. He was certain of one thing: they were all Catholic. Walsingham began to feel as if he was witnessing the hatching of something. Would they be as foolish to gather in... governmental halls...for insurrection? The sheer effrontery was stunning...was it actually that senseless? In some ways, it was the perfect cover: right under the very noses of the power you wished to topple.

Walsingham was losing sight of their lips as they circled tighter and he had to move delicately around one of the stone columns...when his arm was suddenly grabbed. Walsingham instinctively snatched his hand back, but the grip was good and it forced the grabber to bundle into him: Spit-Jack was leering straight at him. 'Unhand me servant.' He seethed in a whisper as harshly as he could.

'I could, sir. At which time I also announce my findings presented in this my hand, here in the black of dark.' Spit-Jack hushfully intoned.

'What are you doing here?' Walsingham grumbles through gritted teeth.

'With the same suspicious intent I will be asked and I convey upon you, sir? Yes, I've caught my eye upon you, sneaking round like mice from a cat. I asks myself why does a gentleman, so called, sneak upon other gentlemen, so called. I'm sure they would be grateful to know your business as do I.' Spit-Jack says.

Walsingham, stunned he had not noticed the Spit-Jack creep upon him in such unawares, now senses the group of men have stopped talking – do they perceive something afoot in the dark?

Spit-Jack is aware too, and lowers his whisper, pulling his superior closer into him, 'But I seen these foreign fish fuckers before and possess no trust of them.' His words wafted and smelt rancid, as if he had slurped from cold chicken broth, but bad breath was no reason to knock back a man's innovation. Walsingham quickly began building a respect for how he had manoeuvred himself, though wished he would hurry with his ultimatum as the men he observed now appeared unsettled and actively seek out the disruption. 'I desire more from this life than cleaning plates, m'lord.' He says and Walsingham realises the servant's desire to be in his employ. It was definitely a clever, but wholly inconvenient, play. Within a few seconds the pretence would all be up and Walsingham knew he would be revealed as a desperate and embarrassing low level clerk snooping in the shadows for scraps of gossip. If the Spit-Jack gave them up then any enterprise would be dead on the floor before it could walk. Would his blackmailer be prepared to jeopardise his newfound opportunity – Walsingham could not believe it to be so, but then these days had suddenly presented him with some very unexpected turns. 'There I was, certain as seagulls screech, you to be a quick thinker.'

'You would give us both away?' Walsingham almost daring him.

'No, master, only you.'

'I cannot be held ransom.'

Spit-Jack did not say anything, but his eyes seemingly ready to give that a try, and he begins to move out from the dark to give them both up.

Walsingham felt his chest burn, 'Think what we could do. Together.'

The servant walks out into plain sight, had he not heard him?

Getting their attention, the mix of foreigners and London men spin around towards him, as Walsingham holds out in the dark shadow of the pillar. He felt himself concoct twenty reasons why he was there as the men started scalding the servant all at once –

'What business have you here?'

'Tis a bloody servant?'

'What did you hear?'

'Belt his arse and he'll be thankful.'

'Are you alone, wretch?'

The voices stop and Walsingham feels his chest pound so hard he was sure it would give him away even if his blackmailer did not.

Spit-Jack says sorrowfully, 'No trespass here, my lords, I'm but a humble servant. I stumble in the dark only to find...' angling his head towards Walsingham... 'my lost amulet.' He showed them a piece of twisted tin on string to be worn around the neck. They bemoaned his birth as a pox on his father and told him to flee lest he be-fucked by pikes and lances.

Reversing out of the hall with respectful bows, his head leered up finally towards Walsingham just as he disappears and his interestingly worn face gives a clear message, you are in my debt. Walsingham nods.

As the assembled watched the servant leave, no wiser that he had left an eavesdropper of immense competence in their midst, somebody entered at the opposite end of the hall. A man trying to hide his presence strides in quickly to address them. All Walsingham could see was that he wore a four cornered hat flopped down over his face. They all quickly forgot the servant's interruption and smooched around this man like trout in the fishery ponds at feeding time. Four cornered hat smoothly takes Ridolfi to one side. They share words, Walsingham watching intently, their lips quivering messages that he rapidly attempts to unravel: the undertaking ready... Whenceforth monies...set in motion....rally...Is thou ready?

Pleased and abated, the four cornered hat's laughing grin jolts Walsingham out of his concentrating trance, like being awoken by a bell in the night. Though jarring, he is not distracted and watches the two men's faces, the glint in the hat wearer's eyes, devilish.

Those eyes.

Walsingham twinges: a spectral spirit from his past, suddenly finding himself back to that dreaded day in 1553 with Warne burning at the stake, his feet like sizzling joints of meat, Robbie's arm, the boy's wailing. It was him. The old Captain of the Guard.

Walsingham falters against the cold dark wall, smacking his back, forcing him to catch his breath. Hatred swells in his chest and neck. Four thousand nights of pain frothing in his mind...their cause only a few paces away. His torturer revealed, but not his identity. Lesser men would have stalked over there, bowed to frustration and let fists resolve a speedy and satisfying victory, smacking his reunited nemesis to the floor and watching the blood ooze from nose and mouth. This was too quick a settlement for the old Captain of the Guard, no. Revenge would be savoured. Seventeen years would not be won in seventeen seconds. It took inner restraint and grinding teeth to calm himself. Composure finally coming when he could foresee the tantalising moment the old Captain of the Guard indemnify him with his own doom. Right now, Walsingham knew, he had to refocus.

Ridolfi and the four cornered hat were winding down their conversation, discussing wine imports and the Englishman was advising the Florentine of a reasonable merchant, not yet hit by the city's Spanish tariffs. He knew this idle chatter were no coded message because their references were too contemporary – it was only two days past that the new wine levies on Spain were effected. Regardless, it was suspiciously clear they were the chiefs in whatever this conspicuous scheme was. What this was he could not yet clarify. Merely suggesting this to the Privy Council would be highly treacherous territory with such powerful and well-connected men. No, he had to be sure and would have to be as certain as convicting his own daughters and accusations as watertight as a ship's hold. This would take a miraculous piecing together.

Ridolfi bid the hat wearer's leave, which slowly dispersed the others, their faces looking confident that a plan – maybe not hatched – had certainly laid. Walsingham tried to read Ridolfi's look, which was continuing to regard the four cornered hat in his departing. Ridolfi flashed a jewelled hand, beckoning an assistant, a countryman of far lesser taste in fashion, no ostrich feather but a peacock's flopping from his cap. They speak rapidly in Italian and though Walsingham can see the words he is not fluent, kicking himself that he once turned down an invite to Milan at the behest of the Duomo's reforming deacon. They do not speak for long but it is Ridolfi's adieu that intrigues him.

Walsingham phonetically murmurs it to himself, 'chair lass he are ray.' Only able to understand a little Italian, he repeats and tweaks it gently to himself in the hope of recognising something, 'share in is he airy.' No sense in English of course, but was the Italian similar to the Spanish *lasciare*? To let. Maybe. He could not recognise the imperfect tense. 'Share in is he airy.' *Che* was it? *Iniziare*. From the Latin – to initiate. Commence. It was his best guess – "let it begin." Just what was beginning? Was he reading into it just what he desired to see? Walsingham was wise enough to know that this was barely evidence or proof positive of an undertaking, but his suspicions were now peaked enough that he could not let it be ignored. Blood from cuts. He glared at the showy Florentine disappearing into the dark caverns of England's governmental building, and as gently as spilled blood on the butcher's floor of straw, Ridolfi and his compatriots seeped away. Their stains etched on the floor of Walsingham's mind.

Choosing the right moment, he too then left.

Sneaking out of the hall he catches a far-off glimpse of a four-cornered hat turn into a small corridor. Seizing the moment, Walsingham dashes after it as quietly as his steps will allow.

A torch flame on the stone wall flaps as Walsingham flights past, turning a sharp corner, and comes face to face with Spit-Jack. This is intolerably awkward, but to his surprise the servant just gestures Walsingham onwards.

'The cellars.' Spit-Jack says, motioning him deeper into the stone labyrinth.

Walsingham nods and with his generous eyes imbues trust in him and they both know that their business together is just beginning. He hurries past, but maintaining a imperturbable dignity. As he hears the swipe of fine leather against smooth cobbles just ahead he realises he has caught the four cornered hat and slows his pace, enabling him to hear better. There is a small hearth, probably used by the Cooks to keep water heated. Walsingham peeks round and sees the four cornered hat, now joined by another, wearing an almost identical hat. He is unable to tell them apart from the one he saw upstairs, in the dark. But he does recognise both men in the generous glow of the fire: Essex and Norfolk. Walsingham hears other approaching voices and knows he cannot remain invisible and has to abandon his new discovery and the secrets they may divulge. One of them, he is unquestionably convinced, must be traitor to the Queen.

Walking back up through the narrow cold corridors, he is afflicted by the possibilities of threats, revolts, plots and rebellions were limitless and the government's understanding non-existent. Complacent, moving easily within the Queen's own walls because no one bothered to look. Walsingham knew his own sphere of confidants would be much more tightly constrained, so much so they could barely breathe without his knowing of it first. He would have to be brutal as nobody was above suspicion.

A blood circle. It would be a bond of those that were within, or a warning of the cost to those who were not.

He is stood there looking at a bowl of oranges, glowing as brightly as if they had trapped the Spanish sun. Maintaining any records would be crucial, but before he could begin compiling folios on every single person who might have known or could know any intelligence pertaining to the harm of Her Majesty, he should write to Cecil with his concerns. Secretly. There could be no risk from now on that any of his endeavours could be discovered, particularly in his own hand. He and Robbie would need to create codes and cyphers together. His blood circle would have to stay very small indeed.

Remembering a trick he saw at the Bavarian ambassador's house in Switzerland, he picks the oranges up. Strolling away with one hand behind his back and juggles, never once dropping them. He settles at a scribe's desk in the silent, temporarily redundant Hall of Commons. He readies two quills, an ink pot and parchment, to begin his next dextrous undertaking.

Using a feather from the left wing of a swan with his right hand, he studiously begins writing whilst with his left he squeezes an orange into a bowl, the juice flushing from the flesh in a chorus of watery wretches. Then with his left hand he takes another swan quill, ensuring he has it from the right wing so its rachis arcs with his opposite arm, and he dips it into the juice, while the right pokes into the gloopy dark ink made from oak apples, iron salts and gum Arabic. Simultaneously, he then scratches ink with his right and writes with juice from his left quill onto separate parchments, writing with both his hands. It took just eight months to master this, cutting a lifetime of letter writing in half – or producing at double the speed. With no error, the right paper is artily inked words while the other, being his left hand and not so fanciful, is a smaller note, the faintest glimpses of words written in orange juice now fading into the parchment. One is for his folio of interactions from that day, recording all conversations, no matter that he saw them by reading lips, and the other is a letter to Cecil, fading with each moment.

Walsingham begins his archive of information, which from now on he would carefully index and, immensely satisfied, folds shut his folio of written report. The first entrant in his new compendium *the Book of Secret Intelligences.*

* *

Portsmouth Point

Sun blazes through ships tarried to sally ports, amess with rigging, rope and beams, the throbbing glow makes them look like kindling in a fire. Among this, the Griffin remains moored. Up high in its crow's nest is Herle, casting his gaze about the town like a farmer at a fallow field. What harvest is there to gain here? He loves and loathes the town of his birth, but it was time to ready the crew for sail because there was nothing to do now except return to London and hope Walsingham had kept good to his word, exonerating him from losing Cecil's faith. He had to make sure he was not in any way implicated in sympathising with Catholics and their perfidious threat. As an agent to the Crown he needed to show good his allegiance for future prosperous maritime contracts. Looking eastwards across the Solent and distant South downs, all silver and green, there stirred within him a feeling that the tide was turning, both politically and in the harbour waters below as the current tugged beneath the boat. He and his crew could pilot the Solent's tides blind, but political, well, he said to himself, that is a very different tide, with many more perils.

His thoughts turn to Walsingham, a scoundrel as devious as any freebooter he had met on the open sea. He was unnerved by him with his stunning calm and conviction. Was <u>he</u> the changing tide? Was Cecil, the government, nay as a England whole finally going to get a grip on the unspoken menace...because of this impertinent outsider? It cannot be so. Can it? Herle knew his own faults, one being a propensity to lash out too quickly, but he was also swift witted enough to see that he had never asked himself so many questions and not know the answers – this Walsingham fellow's annoyance had subtly changed all things. Rubbing his head sweat away, the realisation that it was time to act before the axe would fall was as real as his hangover.

He screamed fifty feet below for them to ready sail.

Frinscombe, the Gaoler, bulbous and grumbling, plods along with his wooden stick that flunks and clunks on the uneven cobbles passing the sally ports. He hears a distant roar from somewhere up on high to set sail and only wishes his mangled leg would allow him one more venture on the waves. Alack, he grinds through his teeth, it will never be.

Hobbling past the victualling store and into his gaol, he lurches over some poor pissed wretch sat at his steps, rebuking them, 'Beshit thyself on elsewhere steps, ye disgrace to thine mother's cunny.' No-one had ever felt sorry for him when he was left orphaned on these streets at four years, but he had made good of himself without worry or imposition to others. He kicks the layabout aside with his good left foot, rolling them over.

His Night-watchmen was asleep at his station, aroused at hearing the old goat cursing then rumbling and mumbling down the stone stairs so slaps himself awake, not wanting a prisoner's beating – or worse, a dock in pay.

Walter was sat upright in the depths of the building, blades of sun sliced through the darkness, which would never bleed the cell out. His own wounds had bled out though, and his skin and clothes were clagged and matted with his dry blood. Standing was not yet an option and he could only just about manage a cough to keep down the paltry meal and drink he was given. Yes, he would live and, God willing, maybe even have no evils that bring about sickness. Provided he kept his nerve, acted his part, Walsingham would be indebted to him for this, and he certainly could not cuss the man, for his predictions were already bearing fruit having made the acquaintance of two detained counterparts – MacKinnon and Bridle – and was confident he could gain their trust imminently.

They had already shared and bonded in mutual horror at the Gaoler's halberd or, moreover, his precise ability to strike in the most excruciating way possible. It was the binds, though, MacKinnon had warned, that were Frinscombe's favourite initiate of pain, whereby he would hang his target from the ceiling until their bones went soft. Conversation inevitably turned to just why they were all here. Williams had told them it was for a drunken brawl in a bawdy house – obviously not that Walsingham had planted him here to find out how present and serious a Catholic threat was in this place and bound for London. Bridle was the insistent one and did not seem convinced a mere slap from a whore had brought about his beatings from the Gaoler. Williams knew at that moment he had convinced them of his disguise for these were not skilled interrogators, just rogues looking to trust like-minded souls.

'Let it be said…there were some different opinions cast. Anti-Papists.' Williams said, smiling through his charade. Bridle spat to the wall in hateful agreement. England would be Catholic again, he suggests, clumsily giving his views away. This was going to be easier than he had first anticipated, Williams thought.

MacKinnon looked hard at Walter, 'And what say you of it?' He knew these dung sticks were trying to assess his loyalties, but he was not going to let them know where he pretended to stand this quick.

'No former soldier of the Queen need share his oaths.' He smirked. MacKinnon and Bridle nod convinced – good God how he loved to act.

'Shit sacks, shut thine faces or it will be with pigs that you forage.' Their gaoler shouts. 'Lest I shall have my prize of you on the binds.'

Walter was satisfied as they all fell into silence.

X

Cheap Ward

ഇാൽ

Leading a man by his leashed neck does not turn heads on his walk through London's market parish of Cheapside. The previous day Frenchman had gone rigid and then collapsed. Fearful he was dead, Beale had put him in Walsingham's cellar, left him, only to find him several hours later padding around like a slowly dying cat without a mew. Rebinding him for their walk to Fyson – the Barber Surgeon – had proven a little difficult as his limbs had lost normal gait and composure. Forcing him, Beale was sure he had inadvertently broken the man's elbow, not that it aroused any reaction from the beast, such is he dead of head. Walking out of Seething Lane, it looked as if a master led his crippling slave. Slavery was not traded anywhere on the city's three hills or within its numerous wards, but owning a slave, publicly punishing or holding them in restraints was acceptable behaviour. So, as Beale paced and yanked his captive along the market thoroughfare, one of the widest streets in the city, nobody gave him any mind.

Left to his own thoughts, he understood the enormity of what Francis had petitioned Cecil and the Privy Council with. It had sunk in what was said on that long coach journey to Portsmouth. He was neither worried nor doubtful that Walsingham's zeal for God, country and Queen was unshakeable in his ambition on the side of right and true. But why, he racked his head, did this holy work mean trudging the filth of the market at finishing hour to take this ghost of a man to a Barber Surgeon? Help get the message, was all Walsingham had urged. Was there such a poultice of remedy that the Barber Surgeon could concoct to bring about words from the half dead?

As the bells of St Mary-le-Bow chimed for the market to close, it stunned Beale to see how deplorable life could be – the number of indigent poor was spawning uncontrollably. Witnessing these wretches was a choking pain to him as they fought over waste and leftovers with London's kites, the voracious birds ever braver as the market traders moved their wares away for the day. On some of the skimpy mothers and their children he noticed a small X-like welt on their arms where the birds had clawed their talons in this life and death scramble for market scraps. The sadness of children having to do battle for cabbage leaves or pork rinds in the dusty tracks just to ram into their slack mouths humbled and saddened him, reminding him of his own struggles in early life. England's economic decline brought about this sad situation, although he could not help but be astonished to see the efficiency of its working for within two hours there would be no mess left on the streets whatsoever. In this great Tudor century and amongst this shame of human existence, he saw London in fact had the cleanest of streets, save for the mud tracks come the rains.

Beale turned into Ironmonger's Lane, the birthplace of Beckett, that sainted Catholic and rebel to King Henry II that so fascinated Walsingham. Passing the majestic Mercer's Hall on the east side of the street,

Beale realised it had been a long time since he had visited with Fyson and was uncertain which of the many overhanging dwellings or shop fronts was actually his. The lane was wide enough only for one cart to pass, although it was just a whistling breeze that passed now, clacking and whinging against the painted wooden signs advertising their trades; pictures of horseshoes, swords, barrels or marlinspikes for the iron trades that still thrived here several centuries on. Finally, he saw the familiar red and white pole of the Barber Surgeon's – indicating bloodletting and bandages. Fyson had added a crude sign notifying the reader that he was good for *ailments, barbering, surgery, wiggery* and *merkins* too. As day departed, the buildings were in a blue dim of shadows and with no light coming from within, only muffled noises informed him that he should perhaps just creep in unannounced.

Inside, no light filtered through – and it really needed to for the operation that was about to happen. Hannah, a halfpenny whore lay upon a table, legs akimbo as if it was business as usual, except it was her undergoing the operation. Porter, an elderly, rakish, man tended her and she does not like his touch, 'Dangle thine twot under thine gaze of a beshitted, brings lack of ease here.' Her toothless attack spluttered at him.

'All we insist is your comfort.' Fyson the Barber Surgeon says, as he steps in with a tiny lamp, the room now glowing mysteriously as outlines of knives, pliers, bowls, kettles, bottles, jars and powders loom in the dark, all science and magic. Hannah writhes a little, so he is firmer, 'Madam, thine undertaking is barely completed with ease, your diligence to stress makes this operation some small trickery.'

Hannah, beginning to regret this decision, spits, 'Lay dormant like your bloated wife is it? You may have her that way, nay shall I surrender ne'er so meekly.'

Fyson remains calm, 'I merely wish you no pain. Can we at least temporarily place your hands in binds to cease your propensities to lash out unwarrantingly?'

Porter looks pleadingly to her, knowing how violent Cheapside whores can – and need to – be. 'Perhaps legs too? Head? Mouth?' He suggests in all reasonableness, fearful of how he might have to explain injuries from a whore to his wife.

'Binds? Off and fuck ye.' Comes her final decision on the matter. 'Stitch me now or by Her Lady's teat I'll send a slicey reckoning on your pricks by dawn tide.'

Fyson and Porter jingle-jangle their delicate paraphernalia towards her with nerves increasing thricefold, trying not to let her see the long needles and paring knife they have in readiness. Fyson asks Porter for the ointment as Hannah lolls her head back knowing that even with the things she has seen in her life she does not want to watch this. Fyson readies the needle and thread, holds up a glass phial to his tiny light, while Porter picks up a small furry triangle – the pubic wig.

'Merkin ready. Preparing lady's fundament for attachment.' Porter declares, as if he was addressing a hundred men, and then takes a deep breath.

Fyson calmly reiterates to Hannah that he is learned at body inks, in case he needs to colour or shape.

Without looking up, Hannah says through gritted gums, 'Colour my cunny? Whores with mouthful of cock make more sense. Nay speak so often. Get on with your purpose.'

Fyson dips the needle and thread into vinegar and jabs it into the crease between her thigh and bald vagina. Hannah kicks the table and growls. He ironically mumbles to himself there is a mere fifteen more stitches to go. On each side.

Beale, wary that you can never be sure what you might find in a Cheapside Barber Surgeon, has his fears for bears renewed with the odd growls he hears. Reasoning it could only be a small one, he makes his way cautiously through the cluttered shop. Then the unmistakable desperate scream of a woman lifts his spirits so he tugs the Frenchman through with haste. As he enters, Fyson and Porter are restraining the screaming prostitute, writhing and expectorating – Beale not at all sure if he witnesses a birth or buggering and the Frenchman has no reaction, a deaf and dumb bystander in this scene of demonic possession.

Fyson, in a raised but oddly calm voice, tries to placate her, 'Hannah, for the love of our Lord, your fundament has suffered an infestation of lice so grievous it may rot your cunny. With this merkin you can continue thine ceaseless lusts.'

Hannah sees Beale and mistakes his confused look for a concerned hero, 'Cease I tells them, pronging my snatch, butchery I charge. Well…aid me, ye numb-fuck.' Her coarse pleas for help continue until Beale runs out of patience – he has no time for this – SMACK. One punch, she is out cold. Beale shakes his knuckles: that's going to need wrapping in watered cloth.

Fyson is instantly relieved, 'Jehovah be praised.'

'Francis Walsingham needs your help.' Beale says, justifying the assault.

'Of course sir.' Fyson says. However both men move quickly to give their attention to the unconscious whore, taking advantage of the small moments they have to tend her natural industry.

After some deft crochet, Hannah wakes and straddles up from the table, rubbing her black eye with one hand and her sore genitals with the other.

Beale smiles to her, 'Hannah – I endow your forgiveness – expediency called for such extremity.'

'T'was not my nose, for I'd have belted you back.' She says, just coming to.

'I may need you...are you still at Venus' ship?' Beale asks her.

'It'll have to be anus, thine twot requires respite.'

'Though I thank ye, tis not my lust to fulfil. I might need you to find someone on behalf of my master, Francis Walsingham.

'Who be that?'

Beale wounded slightly, responds, 'The Member of Parliament for Lyme Regis.'

'Parliament, aye I know it, but I merely recalls any member by scent of cock.' She warns, lifting her skirt and checking herself over, in want of undergarments. He remembers she is half blind. Another of London's tough survivors.

'Then I rely on you honing that art.'

'Aye, find me at the Venus.' The whore says. Limping out, she reasons that the cute little Robbie Beale fellow had never wetted his balls on her so must be of reasonable moral status and, therefore, his steward, Walsingham, would also be. For certain she had participated in government work before – a swift one off the wrist here and a twos-up there, but this sounded different, exciting even, to help find someone on Parliament business.

As Hannah leaves, Beale ensures the Frenchman is lain on the bench restfully as Fyson strokes and mops his head, cleaning it. Attentive, but not caring. He washes the caked blood, sighing at the despicable wounds and wonders aloud if this was the hand of Walsingham. Beale rebuffs the stupidity and reminds Fyson that the Frenchman is officially Queen's witness so must be replenished. A foolish notion – even Porter could see this man was past any surgeon's art, or apothecary for that matter, but what do servants of gentlemen know.

Enquiring how the Frenchman came to be in this way, Beale told them he had not spoken since woolding, just the lolling and moaning. The Barber Surgeon reasoned his brain had died long ago, but his four humours were somehow kept in balance, so lived, like the uncomplaining mule on farmsteads, departed of soul, lust and voice. Fyson had seen deadness of the mind before from his oft visits to St Mary of Bethlehem – Bethlem, or Bedlam as his fellow Barber Surgeons had corrupted it to – where its inmates of similar disport stood blankly in their cells breaking only to bite the wall or scoff their own faeces. Many believed they were being punished for a sinful life and others reasoned their brains had somehow broken. In the Frenchman's case it was clearly physical stress had caused the deterioration. Fascinating how the mind works, the Barber Surgeon and his assistant mused.

Can he do what Walsingham has asked of him, is all Beale concerns them with, 'There is a message he has to deliver, my master believes.' He says diplomatically.

'Did your master Walsingham say if he <u>was</u> the message or that he <u>had</u> a message?'

Beale is lost for a moment. Fyson holds his finger up, signalling to now pay attention to his physical demonstration, which may answer his own question.

Porter takes the brittle stained rags and dunks them in a boiling kettle to melt their stiffness, only to hand them back to Fyson who places them gently over his lost eye and bleeding ears. Porter dismisses himself, hanging up his apron to dry, once a fine white linen garment now a decade of surgical mucus clagging it tight. Fyson sniffs the poor prisoner's head, the blood fresh and gently re-oozing. Parting his hair, he begins to shave his head with such care that it does not emit so much as a flinch from the unsuspecting creature laid down before them. No blood runs as he renders the man's scalp anew and Beale imagines it has probably never seen light since his day of coming into the world. He is wrong. As Fyson shaves closer a scarring is visible and he says, astounded, 'He was right.'

'Walsingham has wrongs, nay is barely himself undone by them.' Beale responds, concentrating his gaze on the Frenchman's head, at a loss to the scar's origins of identity, no ordinary gash of a thrusting dagger nor dent of a blunt rod. Scrutinizing it carefully, closer, they see it appears to be a purposeful shape. Beale dangles Fyson's lantern over the partially bald prisoner and they are both struck by the plain oddity of it, there all along. Beale laughs in disbelief.

'What in Father's fields is it?'

'This,' Beale says looking straight at Fyson, finally grasping the importance, 'could be a key to unlock power.'

* *

Palaces of Westminster

Walsingham folds the scribed papers. One is beautifully inked for his new compendium and the other, now a blank parchment with no trace of his original message. Beale enters in the distance with the Frenchman, they see each other and Walsingham moves straight for the Clerk.

'I require access, if it please your Clerk of the Chamber, for a most pressing issue of her Majesty's concern.'

Not looking him in the eye, he responds, 'How many times do you think I hear that on any given day?' That should remind him of who has the power here, Clerk thinks.

'It only takes one such day to change things forever.'

'You can wait.' He affirms, convinced he is not going to trip and stumble over this one's fine way with words again. Silence, no response. Yes, that showed him, he smugly smiles, these upstart parliamentarians need reminding of their place in the order of things...wait, what was this now, what jape he plays...?

Walsingham's stoic face decides to take this into his own hands and simply proceeds to slide past him towards the Privy Council chamber door, as if he did not even guard.

Suddenly ridiculous in his position, Clerk can only stammer protestations, knowing to pull him back would create such an undignified fuss so is merely left to limply repeat 'No, no you cannot. You must not.' An absurdity made more complete as he hops around Walsingham who moves arrogantly forward like a teasing child, rendering the man of high station powerless and pathetic.

Beale sees this as he drags Frenchman across the hall, becoming more difficult, his body stiffening and unyielding by the hour. He cannot help but think how odd a spectacle the men pose outside such a place as weighty of governmental undertakings as the Privy Council Chamber.

Clerk and Walsingham stop right by the door – a dramatic beat in the chaotic melee. Despite now being in control, Walsingham knows the charade cannot continue through this most meaningful of doors and stops drastically. 'One of two heads will roll if you don't let me in there.' He says without desperation, looking down at the usurped government official. 'I'm prepared to dice it's mine if you do – are you prepared to gamble if you don't?'

Clerk, perhaps still working out if that was a puzzle or just perfectly phrased, allows Walsingham to open the door himself.

Without the full complement of Privy Councillors, it renders the ominous silence all the more striking as the two men make their fumbling entrance. Essex and Howard – without their four cornered hats – roll their eyes while Dudley, Ludlow and Cecil look up expectantly at both men, waiting for them to be announced. None speak and Walsingham knows he cannot stiffen into silence now that he has come this far, so strides resolutely into the room, leaving Clerk agog and with no choice but to dally along behind. It appears to work as the five senior Queen's councillors sit back with a look of expectation, as they might for an important briefing from a foreign ambassador. Walsingham is about to speak whilst walking, Clerk hurrying right up behind him, when he notices one of the doors at the far end of the room is open, slightly ajar, he stammers and falters because he knows it is the Queen's antechamber. His knees suddenly buckle at the sight of a bejewelled finger, regal and womanly, holding parchment, which he sees through the door's smallest of gaps. This faintest glimpse is enough to thwart him dead in his steps, forcing the pursuing Clerk, still pacing merrily behind his tall shadow, to flump straight into him. Each grabs the other in an annoyed and confused state. It makes a peculiar and uneasy exchange in such a serious room. The door is shut by the regal finger.

'Was that...?' Walsingham breathlessly begins, unable to finish and ascertain whether it really was Her Majesty.

Clerk nudges Walsingham aside, giving them even more an air of ridiculous comedy. If the senior men were ever impressed it is now very difficult to tell. 'Francis Walsingham, Member of Parliament for Lyme Regis.' Clerk clears his throat embarrassingly.

Dudley remembers but appears neutral. Other eyes scald him, and it is Cecil whose steam boils over first, 'What in the four kingdoms is this arse-japery before her majesty's council?'

Clerk drops his head in profound shame while Walsingham half looks between his remonstrator and the door that Queen Elizabeth is possibly behind. Not that it would change what he will say, but she must be able to hear them, he supposes, and tries to explain his business, which was so well thought through in his mind, now all flummoxed. Was it really her – or could it be a maid? Reading scrolls? No, that was simply not done. Cecil's reddened stare informs Walsingham he really should start explaining himself, 'He had markings, permanently, on his head. Permanent markings m'lord.' He says as if pinched.

The room is in disbelief and Cecil has had enough. 'Markings?' He rasps. 'What markings? What is your business here?'

'One moment my Lords.' He says, realising he has forgotten his prop. The Clerk now revelling in the foolery, this upstart must be done for, it will never do.

Walsingham quickly ushers in the Frenchman, thrusting him forward to the front, as Beale stays out of the room. The prisoner is greeted by gasps of general horror and they all stand, at first not sure whether to bolt or dive under the table in the midst of the abhorrence before them. This meeting was quickly turning into one of the strangest moments of all their lives.

'Good God, he's a ghost.' Cecil declares.

Dudley winces, 'Is this sorcery?'

'Bepoxed, certainly.' Ludlow says, rushing a kerchief to his mouth.

'The Devil is at play here, Walsingham.' Howard blurts with a sense of panic.

'No, my lords, torture.' Walsingham's momentary bout of buffoonery subsided and he regains control of their attentions, bows the Frenchman's head revealing Fyson's handiwork and the scar. 'A map, my Lords.'

'It's a scar.' Howard dismisses it – and him – with a waft of the hand and sits down, drama over. Ludlow and Essex also sit.

Walsingham brings his puppet closer to their table. The rest now all sit slowly, and cautiously. 'In the Borgia court, messages were sent by being cut and inked onto heads, the cut filled with coal dust or gunpowder. Hair grows back, hiding the message underneath.' Dudley and Essex concur, having heard of these exploits from their military adventures abroad. Howard grinds his teeth, knowing he would look a fool denying it, especially as Cecil wants to hear more. Ludlow still has the kerchief to his mouth.

'Map of what?' Dudley asks. Walsingham goes to their map of England, spread broadly over the table, folds it and folds it again, to concentrate their focus on one particular area: the peninsula in the North: a crude beak shape.

Walsingham points out, 'The marshes, hills and valleys of the river Humber. The Beak.' The five gentlemen and the Clerk look between the map and the Frenchman's head.

Cecil knows this can only mean one thing.

'The Northern Earls are regrouping.'

Howard is cross, but cautious, 'We cannot trust the words of an amateur and this...'

'French messenger.' Dudley states, then with foreboding, 'Why do I feel like Harold Godwinson watching the wind turn?'

'I agree my lord, our moment of decisive action has arrived.' Walsingham says, gleaming inside, his ideas gaining kudos. 'But we don't yet run north as was Godwinson's folly.'

Cecil just stares at the map. 'With France as ally.' He murmurs hauntingly. The seriousness of it drenches them like unforeseen rain on a summer's day, a startling shock of reality that could strike anytime and there is little that can be done.

Essex addresses Cecil directly, 'T'would be fanciful to leap upon conjecture, my Lord.'

Ludlow muffles through his silken mouthpiece, 'Less foolhardy acts have plunged us into civil war.'

These sobering words both elevate and alarm Walsingham, he could never have predicted such language would be used so quickly, but the realisation of just how important his discovery is, widens his chest. Civil war.

Cecil looks to the truth in his old friend Essex's eyes and knows that he must show decisive leadership. He stands and walks calmly to Walsingham, ushering him out. It feels odd, knowing this is how he escorted him out last time.

'The Privy Council thanks you for your time, Walsingham. We must take time to consider these implications. You must gather more evidence.'

When they are out of ear shot, Walsingham makes to shake his hand but instead plants in it the small, folded packet. 'My Lord, to be read over candlelight.' Walsingham looks down into Cecil's eyes, his own are wide and full of meaning. Cecil nods.

The Privy Councillors watch him go, Essex concerned, Howard suspicious, Ludlow relieved he has left, but it is Dudley who speaks confidently, 'You have to give him merit for theory.' He says when Walsingham has left.

'He has painted us a picture without brush or paper. Nothing at all.' Cecil says, perhaps appeasingly, as he taps the pocket of his cloak.

XI

৪০৫৪

Outside the palaces of Westminster, Rider, who owed
Walsingham his kindness from insisting he enjoy a
hearty feast that soaked night, fetches for a stable boy
so his horse can be readied. He was going to serve him
well, he promised.

It was not that Walsingham tipped well, for he did,
but how insistent he was that his cause was the righteous
one. No gentleman had ever cared to talk him through
beliefs, duty or causes of loyalty before. Imagine, he
dared, that people may, in years to come, remember his
part in whatever this great cause was to keep Her
Majesty safe. Not that he could weave it all together in
his head, this great threading of people and events,
though he sure felt he was perhaps the twine or, at the
very least, a needle that would help stitch this great
tapestry. Purpose, Walsingham had said to him, was
how men fulfil their destiny to the realm, to the Queen
and to God. Maybe there was a place in heaven
alongside the powerful men of England for lowly Lynas
Masterman after all, he hoped. His horse brought before
him, he steps up and sweeps his leg over. A voice then
calls after him –

'I have fixed you some bread.'

Lynas looks down and sees a familiar face – Spit-Jack
that served him mutton at Walsingham's request. 'Thank
ye, my good man.'

'Shall be need for such a journey, is it not?'

'Indeed.' Lynas says, puzzled and smiling.

'A long journey north will it be?'

'I thank you again for your kindness. I must away.' Lynas says suspiciously and with renewed belief in himself and his noble position in events, he rides out of the stable yard and out of London. Walsingham's endeavour in his heart.

Spit-Jack watches him go with an all-knowing smile.

* *

Coins jangle on the floor of Portsmouth Gaol and the dice scuttle like rats running into dark corners. It is hard for Walter to accurately say how long has passed since his arrest, as he sits with Bridle and MacKinnon playing knucklebones. It is not uncommon for prisoners of the gaol to have money – how else would they buy extra ale or even a whore for the night, an extra charge Frinscombe, the gaoler, all too often welcomed. Perquisites of my station, he would smugly say to himself as he stuffed more silver groats into his leather purse.

Walter knew if he stuck to short odds he would win through in the end as Bridle and MacKinnon would lose their lucky longer odds eventually. Mathematics never lied, Beale had once reminded him, and the stream was a trickle slower. Williams employed a similar strategy with conversation, ingratiating steadily and then prizing them out. Starting what taverns held the best whores – well that depended on your proclivities, but in Portsmouth there was not really "the best" only ones that wouldn't give you pustules of the groin, he had been told. They were jovially bumbling along with this prized information and keenly recounted to him that 'One whore was so darkly inflicted that no-one went near her snatch, instead she resorts to mouth but that too had caused the unsightly boils to fester round her lips.' Williams could see their air of suspicion evaporate when he had said she was far better off getting the plague and being done with it. Their laughter boomed around the small cell as he collected back his coins. Now, he knew, was the time for coaxing to begin, as he wheezed out the following through trailing laughter, 'That bastard Herle and his crew have all but taken the best whores?'

'What do you know of Herle?' MacKinnon wonders, taking the lead, Bridle again knowing not to speak.

'I knew he stopped God's true work from being done by kidnapping the Frenchman.' Walter says, looking at them, knowing by instinct he had approval, for their silent shared glances confirmed it. MacKinnon rolled double fives, his luck was finished and he even smiled as he handed over his winnings.

'Another game?' MacKinnon asks. Why not, Williams agrees.

* *

Tower Street, just south of Seething Lane, was silent as Walsingham and Beale, lugging the Frenchman behind, made their way from the house. Two days they had waited for word from Cecil. Nothing had been forthcoming. They trudged along a dark track, capturing their portending mood. Anticipating what Cecil might think of his plan concerned them both. Right now though it was the realisation of what they needed to do with the Frenchman. Both Beale and Walsingham understood the poor fellow's life was finished. He had certainly suffered enough indignity and they were not going to simply leave him to the Common Cursitors of London's streets. As dull and dumb as he was, the Frenchman would not register pain, feeling or emotion ever again and he would be picked up and used for some unsightly evil purpose. In these two days past he had slept in a stable, at their feet in a tavern and upon the basement floor, having defecated himself no less than seven times. Beale suggested it would be a kindness to climb him over the highest point of London Bridge and let him drop into the cold and filthy Thames water where his Catholic God could decide his fate, which would not take long. They headed there. Glum and quiet.

They could hear the Thames cascading around the pillars beneath them and led him to a small gap between two building walls on the eastward side. They climbed him up on the ledge and with a gentle nudge watched him flunk into the water, traverse limply downstream, barely struggling to try and keep himself afloat. One more claimant of London's death canal and the first victim to Walsingham's new enterprise. His shaved head finally succumbs silently to the dark water as he levelled with the Tower of London, onwards to the North Sea.

As they walked back, neither man could look at the other for fear of registering the beginning of a tragic, but necessary, tally. Walsingham predicted these terrible trophies would one day be counted against him in the haunting moments that his life's end would bring. He needed to distract himself of whether he could fully justify them for purpose. No greater sin than wastefulness. Beale was empty of his usual spark and pith. They continued on to Seething Lane in complete silence.

* *

Lynas feels the smooth but vigorous energy of his horse as it thunders in the gallop, rasping with relish at once again pumping its legs, free from the fetid stables beneath the Houses of Parliament. Each breath of rider and horse in the thin night air gives them a desire to bound swiftly on. Not even the pains a journey can bring of wind and rain would hold them back now, England's open spaces were theirs. If they were lucky, the moon would enlighten the Middlesex hills' thickened woods on the old London to North road, and its playground of evil could not foil their journey. The forces of God's greatness would be on their side this night. Walsingham had assured him it was so. Lynas Masterman kicked his horse excitedly, and they jerk more swiftly onwards.

* *

Stimpson greets them at the door, he had rigged up an old ship's spyglass to a tarred glass pain to create a long view of the street from within his basement dwelling. Video et taceo – see and do nothing: watching had become an art form.

Stimpson took their cloaks. 'Your guests in cellars be.' He mouthed to Walsingham.

As they descended the creaking stairwell, his host sounded almost sentimental. 'Do you remember that first year of Mary's reign, Robbie?'

'1553, how could I forget.' Beale says.

Walsingham stops before they get to the bottom to enter the gloomy room, a weak light turning it the darkest of orange. 'Dare not ever.'

As they walk in, Beale is taken aback seeing Williams smirking proudly because, manacled to a table, is

MacKinnon and Bridle. He knows not to say anything but has a hundred questions jousting in his mind. Instead, he watches in awe as their master begins to wield a new weapon of his: interrogation.

Walsingham steps forward and MacKinnon tries to be brave. 'If it's to be torture our Lord God shall protect us.' The Prisoner says.

'Dear fellows, you are sure to be wanton of feast after such journeys. Have you not been offered supper or refreshment of drink?'

Stunned a little, the two men look to each other. 'Not the whole day.' Bridle says, licking his lips.

'Walter, you've but grown harsh in your days with me.' Walsingham says.

Williams and Beale know they are mere puppets in this play and surrender to their master's lead so will not speak unless instructed.

'May you forgive me, all we have is fish.' He uncovers a platter in front of them: lamprey, oysters and bream. Tantalising, and just out of reach.

'Poisoned, certainly.' MacKinnon sneers.

Walsingham gets a sharp knife and, with subtly threatening poise, nears them, twirling the blade in his palm, so close to their faces they feel its breeze on their cheeks. With a threatening swipe he slices off a segment of lamprey, dangling it enticingly near them and drops it into his own throat, eats and swallows. Showing them he still stands, Walsingham slides the food nearer to Bridle and MacKinnon so they can reach it through their manacles. It only takes one shared look and they both gorge their faces, keeping dagger stares at Williams. Such is the velocity of their eating, mucus bubbles from their noses and, as they continue to swipe food into their mouths, snuffling and slurping their fill, Stimpson enters with a small jug of weak ale and two tankards, placing it on a table behind them. In no time they have finished, signified by loud belches and the stream of seafood juices down their already darkly soiled under-vestments.

'I thank your kindness. A drink, sir, would sit well.' MacKinnon suggests. Walsingham nods graciously and moves behind them to slowly pour two tankards, the liquid sloshing gently in the cup. Beale a little perplexed and impatient.

'This will offer succour there for all that briney flesh.' He says, bringing the drink near, stopping short of giving it to them. 'Prey tell, how came you to meet Herle and what of Catholic rebellions in the North?'

Bridle spits on the floor, the sudden bad manners after being fed makes Williams move to strike, but the patient Walsingham abates him.

'No, no, Walter. Let these men rest, lest their feast unsettle.' He says with tranquillity.

Beale is amazed at his master's patience, watching him slowly take the drinks back away from them. Bridle and MacKinnon now a little confused as they ogle the drinks, their parched mouths in need of moistening.

Walsingham turns serenely to them, saying, 'Finest salted fish, filling your bellies.' Beale suddenly understands. 'And now drying out your throat and mouth.'

MacKinnon licks his lips, teeth like twigs in dusty earth, his tongue twitching with worry, starting to swell inside his mouth. Bridle exactly the same, and, agitated, begins rubbing his tongue against the inside of his cheek in need of spittle, though he may as well rub sawdust into sand hoping to create water. MacKinnon feels his mouth going gummy, airless and dry.

'My manservant tells me one pinch of salt can be delicately soothed by half a pitcher of ale.' Walsingham says.

Bridle and MacKinnon's mouths fidgeting, their first looks of distress. 'Mack I'm for want of wet.' Bridle gripes, as he struggles hopelessly to move from his tight manacles.

'Ten pinches of salt...well, maybe a gallon of ale will suffice, he tells me.' Walsingham mutters, taking a jug and pouring a little delicately over his fingers in front of them, the dark liquid cascading over his rubbing fingers onto the floor. Bridle tries to move as if to lunge for the floor, but realises the chairs are bolted down, so he must watch the ale seep away into the stones. Its wastefulness bringing tension all around his jaw.

Torment of thirst and the burning of salt on their lips and gums begins to ferment panic. MacKinnon moans for drink and Walsingham merely reminds them both they must have something to tell him. Mackinnon winces his eyes shut, shakes his head violently, snot suddenly flaring from his nostrils, which he now tries to catch with his tongue – the green ooze a quick quenching relief. Walter and Robbie are impressed and disgusted at the desperate sight. Bridle drools, a thick foamy mucus.

'Thine spittle no greater than the brine at the bottom of a fisherman's trawler.' Walsingham states, accentuating his point by dipping a finger in the ale, gently rubbing Bridle's top lip and, like a piranha, he gnashes for the hand.

'Mercy!' Bridle pleas. MacKinnon trying to brave it through, sores already forming at the corners of his mouth, the searing agony of dryness and salty pain grinding in his teeth, like tightly clasped pebbles rubbing together.

Walsingham calmly narrates them through their agony. 'Your first urge will be to rid yourself of the tongue, bite it away and feast from your own blood, alack – this you will only vomit. Not even a starving, thirst crazed man can keep down a pint of his own blood.' MacKinnon and Bridle rock and jolt in their chairs, insane fits as foam froths in their mouths. 'Take the ale...' Walsingham says softly as he brings the jug closer to them, MacKinnon's eyes bloodying by the second as the salt parches all corners of his body. '...after you tell us what we need to know.' He shows the tantalising liquid lapping in the jug, they instinctively gnash for it like squabbling dogs. Williams and Beale mesmerised by the speed in which man succumbs to beast in want of water. Bridle can take no more and screams in desperation. 'Herle. Northern rebellions?' Walsingham shouts back at him.

MacKinnon's face turning green.

'Herle is for Cecil...Ridolfi...' squeaks Bridle. MacKinnon growls, knowing he is soon to either end this life or this scheme. Still he cannot bring himself to talk.

Walsingham goes closer to Bridle, holding the jug near him, as if to pour it into his mouth, stopping just short of doing so. 'Speak and the refreshment of this divine liquid shall be yours to gorge upon and ail you of your salty pain.'

MacKinnon faints, Walsingham nods to Walter who immediately slaps him awake, cutting the man's ear as he does so with his ring. Bridle looks to his comrade of twenty years and knows his betrayal but cannot shed a tear for all his absent moisture. MacKinnon defecates in his breeches and vomits chewed fish down his tunic and faints again.

Walsingham stops Williams from slapping him this time. 'Before we wake your friend once more, we shall hear your tale and then his.' Bridle nods sorrowfully, ready to comply. 'Hasten, for your friend has not long in this life.'

Beale gets ready to record the confession with quill and parchment. This is what his master had meant when he asked if he was prepared to get his hands dirty for England. As the truths came out and he began recording, his initial shock of the interrogation subsided. Instead, he became captivated with the skill by which Walsingham examined them both and danced around the law, particularly enjoying Francis establishing their guilt – "On what authority were you permitted to travel with the Papal Bull Excommunicating the Queen?" If they denied in any way doing so, they would perjure themselves, if they denied acknowledging authority then they had accepted the premise of the question. So clever, Beale thought, were his master's technique of legal entrapments that he concluded no man could be led to think that Walsingham had built the story and tortured them into agreeing with it. He had genuinely found new ground. MacKinnon and Bridle succumbed, answer by answer, to a far superior intellect and Beale happily scribed their transcript of torture, content it was valid legal evidence that would lead to their inevitable incrimination.

* *

Whitehall Palace

That same night, a small dog yaps playfully, circling its master's legs. It had not seen Cecil for some time, whom preferred to stay at his own quarters that were wherever the Queen's court was residing. More recently that had been Whitehall, and even though his main residence was on the Strand not too far to travel back and forth across London each day, he needed to maximise his time with Her Majesty.

Scooping up the terrier in his arms, he had called it Bourne, being the town of his birth, fussing the creature immensely. He took comfort in how delighted it seemed in seeing him. More so than Mildred Cooke, his wife, who was perhaps more used to his absence than the dog.

Fourteen straight weeks he had been apart from them while the government wrestled with famine in the West country and rising vagrancy in the shires and towns. Worse, Mary Queen of Scots being house guest of Her Majesty and kept in some far away country estate at Elizabeth's pleasure was causing more paranoid headaches: a Catholic monarch in England. He need only say those words out loud and it would spin Her Majesty into a fury. His brethren councillors were no better: trembling with anxieties of whether an army would rescue her and usurp the throne; what could it mean for their lands – their money and, perhaps, their religion. It had been a ceaseless and gruelling time. Then...talk about kick a man where he lay – the Pope and the Vatican messaging machine knew exactly what they were doing with the recent Papal Bull that, along with the building threat of rumoured plots, was unnerving the hearts of men. Always rumours, he cursed to himself as he sat and the dog jumped on his lap. You care not for rumours, he muttered to the lick-happy creature, alack, he whispered sorrowfully, I must heed their warning. His thoughts rest on this Walsingham fellow. What had his petition said, "Paranoia of plots to murder Queen Elizabeth are rife, denying us fact or meaningful intelligence." With courage – or naivety – Walsingham boldly declared that evening in the Privy Council Chamber Elizabeth's religious middle way had, well, lost its way. He was the only one brave enough to say so and Cecil, not so much stunned by the revelation, was enthralled by the conviction with which he had. And to men in positions of such power. Cecil could see that Walsingham's timing was incredible – though he had himself confessed to being tipped off by some officer in his network that the Papal edict was coming. He accepted it when Walsingham said Catholic plots would only become more brazen now that they were emboldened by the Pope actively encouraging tyrannicide.

Yes, Walsingham, this obscure fellow had indeed tested his own principles, questioning whether he, her First Minister, was actually keeping his beloved Majesty safe. He counselled her unceasingly, with loyalty and what he hoped wisdom, but was forced to ask of himself whether he was, for the first time, failing Her. Incredible that Walsingham had made him feel this way, talking with such persuasion and not to his own ends like so many a Parliamentarian charlatan, just genuine concern of their mutual mistress. No-one would love and be frustrated more by her than he, Cecil declared to Bourne as he ruffled its ears. He could read the souls of men and in Walsingham there was authenticity. Despite the initial concern of how this low-born Parliamentarian's warped idea was so ill-conceived, he could see it began to have logic.

It was then Cecil remembered the note Walsingham had passed him. It had been a few days hence and he just hoped that some maladroit chamber servant had not thrown it – or worse it had somehow been intercepted by one of his court enemies. He scurried his hands through batches of papers but could not recall where he had placed it. He re-enacted the moment Walsingham gave it to him and remembered putting it in his cloak lining and so fetched it promptly, spinning it round and round in his hands before getting to the inner pockets, relieved to feel it was still there. He set himself down at his small desk to open it.

Blank parchment. Both sides. What merry caper was this? In the meadows of the Almighty...was he purposefully wasting his time? He looks to his candle, hoping his eyesight was not beginning to fail him. "Over candlelight," he heard Walsingham say again, having been precise not to say by it, but over it. Walsingham, he was already learning, chose his words carefully. Cecil held the parchment over the candle, cautious not to burn it, but just so that the heat began to sear and stiffen the paper. Shortly there was a sweet smell like burned fruit, then the faintest fizzing, the dried juice Walsingham had written in was beginning to scorch. Within a few moments the full text appeared, amusing Cecil. Things so simple but yet absent from a lifetime still seem magical when witnessed for the first time. His amusement, though, rapidly screws to sullen consternation as he reads and understands the text, the final words the hardest to accept. He slams the letter on the desk.

Some within your Privy Council cannot be trusted.

XII

ഇൗൠ

Silt and sandy, the Thames estuary is like a rolling grey carpet of waves. The space of no hope at the edge of the world.

Trawler yanks up its sails on this blustery day, arching and bowing on the horizon. By doing so it gave the signal needed onshore, three miles back. As the captain and trawlerman held up his spyglass, Francis Walsingham's words from seventeen years ago came back to him – "One day you will need a powerful friend." Would he ever come good with his word? It certainly seemed like he had manoeuvred himself into more powerful circles, considering he now had him look out for foreign vessels. Seamen are promised favours in return for loyalty too often without recompense, but there was something about Walsingham's conviction that he believed. What he was not going to do was be some pawn in a pathetic power struggle between lowly government clerks. The only other voice he could now hear in his head was his old captain's – "the wealthy and the mighty need us at any price but never let us know our value." Walsingham was, he believed, different.

Then he saw it, tiny specks at first, coming over the edge of the world. He waited a moment just to be sure. There could be no doubt – a flotilla of ten ships. The French. Bastards. Immediately he drops the sails to give the signal he had seen them. Suddenly the small boat lurches to port side as the wind thumps through them, it did not matter what direction the ship began to spin so long as the message had been sent and seen onshore. He looked back and knew word would get back to Walsingham and he would be pleased. It was beginning.

* *

Sun slipped from the sky when, later that day, at the wharves beyond London's east end, outside the city walls, were thick with sloops and merchant vessels of all sizes and in varied states of use: loaded, unloaded, repaired or set for sail in the loud and hectic hustle. Amongst this, walks an uneasy Beale, scanning. Unchecked by the City authorities, he sees the wharves as the pus in London's wound. Even though he was no strict Protestant giving his devotion to the new Puritans, like his master, he did have his own virtues to stand by. He looked scornfully at this parade of the impious, quick to forget their God maybe watching – or worse – do not care even if it is so. Penny pinchmen were tarred here for charging unreasonable duties and unwieldy merchants use gangs to beat the price down. Sailors cavort with sluts and shout shanty songs as they neglect their duty to decency. Lost in their loathsome businesses, no-one gives Beale any mind of trouble as he walks with sheer distaste in his eyes. Amongst all this carnage, he finally sees the one ship that is instantly more intriguing than any other: Venus.

Painted red, with a single sail stitched from ladies' gowns, it has not been seaworthy for many years. It is a small sloop just big enough for the adventures inside. As Beale walks alongside its carnival of colours, he hears a lone lute player begin a lamenting tone that will resonate through the ages:

> *On the good ship Venus*
> *Christ you'd wish you seen us*
> *Our figurehead, a whore in bed,*
> *sucking a dead man's penis...*

As if perfectly serenading him, he gets to the bow and, sure enough, there is that FIGUREHEAD in all its crudely carved glory. Beale walks disbelievingly up the gangplank and onto Venus' main deck. The singing continuing below decks, which he follows as he ventures down into the sloop, seeing the Minstrel on a hammock, swinging and singing, just as gently:

> *When we reached our station*
> *Through skilful navigation*
> *The ship got sunk*
> *In a wave of spunk*
> *From too much fornication.*

Beale is stunned by laughter and the sound of slapped flesh that ripple around this open casket of copulation. Always the man of duty, he is not distracted by his disgust and continues looking for who he came for. He has to tread over, through and around lustful exchanges which appear to be whatever takes your fancy. Seemingly all can be bought here: women, orgies, men-to-men, voyeur or deformed. Gomorrah meets Sodom, he sighs to himself, recoiling just as a prepubescent boy falls to his knees in front of him.

'Sir, I beg thee...' The poor boy says sadly.

'Where is your Whoremaster?' Demands Beale, thinking the boy soliciting, not in want of help. 'Where's Essigia the landlord of this licentious lust house?' The boy looks blankly up to him so Beale gives him a shake, reaffirming his demands. Nothing is forthcoming. A whore, dressed only in woven swan feathers, saunters up to him so he addresses her for sense, 'Is he but numbed with wine?' She shakes her head, clearly numbed herself. 'What's this boy's ailment, woman?'

'A wholly dreadful fable, his anus turned unstable. But by God am I able, to take you on this galley table.' She says.

Rhyming whores? Beale had never believed the mythical tales about this place, but who was he to doubt, as he could see for himself that this lascivious mouth of hell was very much alive and licking its lips. 'Your Master, if you please.' Is all he could manage.

As the poetic prostitute leads Beale on, agog at how such a sordid den had rare and exquisite furnishings and although he has never been to the new stately houses and halls the wealthy in Elizabethan England were building beyond the city, he could not conceive even they contained such opulent oddities. There was a tapestry upon the floor where people trod that he heard tell was sometimes called a rug and which line the floors of the finest Turk harems. Caged birds that sang as if by a pool in heaven, a chess board made from what he could only perceive to be white gold, but which may have horrified him to know was fashioned from the tusks of pachyderms. Trinkets from the unknown world he mused in a murmur.

Rhyming Whore stops outside a noisy quarters and leaves Beale with a wink. There were squawks of pleasure within, though it was not entirely clear from how many the susurrations came.

'Essigia? Present yourself.' Beale asks respectfully. The heaving and sighing from within did not yield. Embarrassed, he persists in knocking, 'You should be running this frigate, not fornicating it.'

A frisky voice chirps, 'Come in and play, whoever you are!'

'Master Beale for want of your ear, not your manhood.' More cries of joy echoed through. Beale impatient now, 'Essigia? I'm here on behalf of Francis Walsingham.' The pleasure stops and there is a rough and tumble of people clambering themselves out of positions, Beale could swear there were four pairs of feet thumping around behind the door. It is opened ajar and Essigia peeps through, a small olive-skinned man with thin eyes and a guilty smile.

With a genteel lisp, he asks shiftily, 'Walthingham return hith eye back to import duty?'

'That is no longer his station in life. He is beset with...' Beale was not at all sure how to word this, '... more magnificent endeavours.'

'He ith not here?'

'No, other grave matters desire his attention.' Beale says. Essigia only hears no and relief overcomes him, so much so that he lapses to hold the door and it swings open. Beale looks no further than the figure he presents himself as and scoffs, 'What sordid sorceries suffer mine eyes?' Essigia looks himself up and down and fails to see why there is shock, for he is merely dressed in leather binds around his chest, buttocks and genitals, nothing more.

'My humble apology, perquisites of one's own station – to enjoy the wares.' Essigia smirkingly says. Then there is a whoosh, crack. Essigia is whipped from behind, his face instantly squirming with repressed pain and his eyes cross with pleasure.

'Should you desire to keep this boat of buggery afloat, untether your manhood and hither.' Beale walks off, his bravado enough to be followed. Essigia untangles himself, puts on a gown and with trepidation slips out to catch Beale above decks in the early evening sky.

* *

As darkness draws its veil upon the alleyways of St Paul's, the pamphleteers and preachers recede into the taverns and hostelries to regale in London's weak mead and over-priced pottage and pies. Williams ventures back to the Ink and Quill tavern where Beale had not so long ago coaxed him to meet Walsingham, and even with his large and tall frame in these darkened rooms he blends effortlessly back in.

Moments later Stimpson cosies in, concealing himself in a distant corner.

Williams greets some old cronies – none matching the description Stimpson was given from Beale, nonetheless he studies them carefully as they offer him a drink and he reasons it will only be a matter of time before any misdeed, if it exists at all, is uncovered in a drunken spill of the tongue. Stimpson's concentration falters when he is prodded by a woman that looks like a goat, clearly she had been talking to him and, as was his default, he failed to hear and answer her. He knew she was some kind of Doxy, no doubt about to trick him into a venture to part with his pennies, so he just waves her off without even bothering for an insult. Shunned, the woman snorts derisions through her nose, vowing she will remember his face.

When this distraction was gone, he could see that the pursuant described by Beale had just arrived and had quickly begun conversing with Williams. It was the caped man, ugly in nose and teeth. Stimpson reads their every word and brands them to memory.

* *

Having ridden now for many hours, Lynas Masterman steps awkwardly from the horse and comforts it, tying the reins to a tree at the foot of a steep hill, dense with pines, their heavy scent green and musky in the cold night. Peaking up along the slope, he is certain there are no bandits or robbers at play here, for this is not ambush territory and the accosted could easily escape or hear their attackers sliding down or struggling up the ridge. Neither could he see signs of lookouts or lone sentries. No, it was safe. He prays thanks for protection from the real dangers of any murky thicket: witchery. All reasonable men knew that the Devil's bidding was obliged in England's darkest corners. Walsingham had told him that as it was the true religion he was serving this very night then he should be assured he would not be struck by evil spirits nor the unwarranted attention of Satan's servants. Emboldened, he carefully began climbing.

With no clear path – not such a bad thing as no man or beast was familiar with this terrain – he circled around brambles and bracken to avoid unnecessary noise. Tonight, he wanted to see no man as he would not be delivering a message but creating one, with whatever news he spied at the precipice of this darkly wooded hill. Did he consider himself espial now? What would be wrong if he did? Had not Moses sent the 12 chieftains under the authority of God's work. Walsingham had explained the story in Numbers chapter 13, telling him how significant exploration was for the Lord's undertaking. Except Walsingham did not want lies to protect the Queen, as they had delivered Moses, neither did the Rider have the luxury of 40 nights but less than 40 hours to get back to London, an incredible feat on horse over such a distance. It only took him fifteen minutes to carefully and quietly climb near to the top and, twenty foot from what he could tell was the plateau, he crawled the rest of the way.

As the ground levelled out, the trees began to thin and passing the foot of the trunks he could see there was no sight of any lookouts. He edged on his elbows until he was able to see the valley below. What he beheld shook and astounded him, a gathered army of what must have been five thousand men and horse. Surely Walsingham and his government brothers had little defence to this – he may well have to present the news in some other way. No, truth is hard and capitulation easy, he could hear Walsingham say. However menacing, it was a spectacular and daunting sight. Their distant campfires made the night look like a fire left to dwindle in the dark, the final embers glowing in red patches: dangerous if provoked. An immense force in the perfect hiding place at the bottom of a valley, the North Sea glistening to the east. If he looked more intently he would have seen the beaked shape of the Humber's estuary, but this was not his remit and he certainly was not privy to Walsingham's tattoo theory. It did not matter, Walsingham had proven himself correct, but even with good riding he would not possess him of this confirmation for at least a further day.

Detail is what his new master needed and he appraised the valley below carefully. He reasoned thirty men could easily comfort themselves around a small fire and he saw at least eighty with many more smoke vents from shelters. Having seen troops and horsemen before, he put the army's size to a more realistic forty-two hundred. As his eyes adjust from the twinkling glows of orange and red fire, he looks for other signs but can see no evidence of siege towers although spots at least four cannon, not an insignificant number when backed by such force. He recoiled as carefully as he had crept there and sure-footed his way back down the slope where his horse was nice and rested, she needed to be for they were to dance their way through the night, eager to deliver Walsingham this news. He petted her trunk then between the eyes, she was ready.

* *

Privy Council Chamber, Whitehall Palace

Cecil pores over the map like a cat might scour the walls thinking there be mice. Dudley, Essex, Ludlow and Howard sit amongst other Privy Councillors. None seem to agree.

Servants outside the doors share sensationalised smiles: if only they could write they would have plenty to sell for gossip to the scandal sheet printers of Paternoster Row.

They hear Cecil inside, weary – the insults and discrediting of one another's views was a distracting and frustrating noise getting them nowhere. Is that what they want? He could not help think, eying Dudley, Essex, Howard and the wet swab Ludlow in turn. Who can he really trust? Why was their opposition to Walsingham so vociferous? Pressing them about Walsingham, they had pointed out the written evidence had lacked. Yes, Cecil had agreed, then countered if we were to organise a secret scheme would we write it down in detail – or moreover carry these plans on our person with any and all involved? He knew they had to argue with him – and each other – for it was why the Queen had chosen them all. Surround yourself with clever men, my Lord Cecil, whether you agree or not, she had so regally advised him at the beginning of her reign.

At this moment, however, Cecil could not find any wisdom in their opposition to Walsingham. There were times when it took some resolve not to chuckle to himself as the Councillors continued to argue on about this fellow that had bumbled in here with his demonic puppet on a leash. He who had written to him on some magic paper where words appear over candlelight. He who had not given him one solid corroborating piece of evidence. He who was now causing consternation and division in the Queen's private council...Francis bloody Walsingham. Cecil sympathised with the Privy Gentleman's heated rebuttals in the chamber, but now it was time to silence them. Cecil slapped the table. As they looked up at him, he pointed out that Walsingham had made a convincing story and it appeared highly plausible: threats to the Queen were very much alive and were perhaps even plotted close to the government. Their eyes and nods acknowledged this, still falling short of accepting it. So why, Cecil pressed them, did they still deny his theory?

It took several moments before any had the bravery to speak.

Then two did at once. 'We trust this man's words?' The voices spluttered. Cecil heard them both clearly, although not sure of who had said it and looks to the entire Council murmuring their approving 'Ayes' to each other. Frustrated at their petty objections without reasoning, he smacks the table again with an open palm, which rattles their goblets, his eyes were round and watered with fury.

'You will hold your noses questioning whether we "trust this man" I see. As I take in the souls gathered here I am poised to wonder who of you has a better notion of what secret enterprises are afoot, endangering your Queen's life?' Then, with increasing aggression, shouts, 'And that's how I see it – not one of you...You of the Privy Council who take your information from your Lords Lieutenant, they from Justices of Peace, the Parish Constables and Nights Watchmen of each and every Hundred, shire, town or hamlet. Not one of you beholds intelligence on the security of Her Majesty nor can you countenance Francis Walsingham by virtue of his current station in life. I am disgraced sirs.' Cecil spins away to not face them, so they cannot see his flustered cheeks and all they are left to look at is his back and the small door that connects to Elizabeth's antechamber. Nothing to concede but their chastisement.

It has been a little too long and Cecil has still not turned round to face them. Essex, Dudley and Howard – the more senior of the Councillors in terms of the Queen's favour – share glances and realise the session is over.

Dudley, with his supine legs and wispy moustache is the dashing darling of the court and it gives him the confidence to be loud and humorous, which is what makes him stand up now. He is not sure why Cecil seems to be defending this amusing and wily Walsingham fellow, but he understands all Cecil's points, so concludes, saying, 'My Lord Cecil, we shall retire with haste to glean from our patchwork of informers, messengers and court riders to what extent we can authenticate or contest the insinuations and claims of this new servant to Her Majesty.'

It was artfully worded and tempered, Cecil knows, though still does not turn to face them as they all leave the room. By God's grace, he thought to himself through tightening chest and neck, Walsingham had best be scrupulous, for he knew that each of the Councillors were leaving only temporarily chastened and would, from this moment on, be anticipating, salivating almost, for either of them to fail.

The chamber is empty of Councillors and Clerk closes its door, leaving Cecil alone. Calmer, much calmer, he walks to the antechamber door and knocks gently.

'Destiny has been thrust upon us, your Majesty.' Cecil says with conviction. The Queen beckons him in to explain.

XIII

∽◌◌

Good ship Venus was listing with increasing intensity at dockside as its sail of stitched together ladies' garments began to billow in the wind blowing up the Thames. Despite the thumping roar and shafts of breeze flaring through the boat, patrons and panderers mind little as their lusts continue unrelentingly. Hannah, striding more comfortably now with her new merkin affixed to her crotch, leads Ridolfi to some cushions, whispering into his ear, soothing his groin.

Watching from across the deck and masking his anxious heart with fake smiles, Essigia pretends to fraternize with his perverse clientele, but never drops his gaze from them. Beale had so thoroughly convinced him of Walsingham's gratitude and assured him that favours could be negotiated as well as encourage blind eyes to be turned, that he was determined to ensure it ended to all their advantages. Essigia willed on the whore and if Hannah delivers he may even give her the night off with a groat to spend as she may delight. His nerves tingle and excite like a hunter may see a hare hop gradually towards a trap.

In a split second it may fall apart: Hannah lunges her hand into Ridolfi's codpiece, but he stops her with his own hand and thwarts her further attempts. Essigia was sure the Florentine preferred women, had he got that wrong, should he have proffered on him a manwhore? Hannah smiles, liking the firm stance he takes, a challenge for her. She cradles his neck and whispers into his ear. He then lets go and she massages him and they lose each other's faces in lustful kissing. Essigia knows his prey is snared. Now he must act and, as he sways through the crowds and nears them, he wonders what Hannah must have said to him. Whatever her sordid devices, she cannot get him too aroused until he tells her what Beale may want to hear – where he has been and who with these past weeks. There was no way that Ridolfi was simply going to give this information up without getting suspicious, so Essigia was going to have to play some games with him. The only certainty anybody ever had on Essigia is that he could certainly play games.

Nobody knew where Essigia hailed from, some said a small village near the Pyrenees, others believed he was a carnival runaway from a Mediterranean port, or even that he was the bastard child of Hector Essigia from Mary Queen of Scots' court. It humoured him to hear the ever-fanciful tales and he revelled and lost himself in his own mystery. It was the only way people would trust his outlandish ideas, it being a quirk of his humble background. You can't blame Essigia for that, they might say, his ancestors after all built a tower to the moon, just as they might explain some strange escapade on the fact he was reared on the breastmilk of mermaids. So it was that this evening's idea did not raise an eye of suspicion amongst his friends or whores in his charge.

Two Summers ago, Essigia and a small number of prostitutes – his Gems as he liked to call them – journeyed upriver by barge to the woods and thickets just outside Richmond. In his usual carefree way, Essigia had stomped through the reeds to the undergrowth, tangling himself in some brambles and, forcing his legs to keep wading through, caused the barbs to lacerate with ease his flimsy hoes and soft legs. Obviously emboldened by the wine heartily quaffed on the two-hour journey, he had not felt the deep cuts and they only began to worry him when his slippers went soggy with blood. After an hour in agony from the stinging gashes, the group had sought a nearby Wise-woman who placed a poultice over his wounds and encouraged him to ingest some, for the pain. Agnes Levet then left them with their basket of bread, cured cheese rinds, leather pouches of mead and this peculiar edible poultice. As they lazed away the afternoon, so numbed and content did he feel that he insisted his Gems try this soothing poultice on their tongue. For the remainder of the day they were rendered useless, such were the effects of the mead and their merriment.

It was not until the following morning when Essigia and his Gems were reflecting on their current state of melancholy that he asked what they remembered of their jolly escapades the night before. As they stitched the memories back together they recalled how their giggles had been plenty but how they had also entered such deep and absorbing conversations and none present held back on honesty with one another. They looked around and nodded solemnly at the secrets of their lives they had shared that previous night. Essigia knew this was not brought about by mead and merriment alone: the poultice, was all he could reason. What a fine potion of magic if ever there was one – it could bring about smiles, laughter and the utmost truth and honesty.

It was complete serendipity then that he recently saw old Agnes from Richmond woods wandering the streets of Tower Street Ward, near Tower Hill. She happened upon her some of that poultice wrapped in the flimsiest of muslin cloth. Essigia emptied a leather pouch and tipped the unguent carefully in because he wanted to take this back to Venus and employ a Physick or even Alchemist to see what the potent concoction might contain, maybe reproduce it to sell as another quirk of the Venus.

That is exactly what he did, but none were able to tell him, so odd and mysterious were the ingredients they tasted on the tips of their tongues or placed in distilled vinegar to see how it might react. After a dozen apothecaries, his supply had dwindled and the small half cupful was now no more than a small ladle's worth. He put it in a small glass vial and hid it for very important occasions. When his services were employed by Walsingham as agent, he knew it was time to use his truth potion on Roberto d'Ridolfi the Florentine banker.

As Hannah plied the Italian envoy with wine she would force him to ingest it by way of her tongue, pushing the unguent to the back of his throat, forcing it down. Essigia warned her to not keep any for herself lest she be absent of mind til morning tide. Now that they were lustfully distracted, Essigia approached them with care, scooped enough to cover his fingertip and pasted it onto Hannah's tongue as he passed and she expertly drove it into Ridolfi's mouth. He had to swallow for her tongue pressed so deep into his throat it almost made him gag. Hannah guided the unsuspecting banker to a cabin, where she was to leave it half an hour and then fetch for Essigia to get some spoken truths from him.

Essigia was delighted with himself, he had accepted Beale's charge but had thought to himself if he could get the information himself and deliver it directly to Walsingham then all the more favour would be granted to him. Skip the middleman. Hannah and Ridolfi fondled their way to the cabin and he could see the tell-tale signs of dribbling from the mouth – the foreigner had no charm or amulet strong enough to defend against English witchery.

His truths will out.

* *

St. Paul's churchyard, Paternoster Row

Stimpson had stayed watching Walter long after the Ugly caped man had left the tavern, clearly acting on some information given over by Williams. Little could he have known it was Beale that was to fair badly as a result of this intelligence. All he could see was how tormented Walter was and Stimpson needed to let the events play out and see what was to become of him. This he knew was what his master would have wanted him to do.

As the tavern was dying down, Williams goes to relieve himself in the gutters outside so Stimpson readied to leave and placed his neck scarf over his mouth and lowered his peak cap, not that Williams would have recognised him for the ales he had now sunk. He saw in Williams a restless soul for guilt. Although he had not been able to read the conversations as well as he may have liked, he had got their gist: there were directions and timings; but no names or clear places. Neither could he make out from each man whom they might serve. This would be the first question Walsingham would ask. It played upon his mind whether to just take the nub of his walking stick and pelt the drunk Williams over the back of the head and insist he tell him what his schemes were this evening tide. But then he was not even confident there had been a traitorous infiltration. What if this were some personal enterprise? He thought about following him home grappling him face down in one of the many streams or open sewers trickling through London to get the answers he needed. No one would question a clumsy drunk face down in a ditch. He had certainly drank his fill – counting five ales to match his one since he had been left alone. It was the strong good ale he was drinking too, not the rancid cow's piss they saved for journeyman travellers or cheap peddlers. About to leave, Stimpson saw a woman enter and garrulously approach Williams.

Dressed in a large woollen shawl that covered her entire head and upper body so that only her nose poked out, he saw she was not dirt poor because her skirt was divided in two showing her underskirt. She hobbled but suffered no ailment of legs as far as he could tell. There were at least three colours amongst her skirts but they looked wet, dark. Walter smiled ironically when he saw her. With urgency the woman was encouraging him to leave – he could only see the body language not her moving lips. She stubbornly refused a drink, the woman looked around the tavern, obviously hoping she was not drawing too much attention, or at least the wrong kind. Stimpson caught her pretty but peculiar face. Her lips were brightened with pink and her cheeks decorated in a smudgy red. If women could not afford vermillion then some would resort to using milk and hen's blood or even wettened brick dust. She was either doxie or whore, then, though it was clear she was not touting because that was illegal in this part of London and Williams never visited prostitutes. Sensing they would leave any moment, he tightened his cape and wound some twine around the bottom of his walking stick, so the deaf man remained quiet.

Stimpson kept his distance as she leaned Williams through the lanes as best she could, apologising to those he abraded. They headed south down St Andrews hill to the river – perhaps she was going to chuck him in, saving them all the nuisance, Stimpson smiled to himself. At the Thames' edge by Baynarde's castle she haloed a wherry, rummaged for his purse, paid them and they were on their way. Stimpson expected them to bob southwards onto Southwark, instead the boat steered eastwards towards London Bridge. There was no straightforward path to follow so he could not keep them in his view and the tide had turned to push the Thames right up its embankments so walking the shoreline was not good either.

Just as their faces were fading from view he could have sworn he saw the wherryman confirm, 'The Venus?' The whore, as Stimpson concluded she now must be, nodded. He could not wait to inform his master, whenever he returned to Seething Lane, knowing where the Venus was moored he knew Walsingham would expect him to follow.

* *

As the night crawled on, it was disappointing, if not humorous, to watch. Sure enough, Essigia recognised all the strange behaviours Ridolfi was exhibiting: the grinning; drooling; eye rolling; blissfully unaware he had been debased by a poultice paste. Ridolfi had proven honest and open to talk as he recounted feelings for his own mother and a terrible practical joke involving an apple cart he and his brother played on the village Friar. As the evening went on, Essigia tried to ask of his recent whereabouts, any underhand dealings... with who...and why, a great tangle of questions that the incumbent was sure to trip on. What he got, however, was largely mumbling and bursts of some recognisable English amongst a lot of Italian.

Essigia was disappointed and felt his endeavours had failed. He knew this meant he could not go to Walsingham directly with such meagre findings. Instead, he would have to relay what pitiful remnants of his interrogation he could to Beale.

XIV

෨෨ლ

As wherrymen approached the eastern land gate of the
Tower of London, they would shout, 'Wary of
Beelzebub's bollock.' Crawl closer to it and you'll be
pronged in surprise, steer below it and t'will be the arse
end of London you go. Such were their superstitions,
warily venturing too close to the tower or too far from
London's boundaries.

This was the agreed meeting place.

'He kept his mind so well guarded.' Essigia began in
his delicate lisp, worried what Beale might do, but
seeing he had no visible weapon – and not aware of his
hidden Grosschedel blade – he kept on. 'No matter
what my whore and wine tried to coax, he all but
resisted. If it please our master Walsingham, there were
some morsels to be prized. He did divers times mention
a "cart loss" in a "bailey." If that might be of use?'
Beale cleared his throat and Essigia took that to mean
this better not be all you have. Essigia scrambled around
his mind. 'He was prone to brag of his fortune, invested
by the pope he claimed, near ten thousand crowns
sayeth he, but I fancied this mere whimsy. It then just
turned to rambling, sir. Wine, he moaned often for and
the only words I picked out between were "Alba" and
"how hard" a "beak" was, I believe.' Essigia dropped
his head in shame. Maybe he was the only one to be so
terribly afflicted by the evil unguent from the Wise-
Woman of Richmond.

'This and no more?' Beale checks.

'I apologise, sir. Please take no affront and assuredly beseech Walsingham if I can be of further assistance to labour services upon me again. I beg thee.' Essigia saw his prospects plummet towards the cesspit as he watches Beale leave and knows the best to hope for is not to be shamed and ostracized by his master.

As he paces away, Beale delights in both what he has been told and in resisting the urge to embrace and kiss the whoremaster Essigia should he give away his lucky find. Best to leave him in the state of repentance he was in. So delighted was he of the discoveries Essigia had given up without realising their potency, Beale could not help but almost skip his way up the hill path around the Tower of London towards Seething Lane.

After speaking with Walsingham and updating him in his warm study, his buoyant mood somewhat drops as the cold night ate into his skin as he waits by the side basement door. How Francis had been rapt with his report from Essigia. To have the "beak" confirmed without the Court Rider's report was gratifying to say the least and they knew that "Alba" was the powerful Spanish Duke who could effortlessly sponsor any such intention on the Queen's life and provide overwhelming force against the English. Neither of them could quite make sense of the "cart loss in a bailey" but they knew Ridolfi's admission alone about connections to the Pope and the bragging of his fortune was enough to warrant charges against him in good time. It was the relaying of the phrase "how hard" that Ridolfi had repeated for which Walsingham saw as nothing short of heavenly intervention. He had smacked Robbie's back, that proud fatherly approval.

Howard. For certain, he was somehow involved. The Florentine fool absent of his senses had not squinted in giving up one of the most powerful men in England and Essigia's ignorance had not picked it up or connected the name. It could not have gone better for them, without doubt a sign in his mind confirming Howard's complicit guilt and they took great relish in it. Delighted as he was that his punt was yielding returns, he told Beale he would need to ensure the two Portsmouth prisoners could corroborate this, which meant going to the basement once again. This is where it became slightly awkward for Beale as he had wanted to seek Walsingham's permission to escort Edith, his housemaid – and sister by law – on her errands. At first Francis thought the boy, as he still called him, was being overly polite and had questioned why he wanted to aid her on a walk she had done a thousand nights before. When Beale blushed, he understood the real nature of his request and he had smirked and given his consent.

Still waiting outside in the gnawing cold, Beale felt his fingers and toes pang. It was nearly an hour when Edith finally appeared. Walking out the door, she slows – but does not stop – upon seeing him and smiles friskily, sashaying past him. She knows his courage has been mustered to ask for her company…and to stand outside in such discomfort. They do not speak and she toys with her shawl and looks back to him, hoping, but not asking, for him to follow and catch up. Beale skips up to her and nudges into her shoulder and she giggles, that sweet sound of playful consent.

Below them, in the cellars, candlelight illuminates MacKinnon and Bridle, both gaunt, drooling wretches.

Walsingham says emphatically, 'Now, gentlemen, let us be certain of the story's truths.' If they could cry they would, but for want of moisture in their bodies. One more exhausting night of torment they doubted they could endure. Walsingham had the names he wanted but not the plans or who else might know of them. He was determined to find out more. The two men do not even try to bravely resist, such have their souls and bodies suffered under Walsingham's guard. They readily spill more of their precious secrets in the dark of his cellar, and Walsingham delights in catching it all in finest quill on parchment to bolster his Book of Secret Intelligences. He lets them drink an abundance of ale instead of only enough to keep them alive these past days.

After their testimony, MacKinnon and Bridle loll mutely in their chained seats, ill-appointed to understand how their narrations had inflamed their culpability. Walsingham knew there were two schools of thought for the use of torture: the first was that it expedited what was needed to be known and the second was its knack in encouraging lost truths. Yes, there was the view that people would tell you anything to cease the agony, but if you interrogated perceptively then your questions could build a story, not invent one. All facts must be accounted for, however long realities took to be established, and he would not be made fool for anyone's ridicule. So he would thoroughly – and painfully – check and check again their stories.

Eventually satisfied, Walsingham got up and knew he had to walk to think how all the affairs he compiled could be neatly explained. Before doing so, he locked his book in a brand-new iron rigged chest.

Had Stimpson not been at the inn watching Williams' lips he would have insisted he should accompany his master as night could be dangerous. Walsingham was tall and confident, however, as he left Seething Lane and headed west, towards Cheapside, along Fenchurch and Lombard street.

He wanted to stand on the streets where his revered historical genius would have once stood. At Ironmonger's Lane, near the old St. Olave's chapel, Walsingham glanced up and around the tight crooked houses and shop fronts imagining if Thomas Becket had ever stopped and wondered at this very spot. The buildings would not have looked in such a lazy state, of course, like old drunks leant against one another in a tavern. All it takes is for one to topple and the whole row would collapse. He saw the signs for Fyson's Barber Surgeon shop and would soon send him thanks and patronage, but now he wanted no company.

Walsingham despised and admired Becket. 400 years hence that "lowly born" cleric and maverick of England rose to prominence and power in such swift grace that he had stunned the governing classes. Yes, that was impressive, he conceded, but his obstinacy and allegiance to the Pope was unshakeable. In Walsingham's eyes this should have been to his sovereign and country not to the papal palaces in Rome. Disgusting and opulent. Unpardonably misguided loyalty up to the end. But – and it really was an impressive preposition – he had to be esteemed for his rise to be in that position: impressive, improbable and unforgettable. For all his misconceived martyrdoms, Becket had used his street smart and passionate zeal to talk unflinchingly to power. That was what Walsingham admired most as his sense of history and portent swells in his mind. He is ready to speak openly and directly to the most powerful man in England: William Cecil.

Scurrying through the night to Westminster, he forgets several streets from him were Beale and Edith.

* *

He held her waist as they walked through the tight lane, the stench of fresh excrement filling their chests. They did not care for the offensive smell caused by two Night-Soil-Men shovelling the slop of human waste from the street privy cess pit into huge barrels on a cart. Thank God I am no Gong Farmer he thought as the rancid smell grew more potent as they closely passed them. It was not going to spoil their night. They had spent it walking around and around, aimless and carefree, keeping each other warm, talking about a possible future. It was only now that Beale felt brave and dropped his hand lower, feeling the strong curve of her arse cheek as she walked.

'And here was I thinking you gentlemanly.' Edith says with a giggle.

CLANG – Beale thuds to the floor as one of the Soil Men slaps him down with his spade and the other snatches Edith, covering her mouth, the scent of shit coursing through her throat and burning her lungs. She looks down to Beale heaped like a dead cat as one of the gong farmers folds him up onto the cart. The other clutches her and whispers into her ear exactly what she should say to her master, Walsingham. Her eyes begin welling, not with tears of sorrow for her temporarily lost lover, but for the vomit inducing odour of the man's hands pressing hard into her mouth, and then for the fear of her stomach not to pass through her mouth. She knew she could not bite him for risk of the countless beshitments her lips and tongue would taste. Writhing against his tight clasp proved pointless and she was now filled with total hatred for him and a hopeless exhaustion. All the while his message was losing its detail on her. It all became unbearable and she managed to loosen a leg from around his and lunge her heel up into his scrotum. Instantly he lets go and bends over double as she flaps to the floor. The other quickly circles round the cart and as she is steadying herself up, he punches her in the middle of the nose. Edith feels her back thud to the floor and her eyes see black. Then she is lifted half up from the floor and, for one bizarre moment, is relieved to hear him remind her of their instructions, 'Temple, noon.'

She was just regaining her vision when a fist hammers her back to the floor, where she will lay throughout the night. Her ears would not hear the cart take Beale away or the old Baker try to fuss and wake her several hours later, deciding to leave her sat upright thinking she was merely a drunk wench.

* *

With his maidservant bleeding on the street floor of some back lane, and his steward carted away, Walsingham hurries into the palaces of Westminster to inform Cecil of his protectorate intelligence. He stops to take a breath. Intentions, a wise soothsayer once told him as a boy, no matter how good they are, merely pave the way to Hell. At this moment Cecil feels to him like

St. Peter determining his fate in the greatest fork in the road of his life.

Unfortunately Cecil was not in a receiving mood as Walsingham is ushered into the Privy Council Chamber by Clerk who begrudgingly leaves, still stunned at his meteoric rise from normality to gaining the ear – albeit suspiciously and without merit – of the Privy Council. Leaving them alone, how many years, he bellyached within, must he keep these doors open for such men?

'What can you tell me now that I did not know yesterday, Walsingham?' Cecil yawns to him.

'I dare not pretend to hold the divinity of soothsaying. Yesterday there is knowledge and today we must use it. History tells me when I am being threatened.' Walsingham says, still catching his breath. Cecil's eyes give him permission to proceed. 'England has nourished Protestantism but it has not brought peace. Paranoia of plots to...' – He thinks better than to say murder – '... displace Queen Elizabeth are rife, denying us fact or meaningful intelligence.' Walsingham knew he was quoting heavily from his initial petition but felt it prudent to reinvigorate the motion. 'In twelve years the tyranny of Catholicism has yet to be expelled, nay festered into a demonic beast, lurking within shadows: nameless and terrifying in all corners of the country, from farmsteads to within these very walls. I can lift the veil of this menace with a secretariat of intelligence. And I shall prove it.' Despite being alone, it felt as if a hundred pair of eyes bore holes through his skull. In a way there were. Cecil as First Minister had to think in a dozen different ways: how some intelligence would or could affect any one area of his government and how it may not for others, what does the Queen need to know

and what should she know. He had to think with a
hundred men's minds.

Walsingham wondered how he would react about his
theory of Privy Councillors that could potentially be
involved in a plot to usurp Queen Elizabeth from power.
Men she had chosen for their loyalty to serve. Perhaps
he needed Cecil to get to this conclusion by himself.
Cecil was sat and moved forward to glare up at him,
behind the oaken table, the map of England now had
notes from the referral Walsingham had made about
"the beak." All in Cecil's hand.

Moving on from Cecil's silence, Walsingham plunges
straight into it, blurting to him that he had cause to
believe Ridolfi, the Pope's banker, had near 12,000
crowns on his person. This was no mere purse of a flashy
extrovert, that amount being several more times than
Cecil's annual stipend. No, these were funds of a nation's
envoy. Cecil pinched his eyes between finger and thumb.
Even though he had sat and listened to Walsingham's
retelling of the entire last few days from Portsmouth to
Venus, to barbers to whores and guesses and half-truths
in between, the First Minister needs affirmation.

'How came you by this?' Cecil tiredly wonders.

'An espial, my Lord.'

Cecil corrected him, 'A whore? As spy?'

Walsingham felt ridiculous stood there in his fine
dark robes having to defend the word of someone who
would sooner swallow yeasty members into her mouth
than seek a reference of good character from these
superiors, so little did she value her own life, but so
much value now being placed on her words.

'Can it be corroborated?' Cecil sharply asks.
Walsingham could feel himself succumbing not to

embarrassment but timidity in revealing to Cecil just exactly how he could back this up. 'Walsingham, we cannot act without...'

'I saw the conversation.' Walsingham thinly says.

'Saw?'

'My expertise lies in reading lips.' For the first time he did not look Cecil in the eyes, knowing the ridicule he has set himself up for.

While chuntering, Cecil clarifies, 'And you expect the Privy Council to believe that? – Not what you heard in voice or read in transcript, but saw in lips? You might have as good and well invented it, sir. You would have me mocked?' Before he could reply, Cecil blusters on, 'Where then, do smirks and gestures come into this – do I take it that a scratch of the nose might mean France readies her forces and picking of the arse that Scotland is about to march south?'

Walsingham does well not to laugh, but Cecil's reddening face made him realise that would not have been the best protocol to break at this point, his voice now hoarse. The quick-thinking lawyer and master of two languages was left with little colourful response, only his logical reason. 'I am certain he has an agent in correspondence with the Duke of Alba to invade from Netherlands with 10,000 men, to usurp Her Majesty and for marriage betwixt Mary Queen Of the Scots.'

Cecil stares at Walsingham, waiting for him to finish, their eyes locked.

'Invasion. And Mary marry? Marry...who?' Cecil ponders searchingly, looking about the room as if the answer to these hides under a book or scroll someplace.

'This I have not ascertained.'

'Well let's see them, then.'

'See…my Lord?' Walsingham stutters.

'The correspondence.' Cecil says.

'It is sourced from…my Agents.'

'The prisoners?'

All Walsingham can do is nod.

'Whom you tortured?'

Walsingham looks up, saying indignantly, 'Coerced, my Lord. We need to advise the Queen, I know of only facts, not timeframes.'

'Oh, we need to advise Her Majesty, do we?' Cecil says, that last "we" with a condescension used all too well to insufferable insubordinates. Walsingham rapidly sees his station crumbling into dust as Cecil laughs chidingly, before deciding to bring this all into context, 'You want me to act on the words of a prostitute, prisoner and your supposed skill of reading lips taught by a cripple of the ears? You're downright blind with ambition, nay artlessness.'

'Your Grace granted my request for an audience.' Walsingham exclaims, perhaps a little too tartly as he sees Cecil turn his unique shade of red once more.

'You are dismissed, sirrah.' Cecil finally shouts, once and for all.

Gloom outside the Privy Council Chamber is starkly dense.

As Walsingham steps out, a shaft of light slithers through, illuminating the hall. The smoothly sauntering bird of prey now suddenly pitiable, doleful in the brilliant light. Walsingham feels his wings clipped in disgrace. How could he have been so foolish as to not go with more evidence.

Clump. The door closes and plummets him into darkness.

'Sir?' Calls a voice from somewhere in the bleakness of the cavernous hall.

Walsingham squints his eyes and makes out that familiar odorous letch, the Spit-Jack.

'You, of all people, right now is...' Walsingham starts, realising he has likely had his ear near to the door all along, hearing his downfall.

'I think it be just the right time, I've brought you your Rider.' Sure enough his Court Rider, Lynas Masterman, is stood, humbly bowing. 'And he has just what you need.'

Without even hearing any more, Walsingham drags the stunned Court Rider into the Privy Council Chamber. They both knew that Cecil could rightly throw them into the Tower of London for what they were about to do, but Walsingham does not stop. The determination Lynas sees in his raptorial glower, means he does not move to prevent him either.

They barge in.

'Proof positive, my lord.' He says confrontationally.

Cecil has not the energy to shout, only a whimsical disbelieving smile, 'Of what?' He tires.

'Rebellion. Starting in the north.' Walsingham thrusting Masterman forward by the shoulder.

'Tis truth, m'lord.' Masterman cowers. 'In the north.'

Cecil is about to rebuke him, then he recognises the Rider's livery and his face, quickly changing his countenance. 'The Beak.' The wise man is haunted, as if he has just been told the exact date of his death. 'With these accusations...' Cecil murmurs, looking at the door that Walsingham was sure once had the Queen behind it listening in, '...it will cause civil war.' Cecil is not merely slicing down his arguments now but testing his broader comprehension of their implications.

Walsingham dismisses Masterman and sees the smug face of Spit-Jack before the door closes on them both – he has certainly proven his worth.

'Civil war.' Cecil says again, as if he can see the soldiers dead on the battlefields.

Walsingham understands perfectly. There have been too many sleepless nights spent thinking his ideas through and his evidence was mounting too rigidly to let this opportunity slip. He needs to convey that he is now completely ready to handle the utter magnitude of it all. With slow confidence he looks directly at Cecil. 'There is less danger in fearing too much than too little.'

Cecil huffs a smile and looks to the smaller door, which has now opened, slightly ajar.

Walsingham's eyes widen and his heart quickens. The bejewelled finger delicately beckons him in. Is it a spectral vision? Did he imagine it?

No, Cecil motions for him to move towards it. Walsingham treads gently forward, disguising the quiver in his knees and, with diffidence, looks to Cecil who moves to it and gently pushes open the door. His petition, his love and loyalty, gumption and dedication have all paved the way to this moment.

The Queen has summoned him.

ജ&ൽ

PART TWO

Brotherhood
of Shadows

March – May 1570

ജ&ൽ

I

Aldgate Ward

25ᵗʰ March 1570

ᏻᏚᏁᏚ

Whispers woke him, suspicious in their hushed and disguised tones. It was the coarse noise from scuffing shoes that finally ripped through his unconscious and ensured he would not lull back into sleep. Is that what it was – a sleep? Even drink could not account for all the pain in his head, so he must have passed out, but how? Chair. He was on a chair. Feeling through it, he could tell it was stone on the floor. Were they outside? In a dungeon? He could not perceive whether his eyes were covered, he was unsure if his eyes were even able to open. Sensing it was dark but not cold, he reasoned it must be a basement. The pain in his head whirred loudly and he lolled his head forward, heavy and empty, the temples feeling like they were going to burst with the swelling ache all around. His scalp so sensitive he worried it would be agonising just to be gently brushed, as Edith had done earlier with her tiny fingers. How long ago was that? Edith? He must have mumbled this aloud as the whisperers informed each other he was awake. Where was she? Where was he for that matter? He tried to ask but the words could not leave his mouth, only what tasted like warm water from an iron kettle dribbled from his lips.

Blood. It was then he remembered the almighty, almost neck-breaking, thud to the back of the head before falling to the floor…of the lane. This is where he gnarled his nose and mouth. What state his face must now present with – was he destined to remain in bachelordom?

'He's coming round, get the bucket.' Suddenly the wash of cold water over him snaps his body rigid, everything tight in the chair. Surprised, he feels he is not tied so his hands freely wipe his face and his legs comfortably alter position, though he still struggles to see. 'Where be your master, Robert Beale?' He did not recognise the voice that spoke. 'Where is Francis Walsingham?'

'I cannot see.' Beale responds limply, which they took as sarcasm, but he was buying time, assessing just what kind of situation he was in – who were these servants of malice? What could they possibly expect of him?

'That will pass.' The voice impatiently says, waiting for an answer.

'Where am I? – Where's Edith?'

'The questions shall remain ours. In good time you shall have answers to yours.' Voice replies, its calmness unsettling him, as he feels the agony of light flaring into his eyes. He begins to see the blur of shapes, outlines. He tries hard to focus but cannot tell if he was looking at a table or a large dog before him. 'First, I insist you indulge my questions: where is your master?'

'It is no great secret that he attends my Lord Cecil at the Privy Council.' Beale says honestly.

'For what purpose?'

'For what purpose do you wish to know? Sirs, I am aide to a member of Parliament for Lyme Regis assisting in governmental business, if harm was to become of my person…' He stops on purpose, letting that thought stir in their minds for a moment and to purvey innocence.

'What do you think would happen if harm were to become of your person?' The voice was surprisingly playful, as if he were happy to gradually raise the stakes. 'You are no prisoner, there are no binds, we came to the aid of a man being robbed and commonly assaulted by two vile bandits who absconded with his lover.'

Beale realises his own play has forced him into a corner. They know he is associated to Francis, that is why he is here, they were not concerned with ordinary Parliament business so now he has to think like the mathematician he is and let them divulge why they want him, then he can calculate his resolution.

Seeing him go word shy, the voice took the lead again, 'Your master has presented a petition that suggests he has information on plots and does linger at the palaces of Whitehall this night, poisoning ears with theories of nonsuch.'

'If that were so, why are you beside agitation in questioning me of it?' Beale was thinking of adding an insult. He begins to realise his captors must place little value in him and, besides, he could now make out the men for the first time: one, colourfully and tastefully dressed with short, dark, curly hair, clearly it was not him who had spoken for he was of foreign footing; the second stunned him – the caped man, ugly in nose and teeth, that had been talking to Williams before they met at the Ink and Quill tavern all those many days ago in St. Paul's. Beale tries not to act surprised and hears himself feebly say, 'You…' Clearly neither heard him. He took the opportunity to look about the room as it came more into focus: he saw no weapons or instruments of torture, two capes and one cap, with a peacock feather in it.

Ugly whispers to the Foreigner whose short beard glistens in the dewy room. He finally answers Beale's question, 'Because you and your master meddle in unsettling the peace.'

'If there are plots to remove and replace our Queen then you would call that "unsettling the peace?"' He was being careful not to accept the premise of their questions that he was somehow involved in any uncovering of Walsingham's doing.

The only man to speak so far, neared Beale, and he cannot help but squirm at his unforgettable ugliness that got right into his face, saying, 'Peace is not stirring up hatred and trying to divide the country.'

Beale was chasing several different thoughts. First, what a preposterous argument, giving away his allegiances. What could this wretch possibly think he is achieving by capturing and questioning him? What was his connection to Williams? What had they discussed that night in the tavern? Was their actor friend working against Walsingham? Worse, had they been betrayed by Williams? – Who else knew of Walsingham's whereabouts and more…his desire for Edith? His final thought rested on that night in Walsingham's study. What was it Williams had said about whom he serves – "the fattest purse of groats." As much as he sought an answer to these stomach-churning questions, he resists the urge to speak out in fear of giving away all he knew. Beale does well to sit on his new seething hatred for Walter Williams.

With his improving eyesight he was able to get a better idea of where he was. Definitely a cellar but not of a tavern for there was no noise above or empty casks here below. Perhaps they were beneath a small warehouse or merchant store closed up for the night. That might explain the foreign man that had yet to speak. The floor and walls showed no damp or small deposits of clay or sand in the bricks, a sure sign of being close to the river. It was dusty with dry mud. They were on higher ground, one of London's hills – Cornhill maybe, or in the west near Smithfield or even at Aldgate. The aeld gate, that ancient freeway, yes, this seemed far more plausible as it was closer to where he was taken from, being still late of the night. He tried to recollect what sort of buildings were around Aldgate, where was it best to take a prisoner and interrogate them for want of no attention. There was the Monte Jovis Inn with its fine horse yard, but he had already established it was too quiet here to be beneath a tavern or even stables. Small stores and victualling supplies made up the rest of the area. Some cook houses too – where it was once rumoured Elizabeth herself had eaten pork and peas upon her release from the Tower many years ago. There was no smell nor trace of food, let alone cooking. Then it struck him. Northumberland House. The grand gabled town house situated halfway up the lane leading to the aeld gate, the last London home of Thomas Percy, the Earl of Northumberland whose forces had been obliterated and scattered by Essex in the failed rebellion of 1569. He congratulated himself for listening so intently to Francis over the weeks gone past.

Perspiration then came in full, burning waves. Was he now suddenly caught in the midst of another rebellion and was prisoner in the headquarters of its plotters? Were the basements of this abandoned home being used by a desperate band of Catholic sympathisers harassing an assistant to a lowly member of Parliament with a lofty idea to protect the Queen? He was delighted with himself for putting this theory together, now grasping the incredible enormity of what he was involved with. His armpits leaked.

'What know you of your master's plans?' Ugly in nose and teeth came at him again.

Beale could not believe their desperation. 'It is your belief a master confides to the servant with his affairs?'

'Oh we're certain of your import, you sell thyself shy of your true value.'

'Value? For what?' Beale clucks at them.

'Your modesty is tender, alack we are not to be fooled.' Ugly says, still the sole interrogator.

Beale was more bored than concerned when he asked, 'What are your intentions with me?'

The man with dark, curly hair gave Ugly a folded parchment, which he ceremoniously opened, and then read, '"What I propose will lift the veil on this menace: a secretariat dedicated to gathering real intelligence for the Crown."'

Beale for the first time tries not to register genuine shock – Walsingham's proposal to the Privy Council, it was not the original scroll, but nevertheless there was a breach of government privacy here, someone had copied and passed this on. An Agent within the Privy Council chamber that would see to the removal or assassination of their Queen. It cannot be so. What knave or dirt sucking pig gland clerk would do such a thing? Anger ground Beale's teeth. From now on any correspondence must be encoded and he instantly thought of several ciphers he could use. He would advise Walsingham to select one man to be his pen, his mouth, his eye, his ear and therefore keeper of his most secret cabinet.

His two captors laughed as he read it again and Beale blushed slightly at hearing its loftiness through someone else's lips, it sounded naïve, ludicrous even. He then felt his concealed Grosschedel blade and is empowered to snipe, 'If it warrants your attention, it cannot be entirely baseless. The need is prescient.'

'Just tell us what you know of it.' Ugly yaps frustratingly.

'This I will tell you…should I break my appointment with Walsingham this night, he will call upon the Night's watch of Aldgate ward to search with a keen eye and be they discover me harmed, further questions should await for the faces I now recognise in you.'

Fury rages from the Foreign man's neck to his cheeks and he contains himself no longer, unsheathing a shimmering dagger and lurches towards Beale. 'What say they even find you alive?' He rasps, in good, but thickly accented, English. Holding the blade to Beale's mouth, he continues threateningly, 'I could fix it you never say anything again, clever or otherwise.'

Maybe a Mediterranean accent, Beale thought. As the blade was pressed more firmly into his mouth he felt his teeth began to grind on the metal and his bottom lip was delicately sliced. Now his eyes widened in horror – was this frenzied foreigner going to cut out his tongue? Even though he was not tied, the man was kneeling on his lap and being taller with thicker arms he pressed easily down upon Beale, his own blade impossible to grasp. Any quick or sudden move, Beale's lower jaw would be hacked off in the melee. 'Say one more keen word, you slave of a whore.' Foreigner hissed. At this point Ugly crouches beside him to whisper into his ear.

'You've already seen we can pick you off the streets whenever we want and dump you just as quick. We understand your master may have you tethered to a firm leash and not be in the business of letting you know his affairs. This concerns us little. From here on in, you will be in our pay and whenever we decide to take you from your evening, from Edith, or from your quarters, you will recount to us exactly the gossips we cherish on what you know on this secretariat of intelligence he designs. Could we be any clearer?'

Beale chokes back his blood dribbling from his lip into his mouth and looks piercingly at them both, knowing he has little choice but to concede, though he makes no response. His frustration at the idea Francis could be entering a trap at any point and it be of his own doing brought a huge sense of failure and powerlessness over him, surging through his hands, quaking into fists. It was hopelessly lost, the knees of his interrogator pressed deep into his thighs and he knew the brute would savagely slice him apart if he retaliated or rebuffed.

'Could we be any clearer?' Prompted Foreigner this time. His dagger pressed harder into Beale's open mouth until he moaned imploringly, closed his eyes, choked back his anguish, nodded carefully and mumbled over the blade and blood that he understood.

After an agonizing moment, Foreigner stands up, wiping the blade on Beale's doublet, convinced their interrogation had worked, sniffing loudly and jolting his head to Ugly that Beale could go. He lifts Beale by the arm pits, wobbling as he is left to stand alone.

'We will see you again, Robert Beale.' Ugly says, about to push him towards the door.

'Wait.' Beale says, turning, now thinking just how this will work in practicality. 'If you are to snatch me at any point – how could I either verify or deny the intelligence you have.' Clearly both men had not thought about corroborating what Beale would tell them. 'You would need to know proof positive that what I say are the motions of events laid down by Walsingham. If my life is at risk I must know it to be certain.' Both men looked to him to continue. 'It must be information only he and I can affirm.'

'And how would this be so?' Foreigner asks, revealing himself here to be the leader of the two.

'I encourage his correspondence to be encoded.' Beale offers.

'Can you write Italian? We speak and read such.' Ugly says.

'So can half the merchants of London. No, I will invent one.'

'How does this enable us?' Foreigner still unsure.

'I shall give you the cipher.' Their puzzled faces frustrate him, but there was the faintest, most curious, glint in Beale's eyes as he went on to explain. 'You must have heard of a Caesar wheel? Each letter holds a number value and if listed around two different circles can be matched, enabling us to write in numbers that would appear as unmeaning to the unknowing onlooker. And you would have this cipher.' Their silence made him certain they were listening.

Both men did not look at the other in their consideration. Neither gives any signal they were happy with the proposal for several moments.

Finally Foreigner turns to Ugly, 'Confronteremo le informazioni che otteniamo da Carlos Bailey.' So quick was his patter that Beale thought the man was cursing as someone might if they had scolded their fingers. It nearly made him miss what he said at the end. It was the second time he had heard it and there could be no mistaking it – the accented "Carlos Bailey" not cart loss, but a name.

'Aye.' Says Ugly and there was a profound moment between them.

'La fratellanza.' Foreigner responds.

'Amen.' Ugly closes his eyes.

'You write.' Foreigner instructs Beale gruffly.

'Write what…the cipher?'

'Yes, the code. Do now.'

'I will need two parchments.' Beale says, not believing how easily they had played into his hands.

II

Palace of Whitehall,
Westminster - the same evening

෨෨

Even Ursula's clever tailoring could not hide his trembling. The apprehension from just being stood by the door was enough to make him feel as if he was floating yet anchored firmly to the ground. These intensely odd sensations rose in his belly as he shuffled into her antechamber. He could never have imagined this was what it was like before entering the presence of God's anointed representative on earth. Then he saw her.

Queen Elizabeth, gleaming like an amber sceptre, radiated majesty in a gown of white so brilliant it looked blue, twinkling with its silver threaded decorations and crochet sapphires. There could have been no formal public occasion that day so this was considered a simple dress. Of course, he had no idea of it and could only tell she had clearly been outside, for her luxuriant velvet cloak rested upon a wooden bust nearby. A moderate dress indeed for an evening's walk. As she turned to straighten herself, the delicate chemise and stiffened corset of silver made her glimmer like trickling water in a sunny stream. Her neck and wrist ruffs a cream colour embroidered with gold, but not yet starched so they flopped a little and gave off the appearance she was loosely holding a handkerchief. She reached to pick up a pomander posy to help thwart miasma or any other foulness in the air that might bring about an imbalance of her four humours. It was then he saw the huge ruby ring that, when caught by sharp light, would project red beams onto the walls. Incredibly, he could also see it contained two miniature enamelled portraits of her mother, Anne Boleyn, and herself.

She simply stunned him. Words evaporated so he decides to lose himself in a theatrical bow. Swooshing silently into his stoop, it was then he caught a waft of vinegar, probably mixed with the lead paint that she had begun to use on her face to cover the smallpox scars that had not healed from eight years prior. He ignores this and continues revelling in the moment. She is everything he expects, still plenty youthful in her near forty years, glowing white, slim in waist but appearing so majestically it almost makes her look manly, authoritative, in her beauty.

This is the moment he has been waiting for his entire adult life...and so he steps forward, committing himself and his ideas, no turning back. Almost stammering, he does not know what to do, how to greet her, and finds himself dropping his head to avoid eye contact and sees her glistening slippers and the gloriously decorated dress in more detail. Her hand, that bejewelled finger, rising slowly up as if to say he should lift his head, so he does.

'Are we in mourning? She says with sharp quietness.

'Majesty?'

'You are attired in black. Bedecked, you say. I shall call you my Moor.'

Walsingham is a little muddled, they seemed to have jumped straight into direct, familiar, conversation, he had thought Cecil would somehow be their medium. He looks to Cecil for approval to speak, but he is passive. 'I see. Thank you, your majesty. My wife tailored it.'

'You say. Your second wife, mother of your two daughters?'

Her intelligence is good. He blushes as her seven maids busy themselves preparing her food and easing her comfort from the trials of the day, but knows their ears are wide open. In fact, he may well one day count on them being. 'Yes, your Majesty, you are well informed.'

'I intend to always be. You say.' Elizabeth says as if disinterested.

He looks up to her, surprised at her voice, tight and high, annunciating her "Ls" as if her tongue was momentarily stuck, her tone almost musical. Her "Ss" with a delicate lisp. "You say" she had said – was he supposed to speak then or was it a mere natural inflection. Safer to wait.

Two maids removed the royal earrings then mopped and petted her hands as she spoke, looking right to him. 'Your fleeing of England finds you well returned and amply positioned these years past?'

'I thank God for my safe return and to serve Your Majesty's parliament.'

'You say. Your passage took you through the Low Countries, France, German principalities and bishoprics, as well as Spain and some Italian states?' Before he could confirm, Elizabeth blurted out random phrases in Flemish, High Dutch, German, French, Italian and Spanish.

Walsingham was shocked and stymied into further silence.

'I know little of Germanic languages, so vulgar, as if one was purging the guts. French and Spanish I am akin. If only we spoke the ancient languages of Greece and Roman scholars.' Her Majesty announces as if daydreaming. Walsingham had not expected such small talk other than to impress upon him her knowledge of languages. 'I may not have travelled as you have, Walsingham, but I understand these countries far better. They have all seen war and would not so easily wage it even with a country that is not so well prepared for it as ours. You say.'

He looks to Cecil, before haltingly saying, 'Yes, your Majesty. Though some may feel empowered by the Pope's blessing.'

'That low clerk of God in Rome has issued these during my reign before.' She says, dismissing her ladies in waiting.

'As it may be, alack not whilst a Catholic queen resides in England.' He says.

'Mary Queen of the Scots is no threat.' Elizabeth states.

'Not only a rallying cry for dissenting Catholics in England, but also for foreign princes to marry.' Walsingham responds with a twinge of disbelief, she must have considered this.

'Well, Walsingham, you say. What is proposed we do next?'

'We watch, your Majesty.' He says, before adding with solemnity, 'From the shadows.'

'You have the right clothes.' The Queen stifles a chortle. Then after a moment rueing, she shakes her head, suddenly disliking the idea, 'As if I had snuck into my own passion play? I wait and watch mine own execution slowly proceed before me, powerless, you say?'

'No, your majesty. We are waiting to ensnare, proceeding in the act so we can respond swiftly and decisively.'

'There are persons of suspicions?' The Queen asks snappily.

'Yes, your majesty.'

'Why not respond swiftly and decisively now, you say? Who? You say?'

Walsingham was now beginning to be a little lost with her conversational style – did she want to him answer why they should not act or who his suspicions fell to? He saw Cecil was uneasy at the pause.

'You say?' She adds, checking over what meats had been presented to her for choosing.

'Your majesty,' Walsingham began, freewheeling somewhat, 'it is not known to what ends the true nature of the threat...'

'You say,' Elizabeth interrupted, never flustering in voice or person, just impatient, 'upon your word, you shall create a "secretariat" for the gathering of intelligence to aid our Crown? Then, as now before your sovereign absent of ideas, you say?' It was clear she was chastising him, and she looks to her First minister, unimpressed.

Cecil knows he has to jump in here, 'Walsingham has a theory, Majesty...'

'Your Privy Council.' Walsingham blurts, as if he has just beaten a drum. Cecil looks directly at his Queen, this may not go well without an explanation. Elizabeth now has a peculiar smile on her face.

'The Queen's most trusted advisors? You say.' Elizabeth steps closer to Walsingham. 'Is this from one of your scandal sheets?' It is not clear who she is talking to.

'No, your majesty,' Walsingham starts, not realising that he must justify himself twice over, had Cecil not advised her, '…I have countenanced the evidence…'

She can hear no more, 'With whores? Deaf men, drunkard sea captains and traitorous prisoners?' Walsingham drops his head – Cecil had advised her. 'You cannot expect me to simply accept your assertion. I acknowledge my many enemies, but a traitor from my Privy Council merely on the words of these low-born dung sniffers. How might this hold up in a judicial court – the Star Chamber would unquestionably accept your evidence?' The Queen catches her breath, hurriedly taking off her slippers. 'And who have you evidence against? Essex, Ludlow, Norfolk – the Queen's own cousin, or every one's favourite vestibule of loathing, Dudley or is it the First Minister, here, you suspect?' The slippers now clutched in her fists – he had heard rumours she chucks them at displeasing courtiers.

'There is a compelling case, your Majesty…' He begins in embarrassment.

Elizabeth makes sure Walsingham and Cecil know she addresses them both now, 'You will come to me with more than hearsays. You say. Aye, the Duke of Norfolk, Lord Essex, even that little girl Ludlow, and their agents have been acquitted once before not a year gone. I will not have but one guess, mark me. Aye, you will watch and you shall account all you see and your discoveries will pass through no man's lips other than your own. I will neither imprison, execute or scourge without representation. The only time I shall hear of your name is whence I drag you from your undertaking. In the shadows indeed Walsingham. From within shadows of shadows.' She places the slippers down and instead chooses some meat and fine bread, taking it to the other side of the room to nibble at, with her back turned.

Instinctively Walsingham knows not to speak and waits for her to finish, which she does by discarding half of it on a small table.

Elizabeth walks back to where she had initially stood and stares hard at them, finishing on Walsingham, purposefully, and threateningly, moving closer to him. 'Are you my serpent Walsingham?'

Serpent? He was perplexed though does not speak because Her Majesty's temper glowed like her hair. Serpent...were they not allegorical of women, futility and even man's virility. Or even the Devil? He was not sure where an answer would land him, he feigns innocence, 'Majesty?'

Elizabeth gracefully picks her teeth, brown with some missing, never taking her gaze from him. 'Those great mythical tormentors, creatures of portent and danger. Lurking in the realms of darkened waters, underground, unseen. Will you lay in wait, Walsingham, for weeks, months or years to ensnare your prey? No matter how dangerously close thine enemy walks, have you the patience to strike prudently or precipitously, sir? Will you be our new guardian of the divine, the waters of life, protecting against those heathens who shalt dare to desecrate our holy source in this well of life, the royal body, England. Or are you such a schematic that it is your own interests you serve, sir?' She stops as an actor might on the stages in taverns, awaiting applause. Walsingham knows these are both a warning to heed and a compliment to accept. It was also the first time that he realised Her Majesty or her government had little clue of just how big these threats to her person actually were. She was waiting for him to respond. He thought of his antihero, Becket, how might he have shown his dedication to his liege lord when questioned so abrasively. Walsingham decides to bow and look directly at Queen Elizabeth –

'I am ready to die for my sovereign that in my blood England may obtain liberty and peace.'

'It is your proof undeniable I seek sir, not your sacrifice.' Elizabeth gruffly says.

'With duty and adroitness I will amass the intelligence to ease both her heart and judiciary.' He responds.

Elizabeth wheezes, as if to say we shall see. Walsingham rises and sees a half smile from Cecil, he knows Her Majesty, and this could have worked.

She then speaks. 'It is from Numbers 13 that I quote, "And the lord spake unto Moses, saying, send thou men out, to search the land of Canaan which I give unto the children of Israel." As our Lord commanded Moses, I now command you, pretended master of espials, journey forth to discover what discernments you find against us.' She gestures herself and the entire palace in one smooth hand, 'From shadows in the shadows of shadows.'

III

Seething Lane

ഗ്രരു

Pressing her ear against the wall, the plaster is scratchy against Frances' cheek, and she can smell the horsehair mixed in to insulate and bind it tighter. Listening intently, not to pry or snoop with the curiosity that itches girls, but to see if she was done for. It did not matter how late it was, she would not tire – what were a few more hours in the eternity of purgatory.

Hearing her father return home that night stirred in her stomach a mixture of excitement and distress. Mary was asleep with the Lord's blessing as Frances held her ear keenly to the walls, hearing the muffled dull tones over her pounding heart. Being in the middle of the house, she was in perfect position to listen to guests downstairs or her father up in his study.

Frances' concern had begun when Edith had rushed into the house earlier that morning on this long day, saying she had lost Robbie from the night before. True enough, he had not surfaced all day and then when her father came back in an odd temper all her worse distresses were confirmed. It could mean just one thing: the good luck charm had curdled into a sour spell and she had brought a curse upon her house. Since that March morning at the wishing well, her father's fortunes had spoiled, starting with that meeting with that usurper John Stow, was all she could hear herself grindingly repeat. Now Edith was injured and Robbie Beale missing, then Papa losing grace at his governmental posting, by the sounds of what she had eavesdropped. Dark happenstance was all around her and becoming too much to bear. The thought of what she had done made her throat throb with the pain of trying not to cry.

Frances took a deep breath away from listening at the wall for she knew if she did not compose herself she might well go into an uncontrollable stupor, and she had never done that before. Instead of succumbing to upset she managed restraint, collected herself, and carried on listening to learn of clues that her accidental evil enterprise may have been discovered.

Her father was furious. That much she could make out. With himself it seemed. Edith had been hurt and he had somehow got her into that situation. Despite his trying and oftentimes asking Edith she could not recount or recognise the faces, nor did she know where Beale had been taken. Amidst the howls of upset, she heard Edith tell her brother by law that there was a message, a meeting place – tomorrow, midday, at Temple Bar. Frances had to agree with her mother when she heard her say it was probably not a good idea to go – what would happen if they took him, her father, as well?

Yet there was no mention of an ill-fated curse or suspicion of maleficent magic. She was almost delighted to hear her father miserably say that the Walsingham fortunes were as temperate as the English weather. Exoneration when one is guilty seems all the more sweeter, she grins.

As Edith sobbed, she could hear her father's calm voice go on to explain to her mother why his meeting with the Queen had not gone so well. *Papa had met the*

Queen? Frances almost collapsed to the floor and had to cover her mouth from screeching, stuffing in her curly brown hair as she did so. Before she chewed any of it in excitement, she listened for more detail but they had begun to move and she could only catch that it had not gone well. Had he touched her, she wondered – for it was said she could heal people just by touching them. Was her hair as golden as they say of it? What must her voice be like or does someone speak for her? Frances was suddenly and dreadfully envious of her father, then quickly remonstrated herself for there was already too much sin in this house, of her doing, to include envy too.

As her father tramped up the stairs, she heard him bemoan his discussion of ideas with the Queen and it was not good enough that he has to prove himself. This Frances did not understand but could tell it was serious with the sympathy her mother was offering. Then she did catch something that shocked her: the country remained in peril – an army was likely mustering in the north and there were foreign ships in English waters. Frances severally swallows, listening nervously and intently to her father wonder how could the Queen ignore the size of forces already in the country. His pleas were so loud that she felt the boards beneath her tremble. Even without her parents' urgent voices, Frances knew this was deathly serious and for the first time in her life she felt her forehead was damp with sweat. Although she was quick to count her blessings there was still no mention of her own maleficent errors.

Were they about to employ a witchfinder? Imagine the scandal, she trembled. The Old Crone who gave her the words and herbs had not foreseen this. What had she done to her sister, to herself, to the family, to these lives that could be affected by this? As Francis Walsingham's daughter, she understood enough about the ways of the world that you do not play with the holy order of things. God has a will and it cannot be shaken from dalliances into charms or witchery, no matter if it was intentioned as white magic or not. It was not the thought of her being either pressed to death or burnt at the stake that now terrified her, but that she had let him down. Father! Frances quivered.

She heard them walk up the narrow wooden stairs towards his study and she imagined his face, those deep sorrowful eyes looking to her in disappointment. It was too much to take and all she could do was choke back the tears that came fat and squalling through her eyes as her chest and neck heaved to repress the noise. Sliding with her silent sorrow onto the floor, she grabbed and tugged at whatever furniture was closest to her. Mary still did not stir and, in all thankfulness, her mother or father had not heard and carried on up to his study.

After the tears ran dry and her throat rasped, she sat upright in the middle of the floor. She had no idea how long she had been crying. One of her stockings was around her ankle, such was her writhing and wrestling of her legs in the tumult. Relieved she had not torn the stocking to add to the list of wrongs she tugs it back up her leg, the only right thing left to do was to tell Papa the truth. May he, and God, forgive her.

Quietly leaving her room, she climbs the stairs and took, what she was certain to be, her last breaths of freedom.

Suddenly there was a bang from downstairs interrupting her purpose, as if a large slab of wood had slapped to the floor. Then shouting, someone was calling, 'Francis...Francis?' Her mother and father came bounding out of the study.

'Frances get to bed.' Ursula shouted at her as she raced down the steps past her and the girl stood nervously watching their troubled faces.

Robbie was back, her father exclaims elatedly.

Frances slumped onto one of the steps, relief surging over her from different directions – Robbie was safe, it was not all doom and disaster after all. She heard him gallop up the stairs and her parents double back into the study as he flew up past her. Joyous day, she clapped quickly. Of course this meant, most significantly, she did not have to confess, just yet. With a mixture of relief and amazement, she smiled and promised herself, for certain this time, she would listen extra hard at the next sermon and pray most sincerely in the thanksgiving. Frances strolls back to her room and closes the door quietly before reaffirming her promise. Then, because she could, decided to carry on listening.

Robbie took three steps at a time as he flew up the stairs of Seething Lane. Doing so with such keen haste he does not see Frances stood to one side or the beautiful smile she gave him that he would have been sure was not entirely made of affectionate relief at his safety. As he barges into the study, Ursula wraps her arms around him as Walsingham tries to shake his hand through the laughter and exclamations of alleviation. His smile and upright gait told them he was fine, and his urgent eyes looked to his master intimating they need to talk.

Ursula understands she must leave, and does so dutifully, but not before one more motherly tug on Robbie's arm. The larger Walsingham family had been separated before and she could not let that happen again. It was one belief she passionately shared with her husband.

'Your ledger.' Robbie says, as the study door closes.

Walsingham reached for the Book of Secret Intelligences and Robbie tells him to find the account of Essigia, where he then explains to him that Cart loss...Carlos...was actually Charles Bailey. Neither of them had heard the name before, other than in these two instances. Walsingham added a notation to the entry. Robbie also excitedly informs him of his foil to his captors.

'They are of keen apprehension that I am in their service or employ. Never could I be, you understand, but I had to convince them. So, from now on, we write in code to which they believe they are the only ones to possess its cipher.' Robbie says excitedly.

'And you are to create this code?'

Beale could not help but laugh at its ridiculousness when he said, 'Yes.'

'Our purposeful misinformation could hasten the identity of their masters. Well done Robbie, this is an incredible development. I am only too sorry you were injured to get us there. I assume there were no clues to their identity?'

'I recognised the accent as possibly Italian,' he faltered, 'but could not pick out his words, until the name and then "fratell...fratellonse?" I'm sorry, I lack to recall.' Beale says helplessly.

Italian, Walsingham knew, had already infiltrated this connivance in some way. Alas there were hundreds, nay thousands, of Italian merchants living, working and travelling into London every month. "Fratell" was possibly brother, though definitely not the term used between priests, but literal brothers, or men of brethren. He wrote it down but did not relay these ideas to Beale. 'You are certain from your encounter there are indeed plots to vanquish Her Majesty?' He asks.

'They are certain you form the only formal opposition to their endeavours, such that you are considered a threat to whatever their cause may be.' Beale answers.

'I see.'

Beale was not sure why this had not raised Walsingham's mood, saying, 'This news serves to bolster our cause, does it not?'

His hope does not seem to lift Walsingham's spirits. 'My reception at the Privy Council...the Queen, it did not yield the support I had expected.'

'You met the Queen?' Beale chokes. 'Did you touch her?' Realising his childishness, he has an apologetic tone, 'Well, it shows me the Council must take your sincerity as first rate to even put you before Her Majesty.'

'That is maybe, but Her Majesty, the government, cannot be seen to support rumours where hard facts are necessity. Alack, we indeed miss.' Walsingham says impishly.

'It is neither conviction in support nor against our theories.' Beale says as both men now sit. 'But a belief in them. You are not chained to some lowly dungeon wall or racked on suspicion of evil heresy.' Beale laughs, upbeat at himself and Walsingham grins.

'This will take time,' Walsingham concedes, leafing through the early pages of his book and adding some more names at its rear, 'and we are amassing a register of our own agents to aid our cause.' He then looks at

Robbie. 'Of which you are my most valued and trusted.' Then, with a playful smile, he says, 'il doppio agente.'

Beale watches contentedly as Walsingham scribes into his book and knew enough Italian to think his quip as "double agent" was rather pertinent, given his thoughts on whether Williams had betrayed them. He could not let this go unresolved.

'What will you do with Walter?' Beale asks with the sincerest tone he can muster.

Walsingham puts his quill down. 'He is a drunkard with debts. He betrayed you. He will do my bidding as a result.'

This gags Robbie a little – bidding, what does that mean?

Walsingham sees, but will not relent. 'Then it will be done and you will forgive him.'

'Forget what could have happened to me, what about Edith, your own kin.' Robbie is livid at him, for the first time that he can remember.

Walsingham understands the anguish and is quick to both ignore the ill manners and then pacify him. 'You are my kin. There is a right and a wrong way to deal with his chastisement.' Looking at him and then continuing seriously, 'We need his capabilities – you saw how he coaxed the prisoners. His foolish mistake cost you pain but has also presented us with an opportunity.'

'Can he be trusted from now on?' Beale demands.

'Stimpson follows him as we speak and will do so until he is kept from harming himself – or others. Now be reunited with Edith and ready yourself for our meeting at Temple Bar midday on the morrow.'

Walsingham watches Robbie leave somehow dispirited with events. Empathising, he reflects on how two weeks ago there was peace in all his diligences, now he had brought uncertainty, calamity and danger: the Walsingham name and reputation as a legal and parliamentarian aficionado had become questionable; Edith, his own sister by law had been molested; Beale, whom he had sworn to keep safe, was filched from his very hands and may yet be further compromised; could his old acquaintance Williams be compromised as well, let alone all the other agents and informers he had now sprawling under his net? Trust was the greatest surety between fellow men and there was now a gape upon him like an unholy scar. The more his investigation and suspicion seeped from this festering wound, the less he could rely and depend on others. As his old Nanna had once said to him as a boy, be careful what you wish for. This, all he could reason, was brought upon by himself. Had he known that his beloved daughter Frances was keenly listening in to some of his business, the betrayals might have felt complete.

Now was not the time for sensitivity, so notwithstanding these blows, he rectified himself with the assurance his cause was the just one. He knew with equal rationality, that there could only be one way in which he would know for absolute certain. Comforting himself asleep, therefore, he promises to seek counsel for his spiritual convictions by visiting his pastor from St. Olave's church before the meeting at Temple Bar.

IV

৪০৫৪

Mist swirls whimsically about him as he leaves Seething Lane that following morning. All that happened these days past frolic in his mind: ships spotted off the coast; Beale; Walter; his near-disastrous first meeting with Her Majesty; the gathered army in the North. Saints miracle, then, he was not succumbed by these stirrings and was soothed by hearing the rumpus southwards as he headed down the lane.

Fog drooped from rooves and around the alleyways of the narrower lane that Walsingham glided into like a sleek-sailed ketch on a grey lake. The shouting and hullaballoo from there was not unusual. He listened intently for the familiar voice as he eased along. Though many fine houses bedecked either side of this tighter lane, there were also tired timber basements and lofts with hops, barley oats and dried bog myrtle piled high. All ready for brewing in the small vats that had wafted their steamy yeast up and down this straw laden street for centuries. On colder days it made the fog look far gloopier. Beer Lane was Pastor Emmanuel's favourite spot.

An interesting gathering place: drunkards pay fipenny for a keg of spoiled ale, no use to London's taverns; other gluggers all the more foolish to then pay them for their share; and Pastor Emmanuel who was brave enough to converse and argue with these absurdists. As the alewives and brewers mulched and boiled their liquids into weak beer, this odd little congregation would sit, sup their rancid prize, amuse and abuse each other on the ills of the day.

Pastor Emmanuel not only liked the challenge, he also felt their hearts were heavy with sin so needed slackening – what harm could it do than undertake the Lord's work and enjoy free ale? Being a tall man, he often avoided abuse, and although in his fifties with a thick head of grey hair brushed back and silver bristles hiding most of his face, he had always kept his back and legs straight. He was nicknamed the Giant Priest, even though he was a strict protestant Rector, but ironically called himself Pastor to remove the loftiness of his title. A clever man, it was his eyes that caught everyone's attention. Soft and milky blue gave everyone cause to instantly trust him and added further legend that he descended from giants of the icy northern seas where everyone was tall, light haired and blue eyed. Had anyone been able to research his ancestry they would have discovered his Nordic descent, perhaps being the only reason why he was able to wear just a basic smock in the cold Winter months without complaint.

The Giant Priest's hand combs out the spillage of ale in his white bristles and he regards his small flock sat on barrels and carts in the cramped lane, saying, 'As our Lord says, in Ephesians 5:18 "And be not drunk with wine, but be filled with the Spirit." Nay spirit of a bottle but the love of our Lord.'

The four other men chant Amen. They offer him another cup, but Emmanuel declines and as they proffer their leather tankards and glug back the beer, he sees Walsingham stood still, a few yards away, as if he had just then floated there. Emmanuel stands, dressed just in plain chasuble with no dalmatic, the two men look all but mirror images of each other in their black attire. Walsingham highly values the man's spiritual wisdom and lack of popery in his worship. Likewise Emmanuel trusts this focused and dutiful servant to God and country. Not that they assumed friendship as each venerated the other's office too much, but the respect ran deep.

Walsingham speaks first. 'My suspicions were right to find you here.'

The Giant Priest supposes correctly that he wants to privately talk so he turns to his limp flock, 'As Peter declares "Be sober, be vigilant; because your adversary the devil, as a roaring lion, walketh about, seeking whom he may devour." Fight not each other. But together. God bless the Queen.' Another round of quieter Amens bids him away and he leaves them to contemplate his words for that morning. He ushers Walsingham back up the lane to his small church.

At the top of Seething Lane as they are about to turn left on Hart Street and enter the cramped St. Olave's church, something pecked at Walsingham's mind. From his very own street it felt as if he was being watched. He quickly turned but could not see anything of alarm. Would it be this way from now on he thought – will I watch and be watched?

Having sat themselves comfortably in Emmanuel's plain, pokey, vestry, Walsingham wondered at its size, knowing for sure that the two men could stand, hold out their hands and be able to touch each wall.

'What ails you this tide?' Emmanuel asks.

'There are limits to which I can converse, and even greater limits as pertains the detail I can give.'

Walsingham says and the Pastor nods, as if he has heard his preamble before.

'God is your only judge. Not I.' Emmanuel acknowledges and studies Walsingham closely, there is an air of insecurity but does not guess where or why. 'What ails you this day, my son?'

They could only be about ten years apart, but the pastor's fatherly manner is convincing, and despite not being able to give particulars, Walsingham relaxes knowing they will both be candid. Compiling his thoughts, his conviction is not lost in the cause he pursues, nor his inner resolve from the nightmares he sees and the sufferings he and his family have endured. All are reignited as he wrestles with an infirmity of his mind: his tough spirit seemingly dwindling. From his days mingling with lawyers at Gray's Inn, he is supposed to seek succour from their motto *without fear or favour rules men's causes aright.* Perhaps these do give him solace, but not answers of spiritual certainty – he had to believe he was doing the work of God. Could he survive the tests his Creator was starting to throw at him?

'I am certain our cause aright.' Walsingham says without realising he was speaking aloud just yet.

'You will summon the strength to continue.' The Pastor says calmly. 'With God's help.'

Aye, Walsingham smiles and without wanting to sound doubtful he looked as if to say "when?"

Emmanuel peers comfortingly right into his eyes, while saying, 'Ephesians 6:10-18 we are taught how strong and mighty His power is through the Armour of God. Put this on, Francis Walsingham, so that you can take your stand against the Devil's schemes. For there is no struggle against flesh and blood, but against our rulers, against the authorities, against the powers of dark, spiritual forces of evil in the heavenly realms. Therefore, our Lord's servant, Francis Walsingham, He is telling you to put on that full armour of God, so when the day of evil comes, you will stand your ground. If by yourself or with a legion of devoted, you will stand firm then, with the belt of truth buckled around your waist, the breastplate of righteousness intact, the shield of faith with which you shall extinguish all the flaming arrows of the evil one. Then, take the helmet of salvation and the sword of the Spirit, which is the word and work of God. Pray, yes, thou be alert. Always.'

Walsingham clasps his hands together and says, 'Amen.' Pastor Emmanuel gently does the same but places them over Walsingham's hands and his eyes look quizzically at him. 'Pastor?' Walsingham asks, suddenly troubled.

'Alert, Francis.'

'Yes, always.'

He had not understood him just yet. 'I am honoured and righted that you attend my church.' Emmanuel starts, still not letting go of Walsingham's hands, 'You must send a member of your household to the church at the other end of your street.'

'All Hallows? – Why?' Walsingham was puzzled and could not at all guess why he would encourage this, with its more papist leanings.

'If idle speculations are to be believed...they smuggle more than Popish books.'

* *

Temple Bar

As they cross the bridge over the narrow, murky Fleet river onto Fleet Street, passing St. Bride's church, Walsingham explains to Beale that it has been wrongly assumed Temple Bar was named because of an old Roman temple. With certainty, he goes on to state, it was for the Knights Templar church – and Temple Bar was where London city and the city of Westminster's boundaries meet. Beale did not have the heart to tell his master that all this he knew. Taking his silence for interest, Walsingham continues that The Knights Templar were a medieval Catholic security force, being some of the most skilled warriors in an age when that mattered. What impressed him most, and what he tried to impress upon Beale now, was how critical they were in furthering the wealth of Christendom. Another part of the great corruption of the Catholic church, Walsingham spurns, disgusted and appalled at how they monetarised the word of God. Impressive, perhaps, though unforgivable. Beale did not know much about the Knights Templar and now nodded with interest.

Walsingham stops and steers them into a tiny courtyard where they stand and observe.

A stern timber sheltered frame stood astride the Fleet Street and Temple Bar junction fifty yards from them.

Beale nods Walsingham in its direction, 'One could see how it might supposedly be used as a checkpoint between the two cities, but does it not feel as if it was more an opportunity for corruption and danger than for customs and security? Think upon what they see come and go each day.' Beale suggests, seeing his master think this a perceptive observation, intrigued. Beale, however, was growing increasingly uncomfortable. Something did not sit right with him and unease surges through him.

'We are out in the open,' Beale jitters, whispering now, 'I feel cornered, as if a net is about to be cast over, in this small pond. Nowhere to escape – it was after all my captors' suggestion for such a time and place.'

Walsingham twitches his eyes about the place.

Distant midday bells sound. After their hum dissolves, they wait silently. For who – or what – they were supposed to meet does not present. There were not many people about, which riles Beale's agitation even more, increasingly feeling as if they are being watched, though none that they could see. It was getting quieter, too, as if the streets had been slowly clearing up to the point the bells rang. A well's bucket swayed squeakily, and a dirt flecked horse thudded slowly past, its hooves sucking and thumping the mud with each tread along the broad slimy street. Door flinging open nearby startles them both to curse the Pope in Rome as, slightly relieved, they then see a mother angrily chase her two children back into their shack, calling after them that they were little pig runts.

Walsingham glances around, the entire area was grey, the clouds above them were bloated and black, the buildings were sad as if built from materials others did not want. Dirty, ancient, and uneven stone were meagre excuses for house walls, propped up with macerated timber beams. There was a thick smell of clay in the air, heavy and old. Unease squeezed their chests.

'Why was Edith given a message to meet here?' Beale asks, continuing his hushed tones.

'Maybe we were not to meet.' Walsingham says.

'Then...what for?'

'To see or witness *someone* or *something* at this time in this place.'

'The bells have blasted, midday has gone, should I dare catch sight of those ill-bred hag seed turds...' Beale grinds through clenched teeth, believing he was the victim of some devilish jape: first he is robbed from Edith in the street; bludgeoned; then recruited as an agent in the pay of Catholics –what Catholics he did not know; and now he has led his master here. In anger borne from embarrassment, he mutters they would do better to make more sense of it all by herding cats.

'If this were a trap,' Walsingham leant into him, 'then we would be skewered by now.'

At that moment, in the quiet of the tiny courtyard where they stood, several sounds were heard at once as large doors from different directions opened. Beale and Walsingham darted looks around, it was the churches: Temple Church; St. Dunstan's in the West; and Rolls chapel. Their ornate oaken doors swung open and the area suddenly smelt of incense as people leaked onto the streets and alleyways, heading towards this courtyard and up into their houses or down to the river to holler for wherries.

'It is the Catholic mass.' Walsingham realises. 'Celebrating the Annunciation.' He rubs his chin with a clenched fist. 'They are trying to warn us.' He muses, looking at what must have been near three hundred Catholics fill the lanes around them.

'What?' Beale snappily asks.

'It is the Annunciation – the last Catholic feast day in March, marking Gabriel telling Mary she was to have a virgin born son.' Walsingham was watching the crowds, knowing he will find people of interest.

'I know what the Annunciation is – you say they are trying to warn us – about what?' Beale feels uncomfortable surrounded by so many Catholics.

'Look' – Walsingham directs Beale's attention to some recognisable faces – members of the Privy Council, including Essex, Howard and the Clerk of the Privy Chamber talking to Ludlow, spread amongst the throng. He even sees Ridolfi and the Fat Parliamentarian that wheezed so heavily next to him outside the Privy Council chambers – no wonder he had complained so mightily of the Protestant elements of government that morn. Though none are walking together, nor conspiring their menacing intents, Walsingham cannot help but ponder that they are here. Some of London's most powerful, all gathered as one Catholic entity. Praise be that he sees neither Dudley or Cecil in this great uncovering of Catholic sympathisers, lest the betrayals of faith of his own government be complete. Sensing Beale's attention on him, he says, 'We are being warned off, Robbie.' More people stream onto the streets from the smaller churches beyond the main thoroughfares. 'Destiny this day was of no meeting or appointment, just a mere show of Catholic might.'

Neither men moves for many moments, a stony island in a sea of pomp and pageantry. Nobody notices them, nor cares to, much to their relief. The two men cannot help but be impressed with the banners held by the children, beautifully stitched scenes of Gabriel appearing before Mary, some have Latin verses in gilt and there are portraits of Saints on bunting. They notice one or two have the same tiny emblems woven into them – a cross inside a rose.

From a different direction, Beale spots his foreign captor nonchalantly escorting two finely dressed ladies. His peacock feather giving him away. Then perhaps ten yards behind he sees Walter walking by himself. Beale points all this out to Walsingham who gently tugs Beale's arm, intimating him to hold back.

'We are indeed being warned.' Walsingham says. 'And with such a show of strength. These demonstrations mean only one thing – they are feeling threatened.'

'By us?' Beale asks, disbelievingly.

'Must be so.'

They wait for the crowds to disperse, many walking down Middle Temple Lane towards the Thames to journey back across to Southwark or upstream to London Bridge and beyond.

'I think we should pay a visit to the Temple barrier, get an idea of all the commerce and pedalling to pass by this place of Catholic intrigue.' Walsingham nods in the direction of the stern timber frame astride the junction and can see inside the small shelter that there is someone manning the station.

This customs house and security checkpoint was no more than a reinforced hut with room enough for two men to sit around a small table. Under a leather apron and hat sleeps a dishevelled bearded man, snoring like a pair of pigs. On the table is a leather-bound ledger that reads *Duties and Excise Recorder, Temple Barre*.

Walsingham and Beale enter, disgusted at the lacking security. Picking up the book, Beale slams it onto the sleeping leather apron and with a cat-screeching yelp the dishevelled beard is awoken.

'What for Lucifer's lust was that?' He splutters. 'What horse drench hooflicker...?' He demands, standing, wobbling from his sudden besnatching of sleep.

'How dare you speak so, in front of a government minister. Where is Her Majesty's Customs Overseer?' Beale orders, dropping his shoulders and extending his chest, coiling up in readiness for opposition.

'Who asks?' A distraught man in his forties then straddles in behind the three of them, his breeches being tightened at his waist.

'This is Francis Walsingham, MP for Lyme Regis, advisor to the Privy Council.' Beale says with the majesty it deserves.

'My apologies, just then finished relieving myself at the river's privy stool bench. A particularly awkward beshatment...' He sees this is not what the gentlemen desire to know so he finishes fumbling with his breeches and politely asks, 'What business do men of government have at our humble excise post?'

'What are your names and station?' Beale harries.

'Adjutant Isiah Jennings is I and this be our Parish Constable, Olias Fallburn. Tidings.' Despite nerves, both men now sit and look up to Beale and Walsingham. Isiah continues, 'May I petition my lords to what ascertainments my lords are here, my lords?' Stresses splutter his tone as he looks uneasily to his leather-aproned friend.

'You have ledgers accountable Adjutant Jennings?' Beale asks.

'Aye, my lords – all are present and true, my lords.'

'Then we shall peruse and check.' Beale says, handing the ledger to Walsingham who begins looking at entries from two weeks ago.

Fallburn, so far quiet in these proceedings, begins to see an opportunity. 'And what do I report to my Justice of the Peace? He is sure to be concerned of my ascertainments.' His tone now ever so slightly leering.

Walsingham knows what this meant: he was after a bribe. He does not even look up from the ledger when he says, 'If his concerns cause you anxiety then I will impress upon the Lord Lieutenant Wadworth who will quell your Justice of the Peace.' Fallburn's ruse is silenced with Walsingham's dramatic referral to the hierarchy of posts.

Jennings decides to sit in silence as Walsingham points out intriguing ledger entries of names, stock, monies and frequencies to Beale, without uttering a word. The two men know these watchmen are no less toll collectors who have probably done nothing more than skim and alter exchanged goods and monies, not at all aware it is not their crimes that are being investigated. Walsingham is happy to keep them in the dark on this, and his stern face makes it appear as if the most scandalous of offences has taken place and their jitters keep them poised.

Beale has no compunction when he asks, 'Why are there no names for the Italian merchants?'

Jennings shrugs, saying honestly, 'Cannot understand their names, nor their tongue.'

'Yet you list the Flemish trader they exchange with as R.C.Br. Yes?' Beale shows them several common entries over the last two weeks. 'Is it always the same men?'

Jennings and Fallburn do not know what answer is right or wrong, so feel pressured into giving the truth. Yes, they both say at the same time, without conspiring.

Walsingham closes the ledger, placing it on the table and leans on it with two closed fists, bearing both men down. 'You are to keep this pretence going, take whatever bribe you have accepted and speak to no man other than Beale or myself, lest I summon your Lord Lieutenant Wadworth to the Privy Council.' Both men take a gulp of relief before they solemnly nod their acknowledgement.

Outside, as Walsingham and Beale stride eastwards along Fleet Street passing its conduit, gushing a misty leak, Walsingham says to Beale, 'RC – the inscription and motifs from some of the bunting earlier, and the "Br." Do you recall your foreign interrogator, I am certain he said "fratellanza." yes?'

'Indeed.' Confirms Beale, sensing Walsingham was rolling to a great conclusion.

'Charles Bailey, Ridolfi and Italian merchants, so called, could well be Rosicrucians – Rose of the Cross, that ancient and secret brotherhood. Fratellanza means brotherhood. Their threat to us this day has unwittingly led us closer to uncovering their schemes.' Taking a breath, before saying with awe, 'A secret brotherhood is reborn.'

V

꙰

It does not take the two men long to walk back up Fleet Street, through the bricked Ludgate into St. Paul's churchyard. However, neither Walsingham or Beale could answer the other's questions on what this worrying development meant and, most astoundingly, just what the Brotherhood's role was in all this, a faction so veiled in secrecy not even the tribunal of the Spanish inquisition acknowledged it. Walsingham would have to be satisfied to take whatever lead he could from this tiny barb on a huge stem.

Walking amongst the usual hawking and chaffering of pamphleteers and petitioners, they listen to what recent days scandal sheets are reporting, from home or abroad.

'Spanish ban Jews from being physicians.' One scrawny hucksterer squeals, waving their single page with the very same title.

'Earl of Moray assassination begins civil strife in land of Scots.' Another shouts, flapping their scandal sheet.

Amongst the usual slanderous exposé of affairs or corruptions of officials now vociferously pumping from the very heart of London, there was small mention of a murder at Tower Wharf. Nothing, it seemed, caused any bluster about the problems Mary Queen of Scots arrival in England two years ago could cause or how the rebellion of the earls in the North this past year might give rise to worse problems.

Walsingham, despite all he knew was finding out with growing alarm day by day that it mattered not to the populace. In their minds the threat had disappeared. It stunned him. In his discoveries of dreadful conspiracies unravelling under the Pamphleteers very noses, not one chose to report it, let alone suggest dilemmas of any kind could be afoot. Did he have it *so* wrong? Or was he really *that* competent in discovering the so well camouflaged?

Beale must have been thinking similarly for he ruefully quotes Walsingham from their sojourn into Southwark many weeks gone, as he looks about the Pamphleteers and Petitioners, mystifyingly saying, 'Oblivious in oblivion.' As they walk the long arc round the churchyard, he half jokes, 'They only believe and repeat whatever invention is printed on paper.'

Walsingham, smirking his way to another idea, says perkily, 'Do we have any printer friends Robbie?'

'I'm certain we could encourage loyalties to our cause.'

'Then let us direct London's conversation.' Walsingham says. Both men beaming with self-congratulation as they cut into Watling Street, before continuing their long march eastwards across the city: it had been a day of little action, but many ideas.

An hour later, their delight at their most recent initiative had yet to dissipate even with such a lengthy walk. Turning into Seething Lane the first sight they behold is Frances, crying on the steps, consoled by Edith, herself dry with the red riverbeds of tears giving away her recent upset. Now their glee vanishes and both men rush to them, assessing in their embraces if they are physically hurt, which they are not.

Frances tries to explain though her blub and tears overwhelm any sense she makes.

Edith looks to them both, 'Stimpson is dead.' The shock hits Walsingham like a horse's hoof to the chest. Beale grabs his mentor's shoulder condolingly then crouches into Edith to comfort her.

'I am so sorry Papa.' Frances manages. Her father cannot possibly know she means both sorrow and sincere heart-felt apology.

'What do we know?' Is all he can mutter. Ursula must have heard them arrive, and comes to the door, ushering him in as the two girls and Beale stay sat outside on the street, holding each other in disbelief.

His body was discovered this morning, his wife says through a heaving chest. He needs answers to a hundred questions, seeing Ursula is trying her best, he waits for her account. At the eastern end of Tower Wharf, his body was discovered in the early hours of this morning by Oystermen, tangled amidst the ropes underneath a small wooden pier.

'He was tied, bound and thrown to the Thames' mercy?' Walsingham gripes, shaking his head – it was an assassination. Why? Why had he been to the eastern boundary of the city, had he been beyond even? Ursula needs to be hugged and, despite wrestling with these thoughts, he is able to put his arm meaningfully around her shoulders.

'Francis...who would do such a thing?' She implores lamentably. He had not the courage to tell her it had been him to send their loyal manservant to do his bidding, without knowing what dangers he might find.

Little did Walsingham also realise that Stimpson had tracked Williams and the whore to the Good ship

Venus, let alone what he saw transpire and why he ended up drowned nearby.

Her sobbing shook them both and he draws her in tighter. As he did so, Walsingham sensed his world, his empire of trust, was getting smaller, tighter, contracting the blood circle.

He must write to Cecil.

* *

Over the following days Seething Lane changed. Both in the physical and spiritual. Grief had taken over the household. Stimpson's body, after two days laying in peace in their basement, was taken outside the city walls near Smithfield and buried in a churchyard there, for want of space at St. Olave's. It was then that Walsingham had a finger ring cast, as was custom when a close family member died. Even though he was not a direct relative, it was a mark of respect they all felt Stimpson deserved. Usually the ring forged would be a coffin, cross or even the deceased's conjoined initials. Walsingham decided to get a skull and wore it around his tiniest finger, more poignant reminders of what this life of dedication to the Protestant faith had so far cost him, he sighed.

Ursula and Francis had seen changes in their daughters, as they suddenly – and most urgently – accepted the almightiness of God's plan. The parents were delightfully surprised when Frances and Mary ventured to Pastor Emmanuel's church to help with their grief and seek much solace in the Lord's word. They had never witnessed such keen attention to the teachings of the Bible – and at such a young age. Frances had seemed extra vigilant in helping her younger sister on the path to righteousness. Her penitence, she insisted it be known from here on in. Walsingham noticed, too, how others dealt with grief in different ways. Edith was seeking increasing consolation from Robbie and the head of the household was pleased to see this develop. Ursula had to turn a blind eye one late night as Robbie snuck away from Edith's quarters in the back rooms. She dare not mention it to Francis, who could not be distracted from his own late nights and early mornings in his study. In deep, dark, thought. Ursula did, however, seek to remind her sprightly and excitable little sister that she need exercise care and caution lest her and Robbie stumble into parenthood.

Walsingham may have naively or innocently missed the realities of what was going on around his household for the plain fact he was making other, greater, changes.

To begin with, there was a great addition of furniture. As he put it to Ursula, a justifiable necessity in his great cause. Ursula paid no mind to it when one day he decided to visit Cheapside and kill two birds with a single stone by first seeing his old acquaintance, now agent, Fyson the Barber Surgeon. He was keen to learn what developments he and his alchemist friends had made. Even though Barber Surgeons had their own guild and the alchemists did not, operating somewhat underground due to their clandestine activities such as trying to turn base metals into gold, both groups were happy to share their advances in discoveries. Fyson took delight in showing Walsingham how the tight-knit brethren had evolved the cleaning properties of repeatedly distilling vinegar, but it was the alchemy of something called Aqua Regia – *Regal Water* – that was marvelling the Alchemists and Barber Surgeons of London. Its gloopy yellow-orange potency was such that most metals would dissolve in it. They could make metal disappear, Fyson had exclaimed wildly. Walsingham was not entirely sure of its practical application though nonetheless accepted it was certainly a weapon in the battle for furthering knowledge. Fyson also showed him his workings of wax smelting. Walsingham knew undoubtedly the significance of this.

'Once I know how to melt and reconstitute the wax seals...' Fyson had said, nearly winking at Walsingham, cueing him –

'Then letter packets can be opened and resealed without suspicion.' Walsingham said excitedly, as if a child had just found a gold coin.

When Walsingham asked about inking, and the magics therein, Fyson took great pride in showing him his own latest investigation. Experimenting with different oxides, he explains, grabbing a small piece of vellum that had numerous sketches and random scribblings all over it, he could make ink...appear from nothing. Fyson asked Walsingham to rub the black powder onto a small empty space and to keep smudging it in.

'Do you see?' Fyson asks, with more excitement.

'I've but dirtied the animal skin and the fingers, nothing more.' Said Walsingham, deflated.

'Look.' Fyson then beams. Slowly there appeared white text. 'Another form of ink not visible to the human eye, unless you have the powder, it saves the orange juice and candleflame, where fire is sure to flummox.'

Walsingham left with a small package of the mysterious black powder, pleased that Fyson was continuing to develop ideas to aid his cause and he had yet another way to send and read secret notes. Fyson in turn remained delighted to receive the patronage of a government minister, now clearly on the rise, having already provided him with more business than he had ever known.

Then, it was onto his other bird. Round the corner from Fyson the Barber Surgeon of Ironmonger Lane stood Poultry Compter, the debtors and vagrants gaol. Frinscombe, the Portsmouth gaoler had scribed a letter of introduction for Walsingham to Theophilus Traske. He could not recommend Traske highly enough to accommodate Walsingham in the "sureties he so desired for furniture and sundry fittings to aid your cause." With this letter of introduction and some sketched plans he entered the Compter and was met warmly by a bright-eyed carpenter, covered in dust and sweat. His blond curly locks made him an attractive man but when Walsingham asked after his wife, he replied he was too busy to do battle with women. Studying Walsingham's plans he asked after the size and proximity of his basement where this new furniture would dwell. As Walsingham gave specific dimensions, he seemed happy it could be completed to his liking.

'As well as these fittings,' Walsingham added, 'are you able to make smaller items, cabinets, chests or other such stores that have capability of concealed apartments within?'

'My talents are there to be tested.' Traske said, his beaming blue eyes striking in the bleak stony dark of the dungeon house. 'Would you like to see my craftmanship?' He then led Walsingham into the depths of the building, the moans growing louder as the misery, slime and sickness oozed from each and every wall. At the end of a tight, steep, stairwell, there was clanging and fizzing coming from behind a thick oak door, which Traske took them into. Walsingham felt the furnace's warmth from the middle of the underground smithy as a blacksmith smacked heated metal until it bent into the shape he needed, while another oiled whips on a bench of sharpened tools. Two prisoners were dangling from manacles attached to the wall, barely conscious.

'Is this how you see your design?' Traske asked, pointing to what looked to be the bare bones of a big bed with cylinders and ropes at either end.

'Assuredly so.' Walsingham said. Thanking Traske, he made for a quick exit, the fear of illness from the thick miasma that must be spreading around the forsaken gaol was too much to ignore.

Walsingham's next – and most significant – change was to call a conference. Since the sad loss of Stimpson, he had felt it prudent to unify his agents, calibrate their mission to his, like a simple rope pulley – too fast, too tight or pulling in the wrong direction could mean their strength – their united strengths – would be lost. This was risky, he could see that – as his small growing web of agents, espials, informers and messengers might have never previously crossed paths. Doing so now could buckle their purpose. By inviting them to his private home and headquarters, he was also potentially making himself vulnerable. Walsingham had to take precautions. Privately to Beale, he called it a gathering of his principal and most trusted secretaries. Then he had said something Beale found most telling. 'This is our grab the whole tree or not pick a single cherry moment.'

* *

Within a day of being summoned, the conference make it to Seething Lane on time. Ursula and Edith show the curious gathering into the basement, serving scrumpy made from the small orchards above. Frances listened as intently as she could, down through two ceilings, her ear used to the rough plaster now. The sweet tang of liquid apples tickled Beale's nose as he waits with Walsingham on the street outside for the last guest to arrive.

'Why him?' Beale says, almost wining.

'He is still in my employ.' Walsingham was not in the mood to explain himself, distracted by the uniting oddities in his basement.

'And in who else's pay? Doubtless shy to tell us.' Beale not letting it go.

'We will all be at our most vigilant today.' Walsingham trying to close the matter.

'Tell me you don't think he had anything to do with Stimpson's death?'

Walsingham is ruffled and rebukes him, saying, 'You will hold your tongue, Robert, do you understand?' He will not abide questioning at this important time. Beale cannot stand this but knows he must, so continues listening to Walsingham speak. 'My grief will not darken my senses nor the realities of what each situation, each day, brings us.' He says, seeking confirmation from his eyes. Beale is too angry to be sure what he means and decides not to say any more.

Standing in silence for a few moments, they hear creaking from upstairs. 'Frances likes to keep herself informed of the day's affairs.' Walsingham says with a proud smile.

Walter Williams then arrives. His face does not hide his indifference, and he looks dashing, wearing a new tailored cape and a small rapier dangling from his midriff.

'It will be breaking the law if your weapon is unsheathed.' Walsingham politely points out.

'Not if it is to defend myself.' Williams responds, gesturing for them to go downstairs before him, 'No, no, after you, my Graces.'

As the three men enter the basement, Williams sees it is very different from the last time he was there, not only is it full of about a dozen people, but the table and chair that Mackinnon and Bridle were manacled to is gone. In its place is a large bench-like structure. He is surprised to see the labourer still working on it.

Traske absently puts the finishing touches to his work, polishing the stands and tightening the ropes, standing back admiringly, brushing back his curly hair when he is done, wiping it for the final time with pride.

'Are you finished Theophilus?' Asks Walsingham gently.

'Yes, master. I bid you away and shall set to your other draughts.' He leaves and the two ladies follow. Ursula and her husband exchange courteous bows, before she closes the small flimsy door behind them.

Walsingham looks around the gloom of his own basement, he is the only one to stand. Without saying a word, looking to each of the gathered, ensuring he has their eyes before beginning. Blythe, Williams, Beale, his Court Rider, Pastor Emmanuel, Fyson, Hannah and the Spit Jack all look to him with mixed veneration and puzzlement.

'Lives will be lost and saved because of what you all have done and will do. Freedoms will be gained and a holy posterity ensured in this country for your forebears to come. Because of what you all have done and will do.' Walsingham is not distracted by agreements of Amen by Pastor Emmanuel. 'Your destinies have been set on a course of a most righteous undertaking. The names in this room, not all are we acquainted, but we are all united, and this night shall form a bond. A Bond of Protection for Her Majesty, our beloved Queen Elizabeth, to aid in securing this realm of England.' He now looks to each, as he says, 'Edmund Blythe, Walter Williams, Soborn Fyson, Pastor Emmanuel Hendon…' But then falters looking at the Court Rider, all the while Beale scribes and lists the names –

'Masterman, it is Lynas Masterman, your Grace.' Court Rider says.

Walsingham then looks to Spit-Jack with the same faltering look – what is your name?

'Merely a spit-jack that works with cooks, m'lord. Jack fetch, Jack turn, Jack do this, is all I hears, you knows I hears good enough, m'lord.' He rattles to Walsingham, the cheek of it amusing him.

'Then we shall name thee.' Blythe announces. 'Working with cooks you say?' Blythe asks loudly. Spit-Jack nods. 'Then let's call you Jack…Kitchener and be finished with it.' The newly christened Jack Kitchener nods his consent and Beale updates his list.

Walsingham then says, as he looks to – 'And Hannah…?'

'Tis but a paunchy rat spewed abortive witch my mother so called me, aye, without name at its end.' Hannah says honestly. 'Whether in your kindness or dutiful need there is to be an artful change I am of no mind.'

'There is no family name you are aware of?' Walsingham asks a little sadly, thinking of his girls.

'All a-kin to pork-bellied drunkards, nay dung eaters.' She confirms.

'I daren't invent one from that list.' Blythe says and the others laugh, even Hannah.

Wanting to move quickly on, Walsingham says to her, 'Tis a very pretty green dress: Beau-verte – there, we have it: Beauvertier. Hannah Beauvertier.'

'Beauvery?' Hannah clarifies, not necessarily good with her Ts since her top two teeth be missing. 'Hannah Beauvery, yes, bested by no label a puking whitless mare of a mother could give.' She likes it. Beale scribes her name as she said it and presents the list to Walsingham. In the quiet there is a faint creak from upstairs. The father of daughters smirks, looking up, as he then moves to Beale, taking the quill and adding a name.

'With these nine names, we are oathed to this Bond of Protection.' Walsingham declares, readying the parchment for them to sign.

'Nine?' Lynas Masterman, the observant Court Rider, politely asks, counting all eight heads in the room.

There is another creak from above, which then turn into footsteps, coming down the stairs.

'We, a bond of nine.' Walsingham says, knowing full well Masterman can count. At that moment in walks Cecil, resplendent in fox fur and a red and white cape. His buskins and stockings shine like a pearl. The room is thrown into silent confusion as they withhold gasps but remember to stand from their seats and gently bow, remaining so until he speaks. Hannah is the last to do these things and follows everyone's lead, not realising who in the walls of hell it is, but knowing it is better not to say. Fyson subtly helps her out by whispering that this was Sir William Cecil, First Minister of the Privy Council to Her Majesty.

Walsingham hands him the quill and Cecil cannot help but grin at the intrigue that has just played out, sneaking in the back rooms and the dramatic entrance. The Queen's surrogate father signs his name with a flourish and then turns to the bowed heads. 'Ye, arise, thou protectorate bond.' They all slowly do and each swallows or licks their lips in reverence at the stout and wise fellow before them. 'You are now sworn to it, a sacred and unbreakable oath. Lives will be lost and saved, our Queen and our country will be safer. Because of this here bond. You do not exist other than on that parchment, such is your significance and what you may well do.'

They instinctively knew to agree and confirm in unison –

'Yes my Lord.'

'Though we protect, there is no protection for us.' Blythe points out.

'Aye.' Cecil says gently, then points to Beale, 'Is this your mathematician?' Walsingham nods. 'It took me a night and a day to ponder your master's encoded letter to me, and still I failed, surrendering in awe to using your cypher. Very clever, yes.' Beale lets out an embarrassed, appreciative, chuckle. 'Though they will need to increase their intensity if any enemy seen or unseen is to remain foiled.'

'Yes, my lord.' Beale bows.

'This will only ever intensify,' Cecil began, 'and you should heed the leadership of this man.' He ended his look on Walsingham. The Queen's First Minister had not the heart to warn him that following his most recent counsel with Her Majesty, if there was any wrong footing, misplaced accusation, ill begotten evidence, she would manacle Walsingham herself for perjury. His eyes could falsify a smile, and that is what he did. As Cecil readied to leave, he admires Traske's new furnishings. 'A satisfied job, Walsingham?' And with that he quickly tramps up the stairs, thanking and bidding Ursula a merry eve on his way out.

There is not a single closed mouth as Walsingham looks to his Bond of Protection and it sinks in that the most powerful man in England has just endorsed their master and his cause. Their cause. Only when their hearts and eyes begin to slowly fill with emboldened pride, do their mouths close. Even Williams is looking on admiringly, and Hannah, for once, nothing to object. Blythe whistles, perhaps remembering what Walsingham said looking up to him some seventeen years ago, a powerful friend that has amassed a most powerful ally.

After the excitement subsides, they inevitably turn their attentions to Traske's craftsmanship. A different, more subdued emotion settles on their faces, as if they had accepted Walsingham's dominance and that this large fitting in his basement was somehow frighteningly emblematic of it all.

'Our Lord Cecil knew of this...thing, what exactly is it, Francis?' Williams asks of the raised wooden frame.

'This is the Duke of Exeter's daughter.' He says coolly, as they all marshal round.

Blythe realises, drops his head and from his stomach sighs, 'The rack.' Hannah and Fyson both with trepidation in their steps and reverence in their eyes, approach it closer, too guarded to touch it. Others look between Walsingham and the torture device.

'Pray God, I never find myself at either end of its terrible binds.' Masterman says, suddenly stirred into the seriousness of what he was looking at and how it related to their undertakings.

After a moment, Walsingham feels the need to quell their apprehensions. 'It is necessary and important in unravelling the Devil's schemes.'

'A yoke and a collar do bow the neck,' comes the sudden sagacious voice of Pastor Emmanuel, manoeuvring himself next to Walsingham, 'so are tortures and torments for an evil servant. Ecclesiasticus chapter 33, verse 26.' He faces them all with an expectant look to ensure they understand. It appears they do.

Beale holds out the list of names for their signature of acceptance.

'Necessary and important.' They each repeat as they sign next to their names on the Bond of Protection, before leaving solemnly, the enormity of this evening's events not lost on any one of them.

As they file slowly out, Walsingham appreciates this will be the last time they are all in the same room together. Hearing the last to flack the wooden stairs above him as they leave, he is left to wonder who will betray him first.

From a small veil covered window two floors above, Frances watches them all file out down Seething Lane's cambered track and tries to make sense of all she has heard this day.

VI

Portsmouth Point

14ᵗʰ April 1570

ဆာ ၁၃

Waves flush onto the night shore as gently as a dying man scratches at the earth on a battlefield, crawling from his fate. Slow, hopeless and inevitable. That is how fate can be, thought the sailor as he gazed at the low moon's glittering reflection on the lapping waves, the pebbles ten thousand gemstones under the cascading water. Could this be an ill omen for the town that looked this night as if it were cast in silver? After all, was that not the colour of Beelzebub's claws, the serpent's tongue, and Death's teeth? He stared searchingly into the night for answers. His eyes were set in his head a little too close together, usually giving the appearance of stern, dull, concentration, but tonight they gleamed as if they were newly minted. Clean-shaven and with curly black hair that shone so brightly in the dark he resembled a jewel-encrusted looking-glass than the weathered midshipman he was.

It must be the time. He checked each of the sentries at the shore's embankment and then at the semaphore tower in Gosport, on the opposite side of the dockyard, across the mouth of the port. Neither lookouts were observantly suspicious, so he silently commanded his six sailors to jump from their small beached boat onto the rocks and pebbles of Portsmouth Point. He follows and they do not rouse so much as a turned lantern in suspicion. Just before dusk they had run aground, knowing the sea would turn come morningtide and sweep them back into the Solent and away, leaving them only this short night for their undertaking. In the silvern dark they needed to be quick and find him.

The strip of land they now began to roam was the Point, the separate, dangerous, dock-side of Portsmouth town's gates. Though majestically moonlit, the immediate rugged skyline was an ungodly brown/grey timber chaos, as if the Creator himself had thrown down the planks in a rage and left them where they lay, ridding himself of the mess forever. He had certainly not been back since. A tiny bluff, one road long, full of taverns and bagnios was where they were certain to find him, being able to camouflage himself amongst the frightful drunkards and despicable fiends. Amongst these very demons of Hades, the small group of sailors were now exploring. Would they recognise *him*? All they had to go on was a brief description that he was a stout, but well-heeled, man, round in face and big of nose, jawed and loose-tongued.

Spreading out and being careful not to attract too much attention, they sullied their faces with beer, ash dust and mulchy seaweed so they could blend in. 'Two hours at the boat.' Their leader with the bone-white smooth face and curly black hair says, as they fan out into the dens of iniquity.

Nobody turns an eye to these new strangers in a town within a town that was used to transient faces, who look, smell and sing like them.

In one tavern, the midshipman's curly black hair swayed from side to side as he pretended to shanty along with the tale of a perjured ship's carpenter who had seduced a virgin then killed her on finding out she was pregnant. No-one cared he did not know the tune, let alone the words, but he drank and swore and stunk just as they did. All the while his beady little eyes that looked as if they were staring at the end of his nose were in fact searching for the man he needed to pick up before the tide turned. If they could not find him within two hours his fate would be left to fend for himself. Maybe forever.

After an hour's singing there was yet no sign of him...and the tide would soon be tugging at the keel of his boat.

Entering another slophouse he could hear the squeal of a woman's voice, 'Who you looking for?'

Squinting his already compact eyes, he could see, beyond her, one of his crew distantly infer that he may have seen who they were looking for. Moving hopefully towards his man, the squealy-voiced woman steps in front of him, large and sweaty.

'Who you looking for?' She yelps again. He assumes her intentions meant what type of girl was he looking for, clearly being the establishment's madame. She would not let his arm go. Relieved, he hears her twitter on, encouraging him to purchase any one of her girls, even if it was just for a frivolous fondling. The price, he had to admit, was temptingly cheaper than he normally would pay in any other port, English or foreign. He forced himself to decline. She is nauseatingly insistent. With her eyes rolling and sweat teaming on her brow, she squeals once more, 'Who you looking for?'

Frustrated and claustrophobic, he swipes her aside, shouting, 'None of your concern, ye beslubbering plump toad-spotted hedge pig.' Ridding himself of the old sweat sack to burble in some other mark's ear, he flung her arms out of the way to get past, but he had now lost sight of his own man. From a table behind him he heard the patrons' disapproval at addressing the madame in this way – even these ghouls have morals, he thought. One even scraped and pranged a metal weapon of some kind on the floor – flunk, clunk, it went. He had no time to show any of these demons a real lesson in manners and knew the time was getting dangerously close to needing that rendezvous. Little did he know the weapon was a halberd, wielded by the only man in the town who knew how to handle it.

Frinscombe watches him go.

Leaving behind more din of chatter and lamentable singing, he had not bargained time to fend off the advances of another whore outside who clawed and cooed at him, so he threatened to thrust her teeth into her tongue lest she move. Beyond, he could see his boat sidling slightly as the sea prepared to slurp it back into the depths. As he dodged past her and towards his boat, not worried about the attention he may draw, he could now see, about to climb the side rigging, there were clearly six men ahead of him: they had found the man they were looking for. Mother Mary be praised, he hummed excitedly and did the sign of the cross as he ran towards them. Just as he neared the boat he was as delighted as he had first hoped and, in relief, excitedly whispers ahead, 'Fratellanza.' They hushed and hurried him up, grinning for their getaway.

Then a gruff voice surprises him, belching from behind, 'Swift one off the wrist?'

Stupefied, his pale face turns, and his black hair flings back across his brow as the swing of the halberd flanks across his head, slapping him to the floor with one almighty deadened-bell-like clang.

The boat and its other sailors are quickly surrounded by a posse. Their new companion, with whom they had only momentarily been acquainted, froze. Frinscombe, swinging his halberd threateningly, treads over the curly black-haired clean-shaven man on the gravelly pebbles, whose eyes now look even closer together. He approaches the men and their recent prize.

'You did well to hide in this here town. Whence your friends and rescuers arrived your secrecy was revealed. Now, Charles Bailly, you are to be taken to London for questioning by your superiors.' Frinscombe says calmly.

Within the group of six standing men, one derisively snorts, stepping forward and, in fabled irony, asks, 'Whom will I owe such treacheries?' The looks amongst his rescuers seem genuine enough, none of them betrayed or sold him down the river. But Charles Bailly does not believe them.

'You've not been deceived, you have been discovered.' Frinscombe says, moving ever closer.

Bailly steps into the moonlight's radiance, he has a fat nose and gappy teeth that make his eyes look wild, as if a dog is in a growl. His voice is educated and faintly eastern, maybe Flemish. 'Discovered? And ye by an ill-nurtured miscreant such as you are.'

'You do me a credit, sir. No, not I.' Frinscombe says, then suddenly flinging the end of his halberd round the head of another one of the sailors, who crunches straight onto the pebbles like a bag of coins. 'I had no knowledge pertaining to your designs in usurping my beloved Queen. No, not I. Neither would I have fathomed who you were or where you intend to be.' He is right up close to him now. Bailly realises he will be unable to swing that almighty weapon at his person and feels momentarily emboldened.

'Then why have you sold your soul to the antichrist?' Bailly hisses to Frinscombe.

'Because Walsingham pays dearly.' And he thrusts the handle upwards under Bailly's jaw, shooting his head quickly upwards, before he crumples unconscious to the beachy floor.

Blythe, one of the posse with Frinscombe, slides from out of the shadows and congratulates the gaoler. 'Indeed a fine catch this night. Tie these men up.' He then addresses the remaining sailors. 'In the name of William Cecil, First Minister and Privy Councillor, we requisition your vessel, which shall be interred at Her Majesty's docks of her choosing, awaiting your sentence.' Blythe motions to another faceless man from the posse in the dark behind him, 'Captain Herle will pilot the ship to London whilst I escort the traitor to meet his spoiler.'

Herle lurches into view, thirsty for an ale to hide his humiliation at taking orders from this fisherman, as he derisively calls him behind his back. What particularly stung was his use of Cecil's authority – something he used to be entrusted with, until this Walsingham nose grinder had tricked and betrayed him with the French prisoner business. There was little that could be done about all that now – and so he alleviated his hard-pressed feelings with the thought that there was bound to be some measure of plunder aboard even so pathetic a sailing vessel as these papists had boarded. Legally it was all his, so long as he shared it with the Queen's purse – and who were they to know how much exactly was contained therein. Swallowing his demotion could end up being a profitable enterprise. As he climbs aboard to check his reward, he decides not yet to plan Walsingham's undoing all by himself and let it roll on to see what may come his way.

'Walsingham will write of his patronage my lord Frinscombe.' Edmund Blythe declares formerly to the no nonsense halberd wielding gaoler.

He grins proudly in return, 'I am but to serve in the endeavours for Her Majesty.'

* *

Westminster

Since departing their basement meeting, forming the Bond of Protection, Beale had conferred with Jack Kitchener and Lynas Masterman twice more in different taverns. Near St. Margaret's church, hidden from prying eyes in Westminster Hall or the Palaces of government, is the sensible location for their conferences, he feels. From their early discussions it was clear both men were not soldiers of initiative. Beale knew they were dedicated and although they understandably had concerns over money, their loyalty could not be questioned. In terms of ideas, though, he realised it was he who was going to have to lead. Telling them the way in which they could assist in obtaining proof positive which leaders were behind any plots was the easy part. First, they had to talk money.

'There be palms to lay heavy for cheeks to turn.' Jack complains. 'Westminster and Whitehall bedecked with servant rogues of this kind, but dutiful rogues as we mention it.' He was almost sniffing out Beale's coin.

'Inns to replace or feed my horse is no humble suffering, sir.' Lynas explains, shaking his empty purse tied to his waist belt. 'No rattle is but the sound of ruin.'

Within several weeks, Beale had seen Walsingham's grand scheme become an undertaking exponentially rising in outgoings and had quickly set in motion ways to make his plans feasible. Beale's prudence in raising funds was quick and masterful, and had to be as the expenses were increasing – Blythe's ship alone was £6 a week to run. This was no insignificant sum. He recalled Walsingham initially paying him an apprentice wage just above the average labourer's earnings of 10shillings and 3pence a week – a mere twelfth of what it cost to cover a median ship each week. Outgoings across their small operation were burgeoning at a stultifying rate. To sponsor their endeavours, therefore, Beale had set up a trading company, which in effect had wealthy merchantmen advance him monies and in return they would receive a share of any confiscated properties or wealth belonging to those falling to Her Majesty's justice, less, of course, what the exchequer took. He raised a great deal of capital in a few short weeks, nearly £2,000. Walsingham was stunned – Hampton Court Palace, he had snorted, had cost £50,000 over eleven years to build. Without doubt, they had to be careful not to be governed by the money, Beale soberly pointed out, as investors could be just as enslaving as the Queen's law. This was the first clue to Walsingham that Beale may not necessarily be operating within the scrolled confines of the law. He chose to stare at his one-time apprentice for a short moment, ignore the premise and move the conversation on.

In the oak benched corner of the tavern, Beale was content, on the inside, and seemingly reluctant to haggle and hand over a small purse of groats to Lynas and Jack for their outstanding endeavours to date. More will come, he was sure to pass on, from Walsingham. Asking for their ideas on how to improve their endeavours, however, sees any elation drop from their faces and eyes empty. They both dare not tie the purse to their belts just yet. Beale turns to Kitchener –

'You will see to apprize me of your ascertainments, whether the gossip from the bowels of the building, as you replace the wax of the Clerk desk or clear the goblets from Council chambers.' Beale says in a firm murmur, his fist clenched on the table, a striking resemblance of how severe these matters are.

'I shall do the same with the stablehands, the livery lads, Riders from...' Lynas begins, before Beale snipes him down –

'Our netcast of espials and agents is growing, this we have covered.' It is not meant to, but Masterman is downhearted, hearing only that he is no longer required. 'Your reconnaissance of the North was exceptional. We need to use your purposes elsehow.' Beale adds.

'Shall I return to the North, my lord? There are brothers that ride for nobles and gentry alike, ye, all men of import.' Lynas says, hopeful in his part to play.

'You have family in the north?' Beale asks.

'Nay kin, but brother Riders.'

Beale sits back in delicious realisation. 'You have a netcast of agents, yet unspoiled with loyalties, in the north of England?'

'Aye, though agents may be too forward a notion.' Lynas chuckles.

'All the more they be unwise, better for our purposes, no?' Kitchener asks, looking between them. Beale admires him, Walsingham hit the chisel and split the rock when he said the Spit-Jack was a cunning and useful fellow.

'I should wager they possess an understanding of what message lies therein their saddlebags as they trot from estate to estate, manor to manor.'

'Oh yes my lord, as certain as Satan is a soulless buggerer – we be inquisitive readers and listeners, m'lord.' Masterman says, finishing his mug of mead and beckoning the barkeep for more.

Jack starts laughing to himself, 'The japes you riders must employ – right under your master's noses – the fun and sport you could have.' It breaks their serious conversation, although Beale and Masterman scald his empty headedness with harsh looks. 'No...I just mean... think on this: You are the messengers, yes? You carry the message and return the response, yes? Well what if...you <u>make</u> the message? No suspicion would be aroused, by master, rider or nay?' Their scowls soften.

'Yes.' Beale exhales, slowly and reverently, turning his looks between Kitchener and Masterman, his excitement building.

Masterman clasps his own thigh in realisation, 'We could tell the learned, connected, powerful men in the north...anything we wanted them to think and we shalt spread the word.'

'Three more meads here.' Kitchener shouts to the barkeep as they smirk to one another as if they had just discovered the elixir of life.

'What shall the message be?' Lynas asks.

'This we leave for our master's devising.' Beale says and begins his cyphered message for Walsingham to instruct Cecil of their intentions.

* *

Straightening his thin moustache with his finger and thumb, Robbie felt his high angles of hair as he leaves Kitchener and Masterman behind in the tavern. He thought about visiting Fyson for a meagre trim and a proper shave. Passing a Milliner's maid, she winks at him as she hauls ribbons and cloth across the street. It must be true what Edith had said to him – his face looks roguishly handsome when he smiles.

The quickest walk was along Kings' Street to Charing Cross continuing eastwards. However, catching a cheap wherry at this end of the Thames was the best likeliness at Westminster stairs, Parliament now being dissolved and wherrymen desperate. With his elated mood he decides for the less strenuous river ride and pokes through the tiny lanes behind the massive stone buildings of Westminster, wet and dank in the continuous shade. He could see the yellow brown humps of the river, frolicking as they rolled along, just beyond. A man stands and blocks his way at the end. His captor – Ugly in nose and teeth. He really must discover the name of this rump-faced bag of slutten guts so as to track him and all of his kin down one fateful day. Beale knew he could turn and out run the piss mark, but he questions the achievement of it and guesses his foreigner friend be at the other end behind him. Subtly peering back, sure enough he senses the presence of someone at his rear.

'You knew this time would come.' Ugly says.

'No spade to send me to the floor?' Beale ventures.

'You want?' The foreigner shouts from behind and Beale spins around expecting the worse – and good job, for a spade is then swung at him, which he ducks, hearing it pulverise against the bricks.

'You don't need to do that.' Beale steps backwards towards Ugly, keeping out of swings length. The Foreigner, hatless and sweating, sculks after him, dragging the spade along the unkempt cobbles, clagging and chocking in metallic devilry as he goes.

'What errand has your master got you on, then, boy?' Demands Ugly.

'I'm no boy.' Hisses Beale, as if it was not bad enough he is having to pander with these cocksniffs to now take their insults too. He was about to add how old he actually was, but he just did not know, in lack of parents. Instead, he attempts to insult him – 'I have bedded more women than you've enjoyed shittings.' A terrible effort, and he knew it, and keeps his face made. The teeth and nose of Ugly rise up in one awful crescendo of noisy laughter. With stunning alacrity, both men grab Beale and slam him to the wall, lifting him off the floor by their arms propped under his neck.

'What writings are you making to Walsingham for Cecil that would be of interest to us?' Ugly growls and Beale muffles an unclear answer. Ugly motions to Foreigner to search him. In doing so he takes his purse of a few groats and finds the communication he wrote, in code. They drop him.

'Let me at least make a copy for my master, to complete the deception.' Beale rasps, on all fours. Their response is quick and final, kicking him so he falls over on his back.

'You are done of favours this day.'

VII

࿊

Clouds shift across the sky as if confused whether it should be a Spring or Summer's day. The erratic wind meant the westwards journey was a slow wherry sail up the Thames. So the men decided to walk. Little did they know it was not just the two of them. Despite checking on a number of occasions at the tell-tale junctions, crossings and lane turnings looking for suspicious pursuers, they would not have given this particular espial a second glance. A girl.

Between the Gate House and Serjeants Inn on Fleet Street ran a narrow north-south alley called Crockers Lane that led to the old monastery of the White Friars of Camelites. None who dwelt there knew where the name Crockers came from, nor cared. Its likely connection was to the Roman pottery once made there. To those from beyond the lane there could be little doubt it meant *crocks o' shite* such was it considered the cesspit into which nefarious Londoners drained. Seeking refuge from the prying authorities, this odd lane with its tight timber shacks had become a sanctuary of dubious deeds and controversial arts. Parish Constables instructed Nightswatchmen to avoid the lane and Alderman struck it from their tax registers. Increasingly it was referred to as *Alsatia,* just as the French region of Alsace, which operated outside of legislative and judicial stipulations, was called, so was this small pariah lane of London. Despite frustrating the Justices of the Peace and Magistrates who were unable to bring prosecutions in an area that legally did not exist, it was too convenient a hiding hole for deviants with wealth and power to crawl into, as they dabbled in murkier areas of the law.

It was behind this perfect shroud of secret researching that the likes of Dr John Dee could conceal themselves.

Little surprise that the two gentlemen felt ill at ease tottering down Crockers Lane, trying to ignore the peculiar glances.

'We must be careful.' Warns one companion to the other. 'For where you may not be harassed by the law, neither do you have its protection.' He knew well of the place they searched for, although this was the first time either man had braved it. In this strangest of lanes, then, walked the strangest of bedfellows. Walter Williams accompanies Clerk of the Privy Council Chamber, Thomas Smythe of Essex.

Walter is deliberating the trail of events that had led him here to walk with a man who had direct access to the Queen's Council, now about to meet one of the most mysterious and well-connected men in all England – Dr John Dee. For years Walter had scratched a living working with a travelling troupe, as a boy during Queen Mary's reign, going from village to village acting in the popular passion plays. Week on week they would traipse the lands of Anglia and Middlesex performing stories from the Bible, with he gradually taking on more demanding roles in these dramatic depictions of scriptural scaremongering. Into Elizabeth's reign this papist tradition was lapsing, becoming unpopular as taverns, particularly in London, were presenting their own plays. Rumours spread that purpose-built theatres were being arranged in Southwark to deliver nothing but these plays. Acting made his chest thump and his eyes see, it was this and nothing more that balanced his four humours. Although, he had to admit, these past few months the intrigue and occasional imbursement of silver had enticed him to keep with this new path and forget the hostilities and threats acting on stage could bring. At least for the moment.

Looking at Thomas Smythe of Essex he wondered what ambitions drove him – was he affected by rumour that his family were descendants of a medieval king's illegitimate issue. Was he looking to right a past wrong? Williams imagined some tanner's daughter having her honour burgled, bent over a dung heap, as he looked over to Smythe fidgeting to find John Dee's abode in this lane of detritus.

At the far end of the lane, labourers slowly dismantled the old Camelite monastic buildings close to the Thames. Elizabeth was brazenly liquidating the Pope's assets in England.

'And she wonders why there's anger.' Thomas says, spitting into the mossy lane.

Walter looked about and saw children, mothers and an old lady dragging a small cart of baskets woven from thick reeds. 'Tell me again the virtues of our visit?'

Smythe stopped to unclog his riding boots of muck. 'Dee's work possess immense benefit to seeing a true Catholic return to the throne.' He has freed his feet from hobbling with the city's crap and continues on down the lane.

'Dee is not a Catholic. He's not even a Protestant?' Williams quizzes.

'Whatever he is or is not, he certainly has political sway. He has the ear of the Queen.' Smythe says.

'You think the Queen's astrologer, genius mathematician – or, as some say, magic summoner – can be controlled?' Walter asks, disbelievingly.

'Given the right master.'

Walter feigns his impress, though still remains unsure how it helps, 'He holds weight in reading horoscopes, I ascertain. How can we trust a man who was convicted for reading tarot cards and charts to the Princesses Mary and Elizabeth…immediately before their brother Edward died?'

'No.' Smythe shuts that door fast. 'He was never found guilty. Examined, yes, by the patriot Bonner.'

'Queen Mary's blood hound?'

'Never convicted. Yes, he be a scryer of futures, and the messages from angels he believes carry the seal of God and truth means he has a mind of the sharpest iron.' Smythe is immovable.

'He has adoration for this Queen?' Williams sounds unconvinced. Smythe concedes with a slight bow of his small head. 'And so he will for the next one.' He says mysteriously.

'Then the dye is cast.' Williams states.

As they continue slowly down the lane, they hear some commotion, and a woman chases away a girl from her yard. She trips and fumbles into both men.

'Ah! For the love of six days – what error here?' Smythe exclaims, pushing the girl away.

She falls into a wall and slumps onto the floor, winded, hair flopping over her face and her cape slipping and ripping. Williams admires her plume of brunette hair, just about seeing her soft brown eyes, beginning to fill with emotion. He picks her up.

'Flee you corruptible mud sucking jabberer before I beat you.' Thomas growls, then wipes the splashed mud from his cape and hands. She turns and runs. Walter looks disappointedly at him – it's just a girl. 'His infernal place must be here somewhere.' Smythe scoffs, moving on.

At a ramshackle wooden hut, Smythe lifts the bolt. They hear a small bell distantly tingle within. Closing the door behind them, they see the latch tied to a length of string that led all the way up the stairs. Following its course, both men tread carefully on the single slatted steps that whined with each boot's incumbencies.

Entering with trepidation there are two sources of light delicately illuminating those parts of the room. The first came from a looking glass reflecting a beam from the second source, which was a glass jar that had in it the tiniest of candles. It amazed them to see such emanated light, as if it were filled with forty lanterns. Magic of the sciences, Thomas whispers.

On a shiny table there were charts and scrolls strewn, unrecognisable to both men. Around these were hunched the long nosed and fluffy bearded face of John Dee. At 43 he could be mistaken for 63, with balding head covered in black skull cap and droopy eyes that had not slept properly in decades. He did not look up to Walter and Thomas who stood there, awaiting his attention.

Thomas, admiring the many diagrams and paintings of the twelve astrological signs, attempts to introduce them, 'Dr Dee, my name...' –

'I know who you are Smythe.' Dee said without looking up, his voice as deep and lagging as logs slowly rolling downhill. 'Why do you have this man in your favour?'

'He is Walter Williams, Dr Dee.'

'I ask not who he is only why he is here? No ally nor friend?' Dee asks, finally stopping what he was doing, straightening, and looking at them both.

'We are assigned by the Privy Council for you to solve a cypher.' Smythe pleas.

'Let me see.' Smythe hands over what Beale gave Ugly and Foreigner. Dee hums. 'Tis a simple cryptogram.'

'Good.' Says Walter innocently.

'Not so.' Dee bites back. 'It makes me wonder what I am missing. Why go to the trouble of making a cryptogram at all if so simple.' He writes what it says and shows them –

Thereto ensure false messages set a plan to proceed not as Cecil were previous warned against. Hither dispatch the forces in the North.

'This makes sense for our purposes, I thank you sir.' Walter says, looking to Smythe, who agrees.

'Mathematics makes sense of all purposes. Whomever crafted this wanted you to think so.' Dee glibly responds.

'And will Math answer questions about the future?' Walter asks, brimming with a discovered confidence.

'And does Walter Williams, a man with dreams and mixed loyalties want to ascertain that future?' Dee intones, the mysterious doctor's eyes fix on Walter with an intensity that makes both visitors slowly retack their stance, altering their feet until they were sure they were more steadfast. Walter towers over him by several inches, but Dee has no concern, slowly walking around his table to speak directly with him. 'Alack – these are not the questions you wish to find of me, are they?' Dee asks flightily.

If Walter was startled or agitated in any way, he was doing well not to reveal so, shaking his head to Dee. Thomas a mere bystander at the closed men.

'Pray tell.' Dee says, never once taking his eyes off Walter.

'You are the astrologer.' Walter calmly answers, knowing his insolence had rammed through the walls of decency. Dee laughs drolly. Walter grins and raises his eyebrows as if to say go ahead.

'I have no issue informing Kings or princes of ill begotten fates and have less concern reading what the stars have in mind for you.' Dee says.

'We thank you for your time, Dr Dee.' Smythe splutters, now in a hurry to get them out of there, embarrassed and worried what was going to happen next in this extraordinary game of who yields first.

'What fate did you report to our Queen?' Walter asks, not at all threatened by the little old man he sees before him or with the discomfort of the Privy Council Clerk.

'Our Queen?' Coos Dee. 'Which one do you refer? For your sakes I bid you answer well.'

It is a clever trap that if Walter says one more word could infer he has no loyalty or – worse – a false loyalty to Elizabeth.

'If you have told Her Majesty she will live and you have forecast a long and fruitful reign, then how do Papal Bulls, her own faltering ministers and the Brotherhood yet thrive this day?' Walter has risen his voice.

'Your cypher has all the answers you need. Besides,' The old wise man creepily starts, 'none of this will matter in the months ahead. London will once again bow to lament. I bid you eveningtide, sirs.' John Dee finishes as he had started: in a silent stoop over the table studying his archaic wonderments.

Walter and Smythe slowly leave.

'This is on your head. Dare there be rumblings from the Privy Council t'will be you in ill favour.' Smythe distraughtly spits at him as they get outside. They walk fifty minutes to St Paul's and Paternoster Row never making eye contact.

As the enormous steeple comes into view, they hear the screaming and huckstering swirl and rachet around the crescent at the bottom of the old Cathedral.

'The scandal sheets?' Smythe asks, almost shuddering. 'What now?'

'Something anew.' Williams replies urgently. They are both drawn to one fellow flapping his pamphlet and wailing its contents –

'Rebellious forces uncovered in the north. Armed uprising threatens to reignite the Northern Rebellions. Government to dispatch edict to all Noble Houses: Posse Comitatus.' Shouts the pamphleteer.

'Ready for war in the north?' Gawps Smythe and both men look like they have swallowed a plum stone. Perhaps Dee is a Catholic sympathiser after all, thought Walter.

* *

'A big man. This be our search.' Hannah was saying to the Rhyming Whore as they walked across London Bridge. Some knowing eyes were casting them unkind looks whilst some could not wait to finish their daily grind and get to the Venus, wishing they were not out walking with their wives...or husbands. Essigia's Gems cackled the attention away, making their way to Southwark, walking in careless abandon, arm in arm, across the busiest road in London's two cities.

'Big in the area that matters – lest he leave a woman in tatters?' Rhyming Whore asks.

Hannah giggles, 'No, Rhy, big in arms, big in strength.'

'Where is such a man found? My heart's delight shall abound.' Rhy – as the Gem friends liked to call her – says mischievously.

Despite the laughter, they look at each other knowing that even if they did find this man; it may be a fruitless mission should he be unconvinced to return with two doxies. Honey traps enticing men to the dark of an alley or a tavern's bleak backyard was an endemic way in which the Spoon (that which feeds you) would be quickly surrounded and robbed of all their clothing, only to find it at market the next day. The slow walk over the bridge gave them time to hatch out a good plan and ensure the Big Man's services are employed.

Leaving the bridge, not looking up to see the gawping green heads on traitors' spikes, these hearty women turned straight into Southwark's boisterousness, not one bit alarmed. The huckstering, whoring and drinkers frothing their insults continued like the millwheel of life, endless and evermore. They headed for the fenced-off pit that had so shocked Beale but in whose favour they were headed there now.

Just shy of dusktide, the bear baiting had finished and the two Gems watched Batemen drag their dogs onto carts, piled high in their ripped mutilation, like farmers stacking muddened vegetables torn from the earth. Betting, they could hear, was not yet done for there were two events left.

'They be the men we seek? Arms and legs small and meek?' Rhy says, pointing to the Batemen readying the grimy arena.

Hannah shook her head. 'You will know when you see him.'

Rhy suddenly laughs and Hannah turns to see what amuses her – a horse trots out with a monkey strapped atop in a frilled pink kerchief scarf. The other women stood around the fences clap and make sounds as if they had just seen a fresh litter of kittens. Entire crowd then rumbles with anticipation. Three Dobermans pelt towards the horse viciously snapping their snouts at the monkey, the horse panics and flares its hind legs at the dogs. Their sudden blood and injuries do not deter them from their goal: the monkey, now screeching and yelping as the savage black dogs near ever closer. The crowd in spasms of laughter, inciting them on. Eventually one of the Dobermans has enough of the horse's pummels and champs into its rump, distracting it long enough for another dog to snipe its jaw into the leg of the monkey and wrench it from horse and strap. Within seconds they angrily savage the guts from the monkey's rib cage.

'By the count of man…thirty-three was the total.' A voice bellows. Thirty-three seconds was how long the monkey had lasted. Not many had waged it would, the bet makers made good on the monkey's prolonged poor future.

'Now. This is it.' Says Hannah, forgetting her shock at the short drama that had just played out. Rhy grabs Hannah's arm, startled.

The Bear. Its thick black mane, once as beautiful and dark as fresh poured tar was matted and clagged with blood, sweat and mucus, some of its own and the rest from all the other animals who had tried to topple it. The beast that had so haunted Beale lives still, somehow remaining magnificent in its tired and sorrowed eyes.

The Dobermans sit down out of respect. Or fear. The Bear makes a gargling roar when it sees its next opponent.

It was easy to see why he was called the Big Man. Wearing leather armour, sandals and nothing on his legs or arms, he looks more like a deserted Roman soldier than a gladiator in the arena of certain death. At nearly six foot seven he is almost a foot over the next tallest man. His wet brown hair is crudely tied back with leather string. Arms as thick as most men's legs and look like polished wood. As for his legs, they could batter-ram down the gates of Hell.

A bellowing voice has everyone's attention as people flock quickly back round the fenced-off pit for the final event before darkness meant no more. 'Can Hercules tame the beast? All our warrior has to do is last by the count of nineteen.'

As soon as the Bear is unleashed the entire crowd, apart from Rhy, count. She is struck in a divine and lustful way, like she has never felt before.

Dropping to all fours, the animal snarls and runs for him. Hercules waits until the charging bear is dangerously close with his snout diving towards his chest when the man flips sideways thrusting his foot under its jaw as he does.

The Bear does not know what hit it, but is not wounded only stunned.

Four, five, six...the crowd chant with the bear padding towards him, deciding to stand on its hind legs, wowing the crowd.

Swinging both paws, its first misses but the next swipes Hercules into the mud.

Crowd momentarily stops counting with widespread 'ooohs' at the potential horror of the warrior's undoing. They see him fidget and continue...Nine, ten, eleven...

Hercules gets up and the bear fumbles, losing its advantage, hurrying a jab with the left front paw, which seems just playful, is enough to thrust him against the fence, breaking it down in one section, the crowd flee in panic.

Bear's snout jabs for his foot but Hercules lifts himself up and dares to launch a punch that cracks the bear's head sidewards. Very different 'ooohs' from the crowd – now he has raised the ante.

Fifteen, sixteen...furious, the bear bounds on all fours after him and catches him quickly.

'He's done for.' A voice shouts. But Hercules wriggles and in the animal's desperate haste to savage him, the bear lets him go although not without whacking him from side to side in reattempting a grab. Hercules flies left then right, toppling over the fence on twenty, twenty one... There is a huge cheer and Bear is restrained with its tethers by four Batemen. He has done it.

'No wonder Walsingham wanted him.' Hannah observes. Rhy smiles her comely lips over at him, blinks slowly, turns her head to Hannah as if she was talking about him.

Hercules sees all this and is struck by Rhy's auburn hair, tight behind her ears, revealing a bright white neckline leading to a handful of breasts. He feels himself get thick. Taking his leather armour off and scraping the mud from his arm with the help of wet hessian, he approaches the two women.

'Winchester Geese is it?' His drawling West Country accent asks, with a playful smile.

'We're no property of the Bishop of Winchester. That wholly unholy open-arsed molester.' Rhy says.

'We works for no such Hag-born cod-piece sniffer.' Hannah confirms.

'We're of Essigia's Good ship Venus, the ship's great petard sucking a man's penis.' Rhy explains. Both women forthright about their living.

He is half astounded and half grateful for this honesty. 'The Rhyming Whore, forgive me. I thought that be just legend.' He says. Rhy smiles and her eyes revealing. 'The name's Nevon, Titus Nevon. My friends call me Hercules.'

'On account of your attire been short dresses I don't doubt?' Hannah scoffs. Hercules and Rhy laugh, but Hannah wants to get straight to business. 'How much you make?'

'Fipenny, maybe six, a fight. If bets are high then I've had a shilling a day for seven straight in my time. Is that all you want me for is it?'

'The only interest we have of your money is for you to make more.' Hannah says.

'There are plenty of other offers, deep goes the Council's coffers.' Rhy adds, giving him another smile and flush slightly when he reciprocates.

Staring straight at Rhy, but talking to Hannah, Titus says, 'You expect me to believe you are in the employ of Her Majesty's government, then disavow me of my sense and assets in some blind alley.' The tone he uses is not accusatory, more what fool they must think of him. His chest tingles seeing how Rhy's neck and cheeks have gone rosy. What a beautiful sight the blush is, he hums to himself.

'You would be needed for protection, an errand in the North. Accompanying riders is all it be. Then as my master commands.' Hannah says, as Rhy now slopes to his side, beginning to stroke his smooth pillar-like arms, then continues, 'This be a job for the strong, the hero, nay a man of adventures. A real Hercules.'

'I shall meet your master.' He says, stroking Rhy's hair.

VIII

৪০০৪

Why such thoughts enter her head she will never know. Was it the Devil in her, as her mother had always professed it was when she committed such wickednesses throughout her life. Or was it just that morning at the old Roman well, all those weeks ago: the Tussie-mussie; those words of conjuring; and the awakening of unknown spirits. Maybe it was all of it. This could well be Frances Walsingham's destiny, she thought to herself.

Nonetheless she was here, not knowing why, deciding to continue in her pursuit, convinced the two gentlemen had not yet seen her. From the moment Frances saw Walter Williams, from a tiny gap in the window leaving Seething Lane, after her father had held that meeting with the Bond of Protection, she had felt there was something corruptible about him. Maybe it does take one to know one, she conceded to herself with a devilish smirk. When, quite by chance, she saw him on Cheapside, with another man with an equally suspicious smile many days later her curiosity just had to be satisfied.

Two streets from their house was Mynchen Lane, sometimes called Mincing, where Ursula liked to hunt the Genoese traders' imports for the best drinkable wines, not trusting Edith's selections. Bored, it was here that Frances decided to undertake her own hunting: for the old wise woman that had sold her the wish charm, nearby in amongst the grocers and herbalists of Rodd Lane. Sneaking away when Ursula, Edith and Mary's backs were turned was an easy trick which she had done often without getting into trouble – she would always meet back at Seething Lane and her mother trusted her to do so.

It was on Tower Street as she skipped westwards towards Rodd Lane that she saw Williams walking the same way on the other side with purpose in his eyes and a redheaded stern looking man. Her intrigue fought down her common sense and she pursues them with the care and suspicion she had been taught by her father. Without Mary, she had to try and do both follow and front. Fortunately for her, they had avoided many of the checkpoints across the City. They eventually came to the lane called Crockers, almost half way to Westminster, she was mightily disappointed, and now very tired. Thinking they were leading her to an underground palace with rooms full of gold, she huffed and grumped, inadvertently becoming sloppy in her new, incidental, station as tracking espial. She sees the red-headed man, Smythe, looking for something but she is then shouted at by a woman for standing idle at her stall. Frances looks to her feet that are upon some small woven mats and is shooed away. Attempting to apologise, the hag only thinks the girl is giving her cheek so reaches to slap her. Frances is nimble. Ducking and running, she eludes the mat-seller, but Frances buckles her feet on the uneven cobbles, almost cartwheeling...into the two men she was following. Her father's friend and his companion.

They both bear down on her.

Amongst the muck and moss, slipping and backtracking, she accepts she is now absolutely, no doubt about it, done for. This is how her life ends. She closes her eyes and they fill but she has no the time to cry.

Red bristled face is shouting at her, 'For the love of six days – what error here?' He pushes her away, this time her knee buckles on a post, she smacks the wall and bundles onto the floor, her stupid cape snagging and making it worse. She braces herself as her father's friend comes near her, he is going to strike for sure and she is surprised when he just delicately touches her hair, stunting her from moving. Picking her up easily, she goes droopy with expectance.

'Flee you corruptible mud sucking jabberer before I beat you.' Red head growls his winy accent thinning her ears, wiping the splashed mud from his cape and hands as if she was the filth.

Frances thanks God, even though she did not have time to ask for His help, she does not question His divine intervention, turns and runs for nearly twenty minutes. Out of breath, she plods into Mynchen Lane, Ursula, Edith and Mary now absent, the vintners closing their stalls. It was getting late, she swallows. The rest of the way home, she wonders how she will ever get into heaven now.

* *

Beyond the shallow southern banks of the Thames at Southwark lay the Marshalsea. Renowned throughout London's 200,000 populace as a diabolically overcrowded prison, it was initially a court and holding place for debtors and the increasingly more vile offenders against the state were housed here. Charles Bailly among them.

Walsingham was keen to question him as soon as he had arrived and knew he could smuggle him in to his basement whilst Ursula, Edith and his daughters visit Pastor Emmanuel and later the wine merchants in Mynchen before he could begin exerting his scrutiny. It was simply not done to introduce a traitor so brazenly, let alone the dire interrogation that would commence whilst they played innocently in the orchard or read their prayers. Walsingham was eager to test his new rack, deeming it great providence he had one and the Marshalsea did not.

He was in buoyant mood walking with Beale and Nevon to collect the prisoner. Beale had said he liked this new fellow, the bear wrestler, though was lost in the hurdy gurdy of his West Country conversation, too soft and curdling for his ears. Walsingham could understand the man perfectly well, his humbler Dorsetshire days easing the encounter.

The three of them had to wait an hour as Messengers went back and forth between the gaoler and Robert Dudley's secretary, being the sponsor releasing the prisoner into Walsingham's care. It would have taken longer if Beale had not sweetened the gaoler with twenty groats. Another ledger entry to be deducted from his investors.

Titus grabbed Bailly by the wrists, which were tied behind his back, and yanks them up, almost disjointing his arms from his pits as he is bolstered off the ground. 'Any slippery swan shittings from you, my handsome, and I'll ride yer arms up round yer head til yer skin rolls off yer back like a nightshirt. Yer follow me?' Bailly can only squeak a yes before he is returned to a position enabling him to walk with a little more comfort.

They arrive at Seething Lane without harassment of rescuers or distraction from the plotter Bailly himself.

Robbie had thought at one point he eyed two suspect men monitoring their moves and readied his Grosschedel blade. Nevon had also spotted them and had given one of his Herculean growls and was such that they never saw their faces again. The only plot, Walsingham thought with acidic irony, that he had managed to foil so far.

Walking into Seething Lane, the Catholic fugitive must have thought his luck was changing and Walsingham somehow a ruse to remove him from that rat nest Marshalsea. The pleasant sized house could easily have been a safe holding place until he was whisked away to the North to inspire Catholic nobles to another rebellion. Yes, he could see it now, a good feast and perhaps even some wine would be most welcome, he even smelt the beef dripping from the kitchen below. His fervent prayers to Mary the Holy Mother had been answered. Waiting patiently for his ropes to be untied, he stretches his limbs with relief when Beale once more unsheathed his Germanic blade and swipes the rope effortlessly apart. Bailly caresses his hands and is about to thank and compliment them on a fine deception –

'Down there.' Beale orders as Titus picks him up by the back of his neck and his breaches, lifting him downstairs like a mischievous child. Bailly's complacency – and pride – slipping quickly away.

In the basement the realisation quickly hits Bailly this was no safe house and there were no rescue routes through the night to a welcoming northern nobleman's house. Neither was there a feast.

'What do you want?' He asks, like a bird with clipped wings, floppy and pitiable.

Walsingham walks down the stairs. 'It is very simple: information.' He says, entering the room.

'I shan't say a thing.'

'Oh, I think you will.' Walsingham walks to his instrument of truth, picking up a cloth in a bucket and giving the wood a final polish.

Beef dripping, Bailly realises – that was what he could smell – fat to grease the ghastly wheels of this contraption. He had heard tell England used them though had never seen one and had certainly not thought his God may forsake him to suffer one. Looking around the room he saw no possible sign of heavenly help in the dank gloom and accepted there was much misery ahead.

Titus shoves him towards the rack, barking, 'Undress.'

'What?' Bailly asks, suddenly coy.

'If you keep yourself dressed, your garments will rip and cut into your skin in want of infection.' Walsingham advises, as if he was preparing him for a shave.

'No, far better to bleed from the inside.' Beale says, slightly surprising himself with the vindictiveness, frustration beginning to seethe from within. The past month's close calls, guesses and lacking pay-offs were scratching at his temperament. This, their prisoner, was the closest they had come to finally obtaining places and names. He was going to revel in scribing the revelations, identities of plotters, co-conspirators in the vile plans to murder his beloved Queen. Above all, it would serve as a job entirely well done for Francis Walsingham.

'What do you want to know?' Bailly whimpers. All three men turn to him stunned. 'I shall tell you, without barricades of lies.'

Walsingham sees through it. 'We are not interested in your stories, only your facts marry ours.' Then intimates he should get on the rack now. Beale and Nevon rip his flimsy doublet off and jostle him onto the long wooden bench, binding his limbs at either end. 'Tension.' Walsingham says...and thus begins the Catholic stowaway's agony.

Titus a quarter turns the wooden ratchet to regulate rigidity. Bailly huffs as his body lays tort across the MP's basement. Now, Walsingham thought, we can unravel suspicions and make confirmation of evil doings.

'Who entitles themselves the Brotherhood?' He asks.

'Tis no secret, they are emboldened to restore the Catholic faith in any place of heresy.' Bailly whimpers, wriggling his body, never able to loosen his binds.

'Who are you masters within the Brotherhood?'

It was clear he was not going to respond, so Walsingham orders Titus to strengthen the turn. Straining, the rope's engrained dust escapes, twirling into the air as if it were the tiny smoke of a miniature chimney. Bailly writhes and screeches in wild pain. He has never felt this before, not at all close to the sensations he first suspected it might be. Suddenly his entire chest is covered in a film of sweat as his elbows, shoulders and hips redden as the stress mounts and tightens inside his body.

'I ask again...who are your masters within the Brotherhood?'

It looks as if he is not going to answer again and seeing Walsingham give the order to strengthen the turn once more, Bailly has to stop him. 'No. No...wait...' He implores. 'I learn no names, I cannot ascertain to determine the cyphers I carry.'

'Cyphers? You had encoded letters? From whom and to where were they destined?' Walsingham asks though does not wait for an answer, nodding to strengthen the rack. Bailly's skin wrenches as if it could no longer hold his innards. Elbow sinews crick and split between screams.

'I am entrusted...' He begins through tears of shame and pain, 'by my...Florentine...behalf...Mary of...Scots.'

Ridolfi, Walsingham jeers to Beale. This would be irrefutable written evidence. 'Where? Where are they – you had no such papers at Portsmouth upon capture?' Walsingham presses.

'Burned.'

'Who to? Who was the intended?' Walsingham excitedly asks, Titus taking this as a cue to retighten the ropes. Bailly arches his entire body up in agonising response.

'Mary...from Ridolfi ...tis all I know.'

'Jar him.' Walsingham says to Titus. The burly bear wrestler lodges a long wooden rod between two cogs, jamming the rack's ropes tight where they are, fixing Bailly in a permanent state of creaking rigidity.

Walsingham encourages Beale and Nevon out of the basement. His plan, he tells them quietly upstairs, is to leave Bailly to dwell on his answers. He will then re-ask the questions and do the same again and again until he falters in his exact response. Beale sighs, they were in for a long evening and night. Not, Walsingham mutters, as long as their prisoner was in for.

'What of screaming?' Titus asks. 'Would Nightswatchmen or Parish Constables not become alerted?'

'Thanks to Beale's artful economies, they could be comforted in my employ.' Walsingham says, motioning them to return downstairs. 'These several moments will feel like days to his rupturing skin.'

'But the children? The household?' Titus says concerned.

Beale chucks him a small ball of thick string. 'For the mouth.' He glibly says, turning to Walsingham, 'Of course, Ridolfi writing to Mary does not implicate her in the plots.' Walsingham gratingly understands this to be true as they return silently to the basement.

Titus was right to be concerned, Charles Bailly or no man could endure pains beheld from the rack. Walsingham only had to revisit his questions once before the torture satisfied the responses.

Walsingham knew it was pointless to pursue whether Mary had indeed entrusted ciphers to Ridolfi. Yes, it made sense – he was a powerful man with the Vatican's ear and a stunning network of Catholic connections running through Europe into the veins of London. However, proving Mary's active involvement was now almost impossible. She would not risk her life and Catholics would not let her be implicated. Besides, what had Bailly himself said, albeit stutteringly – "by my Florentine man on behalf of good Queen Mary of the Scots." On behalf of is just not the same as saying she willed it to be so. Maybe they were a thousand miles from implicating Mary by proof at law, but they were stepping closer to uncovering the role of the dangerous Brotherhood.

Walsingham breathes deeply through his chest, he was not just seeing ghosts in the dark.

The interrogation had made clear Bailly was a middleman and did not know if the plan was to bring five or ten thousand men, neither did he know if it was to be Harwich or Portsmouth through which the foreign Catholic forces would enter with Fernando Alvarez de Toledo, the 3rd Duke of Alba. It did not matter. Bailly had stunningly implicated Ridolfi and also the Pope. Walsingham and Beale were silently satisfied a Catholic plot was discovered.

Thinking aloud to Beale, Walsingham pressed the issue of whether the plot were to succeed who would Mary marry? Surely not Howard, or Essex? What if Elizabeth, God forbid it in an eternity, was killed?

They racked Bailly some more to see if there were answers. Even after hearing his collar bone snap the man did not surrender any more. Angry, Walsingham dismisses Beale and Nevon for the night and looks at Bailly, scorning him, 'You will stay as you are in the hope you see the error of your delay.' Then he stuffs the knotted rope the size of an apple in his mouth and shuts him in the darkness.

Sitting in his study with the familiar candle glow slanting and swaying on the wall, he held no remorse for the Catholic traitor in his basement, limbs tearing and weakening by the minute. Bailly had openly confessed to willing his Queen dead, hoping to return this country to a Catholic heresy and perhaps plunging it into a Civil war that might rip families apart – from which England may never recover. What, therefore, were a few torn limbs of an incendiary scandalmonger like Bailly? No, Walsingham thought, he would have no trouble sleeping tonight. Bones, he smiles in wonder to himself, nestling to sleep, really do snap.

Two floors below, through a wet and sinewy ball of rope, frustration blows the stringed knot in his mouth. Please, he begged from drying throat, I will comply, whatever you need to know. He could hear his own sounds and knew they made no noise but he had to keep trying for the torment of living beyond the night was beyond capable thought.

The following morning, Titus, Beale and Walsingham enter the basement and see his ragged and puckered brown body like fallen autumn twigs. Brittle and empty of life, good for nothing more than the fire.

Nevon chucks the remnants of an ale jug over him, which shocks him awake. They remove the knot of string from his arid mouth, hearing his jaw click several times as he adjusts it. He reignites his pleas that he will tell them all they wish just to free him from this agony so he may again walk as any man might.

Walsingham soothes him with a wet woollen swab as Titus gently rounds the rack's pressure to enliven once more the torment in his bones.

'You know the secrecies I desire.' Walsingham whispers in his ear, dampening his forehead, perplexing Bailly of his real intentions as the pain intensifies in his wrists, shoulders and knees.

'I swear on all that I believe and that which may divide us, I know not names...the Brotherhood is of one sure abode.' Bailly says, after many painful stuttering attempts.

'Yes...' Walsingham reassuringly encourages, as a midwife might to the woman in-between screams and the push. '...we are listening.'

As Bailly describes the house near Temple Bar where Walsingham and Beale had been near to very recently, they knew it made sense. An area of stronghold for the Brotherhood, it also sickened and maddened them to a frenzy that it was right under their noses. What else had they missed? Walsingham felt the noose tightening around them as time slips away. What Charles Bailly then says between the tears of repent alarms beyond any had thought possible.

'What is started will begin.' Bailly warns hauntingly. He then falls unconscious.

'How do I dispose of him m'lords?' Titus asks, looking at the black and blue body of Bailly, redundant meat.

Beale, sickened by Bailly's admissions, spikily says, 'I have pig farmer acquaintances that will rid him of his entrails in minutes.'

'I'll break his neck then.' Titus says, cracking his knuckles in readiness.

'No.' Walsingham's voice is soft, as he looks to them both, 'We do not kill to feel safe. He returns to the Marshalsea. There is no value in his death.'

IX

𝕤𝕠𝕔𝕣

With youthful exhilaration, Beale leads Walsingham out of Seething Lane when they suddenly see the bedraggled, sobbing, girl limp towards them.

Frances.

She falls into her father's arms and wails deeply – relief, exhaustion and fear.

Walsingham cannot help but think every time he leaves the house there is melancholy – life was never so feverish at the Kent estates or while Lyme Regis' ambitionless MP.

Her fatigue musters no explanation, 'May you and the Lord Jesus forgive me.' Frances manages. Overwrought, her head boils to an unbearable heat, eyes give way, and she faints. The two men manage to catch and easily prop her up. Walsingham looks about as he ushers them inside and then to her room.

Within minutes she awakes from her bed, seeing her father's soft brown eyes studying her flushed face. She cannot understand why he smiles so lovingly when she has so much hate for herself.

'Father…' She stutters before her dry throat scratches away whatever was coming next.

'Will a wet cold swab suffice, sir?' Beale asks, handing his master the rag.

'Thank you Robbie.' He dabs his daughter's head with it. Within moments he could turn from razor sharp interrogator to linen soft coddler. Frances hungrily grabs it and wrings the liquid down into her throat, the instant relief causes her to exhale in gushes.

'Mother?' She asks in a panic.

'Your mother is close by.' Walsingham says trying to sooth her head and body back onto the stuffed straw mattress to lay still awhile. This is not what she means and her perplexed worry prompts him with quiet firmness to say, 'Rest Frances.'

She could not understand his calm. 'I am disgraced, my lord.'

'Never. You are safe now. Worry not my blessed one.'

Always so reasonable. Her heart was twisting inside. Yes, this made her a fortunate girl, she knew that – what fathers of other girls did unto them for errant behaviour was almost unspeakable. Her friend Mercy once had a black eye and could not sit down for two days for the flanking her perch had taken from her father's broom. He had never once struck them, she thinks, as she studies the firm moustache and long ears that give rise to his forgiving smile. Yes, the tours of the execution sites were fear enough, she supposed. It was mother whom he left the administering of errors to and Ursula was not shy of using the latch on her. The old dog lead that was now used to keep the kitchen window shutter ajar doubling as a tool to swipe backsides of little girls who were remiss in their manners.

'Papa tis all my fault.'

'Rest, Frances. I insist.'

In a half state of exhaustion and frustration, the adventurous nine-year-old waved her hand at him to be quiet. 'I should not have done it. Such mistake, such error – can it ever be righted? Will I be forgiven in the eyes of the Lord?' She says blurrily.

This amends his attention. 'What do you mean? What is it you think you have done?' Walsingham asks in almost convincing calm.

Tears begin to leak and she could only mumble all the names and events of things gone wrong over the past months – Edith attacked, Stimpson dead, her own father's humiliation at the Queen's pleasure, Beale's abduction; oh the sorrow, oh the sin, she wails...all she alone must pay for. Walsingham makes no sense to it, between the inaudible, breathless cries. 'And now this.' She heaves noisily from her throat.

'What?' Asking without his usual deference to patience.

'I followed him.'

'Who?'

'Your friend.' She explains, going on to recount where she had seen them and where she followed them to, describing both men with such detail Beale thought she must be looking at a portrait.

'Walter Williams, Thomas Smythe...' Beale says markedly and sits at the end of the bed, then quickly stands again as the anger rages through him. He checks for his blade. 'That bastard has long enough dined with the Devil and now he must pay.'

Walsingham does not rise quick enough to confront him from leaving as Frances snatches at his arm, dragging him back momentarily.

'Take me to mother for the latch, I must account for my sins.' She begs. By the time Walsingham moves from her it is all he can do to hear the front door slam so hard it rebounds out of its bolt and swings back open. He must stop Beale before his youthful blunders plunge them both into a mess even he cannot talk them out of.

* *

Racing through Paternoster Row, he barges into the Ink and Quill tavern so quick he fails to see the toothless Versifier singing his same old songs, who had momentarily stopped in panic on seeming him. Beale cannot find Walter in any of the darkened den's corners. He is furious, betrayals are worsened by being made fool of. Where else might he be? The Rose tavern in Southwark, across the water, maybe – being the only place where plays are performed...or at Temple Bar where they had seen him mingling with so many Catholics. Yes, there. His impatience would need a horse.

Paying the barkeep sixpence too much for the lease of a horse, he tugs the reins tightly, veering out of the small cramped stable yard. He gets the animal racing as quickly as it will let him through the throngs of people, buoyed on by the jabbering of pamphleteers and their scandal sheets, 'Rebellious forces uncovered in the north. Armed uprising threatens to reignite the Northern Rebellions. Government to dispatch edict to all Noble Houses: Posse Comitatus.' Robbie Beale angrily kicks the horse.

Within minutes he is at Temple Bar, the wooden scaffold again has snoring from inside. He has not the time, and too much fury, to deal with these miscreants and sits upon the horse near to where he and Walsingham stood, looking to the churches, peaceful and bold with their oak doors closed. No sign of the traitor. About to kick the horse on, out of the corner of his eye, a feather flickers above the small crowd: the plume of a peacock. It is him, the Foreigner...strolling with Ugly...without thinking twice he exhorts the horse into a violent canter.

Ugly is the first to see him and does not have time to think as the thudding beast bounds rapidly at them. Carters and peddlars scatter and Foreigner leaps out of the way, but Ugly makes a poor choice in trying to duck the animal, the horse rises up and pelts him with its hooves. Beale expertly circles his left leg round, spins off, grabs Ugly with both hands and rams his forehead into the man's nose, channelling anger from a thousand fishwife slaps. Blood instantly gushes down over Ugly's mouth and neck, as he crumples, disorientated, to the wet floor. Turning to Foreigner, stunned that Beale's iron head has rendered his hideous companion unsightlier, he rethinks advancing on him. When Beale gets out his Grosschedel with a snarling face springing towards him, Foreigner scrambles backwards over a spilled cart, hoping for respite, the smaller man bears closer down on him. Beale lunges with such force in his shoulders that he barges the man backwards into the wall, now clutching his neck and priming the needle-sharp blade under Foreigner's armpit.

'Where's Walter Williams?' Beale hisses. 'Tell me where he is you open-arsed vessel before I slice off your arm like the pond pike you are.' Beale pierces the embroidered leather garment and Foreigner can feel his soft skin prick under the armpit. He knows any shillyshally here would render him without use of an arm.

'Northumberland House.' Foreigner concedes. Beale lets him slowly go, then thunder cracks him with the pommel of his blade, collapsing him to the floor, his peacock hat falling over his face, little dignity in his moment of shame. He looks to his former abductors, wrinkled wastrels on the floor, cursing them, climbs back on the horse and hurries to the place they took him, the Earl of Northumberland's former residence. Evidently, a Catholic hideaway.

Arriving near the Aeldgate, he dismounts and does not even bother to tie up the horse. Emboldened by his demolition of the two men, he draws his blade and kicks at the door with the bottom of his foot, not even announcing himself. It swings noisily open, rattling the cabinet next to it, the pewter plates clattering onto the floor. He is announced now. Kitchenhand dashes in and drops her basket of bread.

'Where are they?' He shouts at her – though he has no idea who he was looking for, just that he wanted Walter. Kitchenhand panics and flees. He remembers he was in a basement after his capture, so begins searching. He hears a voice shouting from another room.

'What's the commotion there?'

Beale runs to its origin and there, at the other end of a grand gallery is Walter, sat with another man concealed from his view. Beale moves around the long table. Poised for retribution and his blade guiding the way, 'My guts may spill here this night, I shall have satisfaction and commit your blood to a traitor's death.' He flairs.

'Robert...'

Williams lips did not move. The man sat and concealed in the chair stands and faces him.

Walsingham.

Immobilised. No, it cannot be. Beale stops, his blade nearly slipping from his grasp. Astonished and stunned into silence, he can only look to his master, the betrayal too fanciful and despicable to be of this world. Beale cannot put all this together – was this some ruse, some plot within a plot, did Francis think him a traitor and he was on the outside? – Is that why he had smirked when he had joked "Double Agent?" No, and a thousand times no, it cannot be.

His face must say it all as Walsingham moves in-between both men, unsure what they will end up doing.

Beale feels his blade falling from his fumbling fingers and he staggers slightly as he moves to regrip it. Both Williams and Walsingham mistake this for him readying to thrust so Walter draws a sword hanging on the back of a chair. Walsingham holds both arms out between them as if to suggest either would have to go through him first. The blood circle suddenly very real and present.

'By accident of action, by months of betrayal,' Beale snarls, 'we are where we are because of Walter.' His scorn is turned towards Walsingham – 'You would stand by this man?' He fumes, uncaring of manners or respectful station.

'I understand your bane and distress, Robbie... Walter is for our cause.'

Beale cannot chew this sinewy thought, shouting, 'Be that shard born incontinent harlot that spawned his lies, I shall not let mine ears rest upon his mistruths.' Then turns to Walter as his voice booms louder, 'What mysticisms have you concocted and fed him to think so unseeingly? How can you be of our cause?'

Williams has taken the insults and insinuations well, which unsettles Beale, who only sees Walsingham is looking at the floor.

'It is I that have caused these treacheries.' His mentor, father figure and hero says quietly.

'What sayeth here?' Beale asks impatiently.

'All this while, Walter has been under my purview.' Walsingham confesses.

'All this…Edith…the assaults…me?' He chokes on his words. Then realises with horror – 'And…Stimpson?'

'No.' Walsingham firmly says. 'Not of his invention.'

'Is that what he says.' Beale leers at Walter.

Finally Walter snaps, those Plantagenet lookalikes coming furiously to life in his hectic eyes – 'I shall sit and suffer your tantrums as you orientate yourself with how far we have penetrated the treacheries in Her Majesty's government, though I shall not let you accuse me of murdering a good man.'

Beale spins away, whacking a bowl to the wall, unable to look at either of them for a good while. It was empty and takes several long moments to stop spinning on the floor. He finds a stool and buries his head into his hands, massaging his eyes and snorting air through the fingers. Neither Francis nor Walter move. Is the reason he is so upset because he has been so utterly fooled – or is it because Walsingham did not let him into the deception? Tormented, he turns to them, saying, 'Well, you had me swindled.' He fills a carved wooden beaker with whatever ale was left on a table near him and glugs it down with carelessness.

Walsingham feels he should speak. 'I and I alone could be the only one to know. It was not about trust, just surety. We have set our traps, Robbie: the pamphlets; the court riders North by now; Blythe and Herle to soon harry the foreign supply ships. You and I have set these traps and Walter was yet one more masterful stroke, subverting the seditions that threaten our very existence.' Walsingham says, before sitting on a bench opposite him. Williams does not intercede in their private moment, so quietly and subtly replaces his sword into its scabbard. Walsingham looks intently across to Robbie, then says, 'My secrecies scuppered by my own daughter and the passionate, loyal, zeal of my kin, trustee and whom I proudly name my progeny.'

The compliment warms Robert Beale's chest, oh to be called his son, and he wryly huffs a smile, shaking his head at the never-ending cunning of his master. Then a thought snatches his love and he jerks up, 'You know then?'

'Know what?'

'From whom deceits and treasons are borne within the Council? – The vile betrayers of the Queen?'

'Aye.' Says Walsingham irrefutably. 'And so, we can all now finally act.'

ഇ൬

PART THREE

King Death

May 1570 – June 1572

ഇ൬

I

Venus – East London

21st May 1570

ॐ

Dark blue with an icy wind flecking up, the Thames at night feels mystical to Essigia, as if he were peering into the water cauldron of the ancient Gods. At their mercy stands just a man, humble whoremaster, he thought doomily, the waters swirling with portent of dangerous times ahead. With the river reeling underneath and around the Venus, he looks up from the halfdeck to the old unused crow's nest on the mizzen mast and imagines the storms She must have endured, the new horizons doubtless seen by excited crews past. Waiting for his Gems to finish off their last benefactors, anticipating they were not long from their own fun to commence this night, maybe cards or the dice game nine men's morris to wager bets, laughs and the best mead or Porto wine.

Then that gut gnawing sound that might put pay to such anticipations – the gangplank creaking under yet another horny bastard's filthy boots.

'Try again tomorrow, your lusts must wait a night.' Essigia says without looking up. Alack – the boots keep coming. 'Come back tomorrow.' He says firmly, looking up to see just what milk-headed dolt was prone to deafness of ear or thought. It was the Florentine merchant, or banker – or whatever Beale had said he was – still walking up, towards him. Roberto D'Ridolfi was without his hallmark ostrich feather hat, merely plain and dim in his subdued dress, all black breaches and shaded jerkin.

'Dark clothes for a dark purpose?' Essigia playfully asks, about to turn his tone to emanate disappointment that the poor fellow might have to get his balls wet elsewhere, when Ridolfi suddenly grabs him by the throat and pushes him past the mizzen mast to the wooden rails at the boat's edge, tipping him threateningly overboard towards the water. 'What...what ails you, sirrah?' Essigia manages to rasp through his tightly gripped neck clamping his tongue, he could smell citrus, olives and salt, maybe what he had eaten for supper but it could just be the infusion of his body entire, for his sweat was thick in parts.

'The curse that night – what was its purpose? I know you put a curse on my eyes, for I could not see; my mouth, for I was yet speaking ill truths. Why?' Ridolfi growls desperately into his ear. He had put this all together within the last few days: a fellow Brotherhood had been attacked, his own cypher carrier had been intercepted, interrogated and given what secrets away only the Holy Madonna knows. Then there was his – the Pope's – fortune to worry about, if that was discovered and seized his hopes and plans for an invading army and the offer to Mary Queen of Scots a suitable dowry for her husband would all be gone. Leaving him only his rotten old merchant boat full of soured olives from Sicily. No, something was wrong and it stemmed from his night of forgotten lusts with that merkined whore Hannah. He would have an answer from this pox of a pimp if he had to squeeze it from him. Sweat seeps through his leather jerkin as he demands, 'What wizard are you? Nay, what witch of Satan do you serve?' Essigia's cowering face emboldens him to press, 'Do you compact the Devil?'

Despite trembling, Essigia knows exactly to what night he was referring to, and how Hannah had fed him with a kiss of the poultice. Asserting witchcraft is dangerously serious – was it nothing more than a clever blend of herbs? He himself had certainly not felt witched that day with his Gems in Richmond woods when he was given a keen sense of the concoction's potency.

Ridolfi clasped harder with his big clay-brown hand and Essigia's slender neck contracted tighter.

'It was a wise woman...' Essigia gurgles. Ridolfi slenderly relents, so he can say easier, 'I know not her name, oft Cheapside, or Mynchen Lane, selling her remedies and pomanders.' He was not ready to give up Walsingham's servant Beale just yet.

In frustration, Ridolfi growls and recontracts Essigia's neck, this nonsense will not avow him of his mounting problems. No, he should rid himself of this here dreadful link to being uncovered.

'I know your loyalties.' Ridolfi murmurs, approachingly, near licking his ear he is so close. 'Your betrayals sewing lies in the ears of servants to Her Majesty's government.'

Essigia has never been a liar but knows whatever he says now will not disabuse his aggressor of that notion this night. He wonders if the Thames will be his grave or he was to be merely draped in death over the sidearm. Then he sees a friendly face from the deck below and distantly half smiles.

Not waiting for a response or denial and affronted by the gall of this pimp to now smirk at him, Ridolfi drives a dagger under Essigia's chin with a dreadful shlunk sound, it rips up through his jaw to the back of his throat. Blood fills the whoremaster's mouth and floods over his white doublet. He looks down at himself, a vomit stain from hell. Reflexing, he grips Ridolfi's arms, the look from his beseeching eyes 'why?'

Ridolfi returns it with stone cold intent, these piercing brown eyes pointedly gazing between a sharp-edged nose with beads of sweat dripping onto piercing black bristles. Essigia realises this will be the last sight he beholds on this mortal absurdity he has called an existence. He clucks his last gasps, ankles slipping underneath him, he wants to say how cruel this life has been: abandoned he was coming into this world and alone he will be leaving it. There is no time and he thuds onto the half deck, lolling against the ratline ropes. Dead.

Ridolfi ogles this evening's accomplishment, suddenly startled by a scream that comes from beyond.

Rhy, just finished with a benefactor, had delicately emerged onto the main deck just below Ridolfi leering over Essigia. Such was her yowl she cannot scream again and just gasps from deep inside, looking at his body crumpling against the deck and ropes. Spasming in shock, a little semen slides down the inside of her thigh, her body ridding all evils, her heart feeling like it has stopped pumping.

It takes Ridolfi too long to decide whether he should run this wench through too, as the other Gems now surface from their depraved enterprises and see Rhy transfixed in horror, there is no other option. He runs from the brothel boat Venus, leaving the abomination he has committed for someone else to scrub clean, comforted the Holy Madonna will forgive him.

* *

Whitehall – two days later

As morning rose, Bourne, his little terrier, was absent from his cot and of no comfort as he had tried to sleep. Normally the dog's tiny heartbeat was a salve to his senses, enabling him to rest unmolested by the loneliness night brings to a man who is never alone. This left him only to dream of his dog, and since dreaming of playing with one's dog was considered a good sign in these uncertain times he still should have woken happy. However, he had not.

In his private quarters near to the Queen's chambers, Cecil changed from his sleeping smock into his robes of state. Deciding against the fox fur, he deemed the ermine sleeker, more regal. It was going to be a serious morning after all. Not that the outfit made the man, he knew, it would save him introducing and reiterating just how important this Privy Council conference was.

The Queen's First Minister looked about his legs for Bourne swirling yappily around as he would normally whenever his master arose. Instead, the terrier was coiled underneath his cot, the fine woven linen quilt ruffled and drooped onto the floor, and from where the dog hid behind. Asking Bourne what's the matter would have ordinarily yipped a response followed closely by it jumping out and dancing at his master's leg. Not today. Cecil could not but help wonder if his four-legged companion could also sense the rumours. Dogs were considered almost as decent scryers as the likes of Dr John Dee and a keen sense of foreboding. Puzzled, he finally bent to the floor and peered under the bed. There was only doom in the poor dog's eyes.

'Do you know it too?' He asks gently. No response emitted. Cecil nods in agreement at how insufferably vexing the recent news may be. He and the dog stare at each other from the floor. What scrotum-mangling timing it all was – just as he was moving forward with balancing the exchequer through clever new taxes on wool exports, developing strategic naval dockyard improvements and compiling a more reliable branch of intelligences promising to really bear fruit. He could be forgiven for thinking, at last, he was finally to have the resources to keep Her Majesty and the realm safe. Alack, as he had once said to his son, little Robert, cruel uncertainties have a way to bind men's hopes. His ambitions for the realm could be scuppered in one turning of the wind. Looking towards his single small window, London was eerily quiet. Had his little terrier Bourne really heralded these omens? Cecil looks intently to the dog, its eyes shining brightly, a sign it was well in its humours, could the cowering animal be foretelling disaster? Cecil goes with his instinct and feels the unnerving thoughts prod him too.

'Messenger?' He shouts beyond his door, down one of the long galleries. A young court page comes running into the room, bowing, confused by the venerable man on his hands and knees, as Cecil looks up and asks, 'Did you write Walsingham of his invite to attend the Privy Council this morningtide?'

'Who, my lord?'

He scrambles to his feet. 'Francis Walsingham.' Cecil says impatiently.

'The former lawyer's clerk? The...Member of Parliament for...?' Messenger, confused, attempts to confirm.

'Yes, yes, he of Lyme Regis, residing at Seething Lane. Well?'

'I thought it an inaccuracy, my lord. An error of judgement, hand and scribe that no low clerk of government doth attend...' He stops talking, seeing Cecil's nostrils flaring. Page realises the fault is all his own.

'Correct the error. As you journey, take precaution lest the terror strike you.'

Page bows. 'Thank you, my lord.' Humbled by Cecil's care.

'Go.' Cecil roars.

Page spins out so quickly he looks like a flapping duck.

* *

'Eracs ton kcatta. Lla ngierof spihs ni eht htron.' Walsingham says as Edmund Blythe hugs into the man he rescued seventeen years ago. Despite their fondness, they are conscious of prying eyes, and ears. 'Yawa erofeb eht rorret sekrits uoy.'

'Aye, the terror.' Blythe sombrely slips back into English as it should be spoken. 'For God's sake stay safe.' He says to Walsingham as he climbs aboard his boat and commands the crew to ready sail. Looking lamentably over London, he imagines if he will ever behold it again.

Herle's new ship is not far from him, already tacking into the wind, will the piggish thoroughgoing captain know his place on this voyage's mission, he wonders.

As Blythe's vessel slips from the edge, Walsingham looks about the wharf, clattering with muddled carts and angry stevedores. Panic brews, he observes: the rumours are spreading fast.

* *

Approaching the Privy Council Chamber and seeing how smug Smythe is, oddly makes him relaxed. Predictably not looking up, Smythe keeps him waiting for his permission to pass. Knowing how sore this must make the arrogant aspirant, Smythe continues to pretend he is busy, making the upstart wait as long as he can. Walsingham lets him enjoy his game, playing along with a cough. Of course, there is no response, so he does it again.

'I am not permitted to let you in, lest you take a cough, tickling throat or the bloody flux near Her Majesty's presence.' The Privy Council Chamber Clerk says airily and with an immovable grudge in his voice. Walsingham knows his smart interplay will not thaw the ice here so merely takes from his hidden side pocket a small journal the size of a playing card and with a thinned piece of charcoal, licks its nib and begins writing. Smythe's game suddenly unravelling as he sees Walsingham's poise in attending these notes.

'For precision's sake, affirm if you please what you said – "I am not permitted to let you in, lest…?"' Walsingham cues him to finish the quote. When Smythe looks properly up and realises he maybe recording this for some kind of judicial posterity, his large gait suddenly shrivels, unnerved by where this snake in the grass' jottings could render him.

'What notes there?' He flaps delicately, flummoxing a tone of lacking care with feigned interest.

'Our Lord Cecil has asked me to report any suppressers to truth.' Walsingham says pointedly, looking right through the man's shifting eyes. Smythe can now only fall upon the one remaining option that this new situation allows: he must stand unceremoniously to one side. Not even looking at his tormentor as he saunters slowly past.

Walsingham feels his stomach churn for the first time since finding out he was summoned as he knocks and enters. Dudley is the first face he sees, smiling at him, comforting his uncertainty. There are several he has not seen before and neither recognises them from portraits in the few noble houses he has visited or the seldom government dwellings he has worked. Essex, Howard, Ludlow and Cecil he does know, their sombreness disconcerting and guarded, like hunters that could easily turn prey.

As Cecil begins, Walsingham slides into the background near a cabinet where parchment and quills are stored. There is travesty across the land, Cecil begins telling them, tired and worn, it seems. 'We are agonised by rumours, perils, plots and conspiracies, a tragedy of calamities that only Satan could invent.' He laments. Walsingham's nerves increasing, knowing that at any moment Cecil could call upon him to explain these threats. He does not, instead continuing in his reserved tone, telling them that, 'For Her Majesty's safety of person, she will away to Windsor until it is secure to resume government business.' Cecil was looking at every man whilst he told them all this. Odd, Walsingham felt, that he would make so public the Queen's itinerary to a room whom some he had already proven, although not identified, could not be trusted. Perhaps he was dipping his toe in the water, fathoming reaction, looking for substantiations.

'Are we under attack?' Dudley asks, confused and concerned by Cecil's delivery.

'Yes.' Cecil says. There are gasps.

What? Who? When? Come the questions from several voices of concern in every part of the chamber.

'Plague is amongst us.' Cecil's trembling voice says. Anxiety and frightened susurrations burble amongst the serious and powerful men. 'There are not yet numbers of the afflicted, the daily toll has commenced.' Cecil warns.

'What will be our first actions?' Essex asks, having lived through more waves of the plague than any man in the small room.

Cecil is still calm, with growing strength in his voice. 'Very quietly but very quickly, you will all move out of the two cities. Parliament is nay in business and the rest shall await its fate.' Cecil says.

Walsingham's heart plummets, he can see all their hard work suddenly shut down with a definite clunk, just as the bells of St Mary-le-Bow strike the end of market, Cecil's tones ring the death knell to any progress his infant Secretariat was making – or is now ever likely to make in this sudden unknown future. Raising his concerns on it now in such a forum would quickly become as noxious as the buboes on the poor souls suffering the evil pestilence. He has to accept in one swing of Cecil's rhetoric axe he has sliced the head from his ability to track this beast from the shadows.

Walsingham finds a stool; he has to sit, half putting his head in his hands, as many of the men sat were also doing. He is opposite Thomas Howard, the Duke of Norfolk. All he can think of is John Warne's burning body screeching out to him. No solace in the sadness of worse times.

Thomas Smythe furtively enters, whispers something into Essex's ear, which he seems to care not for, and then he hands a note to Howard, with the efficiency of an all doing but never seeing court official, leaving as quickly as a mole burrowing back underground.

Except Walsingham does notice. He tries to see if there are giveaway markings on the seal, it is difficult to read the upside down untidy scrawlings of another man, but thanks to his mastery of rehctub, he can. Howard has already planned a retreat to his homestead in the east.

Nothing has been said in the room for several moments and there is a miserable quiet.

'What of these pamphleteers and their spurious perjuries – claiming "Rebellious forces in the north, armed uprising, Posse Comitatus?"' Howard says, his clenched fist resting on the Council's map of England.

'You cannot believe the truth from scandal sheets.' Cecil barks. If Walsingham was focusing, he would have smiled at his and Robbie's handywork, but he was drifting into melancholy and could only think how it felt as if he was once again letting that boy with scalded arm down again. Walsingham presses his top teeth subtly into his clenched fist to stop the anguish. Attend your senses to the talk of these powerful men, he rebukes himself, finally lifting his head and ears to their conversations.

'There is talk of reprisals on Catholics, these scandal sheets could lead to insurrection, rebellions across our land and civil war if there is no government to control from London.' Lord Essex says, a little too calm.

'Aye, tis true.' Ludlow says.

'Catholics are already being abducted.' Norfolk says. 'And tortured.'

Essex cannot contain his disgust, and neither can a third of the room as they cajole their upset from one to the other, tossing their vitriol in the air like hunting dogs playing with a dead fox. In the distracting din, Walsingham glances over to Cecil. He does not look directly back, perhaps choosing not to, or that he cannot.

'The Catholics in England...' Cecil's voice is oddly fractious and loud, dimming the room, and he clears his throat, a pause, which all feels to Walsingham as if he may not be entirely full of the conviction that he normally has. Worse, he can see the news he is about to deliver, makes him very uneasy – '...the Catholics in this country...are peacemakers...and the Queen recognises this.'

A third of the room clap.

Dudley is the first to find Walsingham's eyes. They share consternation: what on holy mother earth is he talking about?

Cecil does not look anywhere but at the map. As the self-congratulating clapping Catholic sympathisers continue, Walsingham looks at Cecil staring fixedly at the map, its borders, shires and coastline suddenly vulnerable, precarious and pathetic. He looks hopefully at the wise First Minister to say or do something, to give him hope all is not lost in his cause. As the room begins to settle, Cecil senses Walsingham's eyes and murmurs, so quietly, that no man could possibly hear him, *Some within your Privy Council cannot be trusted.*

It takes only one lip-reader in the room to receive the message. As crestfallen as he is, Walsingham now understands this is political, Cecil cannot afford to lose the Privy Council, especially in a National emergency. He has told them what they want to hear. For England's sake.

'What are we to do?' Comes a desperate voice, possibly Ludlow's, though Walsingham cannot be sure.

'Each and everyone of you,' Cecil announces, his eyes now finding Walsingham, 'will go to your estates or your constituencies, knowing the peace of the realm is secure and Her Majesty is in fine health.'

'And we give thanks. Aye.' Says Norfolk, the first time there is general agreement in the room. 'What of perfidies within this Council – your own agents and advisors, Protestant rabble rousers?' He sneers, lurking too long a gaze between Dudley and Walsingham. The room falls silent. Flicking and fluffing of the fire is all that can be heard.

Cecil creaks his chair as he slowly stands, saying, 'Religion should be peacemaker not kingmaker. Let no man be in doubt, there is unease and uncertainty across the land. What do you ask of me?' Cecil impassions, each and every soul in the room certain he addresses them directly. 'The Queen has given this realm liberties of religion. With the hearts and minds of men free to choose. The likes of which have never been seen before. The Dogmatists, the bigots and the zealots of this world, nay in Christendom's realm, will be sure to bring this to a calamitous collapse, such that more than one idea will only drive them to distraction and dissatisfaction, urging men to kill and be killed. Our role, in this Privy Council, and advisors herein, are bound by duty to stop that from happening. Your oaths and signatures countenance it. Let no man falter.'

'Ayes' roar around the room as if he has just ordered war, which, in Walsingham's mind, he had.

'Let not these Nicodemus deceive whom they serve.' Norfolk states, as if hurling an accusation without a name.

Walsingham stings on his stool. Nicodemus. He sees Warne and Robbie as a boy, again, in those unforgivable days of 1553. The Captain of the Guard, now the Duke of Norfolk, Thomas Howard, his Angel eyes with a Devil's grin. Him. Whether Norfolk had meant the insult at him or not, Walsingham had heard enough, utterly sickened by the demon from his past, flouting his arrogance and Catholic superiority in the Queen's Privy Council Chamber. He studies the cruel contours of his nemesis' face, now so completely convinced, from instinct alone, Norfolk is amidst the frenzy of evil plots against the Queen. Essex and Ludlow maybe too, but he has a realising glow brewing inside him as it all makes so much sense. But the Duke is a powerful man and so must withhold himself from blurting it out. Walsingham thinks how he could manoeuvre Howard into a trap, calming himself before speaking.

'Should thine Nicodemus not be issued a test, is this not what our Lord would beseech?' Walsingham loftily asks.

'Men of faith do not need tests from so baseless a mortal.' Norfolk deflects with the simpering disinterest of a yawning wolf.

'No, the law may require one.' Walsingham was improvising recklessly here. Howard and Essex look to Cecil as if to ask will you let this underling speak any more out of turn?

'What say you, Walsingham?' Dudley asks, saving Cecil the blushes of having to remonstrate Walsingham as well as look as if he takes his cue from Essex and Norfolk.

The entire chamber turn their heads towards the lowest ranking official, as the fire once again becomes the centre of sound.

Walsingham smirks, an opportunity, 'The Privy Council shall receive my written proposal.' He coolly bows his head to Cecil. It is cordially returned. Walsingham then sees Dudley subtly angling his head, doing the same. He knows by these understated looks alone, the actual declaration of war between Protestant and Catholics in England has just been renewed.

II

꒰ ꒱

Within four days of sailing, ill aware that London was shutting its government down and abandoning them to their own devices, Blythe and Herle had crept up the North Sea's opposing winds and were nearing the French supply ships at the Beak. Their commands from Walsingham committed to memory for fear any written missions be intercepted. They could only hope that their counterparts on land were just as prepared.

Lurking in the dark of night, they lap gently into an inlet, their two boats and two small crews a humble flotilla. A mission so rash they knew history would either record them as fearlessly brave or recklessly foolhardy, provided they even made it past posterity's fateful lance. Herle follows Blythe's lead although is not convinced they were at the agreed meeting point. Grumbling, he acknowledges it was a saving grace that they were early as waiting was now all they had.

The two boats were well within shouting distance of one another, they wisely decided to communicate by masked lantern. Herle openly questioned Blythe's decision to remain at the inlet. They must give at least two days to see if they would receive word to proceed. Impatient to explore the other inlets, Herle had continued to press the point, but always the message remained "Hold firm."

A whole night and day passed without change to any circumstance, including the squalling rain that happened upon them this entire time. Both crews gave small thanks for this though, as it not only gave them cover from the suspicion of any patrolling French ships, but also the opportunity to keep water stocks in good supply.

Checking the rainwater barrels, Herle restlessly questioned whether holding firm was the right course of action. They had to get amongst the enemy.

* *

Lynas Masterman was now familiar with the terrain, it not being three months gone since running his last errand for Francis Walsingham here. Unfortunately he could not rip too fast a pace on his horse as he travelled with Titus Nevon, a big man on a sufferingly small mare. Masterman jokes he who could wrestle bears is yet to wrestle the reins of a horse. By the time they had made their destination, they had lost nearly a day and could only hope their seaward convoy would patiently wait for the agreed signal.

Thankfully it had not taken Masterman long to spread his packet of pamphlets amongst his brethren Rider messengers in the North. From as far south as the Wolds of Lincolnshire, west to Wath-upon-Dearne and north up to Thirsk near the Moors, Walsingham's message of misinformation would spread quickly. Through this huge swathe of land with its noble houses, Catholic strongholds, ale house lofts and back street lodging rooms, it was filled with the news of "Rebellious forces uncovered in the north. Armed uprising threatens to reignite the Northern Rebellions. Government to dispatch edict to all Noble Houses: Posse Comitatus." Rumours accompanying this, care of Walsingham, were a force of over ten thousand armed men marching

North to subdue another Catholic uprising. So swift and seemingly true were these misdirected messages that not one of the Riders were questioned of it and should the hoax be uncovered, Masterman and Nevon would long be disappeared and none of the Northern Riders could be blamed, easily reinstated with trust.

It was not until Masterman and Nevon reached the armed camp he uncovered recently that they would realise any of these endeavours had been successful. As they approach the thick tree-lined precipice, there were no sight or sounds to give a clue that this news had indeed reached the camp. They cautiously get off their horses.

Masterman easily remembers his route through the undergrowth, avoiding the brambles once more, as they creep up under the trees to the brow of the hill, then crawl on their bellies until they see, with failing hearts, the distant campfires still like a giant fire left to dwindle in the dark. The immense force had not grown in size, nor had shrunk in all these weeks, as far as Masterman could tell. How patient the soldiers were, Masterman admires to Titus, ridding himself of a particularly awkward and tacky vine.

'Aye.' Says the wrestler of bears. ''Tis but perfect hiding place in depths of this here valley.' He looks eastwards to the beak shaped inlet to the North Sea. 'Were those ships there on your journey last?'

'Nay, how many do you perceive?'

'No less than five.' Titus says.

'Aye, tis seven.' Masterman says, squinting his left eye, then looking back to the camp. Now worrying the plan was failing at its inception. 'I see no movement to disperse the camp, we need to send word to Blythe to begin his action.' They wriggle back down under the canopy of trees. Lynas holds Titus' arm and they both stop. The big man knows not to say anything though cannot see any clue of what the danger might be. Lynas peers down to the footing of the hill where the horses are tied and can still see them, chewing happily through the dark silhouettes of trees, he is clearly unnerved by something and continues to glance about. Titus senses nothing. It takes a few minutes before Lynas is happy for them to continue.

'You as rattled as a monkjack.' Nevon whispers.

'Perhaps, caution serves me well.' He smiles.

Stroking their horses there was no sense they had been interfered with nor that anyone was watching. The quicker they galloped away the better. Soon enough they were thundering down through meadows and over hedgerows until they reached the shoreline on a small, slanting cliff down to the shore, looking out to the North Sea.

They could see the broadsides of the two boats, pointing Northwards, their own signal that all was well. Thankfully Titus' tinderbox had not got damp on their voyage and he was able to quickly light Lynas' lantern. Masterman used his glove to half conceal the lantern, beaming the message straight to Blythe and Herle's boats. Five long beams signalling to proceed, as agreed.

Neither men heard another horse and rider come to a stop in the dunes below.

* *

Herle was inspecting the water barrels brought on top deck to catch rainwater as their stocks had turned thick green, some land lubber not cleaning them properly after the last voyage. Storms from the previous day had yielded water plenty enough for two days at least with comfortable rations, maybe five. He had a cupful and it tasted sweet and sharp as if he had licked it from a bay leaf. Then as clear as the stars he saw a beam from the westerly shore, the signal had started. He concentrated hard. One, two, three, four...was it not supposed to be five? He carried on staring to its origination. Nothing. He waited. Something was wrong – or was it? He was certain it should have been five. Three was do not proceed, five was proceed. Should he count the first – or had that been just to get his attention, then you counted from there, in which case it <u>was</u> three. Had he missed the first, well then it was five. Herle screams to the heavens 'By Delilah's snatch and Samson's tongue – what have I seen?'

Blythe races up to his top deck amidships to see what the fuss was about. All he heard was shouting of some unholy oaths, Herle's angry voice. Their two boats had drifted closer together and were only fifty yards apart, but even at this range their converse had to be succinct or the detail would be lost in the mellow breeze between them, and they still did not know who was nearby to listen.

'Ho! The boat a-ho.' Blythe shouts over.

'A-ho.' Herle shouts back.

'Three or five?' Blythe asks.

'Four.'

'Four?'

'Aye.'

Blythe refuses to believe Herle is being awkward or even trying to sabotage. Instead, he rationalises he could have missed the first. It did not occur to him there was an introductory signal. 'We go.' He shouts. 'On my lead.' He was not to know it was actually the right decision, nor was he to know what perils lay on shore for the message giver.

Both boats dropped sail and kept close by one another as they steered into deeper waters.

* *

'Halloo?' The voice curiously rose from the shingly sand.

Masterman had just blinked the third beam with his lantern when he looks to Titus to see what this query was.

'Who goes there?' The voice urgently asks, and they can see its figure now running up towards them. Masterman blinks off another beam but the figure is within ten steps of them and he has to throw down the lantern, extinguishing its light.

'Two lost travellers and no more.' Masterman says, faking his distress. Titus looks to Lynas, give me the signal when to act and I shall piledrive this irksome fellow into the sand.

'What business here? Where be your journey's end?' Voice of the figure enquires.

'Raffkham point.' Lynas says quickly.

'Aye, I can perceive from your voice and thine livery you not being from these parts. I confess no knowledge of Raffkham point.' He says scratching his cheek, searching his memory. Lynas thinks it is time to silence this suffering fellow and is about to nod Titus into action when he hears him say, 'Maybe I should ask me entourage.'

Entourage – how many was his travelling company? Before he has time to unleash Titus' force to immobilise him, the man whistles distantwards and five men come running over.

'All be well Harry?' One of them asks.

'These gentlemen are lost on their way to Raffkham point.' Harry, the nosey voice from the dunes, says.

'No knowledge of that sayeth I.' One of them says. Lynas hears two swords slowly unsheathe from their scabbards.

'I ask again. What business here?' Harry demands, as his five companions slowly form a circle around Nevon and Masterman.

Nevon whispers to Masterman, 'Six men, two swords. I have this.'

'Who wants to know?' Masterman asks.

'And what purposes had you to leave your horses and creep through woodland dark, up at Raffleham point?' Harry ponders with an all-knowing smile. Lynas kicks himself at misreading an old boundary marker.

Masterman knows their game is up, having been watched since they had spied the camp. He has to unleash Titus so gives the giant a nod. The wrestler of bears lurches forward. Harry, suddenly daunted, steps back and the other five mistakenly prepare to set upon him. The two swordsmen move first, one gets there quicker and is parried back by Nevon's large leg lunging and kicking him in the chest just as he swings back his arm, flying him straight into the other swordsman. As they squabble their way up from the sandy floor, Titus grabs and flings their heads together and they fall back to the floor, eyes reeling. One of the remaining men feels brave and runs for Titus who shunts his palmed hand straight into his nose, bursting it open all over his face as he too crumples unconscious to the floor. This is enough for the remaining three to panic and run. Titus smells blood and runs, jumps and lands on two of their backs, forcing them onto the pebbles and he grabs each by their scalps and smacks their heads into stones until they no longer scream. Lynas has caught and wrestled Harry to the floor.

Titus strides over with death in his eyes. Harry blubs for mercy, but it is Lynas that thwarts Titus away.

'Not this one. He can answer for all these men.' Lynas says, so Titus picks him up and ties him to the back of their horse and gags him with his own hat.

Lynas looks, laughing, at Titus. 'I beg thee we shall forever be friends, lest I excite your temper.'

Titus heaves the remaining men in varied states of unconscious disorientation together and ties their hands behind their backs and then all their ankles too. 'This be tight enough for bear tethers t'will be good enough for ye cockwart.' He says, before looking out to sea, 'Do you think they got the correct signal?' All three men look out to the two boats, drifting towards the deeper swell.

'What signal?' Harry asks innocently. Titus cuffs him with the back of his hand and that is enough to force his quiet.

'We need to go back to the valley and see if it has all come together.' Lynas says, realising from the six men they have succumbed here that there is infinitely more danger for them all if they do not.

* *

It was not long after they eased away from their mooring in the covering inlet that they had to engage enemy ships. What had Walsingham said to him in London – scare. Not attack. Blythe was ready.

Since sheltering for the few nights at the inlet, they had removed all ensigns and emblems notifying they were English frigates. The crews knew this was risky because even if friendly ships stumble into them, they would not know it and would be well within their rights to either forcibly board or paralyse them at sea.

Both boats signalled to stock their cannon, of which each only had a pitiful ten aboard. If used effectively, though, they could still make a success of their mission. They were not attacking, but 'scaring' the French supply ships into thinking the pamphlets that Lynas had helped spread were indeed true – there were English ships preparing to ambush them and huge forces to encircle their land efforts. It was a giant ruse that Walsingham dreamt up, assuring them it had all the courage of a bull, and no less the same dull stupidity of such beast. Doubtless why it was more convincing, thought Blythe.

Within two hours of setting sail they were able to creep up abroadsides of the last French ship in its convoy and had positioned themselves in such a way it would have been difficult to tell if there were ten more ships beyond them in the dark. Blythe and Herle ordered their ships' cannon to be filled with empty balls – blanks – so that the intimidation was real but the attack was not. A technique that also cleverly avoided the technicality that if any of the ships had been fired on and hit then it would be an act of war. The French Commanding Officers could not very well return to their ports and declare the English had fired on them without so much as a splinter missing from their boats. Besides, Blythe and Herle were versed in maritime comity, which allows for "firing across the bows."

From the French rear-guard it sounded like several thunderstorms were converging on them all at once as the feigned attack began. Scrabbling up the ratline ropes to his crow's nest, the French lookout in the trailing boat could see a haze of smoke and yet another barrage of flame as more shots were fired headlong towards them from the two boats he could see. He ducks, puts on his leather gloves and slides down the rope to report what he had seen. His captain had already made a decision to tack into and out of the wind, in hope of avoiding such an onslaught and protect the remainder of the flotilla ahead of them. Pray God, he said to his pilot, they don't give chase.

Herle was the first to see the plan was working and knew that Blythe's decision to keep firing was the correct one, saving the French no option to turn and face them with their more than likely heavier firepower. Maybe the fisherman was a mariner after all.

The bluff works. Both captains stop firing after they could no longer see the rear-guard and set immediately to their logs to record the accomplishment.

* *

Masterman and Nevon return to the wooded precipice. Harry, their ashamed prisoner strapped unflatteringly over a horse, just coming to, unaware his indignity is complete by Titus deciding to drop the man's breeches and stick a daffodil in his anus.

They again creep up under the trees on their bellies and beheld a very different sight in the valley camp. Titus, this time avoiding the tacky ivy vines but catching his foot in some brambles did not see what Lynas could.

With an amazed exclamation, Lynas sees the panic of a near five-thousand-man army breaking camp. An hour earlier they had heard the sound of cannon at sea in a swathe of constant firing and were now beholding the French ships close to shore, near the armies. They had got word of the attacks they had endured and now, coupled with the news on the pamphlets, were dispersing rapidly. Panicking.

'We've done it.' Lynas excitedly tells Titus, who stops struggling against nature and buries his head in the foliage with sheer relief. He was five yards from seeing their mission come to fruition but would not witness it at all, instead wryly chuckles to have travelled all this way and not know the result. Still, Lynas' confirmation was joyous enough.

The two men shake hands.

They would not know for many months what effect their efforts would have, for plague was changing all men's destines in the South.

III

Scadbury Park – Kent estates

December 1570

༄

Rain, freezing and thick, flacks down upon the sodden farmstead. It had been a long time since the clean, refreshing rains of Spring and Summer had fallen. Now it was just the clag and stomp of cold driving rain trudging England's green into filth. With lifeless eyes he watches while Winter's misery drops like a pall of grief over him and the whole family.

Sat inside with nothing more than contemplations, Walsingham recalls the Summer now past and how, all those months ago, it had once again felt he had to flee his city in a bid to escape an evil clutch. His uncomfortable recollections no longer waited for night to haunt him. Plague, persecutions and powerlessness are what keeps him awake. Pinching his eyes he thinks over the last seven months.

London to Scadbury was a fifteen-mile journey that, with a cart packed full of Winter necessities, took almost two days to travel. A skilled single horseman could ride it in little over two hours, but the Walsinghams – Francis, Ursula, Frances, Mary, Edith and Robbie – did not have that luxury. Thank goodness they made it out before the May rains had clogged the eastern track. The only rejoicing to take from their dreadful circumstances.

Near seven months had now past as Walsingham feels the cold hard skin of his hands, recalling in this cold Winter how he had tried to reassure their collectively sad and uncertain faces in that late Spring sun all would be well at Scadbury. He knew he was doing what was best for his family, as well as following those orders from Cecil. As they had crossed London bridge all those months ago he also sensed that resting up from the plague on his Kent estates for an interminable time would render him impotent.

Looking at the icy rain flanking down on this miserable December day, he thinks back to leaving Whitehall immediately after Cecil's grand speech and the fever he had in his heart with suspicions about Norfolk. Turning into Seething Lane that long ago afternoon, he can still picture seeing Titus, Robbie and Lynas waiting for him outside his house. Their countenance never being what he would want to behold, he could see that now. Through apologetic and exasperated voices, they had yielded nothing in their thorough day and night search for Ridolfi.

'Seeped into the earth, nay the crevices of hell,' He remembers saying to Robbie as he took off his skull cap, rubbed his cropped hair and sat on the single step that enters the house. Sitting there, he had heard the busyness of Ursula's kitchen, from within, the cry of joy as his daughters' playfully screeched, Edith nagging them to tidy as they amuse themselves with blankets and cushions. Assemblance of normalness in his household that would quickly quieten. He remembered reflecting there and then what his dedication had become in setting up an intelligence secretariat to protect the Queen, the realm, his family – everything he held sacred....unravelling before his very eyes after that meeting with Cecil.

Now several months on, he was empty. Ridolfi disappeared. No clear connection to suspicions of Privy Councillors. Neither had several months' assuaged the death of two agents, Stimpson and Essigia. Nor the only link he had to the Brotherhood, sprawling crippled in the Marshalsea, his secrets wholly tortured out of him. Book of Secret Intelligences lain untouched in these desolate months.

His ideas and instigations were dying in a season of death. He was too numb to be angry.

At his last meeting with Cecil he had bluffed a plan to create a legal test of religion, goading the Duke of Norfolk with 'Nicodemus.' It now felt as if all his momentum had been lost. Heavenly creatures alone only knew what mischief and furthering of the Brotherhood was being caused by Howard, Essex or even that priss Ludlow. Unchecked without his small, though significant, spy network in operation. The menace could thrive and prosper. For the enemy never sleeps.

His only boon of self-congratulation and thanksgiving was that he had sent Nevon and Masterman with a mission before London locked itself down. Even as the Summer months throve into Harvest time, and when the wheat fields' crop had turned into hollow crispy stubs, word had still not yet come. The seclusion and confinement of the Queen and her government was as frustrating as it was disquieting. In fear of attracting the plague, Ursula had been tetchy and dismissed outside visitors as unnecessary for many months, excluding the farmhands from surrounding hovels and cottages to till their orchards and fields. Isolation imprisoned them like the unyielding rain does now.

The other Walsinghams were content enough. During the day, Robbie, Edith, Frances and Mary helped with chores around the farm and their manor house home. Ursula had brewed, pickled, salted, baked and cured all she could for fear of a long hard Winter. Walsingham managed to requisition one of the old servant's upstairs room to use as a study and spent some of his days locked away in there until it was black dark, when he could do his proper thinking.

Perhaps these were just the calmer months, he reflected. The soft lull before the deep plunge.

It was Mary that had unsettled and panicked them all when, one afternoon returning from the river collecting water, Ursula noticed swellings under her arms. Fiery red, and feeling warm to the touch, she frenetically tugged off her daughter's dress and petticoats confirming her worse fears: the poor girl's groin and behind her knees were swelled with the red evil. Buboes, those carbuncles of fire. Mary, always so obstinate or ignorant was not as availed by these as her mother, who insisted she rest up in bed, being sure this was the ailment advice any healer would heed.

Walsingham wrote immediately to William Bullein, his physician in London, asking him a great many questions of his daughter's concern, as well as how life fared in the two cities. He received a response that night, opening the letter after it was quickly dunked in vinegar.

Amongst his first advices, ensure she remain in bed alone and that the family should see fit to dab fresh urine onto the pustules, preferably the child's own, if she was of account to expel her liquids. Should the boils be of such discomfort that they need to be lanced, then do so only with a red-hot poker, not to be sliced with any such butchery knife or blade. Her parents appreciated his latest guidance, coming from London's ever-changing ideas in how to battle the pestilence. Ursula had tried other remedies such as boiling marigold flowers and eggs blown through the shell, making a rue for her to drink, which Mary kept in her belly. Unnerving them all, however, it neither made her better or worse. They had only one option: wait.

Bullein went on to answer Walsingham's other questions regarding the broader effects of the plague on Westminster and London. In his opinion, it was not to be as bad as the years 1563-4 when a near 20,000 had died. Though bad enough, the surge in deaths had not been too great, maybe less than five thousand. Nevertheless, Aldermen had commanded their Wards and Parish Constables to paint a blue cross on the doors of the afflicted, as well as an order to kill all wandering cats and dogs, lest they might carry such vileness. As Rhy might have said if she was yet to speak from her mourning of Essigia: slay the stray.

It was the sorrow in Bullein's final words, describing the panic in London, that had shaken Walsingham – *I met with wagons, cartes and horses full loden with young barnes for fear of the black pestilence. You will do well to remain where the Lord keeps you safe.*

Walsingham decided against a premature repatriation to Seething Lane, realising they would need to wait out the Winter in Kent's icy meadows.

During late Summer into Autumn, he had taken to walking his daughters, when Mary was well enough, along the blush green meadows of Scadbury all the way to Foots Cray, the village of his birthplace, further north. The entire area, he announced to the knackered girls, was the Walsingham seat in the grand old county of Kent. Frances tished and sighed at it being a "seat" – more trough or slop bucket, she quietly whispered to Mary who gave away a giggle. It was not as impressive as their Wednesday walks across Tower Hill, but at least there was no vile Stow to interrupt them and they had Papa once again all to themselves.

Then, one day, they heard the horse.

Trudging and lumbering along the track to their meadow, the sisters seeing the awful apparition. An old mule, dropping its head, they would later say, in disgrace, for the cargo it supported. Him. Frances angrily tugs Mary's arm to check she was seeing this unbelievable vision too. Her groan let the older sister know she had.

'Ah!' Rejoiced their father. 'Just on the sun's dial.' He had smiled down to his daughters, who followed with disgusted angry eyes the tired mule's journey towards them.

John Stow looked in good health with fresh eyes and shining teeth as he carefully dismounted the horse. Unfortunately, Frances thought, it did not buck. Before he spoke to their father, he bent to the girls, 'Miss Walsinghams. May I join you this morning?' Mistaking their shivering repulsion for cold, he went into a tiny leather knapsack and brought out two small –

'Marchpanes.' Both girls shrieked with delight. They had not seen sweet treats for many months. These marzipans were sculpted into the rampant white horse – Kent's county symbol. The sisters were genuinely aghast and managed thank yous before nibbling into the delightful delicacy, the tastes of almond, cloves, ginger and nutmeg whelming their mouths. The girls happily turned their backs on the two men, forgetting their hatred and the cold.

'Welcome friend.' Walsingham said.

'It is of comfort to me discovering you are all well.' Stow beams. 'I have given great consideration to your notion of "setting a trap" for the heretic traitors in the Privy Council's midst.' Stow urged them to talk away from the girls, before continuing, 'You will need to help me with the legislative idioms, for it should be acts of law, as contracts or charters cannot be enforceable in the event of moving to trials...and executions. My feeling principal is that we have something.'

Walsingham had stiffened in the cold, hunching his shoulders tightly inwards, 'The way I perceive it, we have two problems. There is prescient need to flush out the diehard Catholics, we need to keep check of them. Then, the increasing use of pamphleteers gives hearty voice to those criticising the government or, wickeder still, Her Majesty.'

'Aye, we will never rid this land of Catholics. Arguably, we nay want to encourage a police state to suppress them deeper underground, making your job yet harder to evolve the secretariat. As far as pamphleteers, printers or publishers, we do not want to suppress them either as they have proven useful for your purposes. We need only see the results from dispersing the North recently to appreciate that.' Stow folds his arms, hoping Walsingham has some suggestions.

'I worry not for my secretariat. That can regrow ever more resourceful. I am concerned Cecil, nay Her Majesty, will not want us to assume so much that we are making a law that pretends we make windows into souls of men. I agree we are not to be so brutal as to assume one man's faith is not as appropriate as another's.' Walsingham worries aloud. 'We need to forbid criticism of the monarchy, as an institution, not making it personal to Queen Elizabeth, neither must it appear as if she has had a temper tantrum, as Parliament may not pass such spitefulness. Certainly, in the interim, we must clarify and apprehend the plotters we know to exist and wish to usurp the Queen.'

'Could we encourage an oath or pledge to Her religion?'

'For every man in the country – the resource would be too demanding. Too costly. Perhaps there is a simpler way to catalogue men's faith and at the same time encourage the prosperity of the Queen's via media religious policy.' Walsingham brewing ideas again.

'A tax. No, a fine? The ambition is great.' Stow says, suddenly snapping his head to Walsingham.

'And the answer now stunningly simple.' Walsingham smiles.

'A recusancy fine for those not attending Her Majesty's services.'

'Have you a journal to scribe this wording?' Walsingham asks and Stow quickly makes for the leather panniers on his horse.

'Should be stated thus: Convicted for not repairing to some Church, chapel, or usual place of Common prayer to hear Divine Service there.' Walsingham was pleased with himself, almost forgetting how that feels.

'What of the criticisms of Her Majesty and her government?'

'The Monarchy.' Walsingham corrects. 'Simpler. Less personal. The office. A Treason act, forbidding the slanders and ill-rooted facts and mistruths against the Royal person or their device of government.' The two men look at each other knowing good work was underway.

After finishing the sweet treats, the succulent flavours dissipated from her mouth, Frances decides to renew her hatred of John Stow as she watches the two men continue to talk.

'This will, of course,' Stow says with smiling realisation, 'endear the offenders out in the open and make them vulnerable. We will strike from surprise.'

'Like the serpent.' Walsingham absently observes, thinking of the Queen.

'What was that?' Stow asks, not certain he heard him right.

Walsingham shakes his head. 'It matters not. You are right. It will lull devoted Catholics from their sanctuaries in refusal to acknowledge the Queen's middle way and though some will pay the fines for not attending the services, generating income, it will strive to force them to act, speak or write out.' He opines.

'I shall furnish you drafts for each in the shortness of time and then onto the Privy Council.' Stow says, bowing.

'No, straight to Cecil.'

Stow smiles at Walsingham's shrewd political play, no interims to meddle and Cecil can take the credit, or blame. He then realises, 'The courts will be pushed to execute traitors no longer for their deeds but for mere words and thoughts alone. The law will discipline an entire generation.' Stow cannot help but admire and frighten himself.

Walsingham turns slowly to him, 'When you operate beyond the laws of England, you no longer afford protection from it.'

Through the many Autumnal weeks that followed, news was slow. Pestilence, rain and the muds had ground life in the Queen's realm to an undignified halt. Walsingham wrote an abundance of correspondence, always duplicating and dispatching by different means to avoid interceptions. He would only hear by return perhaps half of what he had issued. Had the correspondence ever reached its intended, was the Rider collapsed in a faraway ditch, such was the uncertainty of these pestilent times. He would never know.

Robbie had felt the frustration of inaction too, begging his master to leave the family farm and return to Seething Lane in a bid to ascertain what the situation was in London, without endangering the family and then to reignite all their previous enquiries and endeavours. Eventually, Walsingham did succumb and let the lad go, secretly delighted he was all the more vigorous for their intelligence gathering enterprises than he at that present time.

Then, just as his countenance was improving, fate had her cruel way with him.

Only a few days after Beale had left, terrible news greeted the family one morning. Mary, whose buboes and pustules had much dissipated but had not completely subsided, suffered a poor turn. Her fever was so high she thought she saw stoats running up her wall. The hallucinations frightened Edith and Frances who had to be ushered from the room by Walsingham as Ursula tried to comfort the little girl.

Not trusting the village quacks, Walsingham wrote for Bullein once more. It was too late. Ursula came to the three of them in the parlour as they were making rue to treat her.

'Her little heart has not the fight.' She had said, sobbing. Ursula, Edith, Frances and the master of the house held on to each other and spent the rest of the day at Mary's bedside. They decided to keep the fire in her room going despite her cold state. Ursula commented to no-one in particular, 'The warmth will keep the Angels by her side warm.' They had all smiled. Walsingham knew, however, it was to keep the flies from waiting their turn with her little corpse.

This was where fleeing from London all those months ago had got him. Detached...and a daughter dead. He was drunk with anger, often back and forth in his chair, watching the shadows dance on the wall from the candle's flicker, as he had done near a year ago in his study that had set in motion this journey of tumultuous fate. Such was he dry from crying his tears, his mouth ached from jaw grinding, he knew there would be no sleep tonight.

With mounting frustration he invited, with words out loud, memories and nightmares of his past to haunt him once more, knowing what clarity he had hit upon before by such darkness. 'Come! Come, ye, engulf me with your horrors.' He spat to all the shadows in the room where malevolent visions hid. 'Ye, thoust deepest of dark, with thine mystical menace, come present yourself and tell me for what purpose you suffer me.'

Nothing came.

Despair and darkness were tonight only prosperous bedfellows to his desolation.

Many hours after he heard the first owl hoot, he knew all would be in bed, so decided to sit with poor Mary awhile. Her fire was still going, the heartiest billow in the whole house. He caressed her cold cheek, not shaken by its stiffness or lack of colour for he had seen the dead before. It was the sadness of her not waking to tell him to stop fussing her that hit him hardest. He had always insisted on paternal respect from his daughters but he so desperately wanted to be rebuked by her now. Moving his head onto the bed because his tears splash onto her cheek and forehead, he could not bear for her discomfort even in death. His head rested near hers and his howling sorrows truly began. There were growls of shame and fury, tears of guilt and burden. Startling himself and the rest of the household, he would oftentimes bark words of repent, and then names that should never have been spoken were scorned aloud once more. 'Why the girl? Am I not your servant? Am I not your anointed servant's servant? Whyfore Stimpson? Is there not righteousness in our actions? Is it rectitude you seek, oh Lord? The Frenchman – I never even had the courtesy to learn his name – then the prisoners Bridle, MacKinnon, that reckless soul Essigia, ye all children of God.' Walsingham rambles and yells in-between braying tears. Surrounded as he was in death, guilt – he knew very well – was planting itself nicely with his doubts. Pain was not for the slain, only for the ancient bargain of lives lost and the uncertainty of how many more it will take. All this, though, he could still not rationalise – 'My very own Mary?' He implores the unfathomable cosmos above.

As his cries lulled, a sparse blackness comes over him. It was then that Christ's last words from the cross came so completely and derisively to him, and he shouts hauntingly and searchingly in the dark –

'Eloi, eloi lama sabachthani.'

* *

They had heard. His entire household. Exclamations of pain, wails of weeping, throbbing through the walls. No one judged him any poorer for doing so.

It was Frances, though, who listened hardest. Tears of God were said to fill the lakes and oceans, ye we judge him no less. It were his lulls, the ramblings and screeches amongst the tears that concerned her more. The immensity of the man, her father, whom she so treasured, beyond her favourite stockings and dress or toy dog, that she could now hear crumpling, a poor blessed mortal he was. Then the last words she had heard him say following these long days and nights of torture since her sister's death, the entrancing Aramaic of Christ's own tongue, recognising it from Pastor Emmanuel's sermons –

'My God, My God, why have you forsaken me?'

Frances, so completely and absolutely, knew right then and there this really was it – she would finally come clean with her dark truth. She accepted unquestionably all these faults as her own.

Then, nothing. Listening intently, she heard no more of his outpouring, rationalising he had fallen asleep so she would leave it to the morning. Oddly, it was the first time she would sleep peacefully in a long, long, time. Her guilt, unlike her father's, was soon to be availed.

Long after the eggs from the chickens had been collected the following morning, Walsingham finally woke from where he had fallen asleep.

Frances, now astute in her capabilities of listening through walls and doors, and looking into cracks and gaps, saw that her father was alone and awake, undressing his clothes to be washed. Well, she thought, how much trouble was she going to start herself in now?

He was surprised to see her on her own, having not separated from Edith or her mother's side since her sister's death. He sat on a stool near the bed and Frances knelt beside him as they both held one of the cadaver's tiny hands, which was like touching a statue from the tombs in churchyards. Frances did not take long to get right into her confession and asked that he just let her finish before his remonstration or questions commence. Walsingham was tiredly impressed with her astute candour and looked directly at her as she talked, her intense brown curls of hair like the perfect hat, never faltering.

Frances recounted the story as it happened in her head, the timeline askew, she went straight to the Tussie-mussie. No harm had been meant, she was quick to point out, and then did so every other sentence. Mary had only gone along with it. Poor Mary. Frances tried not to sob, though she wanted to. No, she was going to go through with it all this time, the relief was so near to being complete. Then she felt foolish telling him they had said some words. A charm, maybe. She saw her father scowl. The words, oh God, the words, what did he think of that? Was it really that bad – was it the casting of a charm, she could still remember it and knew she had to tell him, 'On parchment my wish is told, but I shall not say what my heart withhold, I beg haste a quick mission, so my life will match my vision.'

Walsingham closed his eyes slowly. No read could she take from his lips, eyebrow or mouth.

Then those horrifying feelings again: what had they – she – done? Was it white magic? Black magic? Did it matter, when one is ignorant of the sorcery conjured? Frances cried a little as she remembered telling her sister that she "cannot betray the secrets of the old Gods, can you Mary?" How the little girl had sworn so seriously she never would. Then...the Gods swallowed their charm in the earth, and now they had swallowed Mary's soul.

Her father stared emptily at her. What little colour he had drained from his slender hooked cheekbones.

'Father?'

'You will tell no-one. Not even your mother.'

The lowness of his voice, unnerving her so incredibly that she was sure her knees would not support her exit. 'Yes.' Frances stammers.

'What is known of this wise-woman? Describe her to me.'

Frances could not see the point, though began to stutter a basic description, and when her father's insistent eyes screwed tightly at her she concentrated more on her choice of words. 'A raggedy black shawl around her head,' she started to say, as if she was giving instructions to Holbein or one of the other great Court artists, 'reveals only part of her fluffy white hair, like the froth of snow at water's edge. Her nose was bumpy and long, as if it was affixed like an old bulbous parsnip. The woman's milky eyes were sallow and heavy, set back into her head with verily pink eyelids. She dare not smile for fear of revealing her absent teeth.'

Impressed as he was with her detailed description, he had to dismiss her without emotion. Frances left silently, softly repeating her apologies and just as softly begging absolution. He could have throttled her and he picked up a stool he was sat on, throwing it across the room upsetting the tray of uneaten foods. Nobody dares come to ease the mess of the noise.

Of all the problems he had right now, witchcraft was not one he could possibly conceive being added to the list. Rumours of such would only covet more death. Almost certainly it was merely a clumsy charm done with the ignorance of early womanhood. Just to be sure and to be exorcised of any possible dark ramifications, he would need to get expert spiritual and celestial advice. It would have to remain one of his biggest secrets for there is no journal weighty enough to burden this favour for his enemies to lustfully use against him. He was too angry to accept his daughter's apology let alone think what her foolish part had been in all this. No, he would return to his business of grief and melancholy.

Staying right where he was for the remainder of the day seemed the best approach for his anger and distraction, never noticing Edith or Ursula bringing him sustenance. Throughout the next night he could only continue to stare at his dead daughter. His thoughts had kicked about so much in the dark he felt the room bleed with light as day begins to break. Was it as if he was given chance anew? What purpose if not to be sacrifices could all the dead at his hands help to serve? He looked at his skull ring on his little finger made to revere Stimpson, realising he would now have to get another for Mary.

All that was now left is to make a vow from these traumas. 'On my soul, I will keep all I can safe, Mary

Walsingham, I oath to you and our Lord Jesus Christ.' He rubbed the skull ring and the other empty little finger where one would go. 'This is a promise I shall keep evermore.'

From this tiny room in the farmstead, he looked at the sun glistening the icy fields, sparkling new for the year ahead.

He was left with a very simple choice as 1571 began: the dead were sacrifices or burdens, which make or break the man. If he was not to give way, surrender and retreat, then the only alternative was to firm himself upright, look fate in the eye, bargain, manipulate and out-fox that great dark despoiler of destinies...King Death.

IV

Seething Lane

January 1571

೮ೲ

Blood dries to the wood like scabs on skin, Beale thinks, scratching and peeling off the remains of Charles Bailly's stain on the rack. He waits for Walsingham to complete his household affairs upstairs, hearing the arguments between the women as the master demands an explanation. It pains him to think of Edith in trouble, though he understands whoever commits wrongs must answer for them. Francis is always fair. Perhaps too fair. There have been times when, in his own unwarranted anger, he himself might have cracked a hand or swiped a birch rod at Edith when Walsingham did not. Was he really as strong-stomached as he thought – he remembers catching himself wincing during the salting of the Catholic prisoners from Portsmouth and, more recently, Charles Bailly's stretching. Just as he was getting to the bottom of his dilemma, he heard his master stomp down the stairs.

'Thank you for your patience, Robbie. I am sorry to have kept you waiting on the day of our reunifying.' He said, clapping his hands together for warmth in the icy basement – clump, chink, went their sound, the two small skull rings clinking together like holy armour.

'It feels too often now I say this – I am delighted to be back in our own company.' Beale says.

'Aye. T'will be whilst the Winter quietens pestilence before Spring has her onset, when I imagine once again our worlds will be turned upside down.' Walsingham says, encouraging them to take up two stools, turning to business.

'It would be prudent to prioritise our next moves.' Beale says, then affirming, 'I have thought of nothing else.' Burying a hand into his jerkin, he flaps several message packets at Walsingham, opened and aged. 'Investors seeking a return that has yet to bear fruit.'

'T'was inevitable.' Walsingham dismisses and Beale agrees. 'We cannot move precipitously to satisfy promissory notes. The Earl of Leicester may be able to protect us and buy time before we are scalded through the courts.'

'Good. My soul is eased. Our next priorities should give way to finding Ridolfi and how we connect Norfolk or Essex – or both – to Mary and the plots.' Beale says with surety.

Walsingham bows his head in agreement, 'Our priorities, yes. We must act precipitously.' He daintily says. Right at this moment none of it was at the forefront of his mind and he did not look at Beale when answering, feigning deep consternation. One thought possessed him: how he will bury these witchcraft substantiations that may come his way. So reckless a daughter she was. That is what the arguments had been about this morning, and many before it. Punishing Frances with house arrest, as he called it, not explaining why to Ursula or Edith – and Frances knew far better than to betray her father, not in any hurry to declare dabbling in the dark arts.

Walsingham saw Robbie's expectant face, having drifted from their conversation. He apologised for being distracted and so much at their table, nay enough time to feast. The pauper's paradox, he called it.

'So trivial the matters we cared not for only a year past.' Beale says with whimsical irony.

'Of course, this all matters not.' Walsingham pointedly remarks as he starts to stand from his stool, saying, 'None will be as import should we have fallen from the Queen's favour. Or Cecil's.' He slowly exasperates, leaning fully on one hand on his knee.

'Why would we though?'

'Because I have been absent from government court these many months, because I am inexperienced in the underhand cunning of Her Majesty's Ministers, because the constriction of our espial network has weakened and frayed in the middle, loosening its grasp.' Walsingham says, paranoid that it could be seen how he may also be talking about himself here, his frustrations letting loose. 'I have been loathe to trust anyone, my own family, my friends, nay everyone with whom I converse, and all the more worse for it as every day that wretch Mary Queen of the Scots sits, supposed prisoner to Her Majesty, waiting for some plot to snatch the Queen's throne in a blood-soaked coup. We know not how more powerful she has yet become. We know not who she may plot and conspire. For her hand in marriage to any nobleman of England or Spain to overthrow our beloved majesty. We know not with whom she communicates under her house arrest. What lurks unseen in the dark...what vile sorceries could be conjured and cast...' Walsingham had both hands on his knees now, supporting his exhausted, sorrowful, weight. Beale struggled to make sense of his master.

'You suspect witchcraft?' He puzzlingly asks.

'Witchcraft? An evil abomination. It shall not be tolerated. She will have to answer for it and to dare bring ill upon the house.' Walsingham shouts.

'The house…I speak of Mary, sir.' Beale pries slowly, unsure of where his master's anger was directed.

Walsingham makes a weakened exclamation, gets up and slaps the wooden rack, pacing the room. He hits the wall, more out of embarrassment from his foolish tirade and potentially giving away his scandalous family crimes. He must keep up the ruse.

'Forgive me, Robbie, it has been nigh a long year. Frustration of inaction when so tantalisingly close.'

'There is nothing yet vanished, my lord.' Beale says, standing to join him. 'We just need to recoil and cast once more our net of gathering. I have maintained commerce with Masterman, Titus, Blythe and even Herle.'

'None of Fyson, the whores or Kitchener?' Walsingham asks.

Beale shakes his head regrettably. 'Nor of Walter.' It feels as if a wound has just opened up again, but he stymies a dig. 'Hitherto I have enquired after the usual taverns and stables to be sure their whereabouts will not go unnoticed.'

'And that is why you are my most trusted and respected servant.'

'Trusted aye, respected nay.' Beale says and Walsingham laughs. A good, true, hearty chortle that makes him realise how stupidly serious he has been taking himself these last days.

'I shall write them all individually. Do they have a new cypher?' He asks. Beale shows him and he scripts out a short note to them, all the while thinking to himself how his most urgent priority is to repress the witchery that may have spewed forth its poisonous intent from within his own family. Emmanuel, he thinks as he writes, will help him.

As he sends Beale one way with the cyphered instructions, he turns down Seething Lane the other, towards Beer Lane. Ursula stops him.

'What of Fyson's message?' She says, embarrassed she is shouting in the lane. A window shutter on the opposite side of their house opens.

Walsingham is sure to speak quietly as he says busily, 'I was not aware he had left such.' With plenty to do this bright morn his eyes encourage her haste.

Ursula quietens herself, 'All it reads is "if you desire another hair inspection, your humblest servant, Soborn Fyson." You could do with a tidying, not so much thinning, it already being such.'

'Yes, thank ye, goodwife.' He says, smiling her away. He knows full well the Barber Surgeon does not mean to invite him for a trim, and, not knowing any cyphers, has invented his own code. Walsingham paces down to Beer lane.

It is not long before he hears those familiar sounds of shouting and hullaballoo that even the plague cannot allay.

Pastor Emmanuel is sat with his usual congregation, although the strong rhetoric and playful mockery has vanished amongst them. He does not even stand when Walsingham coughs his way through the thick brewing fumes, a seven-month absence in the countryside makes his breath weak to the city.

'Emmanuel?' Walsingham asks.

'My lord.' The Pastor meekly responds, the fire in his eyes dying out. 'I have oft prayed for your safe return and alack, supped many an ale to aid the quickness of dissipating my pain.'

'All is not well.'

'Aye.' Emmanuel says sadly, finishing his drink, standing and leading them both away.

Heading past Seething Lane and Walsingham's house, the father can feel his only daughter's eyes burn into him from above, but he refuses to look up, and continues to explain his woes to the Pastor. Emmanuel is neither drunk or sober, grinning inanely, listening and following the thread of Walsingham's eleven-month journey into witchcraft, courtesy of his daughter.

'Do you believe your daughter to be a witch?'

'No.'

'Do you understand her to be under a spell of bewitching?'

'No.'

'Then she is neither witch nor bewitched.' The Pastor says, slumping into a chair in the small vestry, needing to snooze off his morning libations.

Walsingham was half thinking of rattling the man's brains against the holy tabernacle for all the use he was to him. Clearly Pastor Emmanuel had not read the most recent treatise on witchcraft. Walsingham had, and its words haunted him beyond Emmanuel's supposed words of comfort, "Thou who furthers the devil's work affixing conjuring of words to emit magic from one upon another, must endure the wrath of God as all blasphemies must."

No less clear, and fretting at no resolve, Walsingham reasoned there was only one who could definitively help, and he would call upon him momentarily: John Dee. Fyson is on the way.

Wandering through Cheapside, he noted how less busy with scavengers it was. The indigent had grown less. As a moderately wealthy man this should have been of relief to him, but he remembers how Beale choked, describing how the wretches were ragged with pain, skimpy mothers bickering over scraps with their own slack-mouthed children. The plague, it seems, preferred its victim's poor.

Turning into Ironmonger's Lane, he saw Porter adding another service to Fyson's crudely painted sign *ailments, barbering, surgery, wiggery* and *merkins,* to now include *teethed failings.* Walsingham snickered to himself, the art of dentistry had come to Cheapside's alley physicians. He saw how this era of plague had been none too kind to Porter either, already thin, the ageing man had macerated to near a skeleton. Incredibly, he had caught and survived the pestilence, as one in six people did, having let Fyson conduct all manner of researches on him, whilst keeping all visitors at bay.

'Thank ye, your message was of good timing.' Walsingham says entering the dimly lit workshop.

'My Lord, I have much to present.' Fyson says excitedly.

'Amongst which is your cure for plague, I see.'

'Reeburn Porter is of good wharf stock and his humours aligned with the astrological-scope.' Fyson says, blushing.

'It was luck then?'

'Aye.' Fyson laughs and Walsingham follows, 'Do you recall the oxides to reveal disappeared ink? Well, I had the whores use a cheaper, easier alternative, less mess-ridden. You know how tallow candles are clearer, lighter in colour than bees candles? Well, if you write in clear, light wax it is unseen by the eye, paint over it in any dark colour and all is revealed.' Fyson beams at Walsingham.

Delightful as he thinks this is, yet another invisible ink was rather a disappointing way to spend their time apart. Then Walsingham clicks. 'You have secret messages from the whores?' Walsingham breathlessly asks, the best news he could potentially have heard for many months.

'From Hannah and Rhy.' Fyson says, wafting his fingers for Porter to bring them, and the thin man totters in with three rolled letters, two were almost four inches and the other almost eight. 'Any government ministers use of the brothels and bagnios have been wildly paranoid and n'er a set of balls has gotten moist. Been employed in the hours of dark may have warranted suspicion on our girls.'

'They were searched for contraband messages?'

'Searched, aye, but not for messages, any government minister in want of finding weapons that they may be struck down in the dark in their post-expostulations, to be gentlemanly about it, sir.' Fyson says.

Walsingham is almost translating as he says, 'So Hannah and Rhy were thoroughly searched, for weapons, but none were found and nor were there messages?' Walsingham states and Fyson nods. 'Then how did they smuggle the letters...' Walsingham looks at the rolled up thick parchment.

Fyson stumbles in slight embarrassment that he has to explain such impertinences to a gentleman, so Porter just blurts out, 'They never searched their snatches.'

There is a stunned silence.

'What?' Porter asks Fyson, ill-conceived of the offence he may cause.

'The gentleman.' Fyson embarrassingly motions to Walsingham.

'Of course, I beg thine mercy,' Porter begins, 'they never searched their snatches, my lord.'

Walsingham cringes at the rolled-up paper – 'For the love of our almighty…you mean to tell me this has been nestling inside their fundaments?'

'Yes sir, but many days past now, and the trick should remain intact.' Fyson says, innocently sniffing it.

'Proceed with haste.' Walsingham insists, shaking his head.

Fyson unfurls one of the smaller scrolls and takes some blue paint, squalling the brush all over it, instantly revealing white text, which he reads, '"Is it be seen?"' and nothing else. He coughs, a touch embarrassed. 'That is all there is written. Clearly testing the magic, making sure it works…yes.' He grabs the other one, again washing it over with paint and reveals some more text. '"Rhy is to speak it soon."' Fyson cannot look at Walsingham from the fool he feels at wasted parchment scrolls that say not a thing. Instantly, he grabs the final, bigger, one, holding it up admiringly to Walsingham, trying to thaw his cold stare, 'Obviously Rhy has more room than Hannah.' He coughs again, his embarrassment resurfacing.

This time, as he swabs paint over it, there is a lot more writing, clearly legible. Although, as both men read, it makes little sense, written as prose.

High walls secure the trap behind
A large ditch close to their door
Has prevented all attacks before
No fox or rat disturb the ease
They eat, they drink, do what they please.

Fyson is maudlin all of a sudden, saying, 'She has been missing for many weeks now.'

'The Rhyming Whore?'

'Aye.'

'Is Hannah safe?' Walsingham asks urgently.

'Aye, but for worry of her sister whore and no idea if she lives or clogs a shallow grave somewhere.'

Walsingham looks it over again, cautious to touch it, lest his virtue be disturbed. The verse had to be coded. It was original, he was sure of that – what great rhymester would have ever invented such fetid ordure?

He let Fyson tidy his hair and trim his beard to calm his thoughts, although even as he finished he had still not cleared his mind to discover what it may mean. He asks the Barber Surgeon to put it in a fresh packet to conceal it in his long cloak and take with him for further consideration. Before leaving, though, he seeks Fyson's advice on one final matter. He wonders if he has ever seen the wise woman so eloquently described by Frances to him at Scadbury.

Fyson chuckles. 'You've just described any mad old hen that sticks her beak in the stalls of Cheap Ward on a given Friday.'

Of course, Walsingham realises, Mynchen Lane. He bids Fyson a good day and decides he really must go to Dee for his judgement on the matter of his daughter's witchery.

Turning into Crockers Lane's darkened alleys, he could see why he had never ventured to Alsatia before. Stooping his head low to avoid attracting any of Alsatia's characters, he hears an old woman selling cheap buskins so stops outside a slim building made from old bricks that teeters above all others like a child trying to peek into a kitchen shutter. He was reliably informed this would be it, so he lifts the bolt to go straight in, hearing the bell tingle upstairs announcing him.

Walsingham had seen John Dee before, mostly watching him walk to and fro in the government buildings trying to keep himself to himself. They had never met, never feeling the need to converse or curry favour with a man that no one else did either. Despite seemingly having the ear of the Queen whenever he chose to, John Dee was a man not understood by Walsingham. He knew that hearsays and gossips gathered in abundance about Dee – the most exciting of which was that he possessed a crystal as "big as an egg: most bright, clear and glorious." Used mostly for scryings into the futures of men, it was also said to perceive guilt of any soul. Walsingham had heard it tell his seances were so shocking and spooky they rocked even the stoutest of safe Christian theologists. Walsingham felt an urge to be running down the stairs not climbing them. If Dee was enticingly mystical enough for the Queen then it should be suitable for his supernatural problems, having his daughter's soul to save.

Creeping in, Walsingham sees Dee studying charts at the big shiny table, his balding head and fluffy beard closely studying fantastical diagrams of shapes and numbers.

Dee did not look up as he spoke, 'You have some questions, Francis Walsingham?'

'How did you know it was I?'

'I know nothing but what the stars inform me.' Dee stands straight and smiles. 'Or I am not the only one to employ espials?'

Clever, thinks Walsingham, and knows he does not have to be guarded saying, 'If rumours are to be believed then any espial would be too scared to share your audience lest their findings disappoint.'

'Ah, then rumours rule London, not knowledge.' Dee shakes his head and moves slowly to a cabinet, unlocking it and taking out a small linen covered box, continuing as he does, 'I once told Emperor Rudolph II that after forty years of living, my seeking of knowledge had failed from books or living man, useless as they are to requirements. From this moment, Angels and holy intercessions from God will be my tutors. Of course, my care in not crossing these intelligences with those of Demons or the dark succubae is necessity.'

Walsingham, unsure if Dee is Godly divine or dark witch, wonders aloud, 'How can you be certain to listen only to good and not evil, or that evil is not dressed as good?'

'I advise the Queen. My Angels ensure the Divine's message is always heard.' Dee says, revealing his crystal egg. Walsingham almost uncouthly scrabbles around the table. The crystal, the size of a duck's egg more than chicken, is no less impressive, although he hoped it would glimmer more so, being surprisingly duller than the few gemstones he had seen upon persons of the wealthy. It lacked any magical appearance, but then nothing is straightforward in the world of the unknown arts. Dee glances at him. 'Are you ready to begin?'

Walsingham tentatively hands over a crammed purse of monies, a fist of bronze. Dee refuses to take it.

'You are looking for someone.' Dee announces. Walsingham had seen confidence tricks before, he was a Londoner after all, not always living the excluded life of many parliamentarians, and is a little surprised at the amateurism here. He lets Dee continue. 'No. There are more. No dead men's bones here. There are foreign men. An old woman haunts your dreams. A friend. You are burdened, Francis Walsingham.' Dee woos, staring deeply into his hazy crystal egg. Walsingham a little uneasy, beginning to be taken in. 'You are looking to blame or, at the very least, offload these burdens. You are learning blame is a dangerous game. How reckless that be. Death. Death has been around you. Death is an opportunity.' Dee stops and looks at him for the first time since beginning. 'You are worried about the safety of a woman, but she is not family...Her Majesty!' The Queen's astrologer and "most trusted" advisor exclaims. Walsingham knew that a ha'penny-tongue blabber could have said this, but none ever do. He decides to move the conversation on.

'There is a woman I seek, more of your realm than mine...a mystic, herbalist maybe, wise-woman and conjurer most likely.'

'Conjurer?' Dee blasts, as if to say that is not what I am. 'What has she conjured?'

Walsingham could not recall the exact verse so just says, 'Words of a charm to be placed in water with herbs.'

'A kettle or cauldron, with any fur of beast or feather of bird?' Dee asks, concerned.

'No, I believe not. Herbs and flowers was all, my lord.' Walsingham says honestly, and perhaps stammering slightly, for the first time overwhelmed by looming paraphernalia, the darkness of Dee's room.

'Not by you I ascertain. There was no sorcery to emanate maleficent magic, nay, intent to harm, I suspect. Who was this woman?'

After Walsingham describes her, Dee thinks for a moment, but does little more than tell him the same as Fyson.

However, as Dee secretes his dull crystal egg in the dark linen cloth, he asks thinly, 'What reckoning might these un-named persons receive should I announce them to alleviate your guilt?'

'Reckoning? Why, a trial, sirrah.' Walsingham says, ever mindful of following the law. 'Then the full weight of her majesty's justice, should their fate deem it so.'

Without moving or looking at Walsingham, Dee reels away some names, 'Luanne Fairchild, Margaret Gygacks, Agnes Levet or Rosamund Demdyke. They might be who you seek.'

'My Lord?'

'They match the description and are of local London mix.'

'Thank ye.' Walsingham says, a little surprised. The doctor of no studied art nods and shoos him out.

'I hope you find your Privy Councillor; for corruption of our best is the worse.' Dee says without even watching Walsingham leave, returning to his charts on his shiny table.

'I did not say Privy Councillor.' Walsingham states quietly, but the astrologer does not answer.

Walsingham slowly descends Dee's stairs. At the bottom he opens the door, the bell tingles once more as he leaves and the old woman shouting the sale of her wares in the street. A most curious happening, he reflects, shaking his head, looking back up to the teetering building. He had not mentioned the Privy Councillor to him. He has spies for sure, Walsingham realised, just not his own. It mattered not – he was telling him he was close.

V

෪ ෫

It is a strange, sweet sound when a three-inch nail rifles straight into wood on the first swipe of the hammer. Even when you are inside the barrel of the lid hit and sealed into, Harry Snurle thought with a wry smile reserved only for men who are about to face – and must come to accept – their death. Not that he was aware that Masterman and Titus had no intention of killing him, they were just beginning their fun.

Prizing out the cork in the nailed down lid beams a silvery shaft of moonlight down into the barrel.

'I shall not speak to surrender my allies.' Snurle says to them. Weeks he had been dragged to and fro on the naked saddle of a horse, and now the indignity of being stuffed into a barrel.

'No, but you might scream' Titus says as he threaded an adder into the barrel, re-corked the lid, tipped it and kicked it down the steep hill. The spinning screams of a man bitten by snake was a sound that amused both Masterman and Nevon with thigh-slapping regalement.

'Are we reckoning a scream for every bite of venom?' Nevon enquires, as they both begin to make their way down to the bottom of the hill, the barrel surprisingly intact, and deathly still.

'I counted four.' Lynas cackles in disbelief.

'Do we have enough purple vervain?' Nevon asks. Masterman checks his knapsack and shows him a fist's worth of flowers. 'It will have to do.' As they approach the barrel it then rumbles gently. A soft, pained voice from inside.

'Please...I beg thee...' Snurle implores.

'Ah, he does speak, thou promise not.' Nevon blurts, inflating his broad chest before belching, clearly winded from the steep lunging down. He tips the barrel back upright and opens the cork. 'In Lynas' hand here,' he begins in his broadest West Country accent, 'is the only local anti-venom. You sucks the buds and stems see.' Nevon calmly explains, trying not to wince as he catches sight of a snake bite on the man's face. 'Now...let's stop this nonsense of telling us nothing and tell us what we need to know of you and your Lord's ambitions.'

Snurle has no choice, cursing his crew of five so easily bested by these two men on the shore that fateful night, and tells them all he knows.

As a result of his confession, six days later Titus and Masterman, still with Snurle in their capture, had reached Shrewsbury. It took longer than anticipated as they avoided turnpikes, not for lack of money but the barrage of questions that would inevitably come their way regarding their prisoner.

Snurle finally stopped vomiting after every meal, the venom having finally left his body.

'At least it didn't kill you.' Masterman says.

'Aye, we said nothing of the poison within the poison.' Titus laughs. At least the man's spewing prevented him from screaming or idle talk, he just moaned and heaved for six days. Still, they had to drag him with them in case his stories were fantasies. If this were the case, the Bear wrestler had promised, he would rip Snurle's head off and kick it up his trap.

Confirming his story, sure enough there was a draper's in the town as he had told them there would be. It had taken at least three more bites of the snake when Titus had shaken the barrel, more in frustration than amusement, to remedy his lack of answers. Snurle could no longer take it when he felt his arms and legs go into paralysis.

Entering one of England's farthest northern towns they needed a cover story and decided upon travelling brawlers and baiters. No one questioned Titus Nevon, in fact one townsman – a travelling cheese merchant – claimed to even recognise him – or at least the famous stories of him. So long as Snurle, their travelling companion was not ill with plague, the town not yet being infected with the "London disease," they were welcome to rest in a tavern for a night or two.

Their tavern was in the same street as the drapers, a large townhouse that held lofts full of linen and basements with benches for the seamstresses. For a whole day and night they watched the place, counting only one man in the shop and none to come and go, just several women. It would be easy. They would go tonight after tying Snurle by his arms to the beams of the ceiling.

Masterman gives tuppence to the Ostler boy as he comes from checking the horses and to see who might be about the draper's some fifty yards away.

'But one man and no dog.' Ostler says, pocketing the coins delightedly.

At nightfall, Titus and Masterman are ready and approach the house. Titus goes round the back. Masterman knocks the front door and the man of the house answers in his night smock.

'How many women of your house?' He asks the man.

'What business be it of yours?' He puffs at him, looking up and down the street, perhaps about to call out his suspicions. Masterman thrusts his hard leather riding boot up into his soft testicles and the man doubles over with a huge wheeze. Masterman casually rolls the man inside and shuts the door, checking no person saw.

Titus is already stood inside the chamber room clasping two women, covering their mouths with either hand.

'Are there any more women of the house?' Masterman asks.

'Just...the...two.' Comes the man's coughing reply, thinking his balls in his throat.

Titus releases the girls to sit in chairs. 'Scream and we shall pull the old man's plums off like Romans squeezing grapes.' As the two men go upstairs and search the house, the two young women run to the man on the floor. Their older brother.

Linen stacks the lofts, but yield no return. There are two bedrooms, one for the sisters and the other their brother, a single cot in each, they too hide nothing. Titus cannot conceal his thoughts of filth at the sisters sharing a bed. Lynas rolls his eyes, shrugging his shoulders, exasperated. Then he remembers – what was it Theophilus Traske, Walsingham's Gaol Carpenter agent, told them well – knock and smite the wood, listen for the emptiness of holes within. Explaining this to Titus, they both tapped, knocked and nudged every wood surface throughout the upstairs. Even with careful ears and concentrated senses they were convinced nothing was kept from their sights. They returned downstairs where the man of the house was now sat up, albeit in agonising writhes on the floor. Titus nods for Lynas to try the cellars and explore without him, lest the draper feel emboldened to try his luck and escape to raise the hue and cry.

Several rows of benches line the basement and, as he checks the wood's density, he speculates this is a fair and profitable concern they had going: drapery was a pretty money churner no doubt. Lack of hollowed wood, though, he moves on. Amongst the countless folds of linen, now beautifully sewn he has a snap thought – what if they had been stitched together to conceal whatever was their enterprise here. No one would think to look amongst tightly woven drapes. Randomly he dove his hand into a pile and sliced some folds open, an hour's beautiful craftwomanship ruined. Nothing. A different bench, a different pile of stitched linen, the same result.

Frustrated, Lynas throws a stool at a hanging bench where an ornately woven drape had been dyed and was now settling. It rocked. The wet still dripping from its edges onto the floor, making it too heavy to stabilize and as the rocking picked up momentum, it tipped backward, clattering behind two rows of benches.

Lynas looks up in resplendent shock.

'Everything as it should be down there?' Came Titus' shout from above. 'Lynas?'

'God's blood, fetch yourself here.' He hollers back up.

Titus warns the sisters about their brother's plums again and runs down, unsure from Lynas' voice if there is alarm or not. Darting into the basement he freezes when he sees it, gawping at Lynas.

'If I did not hate its origins so, I would fair it a marvel of artistry.' Lynas reverently splutters. Titus has only a meagre understanding of the sight he beholds, so appreciates what Lynas means. A Catholic altar – in all its majestical splendour. Titus just looks at what glimmers.

Lynas recognises the Purificator, telling Titus that is how the Priest cleans the Chalice, pointing out its silver so pristine it looks like glass. The whole kit was there – a golden Ciborium and the Cruets for the wine and water, still with their liquids in and the crisp clean linen of the Corporal was bright and tort. It was either shortly to be used or very recently had been.

'The fuss of it.' Titus says.

Lynas walks to the trinkets, appraising them, it would take four labourers five years to earn enough to buy the collection.

'What does it all mean?' Titus asks.

'The Catholic church is being driven underground.' Lynas says.

'This cannot be why we have journeyed here? Because some cloth stitcher has his mass.' Says the huge man, disappointed and deterred. They head back upstairs.

'No, there will be more.' Lynas says, yomping back up the wooden steps in jumps of three.

'We found your Catholic church,' Titus growls, 'but where's the rest?'

The Draper rolls round onto his back, with murder intent in his eyes.

'They won't tell us.' Lynas says. Titus puts a poker in the fire, his grin says to them all oh yes they will.

'No.' One of the sisters says, sensing his purpose. She nods at the chimney. Titus smirks and goes straight over, crouches down and reaches up behind the stack, the flames licking his arm, and quickly finds something, dragging it out: a small shoe.

'A child's buskin?' He barks.

'To ward off witchcraft. Further up.' The same woman says. He gets back in there and rams his hand yet further up, feeling leather once again, flames singeing his arm hair, this time it is bigger, much heavier and, tugging harshly, drops it straight into the fire. He has to use both hands to lift it out and it clinks on the floor.

'That is a lot of coin.' Lynas says excitedly.

'This is no bag of coin.' Titus rasps, opening it to reveal ten gold bars. 'Satan's spunk.' Is all he can whisper.

Lynas joins him, nodding apologies over to the ladies.

'Wait til you grasp your sight of this...' Titus plumps, holding a parchment aloft. 'Ridolfi.'

Suddenly both girls charge at the two men, all nails and teeth, followed by their brother, the three of them cleverly conspiring when Lynas and Titus had been distracted by the gold and Ridolfi's parchment note.

The sisters went straight for Titus, snapping their jaws and tensing their nails straight into his arms, chest and neck. Scratching and biting for their lives. Their draper brother hobbles with haste and throws himself haphazardly into Lynas, toppling him into the fire grate, searing coals writhing about both men.

Lynas tries to grab the poker but the draper sees and takes it first, about to hit him but his backswing is stung short by the bricks around them and he manages only a prang to the top of Lynas' head. This enables Lynas to wriggle into a better position and launch his knee into the draper's already delicate testicles, the pain suffocating him in loud gushes. Lynas pushes him off, takes the poker and flanks him with it between his neck and shoulder, having seen a Nightwatchman paralyze someone in this way before. The man is disabled on the floor and will not be bothering them further. Lynas turns to the two women spinning from Titus as he twists, trying to battle them off. A spectacular sight, like a drunk, deranged maypole dance, he almost giggles before grabbing one of them by the ankles, snapping her backwards and onto the floor face down, her open screaming mouth dunking into the slabbed floor. The teeth in her upper mouth scraping out onto the stone, blood squelching all about her, like stamped strawberries. He feels bad for doing it, but has to boot her in her breasts to still the wretch or he too will feel the scratches and half bites of a demon woman possessed. Titus now has the other woman pressed against the wall by her throat, her feet twenty inches off the floor while he takes a breath, as the young woman loses hers.

'You can't kill her, Titus.' Lynas says looking at the brother and sister unconscious on the floor. 'They will have to live with these torments and pray Walsingham does not seek judicial revenge and hunt them down. For my part, I am done with Shrewsbury and permit our leave, never to venture here again.'

Titus looks at the girl, reddening fast. He decides to throw her against another wall five feet away, she flaps into it and crumples to the floor like a panicking bird hitting a windowless kitchen wall.

The draper's house and workshop is peaceful in its dim lights from within, only a dying fire and toppled candles evidence of disquiet and the chaos of the brawl they leave stealthily behind them, their only dilemma figuring how they were going to get Ridolfi's gold and cyphers from a staunchly loyal Catholic north to their safe Protestant London.

* *

Leaving what felt like an hour before he moved or made a sound, he could endure it no longer. From inside the concealed cabinet his jet-black hair was pinching and scraping against the unvarnished wood. Looking himself over, he could only sardonically smart that it was not long ago he wore a fine embroidered tunic and a prim ostrich feather in his hat.

There was no noise from the cellar of the draper's now. It was wise to free himself from the confined inners of the well-crafted cabinet that Lynas had not searched properly. Ridolfi unfurls out and creaks his back as he stands. He too leaves the chaos of the drapers behind him, determined to blend into the shadows forever and escape England.

* *

Greenwich

'Dry gripes astern.' Comes the drunken slurred voice followed by riotous laughter all around the packed tavern. The Mermaid's Ring was a shipwright's alehouse further east of the ancient city. Edmund Blythe and William Herle had cemented their cracks of mistrust at sea and now, with both their ships undergoing repairs, were prepared to sink ales and share each other's company. The tavern had another crew of a naval great. A God of the seas to many, including the drinkers sat listening to him now.

John Hawkins was a skimpy faced fellow with perfectly round eyes and slender neck, like a girl's – no wonder, so many had asserted, he had progressed quickly through the ranks of seamanship with such a pretty neck and so innocent a pair of eyes. He has just finished his amusing story from the battle of San Juan de Ulua, the only good thing to come from that defeat and lost colony in the Southern Atlantic seas. He was a man so widely travelled in that part of the world, cartographers came to him for clarification of their maps. Herle and Blythe were listening, smiling and laughing in the right places, not ones to upset his crew or his many devotees. Hawkins was no liar, nor exaggerator, but they both concluded he rather enjoys talking about himself. 'Dry gripes astern.' Hawkins says again. 'That's what I told her.' They all laugh at the oft repeated tale adapted by any returning voyage from overseas, complaining of his pipes suspiciously not working properly.

His berry eyes fix on Blythe and Herle as the laughter dies down. After several murmurings between him and one of his subordinates, they are invited to his snug and have no hesitation in doing so. As usual in a tavern of any kind, they will be mindful of what they speak, but settle happily in at his prestigious court.

'Captain Herle of the Griffin, Captain Blythe of nonesuch.' Hawkins whines in his high voice. Blythe cannot tell if it is educated or put on, but Herle knows a gentleman sailor when he sees one. 'Why no name?' Hawkins asks Blythe.

'I am but a humble trawlerman, your grace.'

'With ten cannon aboard.' Hawkins grins into his porter ale as his cronies close by laugh gruffly. 'My-my, what hostile fish you seek. And what of you, Captain Herle, what are you not doing with ten cannon aboard the Griffin?'

'We merely protect against French piracy in our own waters.' Herle says steadfastly, though not aggressively.

'Ye, English waters are yet to be safe for true seafaring men.' Hawkins admits, nodding with the agreeing sailors amongst him, his own circle of sycophants. Some with long thin pipes, smouldering the new tobacco leaves found on their western ventures, and which were rasping Herle and Blythe's throats, not at all used to its dark mauve haze. Hawkins has anger in his autumn eyes, dull prickliness, 'Nay, and however long it takes we shall claim it back gentlemen.' His followers roar their agreeing chorus as Blythe looks to Herle – do we say anything?

'And for whom would you fight these cherished seas, sir?' Blythe asks.

'Who, sirrah, do all captains fight for on these seas?' Hawkins shouts all about, ending his eyes intently on Herle.

'The Queen.' Herle says.

'Aye, and which one?' Hawkins drops the room's noise.

'We are no Papists sir.' Herle gruffly says.

'Then we shall sup til we can no more and be merry for it.' Hawkins announces as all about celebrate their Englishness and, most importantly, their Protestant loyalty.

Hawkins was a man of his pledging word, and as the evening rolls on with stories and shanties, they do indeed sup. Herle falls into his routine of a bottomless stomach for ale, but Blythe drinks temperately, knowing he could wheedle scraps of information from the ever drunker Hawkins that may prove useful to Walsingham's cause. He was careful not to give anything up himself and would veer Herle away if he felt him on dangerous grounds. With all Walsingham had taught him, it was evident there were no high-level spies amongst them, just fearless adventurers of the seas. What was clear, Hawkins had quite the flotilla of ships at his command, humbling not only their two ships but the ten French their exploits had scared off at The Beak. Twenty he has to his name. Not all anchored along the Thames. Nonetheless twelve at any one point in time was at his disposal to take with him on expeditions.

After their eighth ale, Hawkins was losing control of his tongue and leans in and slobbers into Blythe's ear, 'You yourselves are returned then of heroes as heroes.'

Blythe bows politely, suspecting a trap.

'Your moves in the north were bold, as prickly as a badger's balls, and your Lord Walsingham played it well. A sham and trick so boggling it fooled them all... and worked.' Hawkins slurs with appreciative cackling.

'Well...I would not know about that...' Blythe tries to explain neutrally. Hawkins grabs him tightly on the arm, coming in even closer, the bristles of his triangular beard tickling Blythe's lobe.

'My venture company is in the pay of Howard.' Hawkins says so quietly that his breath just makes shapes in Blythe's ears and he cannot help but sense alarm. Hawkins grips him tighter. 'Worry free, he is not my master, merely investor...I can see the wind change like any good sailor...and Dudley, Cecil are the men of the Council to be in favour with...no? Is that not who your master serves?' Hawkins lets him go, he cannot be bothered with poking and prodding Blythe any longer, he has shown no fear or fragility. 'I have something he wants. And so it is he has for me.'

Hawkins was not long from an inebriated collapse Blythe hopes, knowing he needs to find Walsingham. It was with thanks then, that within the hour, Hawkins passes out, head on the table, giving Blythe and Herle their opportunity to slip out.

Walking up from the wharf, past and round Tower Hill, Blythe says to Walsingham, 'That's all he said.' Walsingham looks to Herle for confirmation. 'He can't remember for the amount of ale he turned to piss.' Blythe dismisses any forthcoming say on the matter from his new maritime adventurer-mate.

'What does he mean by telling me, us?' Blythe asks.

'Walsingham must tell them what Lynas Masterman and Titus Nevon discovered on their recent adventures.' Herle says.

* *

By the time Walsingham had finished recounting Nevon and Lynas' tale, it was obvious that Hawkins had wanted the confiscated gold, which had yet to arrive, let alone be declared to the exchequer. Beale encourages him not to, until they could accord a favourable dividend to their early investors. Walsingham knew, however, Hawkins was in a very good bargaining position, as he had the utmost authority over any of them. His only problem was that he had no idea where it was.

Walsingham tells Blythe and Herle to head straight to Portsmouth and meet with Masterman and Nevon, entrusting the gold to Frinscombe, the town's gaoler.

Walsingham bids farewell to his agents and retires to his study where he stares at Rhy's letter. *High walls secure the trap behind.* This had to be a reference to a palace, a town maybe. *A large ditch close to their door, Has prevented all attacks before* is the moat, the wall of the palace or gates to the city? *No fox or rat disturb the ease* – are these the espials, the agents? *They eat, they drink, do what they please.* It is clearly of vulgar immorality this speaks, but a whore, God bless her merry soul, is who wrote it. To have the mind or cypher of a whore is to be at a loss in the wilderness of sea without charts. Could it be a person she speaks of and not a place? Was it Norfolk, was she telling him something about Thomas Howard? Or was he seeing what he wanted in it and the reality was it happened to be just another letter testing whether or not the system worked, as Hannah had done twice before. *Trap.* Slang he thought for arse. *Walls* were legs. Perhaps she really was describing somebody. Someone with tall legs. *A large ditch close to their door,* he had no idea what that meant in the roguish speak of prostitutes either side of the river. *Has prevented all attacks before,* to prevent attacks could well be sex or sexual favours or the result of sex, a baby maybe. *No fox or rat disturb the ease* – This <u>was</u> about espials, yet undiscovered. *They eat, they drink, do what they please* this was not about vulgarity but of where this indulgence can happen: at Court. Who has tall legs and is trusted at court that may well see Rhy for sexual favours and, arguably, her talented poetic prowess. He sat back and gave thanks for the candle's solace. There was only one. The Queen's lover: Dudley.

VI

℘⃝℞

Jack Kitchener had proven his worth. His knowledge on the comings and goings of all important Courtiers attending Whitehall when the Queen was in residence was proving of immense value to Walsingham. It was two nights ago, just about the time Blythe and Herle were carousing with Hawkins, when Beale had asked for his help to find him a chamber, secluded from the eyes of prudent overseers of the Privy Council. Jack knew just the place.

Beale had hidden his disappointment well as his request for a chamber had been completely ignored and what he was offered was a forgotten tomb of rat droppings. As Jack guaranteed his hiding, some food, a hearty candle and small unsplintered stool for comfort, he would have to be satisfied.

There in the depths of Whitehall Palace as feasting and Privy Council meetings abounded several stairwells above him, he set to it.

Jack ensured he was well fed and was even good enough to provide a stuffed hessian sack for sleep and to empty his chamber pot once a day. It seemed as if Beale was nowhere except beneath the mount of an increasing number of spoiled parchments. 'How fairs thine undertaking master Beale?' Jack asks softly, bringing some cod tails, gizzards and rye bread.

'My mastery is yet to solve it, but I shall. I must.' He says, yawning, and smiling ever so appreciatively at the sustenance.

'Tis but a humble place for which you must undertake this number wizardry.' Jack says, looking about the tiny brick crypt. 'A larger chamber would have made this no modest task.'

'It is not the size of the room, alack the complicated cypher I am presented with. Normally it has been easily figured, and my expertise at intercepting them has proven true.' Beale moans.

'How easy?'

'What are the most common written letters?' Beale asks, weary and inflating his cheeks, puffing.

'I has no time to read, master Beale.'

'No. Of course. You know your alphabet and can understand words?'

'Aye. So, would it be the a, e, i...'

'Vowels – yes.' Beale nods. 'Now apply the math. The letter E. It is used 13% of the time, on average. T is near and A is another most commonly used letter.'

Jack does well to appear as if his attention has held. Beale shows him the transcripts he is trying to decipher. They hurt Jack's eyes with their mumbled letters and no sense sentences.

'These are taking more time as the cypher created is also using numbers for gaps and punctuation, commas and such, which is making it a lot harder to figure out even to my trained eye.' Beale says, determined not to be defeated. 'I am close.'

'Will wine help?'

In the time it took Jack Kitchener to go to the victualling cellars, pick a moderately valued Porto wine, Beale had cracked enough of the code to get the gist. A quick comparison to an older cyphered note and he was in no doubt: they have him. He did not even have time to taste the wine before rushing this news to Walsingham. Wherever he was.

* *

Barely touching the pheasant and eel pie, it was clear the Queen had enjoyed too much wine with the feast.

Cecil watches her closely but chooses not to comment.

Throughout the merry eve she had waddled to her privy garderobe at least four times. 'Quite unheard of.' He hears a Courtier idly mention in a lull between the music and dancing. No doubt rumours would start anew that Her Majesty was with child. Yet not as big in the stomach to match such slanders. Pish – he had not time for those idle chatterers, knowing her mood would clearly affect how receptive she was for Walsingham's two new bills of law that he called the Treason Act and the Recusancy Act. He suddenly felt uncomfortable – and perhaps mean – that he had to foist Walsingham's requests with absence to avoid the Queen's quite unpredictable fury at being pushed into a corner when deciding what to do about potential traitors in her Court, let alone Privy Council. For all her temper tantrums, she understood the law and even though the unofficial line was that Walsingham's net was tightening, her legal and political mind told her it was not, by any means, a unanimous verdict.

Cecil was impressed how Walsingham had included a precis to the acts, co-authored but solely credited to Stow who was well respected by the Privy Council. A shrewd move by Walsingham, not interested in the grandiosity of recognition, merely playing clever to avoid any conflicts of interest it may bear of questions amongst the many that mistrusted him already. It was doubly ingenious, Cecil thought, how he had appealed to her vanity and common sense whilst judging how to squeeze this through the tight and cautious opinions of Parliament, like convincing a cockerel to bait a bull. In both Acts he had mentioned Divine Right and the libertarian peace of her middle way, all of which was threatened, and he shrewdly suggested it was as if the voice of God had been silenced by dark forces in England.

Yes, Cecil thought as the idle chatter meandered on around him, Walsingham had indeed been clever.

Now he had to just pick the right time to approach Her Majesty with it. In this mood she would care not for the textual overlay no matter how refined because during one galloping galliard, the dancers turned in surprise when the Queen ordered the musicians 'Hush or be gone with limping leg.' Normally a devout enthusiast of the dance, she could hear no more music and had complained to her ladies that the Royal head 'does need rest from these braying untimely noises.' For twenty minutes the court was in near silence, save an occasional cough, a stacking of pewter plates and the nervous shuffling of servants. The Queen had not moved and all but Cecil turned their gaze from her, lest it meet her fury.

Time for mentioning was clearly not now.

Robert Dudley, delicately tearing at the roasted pheasant, pulling off a wing to chew in the embarrassing silence, was watching Cecil. Peeking intermittently over at the Duke of Norfolk and Essex who were sat together, speaking only with their eyes. Ludlow looked impatient and fed up at a lowly Courtier's bench.

Cecil was not sure who he could trust and it gnawed at him that Walsingham was right not to either. He sees servant approach Dudley who composedly slides out of the hall. Cecil watches closely. Why does he have to be the only vociferous Protestant on the council – garrulous extrovert that he is, with his long legs the Queen so oft admires. He seethes into his goblet of wine. Why do I have to trust him of all people?

* *

Walsingham was not allowed into the feasting hall, still regarded as mere clerk of government by Her Majesty, so the Royal Chamberlain had not permitted his entrance. He had to send Jack Kitchener to run a message to Dudley, who was never far from Her Majesty's court. In Walsingham's urgency, Jack was not bid the time to tell him he was fetching his steward Robbie Beale a bottle of Porto several staircases below.

Walsingham knows Cecil would not go for this unless he had hard evidence to the very letter that Norfolk was plotting the usurpation of Queen Elizabeth. He could not argue it was unreasonable and naïve of Cecil to expect, alack this is what you get when you work for a paranoid Queen. Not so paranoid that she made the wrong choice, just suspicious of how it would stand up to scrutiny across Europe and in front of God on her day of judgement.

Dudley meets him in a dark foyer and tries explaining to Walsingham that her fear of foreign princes was not irrational. His hushed tones encourage them into Walsingham's favourite corner of shadows, near the Privy Council Chamber. Quiet and dark.

Jack Kitchener walks in the distance, down into the depths.

'Her Majesty should fear Spain or France.' Walsingham says.

'It will always be so.' Dudley responds, as if he has heard this many times before.

'The Pope...emboldened as he is now. You have heard it say what he says of our Lord Cecil: a common man, although very clever, is false, lying in Her Majesty's ears, a great heretic foolish enough to believe that not all the princes of Christendom combined were in a position to violate his country's sovereignty. These are veritable insults, sir.' Walsingham keeps his frustration to a whisper.

'What am I to do of it? Push Cecil to expel all Italian merchants, French traders, the Spanish ambassador? All Catholics in England?' Dudley half laughs.

Walsingham responds like hitting a pillow with an iron pan, a thud of stoic gentle firmness, 'Yes. Guerau de Spes can be connected to all this: Ridolfi, Bailly, Philip II and the Pope. Other than Mary he is the common link. Not the instigator, but the connection. We cannot interrogate a foreign diplomat for risk of reprisals or war, but we can expel and pump the water from the bilge before we are sunk. It will send the Catholic world a message and we could yet still entrap the traitors and plotters.' It was a new name and new thought. A puppet of no concern ready to fall in their dangerous diplomatic brinksmanship.

'If we do this, then the plot would certainly unravel, suspicions heightened and all the connivers scatter.' Dudley flusters in a low voice.

'Not if we act precipitously, sir.' He says.

Dudley thinks for a moment, his short auburn goatee rippling as his mouth seems to do the thinking. 'Tell me what I have to do.'

As Walsingham ignores his excitement at giving instructions to someone several ranks his senior in government, he calmly outlines what the rumoured Queen's lover need do when the Privy Council next convenes.

Dudley takes a half step back when Walsingham finishes. 'You have excelled your own connivance putting this all together, Walsingham.' Dudley says, after a deep breath, letting it sink in. 'How fairs the Rhyming Whore?'

'She is yet to return from absence, my Lord. I will find her.'

Dudley looks at him with almost the eyes of an equal. 'I don't doubt it, sirrah.'

* *

The following day, Beale had not yet caught Walsingham to give him the news and decides to pay a visit to the Temple Bar checkpoint, to confirm his suspicions about the note and gain them further evidence.

Fallburn, the Parish Constable, was not there but Jennings, the Customs Adjutant and slack-jawed drunk, was. Instantly he hands over the ledgers and Beale is surprised to see that, despite Charles Bailly now imprisoned, there is no drop in travels of certain foreign merchants moving in and around the city. The Brotherhood thrives. Beale tears out the last month's ledgers, twelve pages.

Isiah, a little powerless, tries to protest, 'What jape here?' Beale just chucks the book back at him, almost toppling the little fellow over his stool.

On his walk eastwards to Seething Lane, he passes St. Dunstan church on Fleet Street first and then St. Bride's by the small river crossing. Astounded, he sees the Recusancy notices being nailed into signposts and onto the church doors. To not attend the service of a Sunday was to be obliged to pay the Crown a fine. Both churches had the same message and even the very small churches like St. Andrew by the Wardrobe and St. Michael le Querne's near to St. Paul's had them. Francis' law was enacted fast.

At St. Paul's, Beale notices Francis' other law enacted with swift and vandalous abandon. Pamphleteers and printers that had peddled the slightest sniff of anti-monarchy scandal sheets were being attacked or led off to the Fleet Prison. One Printer was force-fed his own printed parchments, the paper could be heard ripping into his throat as it was rammed down with a broom handle. One witty tormentor cruelly observed he could now eat his own words lest they be true. Beale was stunned at the quickness of how things were moving in their favour.

Perhaps Walter was right, he sighed, freedom of speech in England really was leading to the day of judgement. Beale decides to avoid any more assaults and wreckage, so heads north up St. Paul's Alley, into Ivy Lane then onto Cheapside. This takes him straight out to Newgate Market where he was surprised to see yet another furore, this time hearing many women repeatedly screeching 'witches' as four women were rounded up by a Parish Constable and five Rufflers.

These ex-soldier thugs for hire, were earning their meagre wage, slapping and pulling these poor elderly women around, Beale notices with alarm. The Parish Constable ringing a bell and almost rhythmically repeating a chant: 'Luanne Fairchild, Margaret Gygacks, Agnes Levet and Rosamund Demdyke, to answer for witchcraft.' Were these not the names Dr John Dee had given his master? Beale stops and scoffs incredulously, casting his mind over the astonishing sights he has beheld this day. Stunning and terrifying. The new power of Francis Walsingham's word and actions.

As Beale trots on, contemplating it all, he was confused how Walsingham's standing was unchanged from those days a year ago when they had walked and talked through Southwark about his grand scheme, but the man's word, deeds and intimations, clearly had potency with the men who wielded power. Beale finally turns into Seething Lane, with his head held high, for he distinguishes that he too had been instrumental in Walsingham's plans, words, deeds and intimations. Had this also meant in some way he also had wielded this power as well.

Entering the study, he sees Stow and Walsingham sat, poring over ledgers, court documents of the 1569 Northern Rebellion trials and Walsingham's Book of Secret Intelligences. They are cross-referencing names for possible hints or links that they may have previously missed. They barely sense Beale's presence.

Walsingham turns to Stow, 'What charges could Essex face from our researches here?'

'Little, sir.' Stow says sadly. 'He is implicated only in the same way others point the finger when they say tis not me, tis him.'

'What of Howard?'

'There is no written correspondence and there are merely tenuous links from 1569, in that he was in the same vicinity as some of the other plotters. However, if there were witness testimony declaring his disloyalties...'

'Then we would have a chance Her Majesty could prosecute for treason?' Walsingham props forward in his chair.

'If then he would give witness against himself with his perjuries and he claimed to replace Queen Elizabeth with Mary Queen of the Scots as...' Stow is almost embarrassed to continue.

'As his wife?' Smiles Walsingham.

'How would we prove that?' Stow asks.

'The wraith must cometh from its gloomy obscurity.' Walsingham says.

'The wraith?'

'Aye. The unseen. Walter Williams is to be returned from his murk in the shadows.' Remembering how he had read upside down Howard's intentions in the Privy Council study before Cecil told them all to depart London.

The two men now realise Beale has just been stood there listening. They look up to his broad handsome smile that makes them grin in return.

'None of this matters when you see the discoveries of my cypher.' Beale says in a delighted voice.

* *

Dipping his finger into the tankard of sweet port wine he delicately dabs it on her lips, then her tongue, which wraps around it with eyes full of lust, they both know she could full well wrap it around something else. Still she teases the finger. They both see he is enjoying it, laying and watching them from his bed.

Rhy lifts up her petticoats so he gets a peak of her thigh and fluffy merkin between her legs, another of Fyson's invention.

Thomas Howard, the Duke of Norfolk feels his hardened penis and then says the words Rhy was fearful of.

'Hit her.' He commands.

Rhy nods up to the other man that she consents and he backhands her across the left-hand side of her face, not wanting to further ail the bruise she already has on the right.

'No,' Howard says, rubbing himself slowly up and down, 'with a clenched hand. At her mouth. I want her to lick your body with her blood drooling forth.'

Walter Williams looks down to Rhy, she is brave not to whimper, and he feels for her pain, 'Master...' He tries to implore for mercy.

'Just do it.' Howard growls. 'Dare not save your pleasantries for the whore. She deserves it, no?'

Walter who has been playing these sordid games for what feels like a month now is used to being spoken to in such a way, but he is not sure how much more agony Rhy can take. The beatings have become more savage and more frequent. They cannot fake it, else he knows, suspects something and they are turned out onto the street, their ruse of many weeks foiled and their aim of entrapping him lost.

Swallowing hard, Rhy braces herself, though not closing her eyes. Howard would not like that. She is falling in love with the man that is forced to hurt her.

SLAP – her face claps loudly to one side and Rhy flails against the wood flooring, intoxicated with pain. Walter has to pick her up, bringing her to the bed, where he lays and undresses himself, waiting for her to lick him, as their master requires.

Rhy props herself up against one of the four posts on the bed, takes a deep breath, trying not to vomit with giddiness, the blood trickling down her throat and out of her mouth, she crawls onto the bed and leers over Walter like a tired wolf about to go in for the final lunging kill bite. She licks his nipples until they go hard, her blood smearing like a pissed painter flapping his brush in anger.

'Yes.' Howard leers. 'Down.'

Rhy keeps her tongue stiff as she glides down his navel, Walter rasps and stiffens his back, he is genuinely aroused, she can see, as droplets of her blood retrace the path her tongue has taken. Suddenly Rhy arches up in shock, Howard rams himself into her from behind. She closes her eyes and imagines it is Walter as she hurriedly licks and kisses all around his midrift.

'Smack her again.' Howard shouts as he pounds hard, her arse cheeks becoming raw.

None of them hear the footsteps racing up the stairs.

Olias Fallburn, the Parish Constable, Lynas Masterman, Titus Nevon, Edmund Blythe and Herle crash open the door and file in, the menage-a-trois disconnects like bowls pins toppling over.

'On whose authority have you entered a private place?' Howard demands, his eyes dark and tormented.

'I could ask you the same.' Blythe mutters playfully under his breath.

'The Queen's Privy Council.' Masterman says. There is another set of footsteps they can hear. Harry Snurle then enters, his snake bites healing nicely.

'You are under arrest, my Lord.' He says.

'You traitor.' Howard snarls.

'No, my Lord Howard, that would be you sir.' Blythe says.

'I am a Duke, head of the house of Norfolk.'

'Enjoy that head whilst you can.' Walter says from the bed as Howard is dragged away.

* *

'Very clever, Walsingham.' Cecil says, looking with respect at Walter Williams, 'Truly a great actor.' The three of them are alone in the Privy Council chamber. Cecil continues looking at Walter, 'You can countenance your statement, the…rhyming whore – can we otherwise call her your agent, Walsingham? She was never given money to commit acts of fornication is that correct?'

'That is true, my Lord.' Walsingham says, not conferring with Walter, who nods at Cecil, he hopes convincingly – what is one more ruse in a year of a thousand.

'She will likewise countenance all that you say here as testimony?'

'Yes, my Lord.' Walter says, unshakeable this time.

'And just what will that be?' Cecil asks mildly.

'My Lord?' Walter is perplexed.

'Exactly what transpired between the three of you in the many sordid weeks you had infiltrated his life at his estates and halls? The Crown shall learn of every word and deed. Not this night but in the plain day of a formal trial.' Cecil remains quiet in voice and deathly serious in tone.

Walter cannot help but think this will be far worse than his last confession as a young man to a Priest, but so he must. Walsingham reaches for a quill.

'No.' Cecil suddenly thunders, startling both men. 'I shall write this, would not want the Queen's legality to be jeopardised with accusations of conflicting interests. She will trust my hand as representing the truth.'

There is disappointment in Walsingham's eyes – he has brought this great conspiracy to a near end and he is being treated as if he has fabricated a great story from start to finish. It is Walter who offers a sobering and reassuring thought –

'We will lay before you no counterfeit, sir, but the truth as our Lord Jesus Christ will judge it on the last day.'

Cecil's face turns to sunshine. 'Proceed.' He says.

Walter is fluid and articulate, never once needing to take a cue from either Cecil or Walsingham as to the chain of events, his timeline or own motivation. It was pure testimony. From the moment he and Walsingham had fooled their entourage that he had split from them and, in doing so, ensuring autonomy in his actions in pursuing a different line of enquiry: Essex and Howard, the last great unnavigated courses. Thanks to Walsingham's financial backing, Walter had posed as a Catholic merchant, unhappy with the Protestant middle way. With the help of Rhy during the dark months of plague, they had fled the city and had followed Norfolk to his estates, and sought refuge there, ending up as his live-in lovers. This was the only point at which Cecil interrupted, bemoaning the things we do for England.

'However,' Walters goes on, 'Norfolk was shrewd and they never penetrated his inner circle, so to speak, and knew not of his plans. Once they were close to abandoning their fruitless expeditions and planned to run from his estates. Just by chance, a messenger came to his bedchamber late one night, as we were resting from his ceaseless, injurious lusts, reporting some gold had been confiscated from the Shrewsbury drapers. This we thought nothing of until it drove him to such a distracted mood that he dictated a response to the poor messenger boy in such a fury he quite forgot who could hear. "Damnation for the gold purse that would all secure a dowry for my marriage to the Scots Queen in England." This is when we knew we simply must carry on. Many nights later the Duke was beside himself with drink and rambling often. His countenance always turning black, nay evil, and he numerous times cackled at the idea that "when the day is upon us" he himself will whip the Protestant whore with chains marked with L.'

'"L?"' Cecil asks, bemused.

'Lutheran.' Says Walter. Cecil finishes scribing and puts down the quill. He rubs his eyes and signifies gratefully to Walter. He now must be left in peace. It is a moment or two before he speaks to Walsingham.

'Rhy, the female agent, will corroborate?'

'Yes, my Lord.'

'And well she must, for the foiling of perhaps the greatest plot to overthrow Her Majesty has been uncovered. However, the Duke of Norfolk is the Queen's cousin and will resist all charges. An interrogation will not be permissible. We have to hope that the gold, your two agents' testimony, the turning of Snurle, the ruse in the North and turning back the French...all this...we have to hope, is enough to convince Her Majesty.'

VII

Star Chamber, Palace of Westminster

2ⁿᵈ April 1572

ℬℭ

'No more than a formality, certianly?' Beale whispers as the proceedings got under way.

Daniel FitzAlan, the pink floppy face of an elder statesman looks scornfully across to Walsingham listening to Beale. As the chief common-law judge residing in this most exceptional case, he was not going to let two government clerks, as he saw them, disrupt the function with their petty conferences. Walsingham held up his hand in apology.

John Stow then enters and shuffles as quietly as his woollen cloak will allow onto the same bench as Walsingham and Beale. His smile to them is one of collecting their just rewards.

'The counts against Thomas Howard, 4ᵗʰ Duke of Norfolk issue of 20ᵗʰ Earl of Arundel, is that you conspired against Her Majesty and did plan to usurp her throne with a promise in hand of marriage to Mary Queen of the Scots.' FitzAlan chunters through the formal charge, keeping his eye on the scroll in case anything was added. A Clerk of the Star Chamber clarifies all is in order. 'How do you plead?'

Howard stands straight up and stares his peers down in the small room that held four simple benches: one opposite him for FitzAlan; two flanking either side holding four peers on each; and the small one for Norfolk to perch upon, propping him up awkwardly, temporarily, so as he could not – or should not – get comfortable.

'These very charges make a mockery of this land and my love for the Queen.' Norfolk fumes.

'Guilty or not guilty.' FitzAlan points out, tired and dreaming of when he will be finally pensioned off.

'Not guilty.' Barks Norfolk. 'Smirched I say.'

Walsingham leans carefully and very quietly into Beale. 'It is no formality when Her Majesty is present. All the berries will be picked, ripe or nay.'

Beale looks around the small room and can see only the eight Privy Councillors, including Cecil, FitzAlan residing and four others in the gallery. Walsingham's eyes direct him to look up at the narrow mezzanine above them where a small arched window with delicate blue curtains drawn. Beale could instantly sense the Queen was behind them.

With his dignity dying, Norfolk sits, looking around the dozen or so people in the room and shouts again, 'Not guilty, smirched by envious, low born men.' His eyes grow desperate. 'Lay before me an indictment by mine own hand to the treacheries against my beloved Majesty. You cannot, you have not nor will ever. For they do not exist.' He looks about the silent faces of his adjudicators. 'Where is Essex in your indictments?' He shouts.

Cecil looks worryingly up to the mezzanine curtain, a slight twitch Walsingham notes.

Howard will not yield, his countenance restless and charged, 'I am but ruined with these slanders. From a prominent family with many enemies to satisfy.' He curses, looking at Stow and Walsingham. 'A comfortable choice of difficult decisions. Where is Ludlow? Essex? Ye, the goat escapes.'

Cecil smacks the table, before hurling ridicule at him, 'Aye Leviticus tells us of two goats – one was to be sacrificed the other released with the burden of sins and wickedness. Which are you?'

Norfolk wilts.

Walsingham's joy dances deep in his soul and he notices there was no twitch from the curtain above.

Regardless, FitzAlan has heard enough and looks for the first time directly at Norfolk. 'Lest you be unable to sit through this most earnest of hearings then you should be placed in binds of hands and mouth. This would be an embarrassment to all, ye necessary in showing you there is no greater judgement in this land than that which is passed down by this Star Chamber.'

The eight peers of the Privy Council applaud. Beale looks to Walsingham with sparkling eyes, they are going to find him guilty. Walsingham sees the panic in the old Captain of the Guard's eyes, and instinctively, gently, rubs Beale's arm, he bows his head and says a quick short prayer of redemption for John Warne.

Stow, Walsingham and Beale are in a daze as the court sits for five hours to hear evidence compiled by Walsingham, other witnesses and his own enemies of the Court. Through Beale's deciphered messages, recovered from Ridolfi's hideout in Shrewsbury, to Williams and Rhy's substantiations during their infiltration of his family estate, the evidence was impressive. Cecil never once looked challenged or uncomfortable at the evidence lain before his scrutinous peers.

The Star Chamber's conclusions were undeniable that Howard had consorted with Ridolfi and Bailly, and had maintained clear ties to the Brotherhood. Yes, Howard was right, there was no incriminating evidence from his own hand, but both FitzAlan and the Privy Councillors saw right through that as a weak excuse, let alone defence.

Cecil was loudest of all in his confirmation of guilty.

FitzAlan summed it all up, 'Your lands, sir, shall be forfeit to the Crown's holdings, you should be taken to a private courtyard, as befits your station, within the Tower of London, and on the second day of June in the year of our Queen 1572, shall have your head removed from your body. Your remains will be interred at St Peters in the walls of the Tower.'

Before his sentence had finished being read, Norfolk fell to his knees on the floor as Stow, Beale and Walsingham look up at the heavens for thanks. At the same time, Walsingham sees the tiny blue curtain wisp, sucked inwards as a door within had been opened then closed. Walsingham could only assume that the Queen, having heard the verdict, had left her vantage point in an excitable hurry. He would soon learn the truth of it.

Stow says in relief, 'The ghosts of 1569's Northern Rebellion are lain to rest. Once and for all.'

'Amen.' Walsingham concurs, thinking a great many others had too.

'May England rest peacefully from here for evermore.' Beale says, nodding intently to the two gentlemen.

Walsingham can see in Stow's eyes the barest possibilities of that happening. They let Beale – and certainly England – rejoice in the ignorance of this serenity for a little while longer. For now, he rejoiced in seeing the harbinger of his horror step so disgracefully down to the mere pathetic station of a man with nothing, having lost everything.

VIII

Tower Hill

2ⁿᵈ June 1572

ℰℭ

The Royal Barge was sat on the Thames, its gilt edges sensational whenever the sun sears through thickening clouds. Cormorants swooped serenely onto the river, bobbing on their position to dive into the water when they were good and ready. Elizabeth sat with Cecil and Dudley, her maids were on another float nearby. They were watching the Tower of London courtyard from their small boat amongst the diving birds on the mellow river.

Walsingham can see them from his vantage point on Tower Hill, feeling a lowly outsider distracted with his own excitement. This was a day of endings. Rubbing his two shiny skull rings together as he joined his hands, he thought of Stimpson and Mary, the odd martyrs to his own cause preventing the Catholics from terrorising England ever again. This torment – and his own – was about to be silenced because there were going to be two executions. The first was on the public hill, a gallows death for the crowds, and the second, a private one, the beheading of that traitor Thomas Howard.

Walsingham grins with excitement, although Beale drops slightly with disappointment. He had not been invited to the private execution, unlike his master. For the moment they stood temporarily together on Tower Hill as the last preparations were being made on the gallows scaffold. Unbeknownst to him, Frances had taken Stimpson's old spyglass and was using it to watch from Seething Lane.

In silence, the old woman was brought forward.

Walsingham looked at her feathery white hair, it was indeed like the froth of snow at water's edge. So too was her nose bumpy and long, as if affixed like an old bulbous parsnip, all as Frances had described. The woman's eyes were sallow, heavy and full of sorrow as the rope was placed around her neck. Agnes Levet looked out to the small crowd as Sir Gilbert Gerard, the Queen's attorney, read the charges of conjuring spirits, casting spells to spread maleficence along with the more tenuous charge of misdemeanours against a Queen's agent. There were many puzzled faces. Walsingham did not look to see if Beale was among them.

The Executioner without notice thrust the lever and the old woman plunged through the trapdoor's hole.

At her window Frances gasped and almost dropped the spyglass, she could have sworn a holy oath that the old wisewoman looked right at her down the spyglass.

Walsingham was stunned by the soundless crowd and the quiet shifting of the crone's body, expecting a magnificent magical reaction the moment her neck broke, perhaps the sky to turn dark, the ground to shake or ravens to flood the skies – whatever was meant to happen when Satan crawls from the depths to claim back his own. It is why he kept his distance from the executed witch. For several moments nothing did happen, only her body twitched and the crowd's silence amplified the old lady's last gags for life. Then, as she swayed, like an echo of a life once lived, a light rain fluttered down, clamming the crowd and the hanging body's clothes as if to try and drag it all gently into the earth in one slow droop.

Relieved, Walsingham leads them down towards the high stone walls of the Tower of London's outer enclosure at the bottom of the hill. Walsingham was allowed in and Beale had to wait outside, so he went to reserve a wherryman. Afterwards they were to journey across to Southwark to see Titus Nevon in a bear wrestle, which he had so missed and longed to be in.

As Walsingham walks into the Tower of London's courtyard he can see more clearly the Queen, Cecil and Dudley on Her Majesty's barge, now drifting in closer for the main spectacle. Their faces are brilliant and bright in the sun, although they were not smiling or enjoying the day's festivities. Walsingham looks to the terracing that had been especially erected for fifty noblemen and women who were served crab and cockles, an intended stab at the guilty's great, fallen, house. There was even a young pedlar selling souvenir wooden crests of the family livery and tiny models of mermaids – a crude, and some felt cruel, reference to Mary Queen of the Scots. Walsingham paid the girl extra to deliver both vestiges to Seething Lane.

Howard, twitching, was dragged in manacles that locked both his feet and hands. Since the trial, he had lost a lot of weight and his beard was thick with many months growth, the lice within were galling him to distraction. Still, Walsingham did not pity him. His cheeks filled red and his eyes burned into the man that had executed John Warne and scorched Robbie all those years ago. He could still hear the searing of poor little

Robbie's flesh and sense Warne's feet blistering like joints of meat on skillets. Walsingham turns to see if the Queen was watching. She was inattentive, talking with Cecil and Dudley. Howard was fastened to the block, no wish for a speech.

Walsingham could see several of the Tower's prisoners poking their heads out of their tiny cell holes, one of which was Charles Bailly.

'There is one true faith, one true head of the church, the Holy Father...' Howard began to shout, but the executioner had swung back the axe and it came down with such precision, Norfolk's head spun off, wheeling blood all over the scaffold.

The Queen had not seen it. Charles Bailly did, and now glowers at Walsingham. He starts yelling at him. 'It will do more than that to end us.' He began. 'You will not stop the Brotherhood, it rolls around as slowly and certainly as the seasons. We choose when to harvest.'

This seems woeful and beggarly to Walsingham, shouting as he was from his indefinite cell, in no position to wield revenge, his master of any power now with his head in the hand of an executioner, their gold all gone and Ridolfi vanished. Walsingham gives him a pitying smile. It is only when he sees an old, crooked figure stood with another man that a sudden chill overcomes him. All this time Dee and Ludlow had been watching together from a distant vantage and are now both scrutinizing him. Walsingham remembers Ludlow's first snipe in the Privy Chamber – "Woolingham" he had said. He bore his eyes so fixedly at them that they had no choice but to turn away. Others he must always keep his eye on.

* *

From the comfort of his barge's leather seat, Dudley pours himself another goblet of wine, saying, 'It is done.'

'Why do I not think it so.' Cecil murmurs.

The Queen finally looks round and sees Howard's body on the scaffold, the diabolical twitching of the afterlife, like Satan licking his wounds. The Executioner picks up the head and clearly announces to the small, gathered crowd that this is the head of a traitor. She looks amongst the select crowd and sees Walsingham, stood all in black, as reposed as one of the tower's ravens. Her Moor.

'I want to see him.' She says.

Elizabeth disembarks the barge and waits on the small pier leading onto Tower wharf. From twenty yards away Beale can see her and is in awe, though quickly perturbed by the peculiar look of displeasure in her face.

Walsingham walks along the wharf and approaches Cecil, Dudley and Her Majesty.

'Walsingham.' She says curtly, as if she has discovered a scuff of muck on a new dress. He is taken aback.

'Your Majesty. I trust your highness will enjoy the victory to be savoured here today?'

'The Queen's cousin has been killed. I am to mourn a family member and celebrate the loss of a traitor.' She says.

'Your Majesty has grace and dignity.' He says in a bow.

'I saw your face at the trial.' Elizabeth says, as if uncovering some sordid affair and pointing it out to ridicule him. 'You revelled in the undoing of Her Majesty's cousin.' She takes a step right up close to him, Dudley and Cecil both have the same reaction and edge towards them to either hear or break apart what looks like a tavern stand-off. In their haste, they do not hear what the Queen says and only see Walsingham's face give what looks to be a strange smirk, maybe an embarrassed smile.

The sternness of the Queen's eyes puzzle them, however, and Dudley feels he has to soothe the tension. 'There are many successes to be taken from recent events.'

'With many regrets.' Elizabeth taunts. 'And I have my Lord Cecil and all his agents to thank for ensuring the plot was failed, you say.' The Queen shrills, smiling at her First Minister. Cecil is a little embarrassed. 'I shall endow you with the Lordship of Burghley and all its excesses.'

'Your Majesty, my gratitude leaps for joy.' Cecil exults, clasping his hands together and grinning, not at all expecting the day to turn out this way.

'For you, sirrah.' She says, motioning Dudley to hand Walsingham a scroll.

What could this be, Walsingham almost licks his lips in anticipation: titles; deeds to estates; a knighthood; a seat at the Privy Council or even his own government department for the secretariat of secret intelligences?

'You sirrah, will be person Pleni-potentiary as our Ambassador to France, and will leave to begin the posting in the court of Charles IX within the week. We thank you for your service.' The Queen smirks, saying acerbically, 'This is your wish, was it not Walsingham? You have danced with the Devil and there is a price. You wheedled your way into my government, well now enjoy its trappings. Le serpent dans le puits à souhaits.' Then she walks past him and away.

Walsingham is stultifyingly dumbfounded.

Cecil and Dudley can do no more than keep apace with the Queen and have not even the time to stop and console.

Walsingham unravels the scroll in the hope it was japery, alack, his new posting is to begin precipitously. His heart sinks, she does not trust him. His reward, despite the saving of her throne, is banishment, while Cecil adorns her patronage favour and the credit for all his endeavours. Disgraced in victory.

Beale, having seen the interaction, approaches excitedly but is knocked aback when he sees Walsingham's look of sorrow.

As Beale and Walsingham cross the Thames, nothing is said. They are met by Blythe, Herle, Masterman, Hannah and Rhy.

'Titus is already there.' Lynas informs them.

Walsingham sees in their faces excitement and pride, they are keen to celebrate and he is not going to compromise that so does not talk of his impending, forced, departure. His stomach is sick and his mind muddled, he cannot make sense of it. The Southwark crowds are teaming and he remembers their jeering, elbowing and cajoling from two years ago. He stiffens himself in readiness for the pushes, barging, arse-slapping and shit-spitting catcalls that are about to commence in full regaling.

Then something strange happens. He is not sure how, but they recognise his face and like an enchantment of calm, it ripples through the crowd. The cajoling, shouting and insults do not get started. There is no talking at all. Instead, the crowd parts and gaze upon him in silence. Bedecked in black, Walsingham saunters slowly through them, like a priest through a funeral crowd.

Beale cannot contain himself and mutters in his master's ear, 'This is the acknowledgement that merits you.'

There is neither bowing or mockery as he walks by them all. Walsingham recognises the looks in their eyes, reverential respect mixed with a fear of power. He wonders if that is what the Queen is doing – teaching him a lesson that no-one has as much power as she does and he is merely a servant. Not, to the beasts of Southwark, he thinks.

* *

After seeing Titus to victory in his bear wrestling, Walsingham left his agents to celebrate the rest of the night together, he still had business to take care of before setting to the task of readying the family for France.

Returning home, Walsingham led Frances out to the orchard, where she was sure he was going to birch her. Instead, he picked up two spades and kept on walking, through the gap in the fence, up towards the old Roman borehole that she and her sister had used as a wishing well.

He stops them and lifts Frances up so she too could see Agnes' body, not realising this was old news to her. She pretends a gasp and he takes that as not needing to say anything more. Handing a spade to Frances, they begin to dig and turf the mud down into the hole. His only daughter knows she must follow his lead and does so without complaint.

'The Tussie-mussie is forever gone,' he says, 'with all its evil tidings.' He smiles at Frances for the first time in a long while.

'Forever gone.' Frances says, looking despondently into the hole. 'We will never fill it.' She adds, flinging in a man-sized divot.

'No, but we Walsinghams play our part.' And what part had he played these two years past, he wonders. What was all this for? Yes, he had achieved what he had set out to do, but the cost he seemed to still be counting. A different thought then strikes him. 'I never asked Frances – what did you desire to be granted when the charm was cast?'

'I'm sorry Papa, I really am.'

'I believe you...what was your aim – the purpose of the charm – what did you conjure for? What was your wish?'

Frances turns away from him, that pain in her throat swelling inside again. She has to thud the spade into the firm earth and fling more mud pointlessly into the long ancient burrow before she can speak. Looking up at him with watery eyes and a croaking voice she says, 'To stop your screaming at night.'

A musket-ball to the chest, its throb penetrating throughout his body, creates empty sounds and swelling in his ears. All that is left to do in this moment is be a father. Forgetting the many months of incredible upheaval, of his changing political fortunes, the cost to his family and the effect on the realm, for the first time he considers himself. He watches Frances divot more mud into the depths and knows in some ways her intentions, maybe even her conjuring wish at this well had worked. He thinks of Mary, Stimpson, Essigia,

Warne and the young boy Robbie. Their faces scars on his soul, never to heal. He recalls what the Queen had said to him earlier that day – her Serpent in the wishing well – and broods whether it was majestical insult or a livery of honor, the great giving of thanks that can never be acknowledged.

'Francis.' Ursula shouted from the yard.

Walsingham looks to his daughter, 'If there is trouble, she means you.' He smiles and peers once more down into the waterless hole.

Ursula greets him with a warm smile. 'You have a visitor.' She says, then snappily to Frances, 'To the kitchen with Edith.'

In the basement Cecil is waiting for him, still wearing his jerkin and breaches from today – he must have come straight from the Queen's presence.

'My Lord…' Walsingham starts, '…felicitations on your further patronage from the Queen.'

'I am not here to gloat, Walsingham.' He says with concern in his voice.

'I am servant to Her Majesty's First Minister.' Walsingham graciously bows, forgetting his humiliation in front of the Queen earlier.

'Neither am I here in any official capacity.' Cecil says, sitting himself on a small stool.

'My Lord?' Walsingham uncertain now, knowing Her Majesty has as quick a temper as Henry VIII had and was capable of changes in mind so rapid a charging horse might do well to escape it. Lives had been ruined because of her temper. Was he about to share the same fate like so many ill born courtiers before him? 'My Lord? Her Majesty bears poor tidings?'

'Her Majesty does not know I am here.'

'I see.' Walsingham says, unsure whether this was encouraging news or not.

'I will speak plainly.' Cecil says, giving Walsingham only very quick opportunity to acknowledge before continuing, 'The Queen cannot look upon you with good favour. You proved her wrong, and that her cousin was at the root of much of the evil. This will not stand. Her Majesty has sent upstart courtiers to the tower for less…but you…were right. This is the worse punishment she could grant: out of sight out of mind.' Cecil was looking at Walsingham with pity. It made him feel uncomfortable, weak somehow, and more worryingly what was Cecil building to – was he being expelled from government service for good? 'But you were right.' Cecil says again. 'If Her Majesty knew I was here we would both share a cell in the Tower. You will leave for France within the next few days, your legacy is a foiled plot to usurp Her Majesty, a secretariat to gather Crown intelligence…'

'And a banishment from Her Majesty's government.' Walsingham laughs and Cecil smiles.

'A banishment, yes. Not a complete severance. There will be much use for your compendium of intelligence. It must continue compilations.' He breathes deeply before continuing, 'Without endorsement. Do you understand?'

Walsingham does, almost unable to hide the joy in his voice. 'You will have me report directly from France – to you?'

'The Queen has made it clear you are no longer connected to the Privy Council and being Ambassador to France you report to William Howard, 1st Baron Howard of Effingham.' Cecil says soberly. Walsingham understands Cecil was here to ensure he had no illusions of grandeur about his posting to France. 'What you report to him will, I am sure, be prudent to the role Her Majesty has endowed you with. Your holy work.'

'I understand, your grace.' Walsingham says.

'You report to me pertinences for the safety of our realm and Her Majesty's person.' Cecil says with so matter of fact he might tie ribbons on it. 'This being no other business than between the Queen's First Minister and Her new Spymaster.'

Walsingham smirks, the Book of Secret Intelligences will have new chapters yet.

THE END

AUTHOR'S NOTE

ℰᏩℭᎡ

Although spelling variations have been replaced for consistency, original place names and those of the real-life characters have been maintained throughout. Some specifics have lost their way through that vast landscape we call 'History.'

The calendar has been aligned for the modern reader.

Dialect and vernacular may sometimes read as coarse and despicable, reflecting the danger, desperation and realities of the times – 'it's not always pretty, but it is always important.'

ACKNOWLEDGEMENTS

ഔൻ

For your voice of encouragement and objectivity, I want to thank Cheryl Clarke for her early thoughts and observations, as well as Sue Marchment, Caroline Tyler, Spinks and Susan Jenkins who have all given this book their time and interest in helping to complete it. I am forever in appreciation.

There is no doubt that the stunning resource *Agas map of Early Modern London* has been invaluable and inspirational.

The Whites, where would I be without you.

Mrs Gilbert, Ms Eales-White, James Thomas, Bob Kiehl and Gavin Schaffer – you were all my most important History teachers.

Finally, to all my students that have ever had the patience to be taught by me, it is you and your curiosity of the past which has helped keep my fires of interest burning. I sincerely and unequivocally thank you.

CPSIA information can be obtained
at www.ICGtesting.com
Printed in the USA
BVHW071129131021
618834BV00003B/192